THE *Silk* MERCHANT OF *Sychar*

The Silk Merchant of Sychar

© Cindy Williams, 2019

Published by Rhiza Connect, 2019
An imprint of Rhiza Press
PO Box 1519,
Capalaba QLD 4159
Australia
www.rhizapress.com.au

Cover design by Book Whispers and Rhiza Press
Layout by Rhiza Press

Print ISBN: 978-1-925563-78-8

 A catalogue record for this book is available from the National Library of Australia

Scripture quotations taken from The Holy Bible, New International Version®, NIV® Copyright ©1973, 1978, 1984 by Biblica, Inc.® Used by permission. All rights reserved worldwide.

Exod. 20:4; Num. 5:11; Deut. 25:5-10; Jn. 4:4-42; Jn. 8 :32

THE Silk MERCHANT OF Sychar

CINDY WILLIAMS

A wife of noble character who can find?
She is worth far more than rubies.
Her husband has full confidence in her
And lacks nothing of value…
She makes linen garments and sells them,
and supplies the merchants with sashes.
She is clothed with strength and dignity;
She can laugh at the days to come…
Charm is deceptive and beauty is fleeting;
But a woman who fears the Lord is to be praised.
Give her the reward she has earned,
And let her works bring her praise at the city gate.
(Proverbs 31:10-31)

To Daisy, who showed me how to laugh at the days to come.

Part 1

Chapter 1
AD 21

It was the fourth watch of the night and Leah's husband had barely cooled in his tomb. The pain came on fast, clawing at her insides like stripping bark from a tree. She pulled her legs to her chest, desperate to save the precious, fragile life within.

'No, no, my baby. Please no.' She clutched the coarse blanket to her face and curled into a ball. If she just lay still it might pass. Another spasm tore at her insides. Warm fluid seeped between her legs.

'*Ima,*' she cried out. The wetness spread quickly. She squeezed her eyes shut, willing it to stop. Another tearing cramp. She rolled off the bed and stumbled through the curtain to her parents' pallet. It was empty—the embroidered cover smoothed neatly in place. A final shredding spasm, a rush of blood. It pooled on the scrubbed floor in the pre-dawn light, black and curdled.

'Don't leave me. Don't leave me.'

Her legs wavered and crumpled. All that remained was her mournful moaning.

***

'Leah, *mellita,* wake up.' A soft hand smoothed her forehead. Her mother hovered, her face easing into a relieved smile. For a moment Leah could not recall why she was still in bed at this hour. Then she remembered: the merciless contractions and her mother gently washing away the blood and her baby.

'You've slept well, my daughter.' She helped Leah sit up and placed an earthenware cup into her hands. 'A little wine with chamomile; it will restore your strength.'

Leah grimaced at the bitter brew. It might help her body but it would not heal her heart.

'*Ima*, I failed my husband. He was so pleased that at last I was with child. It made him smile, even in his last hours.' She covered her face with her hands. 'Now he's gone, and I've lost our baby too.' Her mother held her close, rubbing her back in slow, soothing circles. 'How can I face his family? All their hopes rested on this one child. I cannot bear the shame.'

'My daughter, you are young and healthy. To lose a child is tragic but it is not the end. Your body will soon recover and you will bear many children.'

'But who will want me?'

'Do not fret about such things now. Today we will honour your husband and you will remember that you have been a good and caring wife to him.'

A tear trickled down Leah's cheek. She had cared for her husband, but she had not loved him. Love took time, her mother had always said. Leah had watched it with her older sisters. Like fruit on the vine, their pinched cheeks and hard bellies had ripened into the warm blush of motherhood. She saw how their husbands glanced their way at family gatherings—the suppressed smiles and hungry eyes. She saw how her sisters responded—a dip of the head, a brush of the hand, a promise of intimacy for later.

Would she ever feel that way? Her moments alone with her husband had been awkward, clumsy attempts at what was surely meant to come naturally. Instead of relaxing in his arms, she would recoil from his limp, clammy hands and breath like rotting fruit. It was not his fault. He had the thirsty disease. It sapped his strength and melted his flesh. No matter what he ate or drank, it all drained out of him. Day and night he trailed outside to relieve himself. Day and night she swept away the mountains of ants which swarmed over each drop of urine as though it were honey.

Did his parents suspect that his life-span might not be long? Did that explain why they had arranged his marriage before he had yet reached his eighteenth year? The pressure to produce an heir, to continue the family name, weighed heavily upon her. The bleeding that unfailingly accompanied every cycle of the moon tormented her. She would catch her mother-in-law beseeching the family's gods and her father-in-law staring at her stomach as if willing a child to grow.

It was that which drove her to the mandrake by the stone wall. The mandrake that her ancestor, Rachel, had been so desperate to obtain that she had allowed her husband to sleep with her sister. The mandrake that promised fertility.

In the town she had spied young wives scurrying away from the shaded house by the willow tree, clutching the magical root. People said that it screamed when you pulled it out of the ground, and that those who heard the scream died. She had never believed such stories. She had ripped up that root with her bare hands and hidden it beneath their bed. Still her womb remained closed. She started to break off tiny pieces and chew them, praying for fertility. Whether it was the mandrake or the prayers that eventually worked, she neither knew nor cared.

She had prepared her husband's wasted body for burial, praising the gods for blessing her with the consolation of new life in this time of death. She was wrong. The gods were capricious and cruel. She pressed her hand to her stomach. Would it ever again swell with new life?

'Come, *mellita*, it is time to rise.' Her mother stroked her matted hair. 'We will eat something and then we will go to the tomb together. I have arranged with your mother-in-law that we will bring the oil and perfume. I thank *Yahweh* that she allowed you to sleep here with us last night, but you must return to your husband's home for this week of mourning.'

'I don't want to leave you, *Ima*. I don't want to see them. I don't want to see anyone.'

'Take courage, my child. I, too, have felt at times like hiding in a cave, away from the world, but your duty as a wife and daughter-in-law must come first. It is only seven days and then you will return. You are strong, Leah. You will survive.'

Leah allowed her mother to brush her hair and braid it into a heavy plait. She dressed in fresh, flowing linen and wrapped a pale shawl about her. She would neither bathe nor cook for the next seven days but would sit on the floor, barefooted, grieving with the parents of her dead husband and for the baby that was no more.

When she emerged from the house, her mother was turning flatbread over the fire. The aroma carried across the vegetable garden, catching up whispers of coriander, rosemary and mint. The plants had wilted in the late summer heat but now the first rains had fallen and they stood tall and green in the centre of the courtyard. Beyond was her favourite fig tree and she settled in its shade at the large wooden meal table.

'This will strengthen you, my daughter.' Her mother placed on the table fragrant golden bread and a thick stew of lentils, garlic, cumin and herbs. She picked up her spoon. It lay leaden in her hand and her stomach stirred in protest. She set her spoon down again and watched her mother piling flatbread higher and higher on the plate. The courtyard gate flew open and in burst Atticus and Calev jostling each other like lion cubs—loose-limbed, broad-shouldered, their faces shiny with sweat, their laughter bouncing around the courtyard.

'Atticus, Calev. *Shalom.*' Her mother set a circle of goat's cheese on a platter. 'I hope you are hungry this morning.'

'We are always hungry, *Ima,*' said Atticus, stealing a flatbread and stuffing a portion in his mouth.

Despite her stern stare, Leah saw the joy in her mother's face; her parents loved all of their five children but especially their only son.

'A good morning's harvesting always stirs the appetite,' she said, ladling generous portions of stew onto two plates. 'Sit over there with your sister. She needs cheering.'

Plates piled high, they joined Leah at the table. They smelt of fresh sweat, olives and grass; a familiar, comforting, men-of-the-soil smell.

'Curse the gods who brought that vile disease upon your husband,' said Calev. 'He was a good man.' The sincerity of his words tightened her throat and tugged at her tears. Calev spoke more with his dagger than his mouth, but Atticus insisted that beyond his brooding brow he was the most faithful of friends.

'He was,' she mumbled, not daring to look up from her food.

'Don't cry, little sister,' said Atticus. 'Calev and I will always look after you, won't we?'

Calev solemnly nodded.

'Is your father coming home to eat?' Leah's mother plucked several figs from the branches above, cut them into quarters and placed them with the cheese.

'He is eating with Marcellus. They have business to discuss.' Atticus scooped up a mouthful of food and wiped the back of his hand across his beard, clearing it of a speck of stew.

'I would wager it's about the oil mill,' said Calev. 'Your father was cursing like the cavalry this morning. He found olive paste on the milling stones already starting to ferment. We scrubbed for hours to clean off the mess.'

'That supervisor should go,' said Atticus. 'One dirty millstone will ruin a whole batch of oil.'

'A dagger at his throat might persuade him.'

'As always, my friend, you are the master of delicacy,' said Atticus.

They continued to discuss the olive harvest and where the barrels of oil might be destined for this season: Capernaum, Athens or Rome. The oil of Samaria was highly sought after, and especially oil from the groves of Marcellus.

His connections spread far and wide – forged during the twenty-five iron-studded, blood-soaked years in command of an auxiliary regiment in the Imperial Roman Army. He had marched from Galatia to Germania, from Carthage to Cyrene. Their father had marched with him. Finally he had stopped here, in the land of his fighting companion, in the shadow of Mount Gerizim and Mount Ebal—where the fertile valleys, rolling hills and temperate climate nourished and nurtured every sown seed and every wearied soul.

'Cease filling your stomach, Atticus. It's time to leave.' Calev drummed his fingers on the table waiting for Atticus to scrape up the last of the goat's cheese with a fig.

'It's a sin to waste such good food.' Atticus licked the remains from his fingers.

'That's one sin we won't have to concern ourselves with while you are around.' Calev slapped Atticus on the back. They broke out in laughter that echoed across the fields as they returned to the olives; laughter that soothed Leah's sad heart and brought a smile to her face.

'It is good to see you revived, my daughter.'

'I am much improved, *Ima*.' She summoned the strength that her mother assured her she had. 'I am ready to visit my husband's grave.'

Chapter 2
The month of Tevet

The sky in the east cast a pomegranate glow over the mist-shrouded land. Leah pulled on her cloak against the cold that had descended overnight, slid on her soft leather boots and stepped out onto the roof. A door creaked. It was at the far side of the large courtyard, where the sheep and goats were kept dry during the freezing winter months. Was it this that had roused her so early from sleep? She hurried down the outer steps. Her mother still slept at this early hour and her father and brother were away. It was she who must check the animals. She lifted the heavy wood that held in place the door to the animals' pen. The musty stench of enclosed animals hit her like a charging ram but amidst it was a shard of fresh, icy air. She peered past the ruminating sheep to the door at the other end of the shelter. It was ajar and the first goat pen was empty. She was sure she had secured both doors last night. Had robbers broken in and taken their prized animals, the ones set apart for the Passover sacrifice? Her father had warned of the danger of thieves at this time of year; the rain and mist were their allies. She carefully secured both doors, took a dagger from the alcove behind the stairs, tucked it into her belt and hastened towards the hills.

It was the month of *Tevet* and snow sprinkled the mountains like salt. For the past few months, since they had laid her husband in the tomb, the rains had fallen in great deluges, gouging deep, muddy furrows in the roads and soaking the ground until it was as sodden as a sponge. They had arrived unseasonably early and had caught some olive grove owners by surprise, but not her father and Marcellus. They had driven their labourers as hard as soldiers in order to gather and press the abundant crop in the shortest span. Everyone had helped:

Atticus, Calev, Leah and her mother. The seasons did not slow for death.

Leah hugged her woollen coat tighter about her and blew a tiny cloud of warm air upwards to warm her nose. Her boots crunched across the grass, brittle with ice. Where were those animals? She strained to hear even a faint bleat. Silence. They had melted into the mist.

She trudged through the olive trees, their barren branches patiently waiting for the warmth of spring. Beyond the terraced olive groves were the rolling hills where the goats loved to graze. If the mist was thin, she would see the roads and tracks that a thief might have taken. Every so often she stopped and called and listened. The goats knew her voice. They would surely answer if they heard her. She reached the muddy road which led upwards to the villa of Marcellus. Her breath came out short and hard and she stopped. There it was—the familiar, mournful call of her goats. A faint cry from the fields below. She lifted her tunic high, tucking it into her belt and freeing her legs to run towards the sound. She gripped the dagger at her waist and raced down the road, dodging the furrows and half-frozen puddles. Murder was a sin but defending your property was not. Despite her mother's protests that it was not right for a good Samaritan girl, her father had taught her the secret dagger skills of a Roman warrior. She could slaughter a sheep, she could sever a sinew, she could save her goats.

The bleats were closer now. She leaped across a deep furrow in the road, and landed on a patch of ice. Her feet splayed out beneath her. She crashed to the ground, the stones gouging her hands and knees. Her dagger clattered to the side. She jumped up to grab it, an instinct born of her father's warning: *Never lose hold of your weapon*, then staggered and collapsed in pain. Her foot would not hold her weight. Blood seeped through the mud on her hands and welled in deep, tattered wounds across both knees. She couldn't just sit here; she needed to get to her animals. Bracing against the pain, she forced herself up and limped a few excruciating steps. Her vision blurred. She slumped to the ground again. Perhaps if she called, the goats would hear and come. She prayed they were on their own. She called as loudly as she could, her voice piercing the crisp winter air, and listened for a response.

Through the clearing mist she saw a dark figure approaching. She gripped her dagger, ready to defend herself. The figure drew nearer. He was a few years older than her, tall and lean and wearing a fine coat. He did not look at all like a goat thief. She readied her dagger under her coat, just to be sure.

'This is not the best place to take a rest,' the stranger said. His bold gaze held hers until she looked away.

'I am not taking a rest. I am searching for my goats. They have been stolen.' She glanced at him to observe his reaction. His mouth turned up at the sides and his eyes danced in the now rising sun. He did not appear guilty.

'You are hurt.' It was a statement, not a question. 'Can you walk?' He knelt down beside her and gently lifted one of her bloodied hands. Her heart fluttered. He should not be touching her; she should not be *letting him*.

'I … I am more concerned about my goats,' she stuttered.

He glanced at her ankle which had swollen purple. 'You cannot walk on that. I will help you. Where do you live?'

Could she trust this stranger? There was no-one around to hear her screams. It had happened before; it was even written into the law: "If a man finds a girl out in the country and though she screams there is no one to rescue her …"

Trust your instinct: it is greater than your fears. Her father's words echoed in her mind. Instinct had saved his life in many battles. Instinct – that mysterious knowing that surpassed logic. She nodded her head towards the terraced slopes below them.

'These are my father's olive groves. Our home is just beyond, but I cannot return without my goats.' She struggled to her feet. He caught her by the elbow, holding her steady. Pain seared her foot but his touch seared more.

'Does it not say in the law that if a man finds his neighbour's animal he must return it and if he finds his donkey or ox fallen on the road he must help it to its feet? I will help you find your goats and then return both you and your animals to your home—but first you must put away your dagger.'

Her face burned at her woeful attempts at concealment. She withdrew her dagger from her coat and tucked it into her belt.

'Are you saying that I am a donkey?' She struggled to free herself from his grip and march back down the road. She managed only a pitiful hobble. He stepped up beside her and again took her elbow.

'I imagine you are as wilful as a donkey but no, I would say that you are more like an ox … a most beautiful ox.'

She did not know whether to feel flattered or insulted, so she kept silent. They stumbled along, moving slower than her brother on his way to the synagogue. Finally the stranger stopped. Before she could protest he had swept her up in his arms, striding down the road and cutting across the wet grass towards the sound of her goats.

'This is better.' His face was radiant and ruddy and so close. 'Perhaps you are not an ox; you are as light as a dove.' His laughter chimed through the olive trees.

Leah closed her eyes. She felt no cold or pain, just his arms like rods of gold holding her. It seemed only a few fragrant moments before they came across the goats nibbling the sparse, frigid grass by the stone wall. The stone wall where the mandrake grew. They raised their heads, their pendulous ears framing innocent, inquisitive eyes. One greeted her with a cry of complaint, a few stalks of grass spilling from its mouth.

'You should be pleased that it is me and not some thief,' she chided the animals. They regarded her as regally as any Roman emperor.

'They do not seem pleased to be found. Let us rest here awhile and let them finish their feasting.' The man lowered her to the ground and taking a goatskin bag from his shoulder, offered her some water. She drank deeply. The water was sweet to taste and fragrant with spices where his lips had touched it. She returned it to him and their fingers brushed.

'I am Leah Marcellus,' she said. 'Who are you and why were you walking across my father's fields at such an early hour?'

'My name is Yosef.' Yosef, a noble name: the name of the son of their patriarch Jacob and nephew of her own namesake. 'I have business in Sychar to conduct for my father. Our land is half a day's journey.' He waved his hand towards the hills stretching south. 'Like you I care for our family's flocks. I must return before nightfall.'

'Do you own many animals?'

'We have fifty-three sheep and forty-two goats—every one of them as haughty as these.' He spoke with confidence and affection and her heart fluttered a thousand wild wings. 'They are a supplement to our olives but this year they are all we have; our olives were ruined by the early rains.'

'You lost the entire crop?'

'Barely enough to light the lamps.' Yosef stabbed his knife into a cake of pressed figs and cleaved off two wedges. He handed one to Leah and they ate silently.

Leah tried not to stare at his lips, so perfectly framed by his beard, and his hair drenched with dew like a young stag come up from the water. He turned to her and she caught her breath, almost choking on the figs. There was fury in his face.

'If only my brother had listened to me. The signs were there in the skies and on the land: the halo around the moon, the turning of the lilac leaves, the heavy scent in the air. I told him the rains were coming but he ignored my warnings. My father listened but what could he do from his bed? We lost everything.' His voice trembled. Was it anger or sorrow? Perhaps both.

'I will pray for your family's fortune.'

It was a gesture of empathy, the soft touch of her hand on his. He stared for a moment at their hands, and then leaned towards her. His lips were so close, so very close. His breath was fragrant like blossoms of henna. Her blood flowed like honey in the heat. Was this how her sisters felt with their husbands? Was this how it was meant to be? But this man was a stranger—a stranger with arms of gold and strong, tender hands.

A tightening of his jaw, a ridging of his brow and he pulled away, his voice strangely hoarse.

'Come, Leah, it is time for me to take you home.'

***

For the next week the snow fell and the ground froze. Leah rested on cushions with her foot bound and raised. She busied her hands with grinding grain, threading dried figs onto strings and weaving yarn dyed with pomegranate and madder. She busied her mind with schemes to find Yosef.

On the morning of the seventh day, the sun burst forth. Leah sat with her legs exposed, watching her mother pour cleansing wine over her grazed knees.

'Your father and brother will surely arrive home today.' Her mother pressed a poultice of olive paste and honey onto the wounds, binding it in place with strips of linen.

Leah nodded and absently trailed a finger over her hand—the hand Yosef had held.

'Leah! Are you still dreaming? Put that young man from your mind. It is like chasing after the wind.'

'But if I ask *Abba*, surely he will consider my request.'

Her mother wrapped her arms around her daughter, nesting her head next to hers. 'Your father loves you and desires to see you content in marriage, as his other daughters are. He may consider your request but it is his duty to choose the best man not only for you but for the family.'

Leah understood. She would be wise to crush these childish feelings; they would lead only to heartache.

The sun was dipping behind Mount Gerizim when the braying of donkeys and the welcome shouts of her father and Atticus rang through the courtyard. Her mother ran to embrace them. Leah hobbled out, leaning on a staff. Atticus saw her first and strode over to hug her.

'What have you been doing, little sister? Leaping from trees again?' He looked at the bandage encasing her still swollen foot. 'That will dampen your pace for a while.'

'It is improving quickly. With this weather I have been able to do nothing but sit for a week.'

Their parents joined them. Her father appeared lively, excited … or was it simply gladness to finally be home?

'We also were hampered by the snow and forced to take shelter in a cave. But fortune was on our side. The owner appeared and took us to his home. Such hospitality! We ate and drank like kings. '

'Their home was filled with colour—on the floor, on the walls, on their clothes,' said Atticus. 'They have a colossal loom and a room full of wool and flax spun as fine as a spider's web.'

Leah laughed. 'So you have taken a liking to women's work. Wait until I tell Calev.'

'Where there is a chance to make money, he will take interest. As for me, I prefer the olive press over the linen loom.'

Atticus and his father fed and tethered the donkeys while the women prepared the evening meal. They pounded the dough into rounds and flipped them onto the fire. They chopped cabbage, leeks, garlic and herbs into a steaming chickpea soup.

Leah went to the storeroom. She poured olive oil into an earthenware flask and scooped salt into a small bowl. She dug out dried figs and sliced off a generous portion of hard cheese. She carried everything carefully to the table where her father stood with his arms wrapped around his wife, kissing her neck. It was hard to imagine those same arms killing men.

She and Atticus would beg him to recount the terrible and heroic tales of his years fighting across the Roman Empire under the command of Marcellus. Once he had been shipwrecked in a wild storm and had pushed the flailing Marcellus onto a floating plank of wood, swimming beside him to safety. In the barbaric north when an arrow had struck Marcellus in the neck, causing him to fall and strike his head on a rock, her father had dragged him out of harm's reach despite a gaping wound in his thigh. Yes, he had killed but he had also saved, and for his bravery he had earned an early discharge and Roman citizenship.

Her mother set the steaming bowl of soup on the table and then firmly removed her husband's hands from her.

'Tonight, my love,' she whispered.

He grinned. 'Come, my beautiful wife and daughter, we have important matters to discuss.'

Important matters? Leah sat at the table and took a spoonful of the thick, nourishing soup. Was it the olive grove with its trees gnarled and barren under the snow, sleeping 'til springtime? Was it a sister sending word she was with child? Was it an important invitation? Her father sliced off a portion of cheese. Leah watched and waited.

'The people we stayed with have a son who I think would make a good husband for you, Leah.'

The soup caught like clay in Leah's mouth. Her throat had clamped shut. A slow panic crept across her, like spiders on her skin.

Her mother gave her a warning glance. For every crop there was a right time to harvest, as for every request there was a right time to ask.

'*Abba*,' she used the word of respect for a father. 'It is not yet the fourth month after the death of my husband. Surely it is too soon for me to consider another husband?'

Her father glared as though she were one of his soldiers questioning his orders.

'Every battle, every business is built on good planning. You will be free to marry again at the next olive harvest and I plan to have a good husband ready to come for you as soon as the first olive falls from the tree.'

'What if I have already met the man I wish to marry?' The words rushed out like sheep at an open gate, before she could think, before she could close her mouth.

'You have not!' His words were a windstorm, the sort that brewed early in the east and burst upon the fallow fields. Her heart flew to her throat and clung tight. Her mother stopped her cup of wine mid-air. Atticus stopped slurping his soup. Her father's face hardened with fear; the fear of family disgrace should his daughter be found with a man not her husband.

'No, *Abba*. I was merely asking if I will be able to consider this man for myself.'

Her father's features softened.

'You will meet him in a few months when they come for *Pesach*. He is a fine young man, the eldest son. I am sure you will see the merits of my choice and will be pleased for us to draw up the marriage contract.'

A shadow slid over her. Her father cared for her as a centurion cared for his men: he cared for her welfare, he cared for her honour, but he did not care for her dissention. If she had any chance of finding Yosef, she would need the wisdom of a serpent.

And the meekness of a lamb.

Chapter 3
AD 22 The month of Nisan - Spring

The month of Nisan arrived; the beginning of a new year. The olive trees had woken from their winter rest and would soon produce blossoms of creamy flowers on their young branches. Leah's foot had healed and she was again able to follow the goats on their rambling across rocky slopes. The night air still held a bite but the days brought sunshine and the promise of new growth.

On the tenth day, in accordance with the law, Leah's father selected a year-old male lamb from their flock and brought it into the household in preparation for *Pesach*, the Passover sacrifice. Leah's sisters, their husbands and their children had descended upon the house in time for the festival. Their chatter and laughter filled the rooms. In the courtyard the children played with the lamb, feeding it tufts of grass and trying to ride on its back.

'Be careful with that lamb,' her father chided. 'He's not a camel for riding on. If you hurt him, I will have to find another.'

The lamb had to be perfect, without blemish, without a bone broken. The children continued to cuddle it and carry it and argue over whose bedside it would be tethered to each night, the younger ones unaware that their beloved, innocent lamb was set aside for sacrifice.

On the thirteenth day of *Nisan* they loaded the donkeys with enough provisions for a week and set out for Mount Gerizim. The roads were full of people, donkeys, sheep and goats, all making their way to the holy mountain. It was a slow journey. No-one was in a hurry. The men walked in clusters of two or three, holding their long staffs, and discussing how each had fared during the winter months. The children darted in and out of the procession, chasing each other, the little ones running to their mothers for comfort when they tripped and scraped their knees.

Leah loosened her head scarf, allowing a few strands of thick, silken hair to escape. Perhaps it would help Yosef to more easily recognise her. Her gaze swept the throngs, searching for a glimpse of the man with the arms of gold and lips of fragrant henna. She had determined to put him out of her mind but each night, in her dreams, he came to her like the sweetest forbidden fruit. She glared at her father strolling ahead with Atticus, Calev and the other men. If she were a man she would be free to marry whomever she wanted. Despite her dark mood, her lips pursed in wry humour; if she were a man she would not be dreaming each night of Yosef.

Like rivulets of water running into a river the people converged on the mountain, trudging up the winding paths that led to the place set apart for the tents. The women set up the goats' hair tents, hammering the ropes into place with heavy wooden mallets and carting woven mats, colourful cushions and eating utensils inside. Each was spacious enough for an entire household.

Leah worked apart with the other menstruating women, setting up a tent at the edge of the community. The worst had passed and her bleeding had tapered to a trickle. In a few days she would again be ceremonially clean and able to return to her family tent. She was in no hurry. The women's tent with its talk of festivals and food and family distracted her from the thought that she would soon meet the man her father had chosen for her. By day's end throngs of ashen tents sprawled across the mountain. Smoke from hundreds of cooking fires drifted upward and the bleating of sheep and donkeys echoed across the valley separating Mount Gerizim from Mount Ebal.

The following morning Leah rose early to gather the bitter herbs required for the *Pesach* meal. She was not alone. Women, young and old, combed the hillside, pinching off flat and curled green leaves and piling them into their baskets. The men too had risen early to dig the slaughter troughs and deep fire pits for roasting the sacrificial lambs.

This day of *Pesach* marked the first day of the Festival of Unleavened Bread. For the next seven days until the twenty-first day of *Nisan* they would remain on Mount Gerizim, doing no work except preparing food for everyone to eat and remembering, each time they ate the unleavened bread, how *Yahweh* had miraculously brought the ancient Israelites out of captivity in Egypt.

Leah wandered away from the other women, taking the path that led to the ancient oak tree. It was quiet on this side of the mountain, far from the thousands of Samaritans busy with their preparations. At the great oak she dropped her basket of bitter greens and stared up at the towering tree. Could this be the great oak under which, thousands of years earlier, Abraham had once pitched his tent and Jacob had hidden his *teraphim*, the forbidden gods of his wives? No one had yet found them. Birds twittered in its massive branches and the sun broke through in golden shafts. She looked across the narrow valley to Mount Ebal, where her ancestors had stood to pronounce curses on anyone who broke the laws of *Yahweh*. One law kept prodding her with possibility: *If a man seduces a virgin who is not pledged to be married and sleeps with her, he must pay the bride-price, and she shall be his wife.*

What if she found Yosef tonight before her father pledged her to be married to this other man? Her heart pulsed at the thought of them lying together in the embrace of this mountain, his arm under her head, their bodies as one. She was not a virgin but surely with the death of her husband she might be considered as one. All the men would be at the festival tonight while the women remained in their tents waiting until their husbands, brothers and sons brought portions of the roasted lamb to eat with the bitter herbs and matzah. If she could find Yosef they could slip away in the dark together and …

Her shoulders slumped, her heart too. Yosef would never agree to dishonour her in that way, even if she found him, even if he remembered her, even if she was not in the midst of her monthly bleeding. Her mouth curled in a sad smile. Here on the holy mountain of blessing, her only fortune was that she slept in the women's tent, set apart from everyone else. It would be easy to slip away unnoticed. Yes, she would go to the festival tonight and search for Yosef. It was her only hope.

As the sun stooped towards the Great Sea, Leah slipped away from the tent of the unclean. Her heart beating with anticipation, she strolled towards the area set aside for the women to care for themselves and then, with a swift glance each way, hurried up the hillside keeping a row of thorn bushes between her and the camp. She passed the great oak and in her haste stumbled over the loose rocks. Women were forbidden from the festival; she dared not be caught. Yet the law said that all the people of the community, the whole assembly, must slaughter the lambs at twilight. Surely women were part of the community? She would not be breaking the Law of Moses, only the law of men.

She slowed her pace and crept into the gloom of a wild olive tree. Across the hillside the multitudes of men gathered in a large open space surrounded by a rough stone wall, their white robes glowing in the final fading rays of sun. Their prayers and chanting songs caught on the chill breeze, low then rising to the heavens, carried on the smoke of the roaring fires. The high priest, dressed in ceremonial gold, stood on a fallen pillar from the temple ruins, reading from the holy scrolls. Several chosen sheep milled about at the high priest's feet, hemmed in by a few young boys. She saw her nephew, his tiny white robed arms flung around the lamb that had slept by his bed in a tearful embrace.

A line of white robed men stood, each with their sharpened knives poised at the throat of a lamb. The sun set, the high priest proclaimed the time of slaughter and the men slit the lambs' throats. Hot red blood gushed forth and splattered scarlet across their white robes. Young men rushed in with bowls to catch the blood. This, they would smear on the top and sides of each tent with a bunch of hyssop, exactly the way their ancestors had on that terrible night in Egypt.

Leah searched the faces for Yosef but he was not among them. She peered through the dusk at the men rejoicing and kissing each other, at the men cleaning the dead lambs with scalding water, at the men pulling slick entrails from the carcasses. No Yosef.

An immense heat blew from the fire pits waiting to receive the skewered sheep. The cloying smell of blood and death hung in the night air like a shroud. Leah pressed her hand over her nose. She had seen death before but not on this scale. It would have been like this on the first Passover in Egypt: the slaying of so many lambs and the sprinkling of their blood on the doorposts so that *Yahweh* would pass over their homes and not strike down every firstborn male.

Her head reeled under a sudden heaviness. Sweat beaded on her brow. She must return to the women before she was missed. She would not find Yosef this night.

A low rumbling sound set her feet to stone. Men's voices approached. She shrank back behind the tree. They were laughing and clapping each other on the back and brandishing their knives in mock battle.

'So tell us, Simeon, did you really attack that Jew on the south road or is it just idle gossip?' The man's swarthy face merged with the darkness.

'I would have slit his throat like a lamb,' said another.

'You can barely slice a pomegranate.' The swarthy one laughed and shoved him towards the tree. Leah squeezed her eyes shut as though that might somehow make her unseen.

'If you women would stop squabbling, I will tell you a story,' said a third voice, as deep and low as the purr of a prowling tiger. 'Judge for yourselves whether it might be true.'

There was a thudding of bodies settling on the ground. Leah opened her eyes and peered at the men sprawled before her. The one with the deep voice started to speak.

'There is a place on the road to Jerusalem where the horses fear to pass. It is a place of deep shadow where it is said the lions lurk. The Samaritans have no fear for they know the lion's heart. He holds his head with stately bearing, always turned northwards towards Mount Gerizim. The king of all creatures, he will not harm those who travel to this holy mountain but beware those vile ones who worship in Jerusalem. He will pursue them at *Pesach* and stalk them each *Sukkot* until they succumb to the truth.'

'So, Simeon, are you saying you are that lion?'

Simeon's teeth glinted like sharp knives in the moonlight. 'I am simply telling you a story that I have heard.' He rose to his feet and stood tall and erect, his hand clasped over his heart. 'I am the responsible eldest son of a respected Samaritan. Would you accuse me of such things?'

He whipped out his dagger and threw it straight at the tree. It struck deep. Leah stifled a gasp and the screaming of her feet telling her to run. Her heart thudded so loud she feared they would hear it. Simeon strolled over and reached out to retrieve the dagger.

He paused. Leah froze. The olive leaves rustled overhead.

Could he sense her presence? All she knew was that if he took one more step he would see her. She held her breath and prayed. Finally he turned away and with a chuckle called to his friends.

'Let us return to the men. We would not want to be caught skulking in the dark.'

As soon as they had gone she hitched up her robe and ran.

The whole assembly ate the roast lamb at midnight, at the very hour when *Yahweh* passed through Egypt striking down every firstborn—both men and animals. The men brought the mouth-watering roast meat in baskets topped with matzah and bitter herbs back to the women waiting in the blood-smeared tents. Atticus brought Leah her portion, placing it on the ground so as not to touch her.

'I am sorry that you cannot eat with us tonight, little sister.'

'It is of no matter; I am content here with the other women. Go now or you may miss the feast.' She took the plate from where he had placed it on the ground and watched him weave his way back through the tents.

Pesach was not a leisurely feast. As prescribed in the law, everyone ate in haste, the men standing with their cloak tucked into their belt, their sandals on their feet and their staff in hand to remember that first *Pesach* when their ancestors had to be ready to leave as soon as the great prophet Moses told them. A peace passed over the mountain, as though *Yahweh* was watching, approving. She stared at the stars flickering like far flung lamps in the clear night sky. Could anything be more beautiful? The God who had made the stars and brought her people out of slavery and into this Promised Land was surely still nearby. One day he would bring the promised Messiah to them. Meanwhile, she prayed he would somehow bring Yosef to her.

***

Leah awoke at dawn to the smell of freshly baked flatbread. She heard the men returning from their night on the mountain, their voices hoarse from the hours of prayer and thanksgiving, yet hearty in their eagerness to taste the delicious food that the women were preparing. It was the first day of the Feast of Unleavened Bread. The next day was a Sabbath which meant that the following day was the day of first fruits—a day when the priests waved a sheaf of the first of the barley harvest along with burnt offerings of a lamb, fine flour mixed with oil, and a fourth of a hin of wine to thank *Yahweh* for the bounty of the land.

Apart from preparing food the law permitted no work—and certainly no marriage transactions—on these sacred days. So it was not until the fourth day of the Feast of Unleavened Bread that Leah, her father and Atticus made their way to the great oak. The air was cool but the sun beamed with the promise of a perfect spring day. They followed the path around the hillside with Leah's father favouring his left leg. The battle injury hampered him only when he walked up and down too many hills. Leah said nothing; he did not appreciate sympathy. After a while he paused, leaving Atticus to stride on ahead.

'Daughter, I wish to speak plainly.' He cleared his throat and shifted his weight to his good leg. 'Although you are a widow, you are beautiful not only in your appearance but in your nature. I am sure this man will approve of you.'

Leah lowered her eyes. Her father did not usually speak to her this way. She felt his gaze upon her, appraising her not just as a daughter but as a woman.

'Your first marriage was a gift to our dear friends and their only son in the hope that you would bear a child to continue the family name. If the gods had spared him I have no doubt you would have succeeded.'

His words scratched at her scars. She prayed he would cease his attempts at encouragement.

'Our alliance with this family is of mutual benefit. Your dowry will assist them through a difficult patch in their affairs and in return we will have a share of the best positioned olive grove in Samaria.'

'If this man is only half as generous of spirit as his parents, he will make you a fine husband. Let us see for ourselves.'

Leah steeled her heart. To him, the matter was settled. It would do no good to dream of Yosef. He had most likely forgotten all about her. She trailed behind her father, preparing herself to meet this stranger, who might soon be her husband. Under the great oak stood two men who, upon seeing them, stepped forward in greeting. The older men clasped shoulders.

'Allow me to present to you my daughter, Leah,' said her father.

The older man bowed his head in respectful acknowledgment. His face was pale and withered, yet kind.

'It is a strong name for a beautiful young woman. Your father did not speak rashly in his praise of you.' He placed his hand on the younger man's shoulder. 'This is my son who has impatiently anticipated this day.'

Leah's breath seized her throat and held tight. It was Simeon; the man with the dagger. She tried to breathe, tried to loosen the chains in her chest. Of the thousands of men in Samaria, how could it be him?

'Shalom, Leah. I am Simeon.' His voice rolled like thunder over far mountains. He bowed his head, branding her with his gaze. It roamed her body, as freely as goats on a hillside, and danced with desire. His beard was neatly trimmed and oiled, his body taut and tall under a richly dyed robe. His teeth did not look like sharpened swords in the light of day but rather neat and white, like a row of shorn sheep. He was indeed handsome.

She lifted her chin, daring him to speak of the night of *Pesach*. 'Peace be upon you.'

'Come, let us discuss matters while these two become acquainted,' said her father and the older men settled under the great oak.

Atticus reclined against a nearby tree and started scraping dirt from his nails with his knife. Simeon and Leah chose a large flat rock overlooking the fields of new grain below and sat a respectable distance apart.

'I am most impressed with your religious fervour. It is an admirable quality in a wife.' There was mischief in Simeon's eyes; *he had seen her that night.*

'And I am most impressed with your discretion.'

'Well answered. You are as wise as you are beautiful.' He stroked his short beard and arched an amused eyebrow. 'Tell me, do you frequently flaunt the rules of our people?'

'Not at all. I carefully follow the law of *Yahweh* as taught to us by the great prophet Moses. However, I am curious to know how you might interpret the law that states the whole assembly of our people must gather for *Pesach*.'

'Should I presume you consider women to be part of the whole assembly?' A grin played on his lips.

'Should I presume you do not?'

'I see that you are skilled in the art of debate. Did your father teach you?'

'He has been most diligent in passing onto his children the skills he acquired while fighting in the Roman auxiliary. And you, Simeon? What are your skills?'

'My father dismisses my skills. He proclaims I am the manager of our olive grove yet he continues to meddle.' His hand shifted to his belt, the habit of all who wore a weapon.

'Perhaps he is merely guiding you with the knowledge gathered over the years. Is not his advice wise?'

'I admit that it has been useful at times.' Simeon stretched his arms above his head and gazed out over the valley. 'There is one decision that he has truly excelled himself in.'

'What might that be?' asked Leah.

He moved nearer, his body so close she could feel his heat. He smelt of straw and incense and danger.

'His choice of my wife.'

Her heart quickened at his breath on her neck. Her skin burned at his touch. She forced herself to slide away.

'Would you defile yourself by sitting so close?' She glanced at Atticus asleep, thankfully, under the tree. She did not need her reputation soiled by Simeon's indiscretion.

He reached out and caught an escaped tendril of hair, leisurely twisting it around his finger. 'Yes, Leah, I would gladly defile myself for you.'

Chapter 4
The month of Av - Summer

The household was humming with anticipation. This was the day Simeon would arrive to take Leah to the home he had prepared for them. No bride knew exactly when her bridegroom would appear. She waited in a state of eager expectation: would he come in the evening or would he arrive sooner? Dinah, Leah's close friend, insisted he would arrive early so there was time to return to his home for the celebrations. But who could be certain?

Leah stood in the centre of her chamber in a white woven tunic. Her mother, sisters and Dinah fluttered around her, arranging her hair in intricate braids, perfuming her skin and adorning her with gems of turquoise, ruby and lapis lazuli. One sister slid a pair of gold and ruby earrings through her ears— the earrings Simeon had presented to her on the day of their betrothal. They glowed a deep, dusk red that sent a murmur of excitement through her. She had not seen Simeon since that day and yet as the weeks passed into months the prospect of becoming his wife had ripened like fruit on a vine.

Dark dreams of blood flooding the floor, of her blanched, dead husband in a sealed stone tomb no longer tortured her sleep. Their marriage had been as passionate as milk in a sun-warmed bath. She had condemned herself as a woman unable to feel. Until Yosef.

Whenever the scent of spices or the bleat of goats brought his face to mind she resolutely pushed it aside. It had been a childish notion to hope that he might return and ask her father for permission to marry. It would have been fruitless if he had. Her father had set his mind on this alliance with Simeon's family. It was Simeon who would be her husband and of him only would she think.

'I have heard he has the face of Apollo,' said Dinah, reclaiming Leah's attention.

'And the virility of Mars,' said one of her sisters, setting the young women to twitter with delight.

Leah rubbed the ruby at her ear. 'He is indeed handsome. As for virility, we shall see tonight.'

They burst into laughter. The sun beamed across the room enveloping Leah in its warmth. Unlike her first husband, she was sure this one would have no trouble consummating their marriage. To no longer be a widow in her father's household, to be a wife again, to bear children; at last she would gain honour.

She wound a turquoise studded bracelet around her arm. It was a gift from her father; a treasure he had acquired from a grateful gem merchant whom their auxiliary regiment had protected in Arabia. It was engraved with lions and tigers and the blue-green gems reminded her of the Great Sea, of waves gliding over smooth rocks and of lands far away. Her new home was not far away. It was only a half day's journey and still within Samaria. She would be amongst olive groves and flocks. She would be amongst people of whom her father approved. She would be the wife of the eldest son in a home that Atticus said was filled with colour. All would be well.

'The bridegroom is coming! The bridegroom is coming!' A voice from the courtyard below called out the traditional words. Leah and her companions rushed to the lattice window to see a procession of young men dressed in rich robes the colour of fire and autumn. They were singing and beating tambourines, a little out of time as some danced and others tugged at a donkey laden with baskets. Behind the group were two oxen pulling a low empty cart ready to transport Leah and her companions to Simeon's home. Leah's mother called her attention away from the window.

'Come, my daughters, we must complete Leah's preparations.' In her hands she held a small alabaster vial. 'Let me anoint you, Leah, for the journey ahead.' She opened the vial and carefully poured a few thick amber drops onto her fingers. 'It is nard blended with lily and rose. I have been saving it for this occasion.'

Leah's hands flew to her mouth and her eyes moistened. Nard was the most precious of perfumes—luxurious, fragrant and costly.

'*Ima*, I did not expect such a gift; it is not my first marriage.'

25

'That is all the more reason.' She pressed her fingertips dripping with the precious perfume on Leah's forehead, on her throat and on the palms of her hands. 'Today you are as pure, as beautiful as any virgin. Your husband is receiving a precious jewel.'

Calmness settled upon her like a dove—nard had that effect.

'It is surely the fragrance of heaven,' said Dinah, tilting her head back to catch the scent.

'Truly from the gods,' agreed her sisters.

Leah's mother frowned. For her there was but one god—*Yahweh*. 'Never forget who you are, Leah—a Samaritan but also a Roman citizen. We are blessed to be able to claim the legal favour of Rome yet not have to worship their gods.' She looked pointedly at her daughters. They embraced all the gods: Samaritan, Roman and those of their Assyrian ancestors. 'Your father shed his blood to earn this privilege that you all now enjoy.'

'Oh, *Ima*, we all know that.' The sisters rolled their eyes at their mother's earnest tone. This was a day to celebrate not cast dark shadows.

Her mother squeezed Leah's hands. 'I am only reminding you before you go away. This marriage is to a good family, I am sure, but you will be far from family and friends. I only seek to remind you of your position, that you are a woman of virtue and value.'

'Thank you, *Ima*, I will remember.' A dart of doubt flitted through her at her mother's concerned tone.

'It is not far. I will visit as frequently as I can.' She squeezed her mother's hands. They were strong and sturdy from years of kneading bread, years of spinning wool, years of tending gardens, yet the olive oil she applied each day had kept them soft. Her new home would also have an abundance of olive oil. For that she was grateful.

The courtyard gates creaked open and they heard the shouts of the men greeting each other. Her mother bustled from the room to attend to the final packing of provisions for the journey. The wedding celebrations would last for a week.

'I hope I look as beautiful as you on my wedding day,' said Dinah, draping a shawl over Leah's head and across her shoulders. It was as fine as gossamer, woven in hyacinth and purple.

'You will, Dinah, and I will be there to see it.' Dinah's betrothal year was nearing completion and her husband had almost finished preparing a room for them attached to his parent's home in Sychar. He would surely come for her before the olive harvest.

'Come along, you two,' called her sister. 'Our father does not have the patience of Jacob.'

Their ancestor Jacob had worked seven years to claim his wife, Rachel, only to be deceived into marrying the older sister. For seven more years he laboured, so great was his love for Rachel. Leah smiled to herself; her father was courageous and tough, but he was not patient.

She led the way out onto the upper terrace and waited for her father to call her. The men had quietened below, Simeon flanked by his friends. They all stared up. She recognised one from the night of *Pesach*, his dark, swarthy face grinning. But it was Simeon who captured her attention. His neatly trimmed and oiled beard glistened. He raised his eyes to hers. A fire rushed to her face, so direct was his gaze.

Her father stood at the bottom of the stairs, his face beaming. He wore his finest clothes and over them the bronze medallion bestowed on him by the Roman procurator of some faraway province.

'Come, my daughter. Your bridegroom is ready for you.'

Leah descended the stairs and grasped her father's hand. He led her towards Simeon, took his hand and placed it over Leah's.

'Simeon, I hand you my daughter, Leah. She is now your wife. Do nothing to grieve her all the days of your life. May *Yahweh* bless you with prosperity and many children.'

He stepped away, leaving the two of them alone. All the friends cheered and broke into song. Simeon helped Leah onto the cart, covered with colourful mats and cushions. He leant close and whispered, 'You are even more beautiful than I remember. Rest well, my beauty. Our room is prepared and I vow that my lips will not sing until they have touched yours.'

Leah dipped her head, hiding her flushed face beneath her shawl. The nard flowed through her body, dissolving every jot of doubt. She sat surrounded by the happy chatter of her sisters, her mother and Dinah. The men led the way singing and dancing along the road while Simeon walked silently, only his eyes dancing with anticipation.

The journey passed quickly over the rolling lowlands past fields and orchards abundant with the summer harvest. With the sun's ebbing heat they turned off the tired road that led south and followed a spacious path lined with spreading trees—a welcome shade. Ahead, guests lined the road clapping and singing in welcome of the bridal party. Leah swallowed and sat a little straighter. This was her new home and these people would be her new family. And what a home it was. It loomed before them, its whitewashed walls glowing in the late afternoon light.

'It's enormous,' said Dinah, her voice hushed.

'Father has surely made a good choice of husband for you, Leah.' Her sister's voice was edged with envy.

'People are not their possessions,' rebuked her mother. She patted Leah's arm. 'I am sure your father chose your husband for his disposition, not his denarii.'

The gates into the inner courtyard stood wide open in welcome. The men led the way in, still singing and dancing, followed by the oxen panting and blowing under the load of the cart, and the guests chatting and exclaiming and pointing at Leah. The cart drew to a halt and Simeon's friends hurried over to unload the baskets of gifts. Simeon took Leah's hand, his eyes gleaming like jewels. They walked past the tables laden with food, past the lamps towering on their stands ready to be lit, past a garden lush with flowers of every colour and stopped before a group attired in robes of splendour.

'Welcome, Leah, to your new home,' said Simeon's father. 'We have looked forward to this day with great anticipation. May I present to you my wife, Mariamne.'

Mariamne took both Leah's hands in hers and kissed them. 'My home is now your home. Welcome, my daughter. May the gods bless you abundantly.'

'Thank you. I am honoured by your gracious words.' As Leah dipped her jewelled head in deference she caught sight of a face radiant and ruddy. Her breath caught sharp and sliced through her heart. That face. The face that sent a thousand sparrows quivering in her chest; the face that sent her blood flowing liquid through her limbs.

The face she had determined to forget.

'And this is my brother, Yosef.'

Yosef stepped forward, his eyes sober and sad. She saw his lips, so perfectly curved, and heard his voice as though from a great distance. She forced herself to stand straight despite the blackness bearing down on her. She tried to focus on his face. She was like Lot's wife, a crumbling pillar of salt ...

'Leah, Leah.' A gentle shaking awakened her. She opened her eyes to see Mariamne hovering over her. 'Come, my dear, take some water.' She helped her to sit up and handed her a small cup. 'I know, it's a special day and with the long journey and the heat it's hardly surprising you were overcome.' She smiled and creases fanned across her translucent skin.

Behind her, Leah heard Simeon's friends teasing him and his deep laugh in response. But it was Yosef's face before her that churned her belly and clenched her heart. Simeon's brother and now her brother-in-law! How could this be? How could she live like this, the wife of his brother? Panic swelled in her throat. She stared at him, standing with a group of men, feigning interest in their words between furtive glances at Leah. She saw his mouth frame the words, 'Forgive me.'

Forgive him? Why had he not come for her himself? Why had he not intervened and stopped Simeon marrying her? Where had he been at *Pesach*? Did he feel nothing for her? She swallowed the water and her panic in one angry gulp and thrust the cup at Mariamne. Mariamne's eyes darted from Leah to Yosef and back to Simeon. Leah bit hard her lip. She would need to conceal, no, crucify any thought, any hope of Yosef. No-one could know, especially not Simeon.

'Simeon. Come and help your wife. She has recovered.' Mariamne's voice held an edge. Anger? Concern? Leah could not discern.

He came to her at once, raising her to her feet. Dinah also hurried to her side and re-arranged the flowers that had fallen from her hair, fastening them in place with smoothing kisses and pats.

'Surely you are not worried?' She whispered to Leah, while fluttering her eyelids at Simeon. 'I would not be.'

Leah nailed a smile in place. 'Of course I am worried. I am worried that if you keep fluttering your eyes at my husband, I will lose him before we are truly married.'

Dinah laughed. 'I think there is little chance of that.'

'You are indeed right,' said Simeon to Dinah. He plucked a creamy white flower from the wreath Leah wore and held it out to Dinah. 'Flowers fade next to you but my eyes are for Leah alone.' He dropped his voice and whispered in Leah's ear. 'And very soon, my body.'

They made their way through the chattering guests, drinking and dancing, smiling and singing and accepting their congratulations. Leah tried to absorb the excitement of the guests. If she did not see Yosef she could pretend he was not here. Yet she felt his eyes upon her. She looked at Simeon, his face glowing with joyful anticipation and pride. He was her husband; she would not fail him.

'May we soon hear the cries of a child in your arms,' said the women, kissing Leah.

'And may we even sooner hear your cries of contentment,' said the men, winking and clasping Simeon on the shoulder.

To the claps and cheers of the guests he led her up the stairs to the flat, tiled roof, past a border of fragrant flowering shrubs to a freshly whitewashed door.

'Does this please you?' Simeon asked, eager for her approval of the room he had prepared.

'You have done well, husband,' she replied, pressing his arm.

The cheering subsided below, the guests returning to their grapes and wine and loaves and lamb, until Simeon's pronouncement of the consummation of their marriage. This time there would be no blood-stained sheet to present to the guests as proof of her purity yet everyone seemed as pleased as if she was truly still a virgin.

Simeon opened the wooden door and led her into their room. It smelt of fresh wood mingled with flowers. It was spacious with woven cushions scattered across a bed laid with pure white linens. He closed the door and pulled her towards him, stealing her breath with the urgency of his kisses. He ripped off his outer garment and loosened her tunic, all the while kissing her lips, her neck, her throat. Her shawl fell to the floor, then her tunic. Unlike her first husband there was no fumbling. His tongue, his lips, his hands were as sure as a wild goat treading the heights of Mount Gerizim. And she gave herself to her husband.

Finally he rolled onto his side and propped himself up on one elbow, entwining his fingers in a strand of her hair and grinning.

'Most husbands demand that their wife be a virgin but I prefer experience to purity. I will be able to attest to my friends that what they say about widows is true.'

'You speak as though you are familiar with the ways of a woman. Have you lain with others?' A chill slid up Leah's spine.

'A man does not live on bread alone. He needs variety to satisfy his appetite.'

'Our law does not respect such behaviour, even for men.' She clutched the linen covering to herself. He spoke as though this was the natural way of men and yet it was most surely not the way of the men that she knew...

Simeon laughed. 'Which of our patriarchs, Abraham, Isaac and Jacob, had only one wife? Surely I am the best of Samaritans for following their ways?'

'Isaac had only one wife.'

His smile hardened and his cheeks reddened. 'And I too have only one wife.' He gripped a handful of her hair, pulling her face close to his. There was a madness in his eyes. 'You will not question me again on this matter.'

She felt a knotting in her throat, a chasm in her chest, turmoil in her mind. How dare he treat her this way? She yearned to retaliate yet her heart told her this was a time for subtlety not screaming. She gently placed her hand on his glowering cheek.

'My husband, let us speak of more pleasant things.' She kissed his lips and felt the madness subside. She released the linen covering still held against her body and his gaze embraced her. He loosened his grip on her hair and stroked it.

'Your hair is the colour of the late harvest,' he murmured, raising the tresses to kiss her neck.

Leah breathed a sigh, more of relief than pleasure, and gave herself once again to her husband. But the name on her lips, the face in her mind, was not Simeon's.

Chapter 5

As soon as the wedding week had ended, Simeon prepared to leave. He did not say where he was going or for how long. She only knew that he was taking the family's finest horse. She pressed a skin of water into his hands and probed as subtly as she could.

'Will you be away for long, my husband?'

Night fell over his face and his mouth set hard like dried mud.

'As long as it takes,' he muttered, turning away from her and heading towards the stable. Leah followed after him.

'What is it you must do? Is it dangerous?'

'Not for me, woman.'

What did he mean? Were others in danger? And from whom? From him?

Her father-in-law shuffled out, leaning on a stick. 'Now, Simeon, as soon as you have delivered the documents, hasten straight back. Linger no longer than necessary in Jerusalem.'

'Do you think I would take pleasure in that city of harlots, Father?'

'I do not know in what you take pleasure, son, but I need you back here, with an answer, before the Sabbath.'

'Do you presume I have forgotten that it is my turn to read the scrolls, Father? I will be back.'

***

Friday evening arrived and still Simeon had not returned. His absence was both a relief and a concern. He had seemed so eager to leave. Had she not pleased him? Was he, at this very moment, lying with another? Since that first night she had been careful not to argue or correct him. In return, Simeon had caressed her with charm

32

and seasoned their nights with a virility that would surely soon produce a child.

During their wedding week he had drunk copious cups of the finely aged wine and feasted on the finest food along with the other guests. Leah had eaten little during the week, twirling the fragrant wine in her cup, picking at the piles of dates and searching for a glimpse of Yosef who had disappeared. It was not until she had watched Simeon dig his heels into the horse and gallop out through the gates that she found herself relaxing, as though she had been holding her breath for a week.

Now as the moon rose over the eastern hills, Leah and Mariamne sat together in the courtyard preparing food for the following day. Simeon's father had retired to bed as soon as he had finished the Sabbath sundown prayers and meal. He would rise again at the fourth watch, along with every other Samaritan man, to pray at the synagogue for three hours until dawn.

'It is a sad sight to see an old man going to the synagogue without his sons,' said Mariamne.

'He is not old.' Leah scooped pomegranate seeds into a pottery dish.

Mariamne gave a weary smile. 'I fear that he has aged beyond his years. The sickness last year has stolen his youth. Even walking seems to tire him. And to see a man without his sons at his side on the Sabbath ...' Her voice faltered and Leah strove to reassure her.

'Did he not say that Yosef would come directly from his flocks to meet him? He will be at the synagogue at the appointed time, I am sure.'

Mariamne nodded her head. 'You are right, daughter. Yosef is a good son.' She picked up a fresh pomegranate from the basket at their feet and sliced it in half. 'Look at me fussing and fretting about my husband when it is your husband who has not yet returned.' She hit the pomegranate, sending the scarlet seeds straight into the bowl. 'It is not the first time that Simeon has been delayed on a journey. Do not be anxious; he can well take care of himself. I only pray he will not miss his turn reading the scriptures and so bring dishonour to our name.'

'He would not do that, would he?'

Mariamne sighed and looked up at the star-lit sky. 'I understand my eldest son no better than I understand the movement of the heavenly bodies. He is strong and capable yet sometimes a dark brooding overshadows him. It has always been so. As the eldest he will inherit the olive grove, the flocks and this whole household. He has the intelligence but not the stability of mind. His emotions sweep him away like the Jordan in full flood. At the last olive harvest he refused to take heed of Yosef's warnings that the rains were coming early and we lost our crop.'

She lifted a charm cut in turquoise from around her neck, reverently resting it on her palm. 'I have prayed constantly for both my sons and now you are here; an answer to my prayers. I see the delight in Simeon's eyes when he looks at you. You are a blessing to our family.'

'I hope this will be so,' replied Leah, lowering her head at such lavish praise and continuing to scrape out the juicy seeds that stained her fingers as red as blood.

The women soon completed the preparation of food for the Sabbath. Leah placed the bowl of pomegranate seeds with the rest of the food: bowls of chickpeas crushed with garlic, parsley and olive oil; cucumbers chopped with mint and soured goat's milk; salted fish, almonds, fresh figs, grapes and a towering pile of flatbread wrapped in cloth.

By the time she climbed the stairs to her room the moon glowed high in the night sky but she was not yet ready for sleep. The air was warm and laden with the scent of ripened figs and grapes. She stood on the roof staring across the slopes with their spreading olive trees and stone wall terraces. The stars drew her gaze. Their movements were indeed mysterious, marking off the seasons and determining a man's destiny. Was Simeon at this moment staring at these same stars … was Yosef? She had found out from Mariamne the reason for his sudden departure from the wedding feast: to see that none of his animals had strayed over a cliff or become stranded in one of the many limestone caves. Would he return to his flocks after synagogue or come home for the Sabbath meal? Like the loom on which Mariamne was teaching her to weave, pushing it first one way and then the other, Leah hoped he would not return yet prayed he would.

A movement among the trees lining the road caught her eye. She glanced at the courtyard gates below. Were they firmly secured? Apart from the two servant girls, she and Mariamne were alone. The men had already left for the synagogue. She had to check. She ran down the stairs and across the courtyard. Both gates were closed but only one was secured. She grabbed the solid wooden bar and dragged it across until it thudded into place. But someone was at the gates, just outside. She heard the snort of a horse, a dragging sound and then a muffled moan.

'Who are you?'

'It's me ... Simeon.'

Her heart steadied its pace. She dragged the wooden bar away from the gate and swung it open. Simeon was slumped over his horse, his arms gripped around the animal's neck. The horse obediently wandered into the courtyard and stopped, waiting for its master to dismount. Simeon swung his leg over and slid to the ground. Leah caught him in her arms.

'What has happened, my husband? You are hurt.' She felt a dampness seeping through his robe.

'Water, I need water.' The words scraped over dried out lips.

She hurried to the water jar and dipped in a large cup. He gulped it down and she refilled it once, twice. After the third refilling he raised his eyes to hers.

'I need to wash before I go to the synagogue.'

'Are you not wounded?' she asked. Blood stained his tunic in dark patches and his bare arms were covered with deep scratches.

'It is nothing,' He wiped his hand across his mouth. He pulled her close and, running his hands through her hair, kissed her. His beard scraped her face. She recoiled at the stench of his breath. Finally he released her. 'My thirst is quenched … for the moment.'

She chose her words with care. 'You were away so long. I feared you had fallen into strife.'

'Fear no longer, my dove. I have returned, as I promised, in time for the Sabbath.' He removed his blood-stained tunic and thrust it at Leah.

'Get rid of this and tell no-one.'

He strode to the water jar and doused himself, wincing as the liquid flowed across a long, dark mark on his chest. Leah brought a clean, linen cloth and pressed it to the wound. Moonlight glistened off his wet skin, over the curve of his shoulders, the sweep of his stomach, and beyond. He grinned and grabbed her around the waist.

'I see you have missed me too.'

'Of course, my husband.' She contrived a smile. 'Now let me dress these wounds so you may be on your way.' She dabbed on wine and oil and fetched him a clean white robe. Giving her a final hungry kiss he hurried through the gates and disappeared into the dark. Leah picked up his discarded tunic, wondering not only how she could conceal it but why? The wound across his chest could not have produced all this blood. It must be the blood of another. Why would he want it kept secret unless …

Chapter 6

Leah woke to the raucous crow of the rooster. She groaned and rolled over keeping her eyes closed. Was it morning already? The Sabbath was a day of rest but also of hospitality. And today, Mariamne and her husband had invited not only their relatives, as was the custom, but also the ruler of the synagogue in honour of Simeon's reading of the law. Had he read well? She prayed so, for his success was her success and his shame was ... *the tunic!* She had still to get rid of it.

She threw back the bed coverings, pulled on her robe and picked up the bundle of rags in which it was hidden. She crept down the stairs to the courtyard below, silently lifted the bars of the gate and slipped outside. The trees of the olive grove stood silent and still, dark, spreading shapes in the glow of pre-dawn. She could not hide the tunic here. One of the hired workers might find it. She needed a more deserted hiding place. She turned towards the hills where only the sheep and goats grazed. She had to hurry. She needed to be back before the men arrived.

Panting up the steep slopes and scrambling over shadowy boulders she finally stopped in front of a rocky outcrop. It loomed above her like a towering fortress, releasing a shower of loose stones from its upper reaches. Before her was a small cave opening – a black mouth in the blanched rock, swallowing the early morning light. She stepped closer and peered into the gloom. No-one would find the tunic here. She tossed the bundle as far as she could into the blackness. A low growl rumbled from deep within the cave. A lion! She stifled a scream. Her father's advice echoed in her ears. *Run when you can. Keep to the open ground. Find a tree.* She flew down the hillside, leaping over the boulders, not daring to look behind. She saw a large spreading oak in the open pasture below. She raced towards it, her chest heaving, her legs screaming to stop. She did not stop until she had scrambled into the highest branches. All was still and quiet in the pasture below but far in the distance, silhouetted by the first rays of dawn, stood a lion with a bundle of bloody rags in its mouth.

Leah gulped in deep breaths. Her heart slowed its frantic beating. She had neither run so fast nor climbed a tree so quickly since she and Atticus were children competing like budding gladiators with their father as their trainer and king. A flock of songbirds settled on a branch, chattering to each other in playful tunes. She breathed in the sweet morning air and a prayer of thanks to *Yahweh*. Did he hear? Had he protected her? The law commanded they make no image of him to worship. Every other god was visible, their images fashioned into amulets, pendants and carved poles set up on the high places beneath spreading oaks. Her father wore an amulet of the Roman god, Mars. Mariamne burnt incense to the Queen of Heaven. *Yahweh* was invisible, untouchable, silent. Was it *Yahweh* who had protected her or simply good fortune?

***

'My daughter, what in the heavens have you been doing?' Mariamne was laying out the food in readiness for the men's return. 'Your cloak is covered in dust, and look at that tear!'

'I did not sleep well. I rose early to walk … not far,' she added, assuring Mariamne that she had not broken the rules of the Sabbath. She lifted the torn fabric. 'I must have caught it in a thornbush.'

'It is easily repaired. Now hurry and bathe. The men will soon be here.'

Relieved that Mariamne had accepted her explanation so readily, Leah filled a small jug with water and hastened up the stairs. Removing her robe she poured the water over herself, washing away the dust. The sun beat on the wet tiles. In the distance she heard men's voices, returning from their prayers, ready to eat.

***

'Leah, get us more wine,' called Simeon, chewing on a flatbread. He was lounging at the table with the other men, debating the portion of law he had just read out. The bowls of food were almost empty but their cups were full. The women sat separately in the shade of the house, discussing food and fabrics, and watching their children pretend to be Roman soldiers with much marching, shouting and laughter. Leah rose from her seat, placing her half-eaten bowl of chickpeas on the ground. Mariamne touched her hand.

'The servant girl can go. Rest here with me.'

'It is no trouble. I will go,' said Leah.

The storeroom was tucked away next to where the animals slept in the winter months. She opened the door and stepped into the cool, spacious room, leaving the door ajar so she could see. Along one wall were numerous barrels of the family's own oil, at the rear were bags of grain ready for roasting or pounding into flour, and along the other wall were three large jars of wine. She picked up an earthenware jug and dipped it into the wine.

'Leah.'

Yosef stood in the doorway, his head wreathed in golden sunlight.

He stepped towards her. 'I had to see you, to talk to you … to explain.'

She stepped back, holding the jug against her like a shield. 'Why did you not come to me? Why did you not tell me?'

'I have thought of nothing else.'

'Then why did you not come?'

His eyes bored into hers, as rich as rain drenched soil. 'I wanted to. I planned to. After I left you I had to tend to my flocks. I spent those days dreaming of you and how I would speak to my father. I was too late. When I returned home the agreement between my father and yours had been sealed.'

'But surely, if you had told him…'

'Leah, you know that Simeon must marry first. He is the heir and he is the one who must bear children to continue the family name. Even if my father had allowed me to marry you, Simeon would not have let me. If he had known of my feelings for you he would have made certain to marry you, just to spite me.' There was a hardness around his mouth, a stiffness, and then it softened. 'My only hope was to stay silent and pray that he would not want you. Then I could have asked my father.'

She crossed her arms in front of her. 'If you had only warned me, I would have refused to marry him.'

'Do you think your father would have acquiesced? He wanted this olive grove and we needed his money.'

Leah sagged with the truth. Her father had consulted her but it was expected that she would say yes. Like the sudden spring rains, tears filled her eyes. 'I do not know if I can bear it; to see you each day as my brother-in-law and not my husband. And ...' the thought struck a violent blow, '... if you marry another...'

Yosef pushed the door shut with his foot and took her in his arms. The darkness wrapped around them like fine wool. He ran his fingers over her face, gently wiping away the tears. 'I will not marry another.' The fragrance of his breath was like spices, his words the sweetest nectar, his lips so close, and yet a bitter barrier held them apart.

'Woman, where's my wine?' Simeon's voice roared from outside. Leah and Yosef sprang apart. Yosef darted into the dark, concealing himself behind the bags of grain.

'I am coming, husband.'

The door swung open and Leah flinched at the brightness. Simeon strode in and grabbed her arm, squeezing it hard.

'We have been waiting for too long. Is this how you treat our guests? I will not be dishonoured in my own home by my wife.' He pushed her against the wall and looked around suspiciously. 'What are you doing here in the dark? Why was the door shut?'

Leah suppressed a shudder. 'It closed of its own accord. I was about to open it when you came.' She prayed he would not hear the wild pounding of her heart. 'I had to search for a jug with which to draw the wine.'

He studied her face as though searching for clues of her unfaithfulness. She held her breath.

'Have you seen Yosef? He also has disappeared.'

'I have been in here the whole time. Why would I have seen him?'

'I do not trust him,' Simeon growled. 'He steals everything of mine; my ideas, my father's favour, the respect I am due as eldest son.'

'I am sure your father favours you both equally.'

Simeon spat on the packed dirt floor. 'My father is a withered old fool. He is out there bowing and scraping to that bleating goat of a synagogue leader. Why should we listen to his "teachings" when he takes no heed of them for himself?'

'What do you mean?' Leah asked, relieved that they were no longer talking about Yosef.

'He stands in his flowing robes demanding obedience to the law yet he lifts those same robes to his servant girls, telling them that it is the way to be closer to *Yahweh*.'

'Where have you heard such things?'

He glared at her. 'Do not question me. I know and that is enough.' He picked up the jug of wine and drank it down, golden liquid spilling from the sides of his mouth. 'Now fill this and bring it to us.' He seized her around the waist and pulled her hard into him, spittle spraying her face. 'I am thirsty for sundown.'

When he was gone Leah hurriedly re-filled the jug of wine and left, not daring to even glance at Yosef.

At sundown when the Sabbath ended and the Samaritan men were once again permitted to lie with their wives, Simeon took Leah to him. His body was relentless, as hard and brutal as the rocks that reared over the ravines of the Jordan. She shut her eyes and imagined honey and spices and Yosef's lips upon hers.

Chapter 7

Soon after, the household loaded oxen and donkeys for the third pilgrimage of the year to Mount Gerizim. On the fifteenth day of the seventh month the Festival of Tabernacles would start. For seven days they would live in sukkot, booths built with branches of olive, palm and willow—a reminder of how their ancestors had lived for forty years after *Yahweh* rescued them from the clutches of the Pharaoh. Each animal laboured under its load of choice fruit from the trees and crops from the land—offerings for the summer harvest. The roads were dusty and teeming with travellers; Samaritans going north to Mount Gerizim and Jews travelling south to the temple in Jerusalem.

A crowd of travellers passed by, speaking in heavily accented Aramaic. One girl, with a scarf wilting over her head, smiled at Leah. 'Shalom, peace be with you.' The girl's face sparkled like a pool in parched sand.

Leah smiled in return, before she could think, before she could suppress it. This girl was similar in age and she, too, was on her way to worship *Yahweh*. Simeon glared at her, his hand poised on his belt. She averted her eyes. They were not meant to smile at Galileans, especially when they were on their way to worship at the wrong place.

Most Jews from Galilee avoided Samaria, preferring to add an extra day to their journey to Jerusalem rather than taking the direct route. A group was safe enough but those who travelled through here on their own risked the abuse of over-zealous Samaritans. Or worse …

What of Simeon's blood-soaked tunic? Was it Jewish blood?

She looked back to check on the others. Yosef walked far behind, assisting his father who struggled to keep up in the sapping summer heat. He handed him a skin of water and took his elbow to steady him. Her heart ran warm. Here was another gem amidst grime, a man who was kind.

The festival week passed quickly. Each day the men made their way up the mountain to the holy rock where the tabernacle had once stood. Each day they chanted their prayers and blessings. Each day Leah cooked and cleaned and wondered if the girl from Galilee was doing exactly the same.

***

Weeks passed and summer slid towards autumn. The olives were ready for harvest and the hillsides teemed with hired workers beating the precious fruit from the trees. Others scooped the dusky purple and green ovals into baskets to take to the press. One afternoon when the sun shone with unseasonable strength, Simeon's father staggered into the courtyard, leading a donkey saddled with baskets of the morning's harvest. Leah dropped her gardening implements and hurried to greet him.

'Father, let me take care of the donkey. Come and rest in the shade. I will bring you water.'

The old man expended a weary smile. 'Thank you, Leah. This day is surely the hottest we have had during the harvest, or perhaps I am not as young as I used to be.'

Indeed he did not look well, his pale face and panting breath. Leah tethered the donkey and hurried to the water barrel to fill a large earthenware cup. It was unfavourably hot for the month of *Cheshvan* and although every day Mariamne had pleaded with her husband to return early to rest, he insisted on leaving at dawn and not returning until dusk.

Leah handed her father-in-law the cup and he raised it to his lips. Water spilled over the side and she saw that his hands were shaking. 'You are toiling too hard. Can you not leave the work to Simeon and Yosef?'

'We cannot risk another failed harvest. If the rains come early as they did last year we will be ruined.' He took another shaky sip. 'I should have listened to Yosef. He reads the weather better than anyone. But it is Simeon who will inherit the groves. How is a young man to learn without responsibility? He chose to wait. He was wrong. I fear he still has much to learn.' He lifted his eyes to Leah's. 'It is good that Simeon has you. Maybe now he will settle, have many children ...'

43

His words tumbled out like a stream over stones, garbled and slurred. 'I will fetch Mariamne,' said Leah. She rushed into the house calling Mariamne's name.

'What is troubling you, daughter?' Mariamne hurried down the stairs holding a broom. She propped it against a wall and looked past Leah into the courtyard, drawing in her breath.

'I gave him some water but he is not well, I fear,' said Leah.

'By the heavens! I told him to come home earlier, not in the heat of the day.' Mariamne hastened to him.

He leaned against the wall of the house, his head resting on his chest. The cup of water had rolled away and his arms hung like weeping branches. Mariamne dropped to her knees beside him and gently touched him. He slumped to the side, his head lolling at an awkward angle. His eyes stared straight ahead, unseeing.

'My husband!' Mariamne tore at her head covering; her eyes squeezed shut, her face contorted in a deathly grimace. She flung her arms around him. 'No. No. No. We need you. I need you.' A wail rose from her, deep and anguished. It echoed around the empty courtyard and cut deep into Leah. She sank beside Mariamne and the two women wept.

That same day, in the cool of evening, they buried him. Simeon and Yosef carried his linen-wrapped body on a bier. Mariamne, Leah and a group of wailing mourners followed. The burial tomb was hewn out of the limestone rock, not far from where Leah had hidden the tunic. She glanced about hoping she would not catch a glimpse of the lion lurking in the shadows or worse still, Simeon's bloody tunic. All she saw were the sombre faces of those who had hastily gathered to grieve.

Simeon emerged from the tomb, his garments gaping where he had rent them—a gesture of grief that extended no further. His face was not jubilant, neither his voice, yet there was a glimmer in his eyes, a stretching of the neck, a poised pressing of fingertips.

'I am deeply humbled by the respect you have shown my father and our family. He was a good man and I pray that I may honour his name in my duties as eldest son. Please return with me to my home where you are all most welcome.' He led the crowd away, accepting their condolences and shoulder clasps of solidarity. A lion with his pride.

Yosef did not follow. He sat on a boulder concealed at the side of the tomb, his head in his hands. Leah came close and he lifted his head. His face was as haggard as the southern desert mountains and her heart swelled with sympathy.

'Blessed be your dear father's memory. May *Yahweh* give you comfort.'

A tightening of his jaw, a fire in his eyes, he took her in his arms, his lips like flaming embers on her neck. 'Leah.' His voice cried out and she held him tighter, kissing his hair, his cheeks, his lips. His hands slid down her back, over the curve of her hips, drawing her closer and closer and closer. Her blood flamed with the heat of his kisses. Her body melted so she felt only Yosef. She wanted only Yosef.

He groaned, a sound of deepest despair, and wrenched himself away, burrowing his knuckles into his brow.

'I will not do this. You are my brother's wife. I will not dishonour you or him by doing the very thing I most desire.'

The truth he spoke tore at her heart, rending it as surely as her torn tunic. Tears veiled her vision; grief veiled her soul. They could not break the Law of Moses.

They could not bring shame upon the family.

Chapter 8
AD 23 The month of Adar

'See how the pattern is taking shape?' Mariamne grasped the wooden weaving comb, pushing the woven threads upwards, tightening the weave. 'The stars are simple but the camels require more patience. Here, you do the next part.'

She passed Leah a ball of fine twined wool, dyed a deep blue. Leah attached the yarn to the weaver's shuttle and stood before the large wooden loom. Most households had a small loom on which to weave rough goats' hair for blankets and sheep's wool or flax for clothing, but the loom before her was larger than any she had seen. It stood in the centre of the room, the coloured threads attached to a cloth beam at the top and anchored by small weights of baked clay at the bottom. Baskets filled with skeins of spun yarn in scarlet, blue and purple lay close by. Other baskets, stacked in a corner, held clumps of dyed fleece and flax fibres waiting to be spun. A luxurious mat covered the floor and across olive wood couches were scattered cushions the colour of sunset. Warm light poured through the open doors.

Mariamne picked up a mass of madder-dyed sheep's wool and attached it to the distaff, preparing to spin it into fine scarlet thread. She grasped the spindle with her fingers, then stopped. There were tears in her eyes. 'He promised that after the next plentiful harvest he would buy me an ivory distaff. We used to laugh about it.' She sniffed and absently stroked the wool.

It had been four months since her husband's death. Four months of storms and snow and sadness. But now as the streams ran fast with the melting of snow and the lilies of the field bloomed in carpets of purple, scarlet and gold, there returned to her face a whisper of joy.

'An ivory distaff? Who has ever heard of such things?' Leah tossed the shuttle through the loom, carrying the thread to the other side like a streak of midnight sky. Pain showered needles into her neck.

'I have heard that the governor of Syria presented his wife with one.' Mariamne studied Leah's face. 'Are you well, my daughter?'

Leah tossed the shuttle back, more gently this time. 'It is nothing.'

She was relieved that the marks of Simeon's hands were hidden beneath her tunic. It would do no good to tell Mariamne that her husband's death had been like an east wind fanning the embers of Simeon's temper. A spilt drop of water, an over-seasoning of salt in the stew, a smile at the wrong moment and his wrath rained upon her. Her attempts to explain or reason only fuelled his fury. The best defence was subservient silence—like a sheep at its shearing. Later he would come to her, tender and remorseful, stroking her wounds and holding her as he had at first. It was then, when the threat of violence had died, that her teeth clenched and her eyes burned with frustrated tears.

Only Yosef's presence made her days bright and bearable. She lowered her eyes at his frequent glances for fear Simeon would see, yet her nights were filled with dreams of his kisses and his arms around her.

'What plant produces such a shade?' she asked, diverting the conversation. 'It is not the red of a setting sun or the blue of the deepest sea or the purple of a king. It is none of that yet it is all of it.'

'It comes not from a plant but from a sea snail.' Mariamne picked up a skein of the blue thread from a linen-lined basket. 'This alone would have required the crushing of two or three thousand murex shells.'

'Two or three thousand? So many snails for so small an amount.'

'Is the sacrifice not worth it?' said Mariamne. 'Look at the clarity; look at the depth. This dye is unlike any other. It is not the muted, fading tones of the earth but the bold, steadfast shade of the sea. The dyers of Tyre and Dora are skilled in their secrets. They can even transform the juice of the murex into the blue of a summer sky.

'How do they do it?'

'It is a secret they guard with their life.'

Leah touched the thread, silently thanking the slayed snails for the secrets they held and their sacrifice. She would weave the precious yarn with care.

That evening Leah and Mariamne sat together in the warmth of the house, dipping bread into bowls of lentil and herb soup. Fragrance filled the room: coriander, cumin and mint. The lentils were tender and sweet. They had pulled the plants from the cold soil, laying them on the roof to dry. Leah had crushed those dry enough and collected a generous bowlful.

'Tomorrow I will show you how to harvest the flax,' said Mariamne. 'The flowers have bloomed and the stems are still green. If we want the finest linen, we must harvest before the Sabbath.'

'Where is the field? I have seen olives and vineyards and grain fields but no flax.'

'The flax plant is greedy; it steals goodness from the soil so we plant in a different place each year. This year, ours is towards the Jerusalem road, where the stream flows free. Once we have pulled up the stalks we will leave them in the water for a week to allow the stems to rot and release the inner fibres. Then we will be able to spin and make beautiful linen!'

Mariamne clapped her hands together and Leah laughed. It was good to hear gladness instead of grief.

Smoke from the fire drifted into the house along with the voices of Simeon and Yosef. There was no laughter, only a grim grumble, like thunder brewing in the far hills.

'Leah!' Simeon shouted from outside. 'Bring us more soup and more wine too.'

Mariamne rose from her seat. 'I will fetch the wine, my daughter.'

Leah hurried outside to where the soup still simmered over the fire. The men barely noticed her as she refilled their bowls with the thick broth.

'Father would not have approved,' said Yosef leaning on his elbows and rubbing his beard.

Simeon threw his wine down his throat and thumped the cup on the table. 'Listen, Yosef, I am in charge now. Father was a fool to solicit the advice of that Jew. Don't you know they delight to see us beg like dogs under a table? I will not pay him a single denarius.'

'He is a merchant of vast influence in Judea,' said Yosef, lacing his fingers tight like the thongs of a soldier's sandals. 'He will bring many buyers for our oil, buyers who are prepared to pay a good price. We must pay him what we owe. If he sends debt collectors from Jerusalem, we will be the shame of Samaria.'

'He would not dare,' growled Simeon, 'if he values his life. Besides, we have barely enough to pay our tax. That vile tax-collector—may the gods strike him with leprosy—keeps as much for himself as he pays to Rome.'

'How could we not have enough? We have produced more jars of oil this season than any other. Father was sure it would more than cover our debts from last year.'

Simeon shoved his stool away and loomed over the table like thunder. 'Father this, father that, father is no more. Do not dare to blame me for the debts of last year; the rains should not have come so early.'

Yosef rose up, his sinews strained, his knuckles white on the table. 'The trouble with you, Simeon, is that you take no advice, not even from your family.'

'Why should I value your advice, little worm? Leave me to conduct the important business and go back to your sheep. It is all you are good for.'

Yosef lunged at Simeon, shoving him hard to the ground. Simeon grinned.

A shudder ran through Leah like a sword; she knew that look well.

Simeon sprang to his feet. 'So you want to fight?' His eyes held a maddened gleam. His hand moved to his belt.

'You are a fool, Simeon. You are ruining this family with your stupidity.' Yosef stood his ground, fists at the ready.

'Simeon! Yosef! Stop your fighting now!' Mariamne strode from the house, her robe swirling like a scythe. She planted herself in front of them and set her hands on her hips. 'It is a disgrace to see brothers fight. Do you want to bring shame on the name of your father? Do you not know that a house divided against itself cannot stand?'

She spoke as sternly as any centurion. Simeon opened his mouth ready to retort. Mariamne held up her hand as though halting a horse and he shut it again.

'And you, Simeon. Do you think that being the leader of this household entitles you to lord it over us? Did you learn nothing from your father? He led by serving and if you want to prosper I advise you to do the same.'

She turned on her heel and marched back into the house, leaving the men stunned into silence. They righted their stools and returned to their seats. Leah hurried over with the soup. She placed a bowl in front of Simeon, and the other before Yosef. Her arm brushed his and they exchanged the briefest of glances. Simeon stirred his soup and stared. Had he discerned their secret? A chill shivered through her. She hastened into the house, his glare blazing a mark on her back.

By the time she and Mariamne had completed their household duties, the men had retired for the night. Simeon had stumbled up the stairs and Leah prayed the wine had sped him into sleep. She extinguished her lamp and stepped silently into their chamber. He lay sprawled on the bed, seemingly asleep. Softly she shut the door. His eyes sprang open.

'So, you've had your fill of my brother, have you? And now you come to me.' He sat up and glared, the whites of his eyes glinting madly in the moonlight.

Leah shrank back against the wall. 'You accuse me falsely, my husband. I have done no such thing.'

His mouth curled like a beast before its prey. 'Men divorce their wives for lesser evils than your harlotry. Do you think I am so foolish as to not notice your absences at the same time as Yosef?' He slid off the bed.

Her heart raced faster like hind's feet in flight. *Run, run, run, run.*

He came towards her, his hands spread wide, his voice a cold, chilling whine. 'I did not wish to believe that my own wife would betray me. I suppressed my suspicions but now all is clear.' The voice was fearfully calm, fearfully strange. It slithered slowly up her spine. Her heart froze, her legs froze, her blood froze.

'If your father and I did not have a business arrangement, I would divorce you tonight,' he spat. 'But as you are more valuable to me as a wife I will settle with teaching you how to behave as one.' He grabbed her arm and twisted it behind her. She cried out in terror and he threw her to the floor.

'You are wrong, Simeon. We have done nothing.'

His foot slammed into her side. She felt a crack. Pain flamed through her body, stealing her breath. She tried to rise, to run.

'We?' he snarled. 'You are even brazen enough to admit it.'

He kicked her again. She fell and her head hit a stone water jug. Her vision hazed. A loud ringing engulfed her. Warmth trickled down the side of her face. She tried to wipe it away. He grabbed her, pulled her to her feet, his face a blur. He slapped her, the sting of a thousand bees. Bile swarmed in her stomach, tears stabbed her eyes. She tried to push him away, to get past him to the door.

He grabbed her by the throat.

'My brother thinks he can have whatever is mine but he will not have you.' His grip tightened around her neck and she struggled for breath. Her heart hammered nails in her chest.

'*Yahweh!*' It was a muffled cry, like a song in a storm, but at the sound of it his hands dropped to his sides as though someone had knocked them away.

His words were hot and fierce in her face. 'You will remember to respect me. And you will stay away from my brother. Now go and cleanse yourself. I do not wish to be defiled by your blood.'

She staggered to the far side of the roof. Pain assailed her on all sides, fear cowered in the corners. She slumped into a crumpled heap and stared at the stars, so still and peaceful. They wavered and blurred and then there was darkness.

A noise awakened her. She inched open her eyes. Simeon was on his hands and knees amidst piles of lentil pods, laid out on mats for drying. He drove his dagger into a roof tile, levering up the mud and straw and extracting a bulging purse. He stuffed it into his belt and stumbled towards the stairs, the coins clinking in protest. She lay completely still, holding her breath, holding her tears, holding her fear. Don't stop, don't stop, don't stop. The entrance gate creaked open and shut. She peered over the edge and saw him striding away. She released a long, weary breath. Now she could relax. Now she could rest. Now she could steel herself for his return.

Chapter 9

She slept through the crow of the rooster and the chorus of birds. It was only Mariamne calling from below that roused her. Warm sunlight streamed through the window. She tried to rise but the movement sent pain searing through her body. She forced herself to sit up, wincing with the effort. Today she and Mariamne were to harvest the flax; it could not wait. She rose to her feet, steadying herself against the wall, waiting for the room to stop swimming. Slowly her vision cleared and the pain in her head retreated to a dull ache. What would she say to Mariamne? How would she explain her injuries? She could not speak against Simeon to his mother. He would surely return this very day. The thought sat like a sack of grain on her shoulders.

Footsteps sounded on the stairs. 'Leah, are you well?' Mariamne's anxious voice preceded her entrance. She pushed open the door and stopped, her eyes widening.

'What has happened, my daughter?' She rushed to Leah's side and placed a gentle hand on her head. 'This cut needs tending at once.' Her gaze fell to Leah's neck and a shadow passed across her face. 'I fear you did not fall.'

Mariamne returned quickly with a soothing poultice of olive oil and bees' honey. She bathed Leah's wounds, a myriad of expressions scudding across her face.

'My husband taught our sons to respect women. He was a good man, an honourable man.' A single, lonely tremor tripped over the word *honourable*. 'We have all suffered grief these past few months and Simeon has borne the added weight of responsibility. I had hoped his darkness of mood would pass. But now this! Oh, my daughter. I did not imagine his anger would turn against you, his wife.'

Leah's lip trembled. She dared not speak. She dared not allow the storm brewing in her heart to burst upon her lips. No man should treat his wife, or even his dog, in this way. She had endured the past months of his anger, his abuse, without a murmur of protest. She had tried to please him, she had tried to understand but his anger had only amplified.

Mariamne fastened the poultice with strips of linen and then clasped her hands around Leah's. 'Truly you are as a daughter to me. You have been a source of strength through these months of sadness and my heart rejoices that your father chose Simeon as your husband.' Her gaze swept the room—the disturbed bed, the upset water jug, a tarnished drop of blood. 'Love takes time to grow between a husband and wife, but if there are … distractions, it can take longer.'

Leah averted her eyes. Had she and Yosef been so indiscreet? Had she deceived herself by believing she could hide her feelings for Yosef? Heat fanned through her body, to the very tips of her fingers, proclaiming the truth of Mariamne's suspicions.

'If I have brought shame to this household by inciting Simeon to anger, I am truly sorry. I fear I have failed as a wife.' *Again*—the unbidden word brought with it a memory of her first husband and a pool of blood on the floor. She took a battered breath.

Mariamne squeezed her hands. 'I have seen the way Simeon looks at you. His heart is truly for you, not against you.'

Leah winced. The way he looked at her brought only fear and trembling. 'I am grateful for your kindness. I will try harder.'

'And I will speak to Simeon before Yosef returns with the sheep for shearing. There is no thought or action that justifies this behaviour.' Mariamne surveyed the grey clouds sweeping in from the west, dimming the sun and threatening rain. 'Perhaps we should wait until tomorrow to visit the flax field. It will allow you to rest. One more day should not hurt.'

'Is it not better to harvest early?' asked Leah. 'Every day the fibres grow a little thicker and our linen less fine. Let us go today.' She did not wish to hinder Mariamne. She did not want stay at home. She definitely did not want to see Simeon.

The women set off towards the Jerusalem road under a soft sprinkle of rain. Leah led the donkey, praying it would not swerve or suddenly stop to nibble the grass beneath the flowering almond trees. The slightest tug on her arm was a sword in her side. Soft, green ears of barley nodded in the fields and lanolin scented the air. Yosef would be gathering his sheep for shearing and soon there would be piles of oil-rich wool to wash, dye and spin. She was glad he had not witnessed Simeon's violence. What could he have done that would not make matters worse? What could any of them do? She sighed and pain pressed hard upon her, pulling tears to her eyes.

Leah could not even breathe without feeling the brand of Simeon.

'Here we are,' said Mariamne, pointing to a field the colour of the sky. The showers had passed and the sun danced off the droplets of rain on the flowers.

'Never have I seen a flax field in such full flower,' said Leah, allowing its radiance to soothe her sadness.

'Each flower lasts only one day—a fleeting moment of beauty. The true value of flax lies not in the flower but in what it produces. It is a comforting thought to an old woman.'

'Old! You are not yet old,' said Leah. A sliver of light slipped through her smile and into her heart.

Mariamne showed her how to pull up the entire flax stalk and lay each on a mat. She showed her how to anchor the flax in the stream with rocks, allowing it to soak until the stems rotted and released their inner fibres. The stream ran close to the road and the donkey gratefully gulped the clear water while the women worked. With each yank of the flax, Leah gritted her teeth, sweat beading on her forehead. They stopped to scoop up water but Leah could barely stretch out her hand. Mariamne studied her with concern.

'I should have insisted you remain at home, my daughter. You are as pale as snow and your breathing is laboured. Here, lie down.' She helped Leah onto a patch of soft grass. Leah lay on her side, relieving the pain. Mariamne put her hands on her hips, surveying their work and the pile of harvested plants.

'There is little left to do. I can finish it by myself. You must rest.'

Leah could not rise. Her whole body bore the memory of Simeon's heavy hand. 'I am sorry, Mariamne.'

Mariamne dropped to her knees beside her. 'No, Leah, I am the one who is sorry for what my son has inflicted on you. It must not happen again.'

Leah closed her eyes and allowed sleep to overtake her. She dreamed of her father in Roman auxiliary uniform stamping on a snake with his tough sandals;

of her mother brushing her hair in smooth, sweeping strokes; of her brother and Calev teasing each other. She could almost hear their voices. They sounded so real.

'Woman, let us help you. That load is too heavy even for a man.'

'Thank you for your kindness. I am most grateful.'

'Are you not Mariamne, the mother-in-law of my sister?'

'Yes, it is I. And you must be Atticus. Forgive me, I did not recognise you. You are far from your home.'

Leah's eyes sprang open. There before her were Atticus and Calev, two soiled angels, their faces grimy with travel, their cloaks caked at the hem with dried mud.

'We have been away many days on my father's business. He has not been well these past months. He asked us to visit you on our return journey, to inspect the olive grove and to see Leah.'

'Atticus!' Leah managed only a croak. She moved to rise and clutched her side. Atticus was with her in an instant.

'Leah, you are not well. Have you hurt yourself?' He turned to Mariamne in query.

It was Calev whose gaze fell upon her neck. His eyes narrowed and he elbowed Atticus. 'This was no accident.'

Leah pressed her fingers to her tender, bruised throat, to where both men now stared. 'I will recover. I just need a little rest.' She laid her hand on Atticus' arm, an assuring touch, assuring him, assuring herself that he was really here.

'Who did this to you?' he demanded.

Leah could not meet his piercing gaze. She could not betray her husband. It would bring shame upon Mariamne, Yosef, the whole family—her family.

'Perhaps it is the will of the gods that you have come,' said Mariamne. She paused. A beat, a breath, a bracing of her hands on the hoe. 'I am ashamed to confess that it was the hand of my son that brought this upon Leah. Since his father died he has been greatly troubled of mind.'

Atticus looked at Leah. 'Did you give Simeon any cause for his actions?'

'Does a woman ever deserve this treatment?' She bristled like a flaming thornbush. 'Our father has never raised his hand to our mother. It is not right.'

Atticus stepped back and his voice softened. 'Not all men are like our father.'

'My husband also was not one to raise his hand,' said Mariamne. 'I did not believe Simeon would ever do such a thing. I intend to speak to him but what is a mother's counsel to an angry son? I fear it may be fruitless.'

Atticus grimaced. 'You are right; this is a matter between men. But I will not discuss this with Simeon until my father has seen the grievous work of his hands.' He turned to Leah. 'You will return home with us.'

'No!' cried Leah. 'I cannot abandon my husband and my home. I beg of you, Atticus, do not act with such haste. I will soon heal and all will be well.' Her words tumbled out surprising even her. Here was a way out, a chance to escape Simeon's wrath, but then what? A widow in her father's house? The dishonour of divorce? She could not bear the shame of failing as a wife yet again.

'Your husband?' Atticus spat. 'He has forfeited the right to be called that. You are a Roman citizen. Your marriage contract is sine manu. It is our father, not Simeon, who has legal authority over you. It is he who decides.'

'Does your father not wish you to inspect the olive grove?' Mariamne spread wide her hands. 'The hour is late and Leah is exhausted. Allow her to rest this night and allow me to offer you the hospitality of our home. If Simeon has returned you can speak to him as you intend.'

Atticus looked sideways at Calev, raising his chin and a questioning eyebrow. Leah caught Calev's curt nod. 'We will accept your offer with thanks, Mariamne,' said Atticus. 'And tonight, Leah, after I have spoken to Simeon, I will decide whether your loyalty is wisdom or foolishness.'

Chapter 10

The light was fading and a chill wind whipped across the courtyard. Atticus and Calev had not yet returned from the olive grove, and Leah prayed they had not come across Simeon. As the hospitable host, and in the presence of the women, he might feel obliged to restrain himself. In the fields, she was not so sure.

She hurried to the storeroom. Wine spilled as she filled the jug; olives dropped as she scooped them into a bowl; she completely forgot the chickpeas. She set the food on the table and threw wood on the fire. On the smoking hotplate a pile of barley kernels, the first of the season, not yet ripe and no good for bread, hissed and sputtered.

The gate swung open and Atticus appeared. The sight of her brother eased her mind but not her thickness of throat. He waved away the wine the servant girl offered.

'Were the trees in good order?' asked Leah. She had not ventured into the grove over the winter months.

'They appear healthy enough although the pruning is careless. It will lessen the crop,' said Atticus, his eyes combing the courtyard. 'Has Simeon returned?'

Leah shook her head. 'Sometimes he stays away for days.'

'So he may not return at all?' He paced back and forth. 'We cannot wait all night for him to show us the record of accounts. Ask Mariamne if we can inspect them ourselves.'

Leah found Mariamne at the hand mill, grinding the grain, scooping the barley kernels into the opening at the top of the millstone and rhythmically turning the mill.

'It is my fault that we do not have flour for the bread,' she said. 'I asked the servant to grind less grain, to preserve our dwindling stores. I pray the barley is not late in ripening.'

'My brother and Calev do not need bread. The vegetables and roasted grain will be enough,' said Leah.

'Do family members deserve less honour than other guests? On the contrary, it is both a duty and a pleasure to provide bread for your brother and his friend. I am glad they have come …' Her voice trailed off and Leah felt the tension in her words.

How would Simeon react to seeing Atticus and Calev, to hearing whatever they might say to him? Was it really better that they were here or would it make things worse? Leah's head throbbed.

'Atticus wishes to see the records of the olive grove. Shall I fetch them?'

'Certainly,' said Mariamne, dusting the flour from her hands. 'I am almost finished here.'

Atticus and Calev spread the scrolls out on the table, pushing the food to one side. They perched on the edge of their stools, poring over the figures. They pointed and murmured and muttered. They did not look happy.

Over the meal they spoke of other things: their father's thriving olive grove but faltering health, Calev's journey to Arabia to trade oil for spices, their sister's new baby, anything except the one thing that hung over them all: Simeon's return. Leah strained to stay upright, her bruised body as heavy as a grain-laden cart.

'We will speak more in the morning, little sister,' said Atticus. 'You should rest.'

Leah showed the men inside to their mats, each covered with one of Mariamne's richly woven blankets. She wished she could sink onto one of them right now. She dreaded the effort of dragging herself up the cold stairs to her room. She dreaded more that somehow Simeon might be there.

The chill wind had not yet abated. It blew across the dark, silent courtyard, fanning the embers of the fading fire. Leah ascended the stairs, one painful step at a time. At the top she slumped down, her head in her hands, hopelessness falling upon her like a great cloak. She had tried to please Simeon, to be a good wife. For his sake, she and Yosef had kept themselves apart. If only he could see that they were for him, not against him. If only he was kinder. But it was like looking at an east wind and hoping it might blow west.

A sound carried high on the breeze, catching up her chin, setting wide her eyes. She crept to the edge of the roof and peered into the night. It was men's laughter—the callous laughter of abundant wine. There were Simeon and his friends, stumbling along, propping each other up and talking in loud growls like a pack of wild dogs. A chill shivered through her and she hurried to the safety of her room.

'Leah!' called Simeon, lumbering up the stairs. 'Come out, my wife.' The men had quietened below, shushing each other like mischievous children. Leah braced herself. She could not avoid her husband forever.

'Simeon, I have been waiting for you.' She reached out her hands to welcome him. He stopped before her, swaying a little and pressing his hand to his forehead.

'My wife, you are so beautiful. Why must you put me through this pain?'

'I have never wished to cause you pain, Simeon.' The knot in her throat pulled tight.

'But you have—you and my brother. That is why I must take you to the priest tonight.'

'The priest?'

'For the test of unfaithfulness.'

Her heart drummed a manic march. 'I have never been unfaithful.'

Simeon scowled. 'So you say, but how can I be sure? *Yahweh* will decide.' He gripped Leah's arm and steered her towards the stairs. 'We must not keep the priest waiting. He has prepared the curses and now waits only for you and a grain offering. Hurry and gather a tenth of an ephah of barley flour.'

Curses? What curses? She had no time to ponder. She had to get the flour and prayed there was enough. She dared not tell Simeon that their stores were nearly depleted. A tenth of an ephah was enough to make four large loaves of leavened bread, enough to feed their small household for at least two days. She prayed that Mariamne had not used all the flour she had ground that evening. She hurried to the storeroom, holding her lamp before her. She found the almost empty sacks of grain, and there, nesting in the loose folds was the bowl of flour, still half full. She measured out the prescribed amount, wrapped it tightly in a clean cloth and returned to the men who sprawled around the glowing embers of the fire.

Simeon snatched the bag of flour from her hand. 'We have waited long enough.' He grabbed her arm and marched her towards the gates, his friends scrambling to their feet and following after them.

'Halt!' Atticus shouted like a centurion. He and Calev strode towards them, their feet without sandals and cloaks askew.

Simeon dropped Leah's arm. His hand fell to his belt, his dagger. His friends also stiffened, alert, on guard. Atticus pushed past the surly group.

'Where are you taking my sister?'

'Your sister?' Simeon froze, for a slurred moment unable to comprehend.

'It's Atticus,' said Leah. 'He arrived today. I have had no opportunity to tell you.'

Simeon's hand relaxed. He stretched his arms wide in welcome. 'Atticus, an unexpected pleasure. Guests are always welcome in my home. I trust that Leah has cared well for you.'

'More than you have for her.' Atticus fixed a stony eye on Simeon. 'She is injured and not by her own hand. And instead of caring for her, you now drag her out in the night. What is so urgent that it cannot wait until day?'

Simeon's lips drew back taut and tight, his teeth bared in a skull-like smile. 'She would not have told you that I had just cause. Your sister is not as pure as she appears. We are taking her before the priest to submit to the test for an unfaithful wife.'

'Unfaithful?' Atticus' voice rose a pitch.

'It's not true,' cried Leah.

Simeon smiled coldly, his eyes bloodshot and bleary. 'We will soon know the truth.' He grasped Atticus on the shoulder, a false gesture of fellowship. 'Surely your concern is with the olives, not my wife? Rest, sleep, enjoy your stay in my home. This is a private matter between husband and wife.'

'The matter does not seem so private.' Atticus eyed the group of friends. 'If they are going, we are going.'

Leah tried to catch Atticus's eye, to show him her gratitude, but it was Calev, half hidden in the dark, who acknowledged her with a grave nod.

***

Simeon and his friends led the way, setting a brisk pace despite their stumbling and stopping every so often to relieve themselves at the side of the road. Atticus and Calev walked behind Leah where Simeon could not hear their muttering.

'Leah, is it true? Does Simeon have just cause?' whispered Atticus.

'I am innocent but he will not believe me,' said Leah, gritting her teeth at the pain reverberating through her bones with each step.

'Why are we letting him do this to her?' growled Calev. 'Look at her. She can hardly walk.'

'We are waiting for an opportune moment. This is not the time. Let him put Leah to the test—she is innocent and she is strong,' replied Atticus.

Her brother's words were like rods of iron, strengthening and encouraging her. If this was what was necessary to stop Simeon's anger, she would willingly submit to it. Not that she had a choice.

'What sort of a husband drags his injured wife out at night, under cover of darkness, to some ancient ritual without witnesses? He is vile, a serpent to be stopped,' muttered Calev. They fell back further continuing their murmurings all the way to the synagogue.

The synagogue stood on the outskirts of the town, built on the highest rise and facing Mount Gerizim, the holy mountain. It was a simple, square building, whitewashed on the outside, glowing in the moonlight.

Simeon led Leah inside, his fingers gripping her arm. She kept her eyes down, following the symmetrical patterns of the mosaic tiles, outlines of order bordering tangled wreaths of flowers, silver trumpets and the golden Menorah of Moses. The priest stood before the altar, his ghostly robe glowing in the lamplight, his pale prayer shawl twisted as though he had thrown it on in a hurry. His beady eyes strayed across her body and she wondered if Simeon was right about him lifting his robes to his serving girls. He muttered a few words and Simeon scurried over to sit on the bench with his friends. Leah stood alone.

'Bow your head.'

Leah obeyed, fastening her eyes on one tiny tile, counting each branch of the sacred golden lamp stand and holding her breath. One. Two. Three. Four. Her eyelids trembled, her teeth clenched tight, her chest cried out for air. Five. Six. Seven. The priest's hand clawed her scarf, tearing it away and tossing it to the ground. His beady eyes darted to the wound on her head and away again. He snatched the cloth that bound her hair and pulled it loose, sending shafts of pain through her scalp. Her hair fell about her shoulders and over her face. She heard Calev's shout of protest and wished that he and Atticus were not there to witness this humiliation. She bit back tears. Only a wayward woman would be seen in public with her hair exposed in such a way.

Anger surged through her like the sea over sand. She had nothing of which to be ashamed. Simeon was the guilty one. He would not have dared to bring her before the community of worshippers in the daylight for fear they would see the marks he had inflicted. He was a coward, hiding in the dark. How much had he paid the priest? They were as evil as each other. She looked at the altar before her. She could not trust these men but surely she could trust *Yahweh*. She raised her head high and waited before the Lord, the grain offering for her husband's jealousy in her hands.

The priest took a clay jar and filled it with holy water. He bent down and scraping dust from the floor, sprinkled it into the water. From the altar he took a scroll on which were written square characters in Aramaic and held it high before him along with the jar of holy water. His face glowed proud and portentous as he barked out his pronouncements.

'Woman, you are here under oath to accept the curses that *Yahweh* brings upon any woman who has been unfaithful. If no man has slept with you and you have not gone astray and become impure while married to your husband, may this bitter water that brings a curse not harm you.' He drew a raspy breath. 'But if you have gone astray while married to your husband and you have defiled yourself by sleeping with a man other than your husband, may this water that brings a curse enter your body and cause your thigh to waste away and your stomach to swell.'

Leah shuddered. Her thigh to waste? Her stomach to swell? That was the curse of barrenness. It would give Simeon every right to divorce her and marry another. To be unable to bear a child was the most shameful of circumstances. To be discarded by your husband because you could not bear a child was worse. She swallowed the nausea that rose up within her and spoke the required words.

'Amen. So be it.'

The priest grabbed the grain offering from her and waved it solemnly before the fire on the altar. Then he flung a handful of flour into the flames, filling the room with an acrid odour. He dripped water over the curses written upon the scroll until the letters dissolved and ran together, and he washed them into the jar of bitter water.

'May this water that brings a curse go into you and cause bitter suffering. However, if you have not defiled yourself, *Yahweh* will clear you of guilt and you will be able to have children.'

Leah shuddered again. *Yahweh* judged not only one's actions but also the thoughts and attitudes of the heart. She and Yosef had determined to stay apart, to respect her marriage to Simeon and to maintain honour in the family. But with every harsh word and blow Simeon quenched the love that might have been his and drove her more and more towards Yosef. Surely *Yahweh* could read her heart as an open book. Would she pass the test or be cursed for her love of another man?

The perverted priest thrust the jar of dirt and curses into her hands. She lifted it to her lips and drank.

***

On the dark journey home Leah thirsted for cool, clear water. Water to wash away the fragments of burnt parchment and grit abrading her throat. Water to soothe her bruises from the previous night's beating. Their progress was slow, too slow for Simeon and his friends. They strode on ahead, eager to return to their revelry.

All was quiet when they entered the courtyard. Simeon and his friends had drunk their fill. Some were sprawled under the grape vine; others fell about the dining table, their cloaks resting in pools of wine. Simeon, too, lay snoring, stretched out by the stairs, clutching a teetering cup of wine. Leah stole past him praying he would not wake, praying he would lie there until morning and then leave. At the second step a hand shackled her ankle. Her heart leapt to her parched throat.

'I've been waiting for you.' He shoved his cup at her, spilling wine over his tunic, over her feet. 'Get me more.' His voice was slurred and slow. His grip around her ankle slackened, his cup fell sideways and a great snore rolled through him. She stepped back into the courtyard, shaking.

'That is enough,' said Atticus, his voice a harsh whisper in her ear. 'You are not safe. Quickly, gather your belongings. You will not stay here a moment longer.'

This time she did not argue. Her brother's words were like the cool, clear water she longed for. Now she could think only of escape. She crept up the stairs, hastily wrapped her belongings in a blanket and stole back down, suppressing the urge to kick her sprawled out husband in the stomach. Calev took her heavy blanket of belongings and swung it over his back. Atticus helped her onto the donkey and silently they slipped away.

Chapter 11

'We will take the hill path,' said Atticus. 'It is rugged but more direct. We must hurry before Simeon discovers you are missing.' Atticus urged the donkey along. It plodded at a steady pace, each roll of its hind-quarters making Leah wince. She patted its sturdy neck, grateful she did not have to walk, hoping it would hurry.

Perhaps an hour had passed when she heard the sound of sheep. With the moon blotted by clouds it was hard to tell both the hour of night and the direction of the sound. The bleating grew louder, a flock of animals approaching. She peered through the darkness. A figure appeared on the hillside above them and Atticus and Calev drew to a halt. The man made his way down a rutted track, trailed by a line of bleating, snorting sheep. He raised his staff in greeting.

'Yosef!' Her spirit soared, like an eagle on the wind.

'Leah?' He stared as though at a ghost. 'What has happened?' He clasped Atticus and Calev on the shoulder. 'My brothers, what are you doing travelling at night? What has happened?'

'Your brother has attacked my sister in a shameful act of jealousy.'

'Attacked? Jealousy?' Yosef searched Leah's face and her heart swelled at his concern.

'Do you not know of what we speak?' asked Atticus. He grimly recounted the events of the evening. 'By his actions he has broken the clauses of the contract between our fathers. He has mishandled the olives as well as his wife. My father must see the evidence for himself.'

'What evidence? Leah, how has he hurt you?'

His voice, so tender and loving, brought pain to her parched throat. She swallowed back tears and raised her chin high exposing the hand marks on her neck. Yosef sucked in a breath.

'Like an animal marked for slaughter,' he muttered, his face as dark as the night. 'Go. A storm is brewing over the mountains. It will arrive before dawn. That is why I am taking this flock home. It is easier to shear dry wool than wet. Simeon has brought disgrace to our father's name. I thank the gods you were there to bring Leah to safety.' He reached for her hand in the dark, secretly squeezing it. Her skin tingled at his touch. He whistled gently to the milling sheep and goats. They lifted their heads, grass still hanging from their mouths, and trotted after him into the night.

The storm started with one drop of rain, then two, bursting like vine ripened grapes on the ground. A sheet of lightning lit up the hills and the path ahead. It roused Leah from her weary stupor. How much longer? She could see no welcoming lights ahead, only roiling dark clouds gathering strength. A burst of thunder shook the ground and the donkey halted.

'Come on.' Atticus soothed the wary animal. 'It's only thunder.' It resumed walking but its ears twitched; one forward, one back, on alert. A donkey's hearing was more acute than any horse; what was it listening for? The rain drops fell heavily now, battering the ground and blotting out their footsteps. She wrapped her scarf tightly about her and drew her cloak over her head. Atticus and Calev bent against the barrage and pushed on. Another rumble of thunder, this time from behind. Leah trembled. Did not the lightning come first? She looked behind. Lightning flashed across the sky and her heart stopped cold. It was not a rumble of thunder but of horses. Horses bearing down upon them like wild beasts.

'Atticus!' she screamed through the storm.

He was already dragging the donkey off the path. 'Hurry!' He pulled her from the donkey and pointed at the dark hills beyond. 'Run and hide amongst the rocks.'

It was too late. The horses were upon them, rearing up their front legs and foaming at the mouth. She shrank back in the darkness, crouching behind a nearby boulder

'So you thought to steal my wife,' Simeon shouted. 'Is this the way a guest treats his host?' He pulled a dagger from his belt, brandishing it before him. His friends did likewise.

Atticus did not flinch. 'You have no wife. My father will see to that when he views the work of your hands on his daughter.'

Simeon laughed and spat on the ground at Atticus' feet. 'He will not forfeit his interest in my orchard for the sake of a woman.'

'He may when he hears of the state of your accounts.'

'How …?' His face contorted in fury. 'That harlot! She has no authority to show you the scrolls.' He wheeled his horse around searching for Leah through the driving rain.

She cowered behind the rock, her heart pummelling her chest.

Atticus stepped closer to Simeon, his voice cold and calm. 'This is neither the place nor the time to debate. Turn your men around and leave while you yet retain some dignity.'

'Dignity! You will see dignity at the point of my dagger.'

He leapt from his horse, throwing himself upon Atticus. His friends leapt to the ground, daggers in hand. Leah clutched her hands to her chest, her shoulders hunching in horror. The panicked horses, the darkness, the pounding rain made it impossible to see what was happening. Atticus and Calev were outnumbered. She had to help. Her father had taught her to fight as well as Atticus. What was she doing cowering in the dark? She needed a weapon.

Stones! They were all around, scattered like hidden gems in the soaking grass. She dropped to her knees, ploughing her hands over the soil and seizing a handful. *Find higher ground.* Her father's battle instructions echoed in her mind. Along the path sprawled a sycamore tree. Bundling the rocks in her cloak she clambered up the slippery, gnarled boughs. The fighting was fierce below. She took hold of a rock. She could not distinguish between the battling figures; a random throw might hit Atticus or Calev. She needed a target. She strained to see, her heart pounding, not for herself but for her brother. She knew how vicious Simeon could be. His crazed curses cut through the night.

And then another shout—from far along the path. It was Yosef, running towards them, his cloak tucked into his belt. Where had he come from? She had no time to consider. He ran directly beneath her and into the thick of the fighting. She could see him breaking men apart, pulling them off each other and flinging them away. One rose up to attack him from behind. She took aim and threw her rock. It hit its mark and the man collapsed to the ground with a cry, clutching between his legs. She heard more cries, then a bone-chilling scream and then silence. Simeon's friends scrambled onto their horses and fled. Only one figure remained standing. She slid down from the tree and ran towards the men on the ground, her heart drumming with dread. It had been the scream of death.

Please not Yosef. Please not Atticus.

The man was on his knees now, bent over another, cradling his head. At the sound of Leah's frantic footsteps, he looked up, his face stricken. It was Calev. In his arms, as limp as a rag, lay Atticus, his eyes closed as though asleep except for a deep slash on his throat. Leah's hands flew to her mouth. 'No!' she cried. Tears spilled from her eyes. Coldness consumed her body. There was blood everywhere, running with the rain in rivers of red across the road. Her legs became like river reeds beneath her. They had killed her brother. Had they also killed Yosef? She saw two bodies slumped in the mud.

'Yosef!' She rushed to his side. He groaned and relief flooded through her. He lay sprawled on the road, his leg bent at an unnatural angle. There was a dark, jagged wound below his knee.

'Leah, you are here!'

She caught him in her arms, sobbing. 'You're not dead, you're not dead.'

'Is Simeon alive?' He strained to see.

How could he care for his brother? If not for him, Atticus would be alive and Yosef would not be lying here like a felled tree. Her lips pressed hard together. He deserved to die.

'Is my brother alive?' said Yosef. 'I must see him.' He dragged himself through the mud.

A movement caught Leah's eye. Simeon's fingers flexed as though he were trying to raise his hand. His dagger lay nearby. Was he trying to reach for it? She lurched forward and grabbed it, wielding it before her. She would strike him if she had to. He opened his mouth straining to speak. A word gurgled in his throat. His eyelids fell shut and with a final shudder he breathed out her name: 'Leah...'

**

The remaining hours of night were a thick mist, where voices and figures formed and faded. She vaguely remembered Calev running for help and returning with a donkey and cart. She vaguely remembered him lifting Yosef onto the cart and handing her a length of wood and some rags.

'Here, tie this to his leg.'

Leah obeyed. Yosef gasped and gritted his teeth.

The men dragged Atticus onto the other donkey, his body lifeless and limp. The taste of vinegar cut through the mist, running over her tongue, down her throat and through her whole bitter body. Atticus, her only beloved brother, had come to rescue her and now he was dead, murdered at the hand of her husband. If only she had not agreed to steal away with him. If only she had stayed. And her unwell father; how would he bear the loss of his only son?

Calev kicked Simeon's body off the road and tossed stones over it. It was a half-hearted effort, a duty executed with disdain, not enough to keep the wild animals at bay and yet she felt neither satisfaction nor concern. Calev caught her eye. His face held no light, only a glowering black grimace. They set off along the path, leaving Simeon's body abandoned, alone. The creaking of the cart, Yosef's mumbled groans and the jolting of her battered body were not enough to keep her awake. She closed her eyes and fell asleep.

The anguished cry of her mother roused her. The cart had stopped and the first rays of dawn streaked the sky. She was home, in her parents' courtyard. The familiarity of it all was a soothing balm, until she saw her mother. Her heart plummeted. She started to shake. Her mother was wailing over not one body, but two. Felled beside Atticus, his fist pressed to his heart, was her father.

Chapter 12

As soon as the week of mourning was over, Leah prepared to return to the home of her husband, to Mariamne and Yosef. She knelt on the floor, in the room of her childhood, absently pushing her belongings into a woven bag. She did not wish to leave. Here, she was welcome, cosseted, consoled within the family; a family that no longer had a father or brother. They had been torn away as a surging sea might sweep men from a ship. How she wished she too could be swept away. During this past week of grieving, guilt had gnawed at her, stooping her shoulders and slowing her steps. Even the presence of Dinah with her stories of Sychar and her copious hugs did not help. Everything, this whole tragedy, was caused by just one thing: her love for Yosef.

At the thought of him her heart skipped like a stone across water, and sank. He had remained here, groaning in pain until several solemn-faced workers from the olive grove had arrived to take him home—home to Mariamne who would be grieving, as was her own mother, at the bitter loss of a son. Yosef, as injured as he was, would bring some comfort but what of Simeon? Had his friends retrieved his body or had they been too late? The lions were hungry at this time of year. She hoped for Mariamne's sake they had found him.

Leah wiped the moisture from her eyes. The wild beasts would not get her father or Atticus. They lay still and silent, side by side in the family tomb. Leah had wept with her sisters and mother; a brood of weeping women bereft of men. Yet that was not entirely true: her sisters had their husbands. It was she and her mother who were widows. Without her father and Atticus, how would her mother manage the olive grove? Would Marcellus take charge? Or would a male relative claim authority over their share of the estate? How she wished she could stay to support her but she was not free to do so. This was no longer her home. She belonged to the house of Simeon and the law demanded that because she had borne him no children, she must marry a close male relative. Their firstborn son would carry on Simeon's name so it would not be blotted out forever. Yosef was the closest relative but would Mariamne allow them to marry?

She pulled the cord tight on the bag and heaved a ragged sigh. Mariamne surely suspected her affection for Yosef; she had implied as much on the morning after Simeon had beaten her. It was this that had driven Simeon to drag her before the priest. Did her love for Yosef condemn her to the curse of a barren womb? They had not lain together but did a kiss make her an adulteress? The law was clear: anyone who committed adultery was forbidden forever to marry their lover. If Mariamne suspected adultery she had every right to deny her Yosef, to cast her off to some other male cousin to fulfil the duty of yibbum.

A moan, like a wind across wasteland, shook her shoulders. If only she had loved Simeon more, if she had shown him more respect, if she had hardened her heart against Yosef. Perhaps then he might have softened towards her, cared for her.

Leah forced herself to rise. She could cry no more tears. She looked around one final time at the welcoming comfort of her childhood home. She was a child no longer.

***

Leah drew her widow's garb closely about her, grateful for the seclusion it offered. She did not want to see the piteous stare of each passing traveller. She and Calev were taking the longer route, along the main road to Jerusalem, and she was grateful that they would not have to pass the sprawling sycamore tree with its memories of murder.

'Do you need to rest?' asked Calev.

Leah shook her head. 'I am quite well. I could walk, you know.'

He had insisted that she ride upon the donkey, as though she were an invalid. Her bruises had healed and the pain in her side had subsided. Her only wounds were on the inside and sitting on a donkey would not help those. Calev shrugged his shoulders, his face as lifeless as the rocks scattered in the fields.

'If that is what you want.'

He led the donkey to the side of the road and stopped. Lifting a skin of water to his lips, he drank deeply and watched Leah dismount. He wiped his mouth and passed the skin to her. The water was cool and refreshing. She stretched her stiff limbs, as glad to be off the donkey as she was sure it was. Even without Leah it carried a heavy load. Calev had packed his possessions, his tent and enough food for a journey of weeks.

'Where do you plan to go?' she asked.

'I have a relative in the east, over the Jordan River. He travels the silk route as a merchant. He has need of men to ride the camels.'

'Can you ride a camel?'

'I will learn.'

'The desert is a harsh place to live.'

'Better the desert where there is hope than here where there is none.' Even now his voice carried the grit of the great arid expanse beyond the Jordan. 'There is nothing left for me here now that your father and Atticus are gone.' He pulled tight the girth straps on the donkey, his face averted, his unspoken accusation hanging in the hot air—*since your husband murdered them.*

She kicked at a stone in the dust. Would she ever be able to lift her head high again? And yet … she chewed her lip … it was her father who had insisted on this marriage. She had submitted to his wishes, not once but twice. First, with the weak, ailing son of a friend and second, to a man consumed with jealousy and violence. Her nails dug into her palms.

Surely her father had been different with his liberal Roman outlook. He had taught her and Atticus equally to read, to run, to wield a dagger. Surely he had believed he was doing the best for her. Surely he had loved her. A salty warmth spread on her tongue. She wiped her lip with the back of her hand. The smear of blood brought with it an odd satisfaction. She raised her head high. She was strong. She would survive. And so would Calev.

***

They entered through the large wooden gates and Leah could not help but hesitate. The courtyard was silent … grieving. She took a deep breath, preparing herself for whatever reaction Mariamne might have. The dogs barked and ran up to them, sniffing and licking and wagging their tails. They seemed pleased to see her.

Mariamne appeared around the far corner of the house carrying a large basket of coloured cloth. At the sight of them, she dropped the basket to the ground and hurried over, her hands outstretched.

'Shalom, my daughter. My heart rejoices to see you.' She clasped Leah to her chest and then stepped back, holding her at arm's length, her face drawn, a sad smile upon her lips. 'And yet my heart grieves for the loss of your brother and father ... and your husband, my son.'

'Is he ...' Leah's voice trailed off, recalling Simeon's body barely covered with stones.

'He is with his father,' Mariamne replied, adding no explanation as to how he had been brought to the family tomb.

'I must go,' said Calev. He spoke through hard-set teeth.

'Please, you must eat something,' said Mariamne. 'You have travelled far to bring my daughter safely home. I cannot send you on your way without food and water.'

Calev's knuckles clenched white around the donkey's lead, his haunted eyes glanced about the courtyard. 'I am sorry. I have a long journey before nightfall. I cannot stay.'

Leah understood. He could not bear to be here, in the home of the man who had murdered his closest friend.

***

After Calev left, Leah and Mariamne sat in the shade of the almond tree. Bees fed on the flowers, their whirring wings sonorous in the silence. How quiet it was without the sound of men. Where was Yosef? Who was tending to him? Her concern must have shown on her face. Mariamne touched her hand.

'Yosef is well but weak. The wound was not clean. We wash it day and night and it is starting to heal.'

'I am relieved to hear that,' said Leah. Her gnawing guilt suddenly burst forth. 'I am so sorry, Mariamne. Everything is my fault. If only I hadn't ...'

'No, my daughter, this is not your burden to carry alone. Simeon was not a good husband. Before you were betrothed I feared it might be so, and yet I hoped ...' She pressed her hand to her brow, closing her eyes. 'I, too, bear responsibility. I loved him as every mother loves her child. He was my firstborn, at least the first who survived.'

There was a catch in her voice; Mariamne too had suffered the loss of an infant.

'Simeon came into this world as violently as he left it. For many days I hovered between this world and the next. When I was finally able to hold him in my arms, I did not wish to. My heart was frozen. I could think only of the child I had lost. Her sweet face still fills my dreams.' Her voice was subdued, drifting on dark, distant clouds. 'When Simeon arrived, he demanded more than I could give.'

'And Yosef?'

'Yosef returned the sun to my soul.' She twirled an almond flower absently in her fingers. 'Their father trained them both up in the way they should go, but Simeon constantly chose the way of the unwise. I tried to love them equally but it was so much easier to love Yosef ... as you yourself know.'

Leah cringed at her candour. She could stay silent no longer. She had to confess. She had to tell the truth.

'Yosef came across me searching for my goats. He helped me find them and from that moment I could think of no-one else. I hoped he would return to discuss marriage with my father. When he did not, I determined to put him from my mind. I accepted my father's choice of a husband but I did not know he was Yosef's brother.' She looked into Mariamne's face, gentle, understanding. Tears sprang to her eyes, spilling down her face. 'I really did try ...'

'I know, my daughter. Yosef has told me everything.' She tossed the flower away. 'My husband and son are gone. We cannot bring them back. It is just the three of us now.' She leaned forward, clasping her hands in her lap. 'I have considered this matter with great care and now I will speak openly. Yosef has assured me that you and he have not lain together.'

'I would never have dishonoured this family, my family, in such a way,' said Leah.

'I did not think so, my daughter.' She took Leah's hand in hers. 'My greatest hope is that you may already carry Simeon's child. We will wait two months. If you are not with child I will assign the duty of yibbum to ...'

Yosef, Yosef, certainly it would be Yosef. He was Simeon's brother, the one appointed by the law to marry the childless widow of the eldest brother, the one whose duty was to father for his dead brother a son to perpetuate the family name. But still she held her breath.

'… Yosef.'

Her heart leapt like a child in the womb. She squeezed Mariamne's hand. 'Thank you.'

'When Yosef recovers, he can inform the elders at the town gate. Only respect my request: before you lie together you must wait two cycles of the moon – for the month of mourning and for a further month.'

Leah climbed the stairs to her room and paused at the door. All was as it had been a week earlier except for the absence of Simeon, the absence of fear. Soon she would be Yosef's wife. How her heart rejoiced. Yet still there were shadows of Simeon everywhere—on the steps where he had sprawled, on the roof where he had cast her aside, in their room where she could still see herself cowering in the corner, hands raised in defence against his blows.

She dipped a cloth in a bowl of water, freshened her face and fastened her hair with a clean strip of linen. She yearned to see Yosef, to see that he was recovering, to see her soon-to-be husband. She did not have to wait long.

'Yosef eats less than a sparrow. Soon he will look like one too,' said Mariamne, folding coloured lengths of cloth into sturdy, cilicium storage bags. 'There, we are finished.'

Leah tied the bags firmly and Mariamne stretched her back. 'Let us pray you can entice him to eat.'

Leah filled a small bowl with dried dates, along with salted olives and a jug of water. She had never been into Yosef's room. It would have been unthinkable. Now she had every reason. She would tend to his wounds for as long as it took him to recover. He lay prostrate on his mat, his bandaged leg resting on a plumped up pillow. His face was pale and gaunt, his dark curls tousled like a young child.

'My son, Leah has returned to us,' said Mariamne.

He raised his head and smiled. The warmth of a thousand suns drenched her soul.

'Shalom, Yosef.' She walked towards him, her eyes never leaving his. She knelt at his side and poured water into a cup. His fingers brushed hers. He raised the cup to his lips.

'Leah, it is good to see you.'

Her throat tightened. Her heart overflowed with joy, sorrow, bitter relief. She trembled, willing her hands to settle in her lap.

Mariamne placed the olives and dates in front of him. 'Will you not eat a little, Yosef? It will strengthen you.' He picked out an olive and placed it in his mouth, a smile spreading across his face like the dawn. 'These are truly good.' He popped one after the other into his mouth, chewing the meaty flesh and spitting the stones into his hand.

'See how his appetite has returned! Leah, you are an answer from the gods.'

The days settled into a steady routine of cooking, weaving, and tending to Yosef. Every day he regained a little more colour, a little more strength. The poultice of balsam and bees' honey soon helped the wound heal leaving only an angry red scar that dulled with each passing day. Each evening Leah retired to her room where, like the waning of the moon, the ghosts of Simeon gradually departed. In their place grew an ever-brightening gleam of anticipation: soon she would truly be Yosef's wife.

Chapter 13

The moon was full. Leah rose from her bed and wrapped a shawl about her shoulders. It was the month of *Nisan* and despite the pleasant days, the nights were still cold. She stepped outside and stared at the stark sky. Was it the full moon, gleaming in glorious splendour, which had awakened her? She heard the faint flutter of moths in the moonlight and the chirp of grasshoppers. All seemed familiar.

She gazed across the courtyard to where Yosef lay and saw the dim glow of a lamp. He was awake. She drew her shawl snugly about her and slipped down the stairs. At the door to his room she hesitated. What would Mariamne think if she discovered her here, alone, at night? But what if Yosef needed help? She would just quickly check and then leave. No harm would be done. She tiptoed inside.

'Yosef?' He was sprawled on his back, hands behind his head, the thin covering moulded to his body. At her voice he sprang upright.

'Leah, what brings you here?'

'I saw the glow of the lamp. I thought you may need help. Are you in pain? Shall I bring you some herbs?' Her words tumbled out like the rushing of a stream, like the rushing of her heart.

He looked at her, his eyes hungry, his voice hoarse. 'I have need of only one thing.' He reached out his hand to her.

'We have promised Mariamne.'

'And yet you are here.' His skin gleamed bronze in the lamplight, across his broad shoulders, across his bare chest. 'Have we not mourned enough?' His eyes burned into hers. 'You are my beautiful wife. Come to me, *mellita*.'

His mouth upon hers was the sweetest spiced wine. She could scarcely believe no-one stood between them. He whispered her name and kissed her neck.

'Leah, let us wait no longer.' His hands slid beneath her robe, easing it from her shoulders, freeing it to fall in a heavy, crumpled heap. He traced her bare skin as one might a fine fresco or a fragile flower. 'So soft, so soft,' he breathed, trailing kisses over her throat, her shoulders, her beating breast. She was a butterfly on the breeze, his touch bearing away her body, her heart, her doubts.

'My husband,' she whispered and he pulled her to him beneath the blanket. The embrace of his arm, the graze of his beard, the heat of his skin, entwining, entwining, entwining. His body held the tang of the earth, the tang of sweet sweat, an oasis of henna and honey. She stifled a cry of joy and drank from the river of life, drank until she was drunk.

At the first pale streak of dawn Leah stole across the silent courtyard and up the stairs to her room. She lay on her bed, contentment filling her to overflowing, spilling through her heart, her mind, her body, like abundant rain softening and soothing and smoothing every ragged and grieving edge. Yosef's love was like no other, pure yet powerful, caring yet confident, as though he had slept with many women, yet she was surely his first. A cloud crossed her thoughts: Yosef was not her first; if only he had been. Her first husband had been a reed in the desert, wilted and weak. Simeon had been a wild ram, driven and cruel. Both had left her parched, thirsting for she knew not what. With Yosef, she would never thirst again.

Already she missed him—the strength of his arms, the graze of his beard, the spice of breath. She would go to him again tonight and the next night and the night after. He was her husband. Except that no-one could know.

A whisper of incense wafted over her. She rose from her bed and wrinkled her brow. Was Mariamne burning incense to the gods? She followed the fragrance to an alcove near the vegetable garden lush with leeks, mint, coriander and thyme. Mariamne knelt before a stone altar, murmuring incantations.

'Leah, you have risen early. Come, join me in my prayers.' She touched the stone basin filled with smoking incense, as though it were the finest alabaster. 'I had it especially built.'

Leah contained her surprise. Mariamne had often referred to the 'gods' but she had not expected her to worship them. 'I did not know that you prayed.'

'Until recently, I have not, and I fear that my faithlessness has caused my misfortune.'

'Is it not enough to worship *Yahweh*?'

Mariamne lifted her palms and her eyes heavenwards. 'How are we women to worship *Yahweh*? By traipsing up the holy mountain three times a year only to sit in our tents while the men offer sacrifices? By cooking every Sabbath while the men pray in the synagogue? Can *Yahweh* hear our cries when we are not permitted to worship him with burnt offerings and sacrifices?'

'Can you not simply pray?'

Mariamne shook her head. 'A true god requires sacrifices. *Yahweh* will only accept sacrifices from men, and he has taken almost all my men from me. There are other gods to whom I will appeal.' She picked up a small bronze statue, cradling it in her hand. The face was familiar.

'Would you worship your husband?' Leah shuddered. The word of the law, taught to her by her father, repeated to her by her mother, came to her: *Do not cast for yourself an idol in the form of anything in heaven above or on earth beneath or in the waters below. Do not bow down to them or worship them.*

'My grandmother told me that our loved ones who have passed to the next life have the ear of the gods. They will speak on our behalf if we appease them with our offerings.' She placed a sheaf of freshly picked herbs and vegetables on the altar, murmured a few words and turned to Leah with a serene smile. 'If only I had known earlier the peace that worship brings, the assurance that the gods are smiling down on us.'

Leah had only ever worshipped *Yahweh*. Yet her father's years of service across the Roman Empire had given him a liberal view of other religions: *Let them worship their gods, and let us worship ours.*

'I am glad for the comfort it brings you. I will leave you to finish your prayers in peace.'

Mariamne took her hand. 'Will you not stay with me a while?'

Leah hesitated but a moment. What harm could it do to kneel here beside Mariamne? She did not have to pray to her gods. She knelt on the woven mat and followed the elder woman's movements, touching her fingertips together in front of her, bowing her head and closing her eyes.

Mariamne chanted the name of Aphrodite, whispering words of petition and praise. Leah thought only of Yosef, whispering words of devotion and love.

When Mariamne finished her prayers and fell silent, Leah opened her eyes. In the palm of her hand Mariamne held a gold pendant tied with a fine leather cord. Engraved on it was the likeness of a half-naked woman, holding her fallen robe with one hand and touching her hair with the other. 'I have been praying that Aphrodite will look with favour upon us. She is the queen of fertility, beauty and love. This household has need of such things.' She rubbed her thumb over the golden coin.

'It is beautiful,' said Leah, avoiding Mariamne's eyes. Love, fertility—could she suspect that she and Yosef had already lain together? 'I have not seen you wear it before.'

'I bought it only recently, in exchange for three of my best rolls of cloth.'

'You sold the blue cloth, the one dyed with the murex?' Had Mariamne truly traded such valuable fabric for one gold pendant?

Mariamne smiled that same serene smile. 'Do not be concerned. There is still cloth on the loom which, with the blessing of Aphrodite, I am sure will surpass in splendour the ones I sold.'

Leah breathed lightly, knowing that Aphrodite, if she were truly a god to be worshipped, had already bestowed her blessing of virility and love.

Later that morning Leah stood over the fire, roasting a portion of the new season's barley for their midday meal. The grains had ripened in time to refill their depleted stores. She shook the heavy pan to stop the grains sticking and gave the other pot on the fire a quick stir. In it bubbled more of the creamy oval grains. These she would dry and store, ready to use in soups and stews, or for a nourishing gruel drizzled with honey from the date palm.

At the scraping of dirt she looked up to see Yosef, propped on two sticks, limping towards her.

'That smells good.' He brushed his face against her hair, a brief moment of intimacy, before resuming a respectable distance between them.

'Do you mean the roasted barley or the fresh air?'

'I mean you,' he whispered, setting Leah once more ablaze.

'Come and sit over here while I finish the barley. It will soon be ready.' Her words were stilted, as though she were on a stage, saying one thing and thinking another. How hard it was not to kiss him, to hold him. She brought him a cup of water and it seemed he had read her mind.

He leaned towards her and said in a low voice, 'Waiting only makes the moment sweeter.'

'Tonight,' Leah whispered and quickly returned to the fire. She did not want the servants to see.

The day dragged as slowly as an old ox. At the meal, at the barley field and later at the loom, Leah nodded while Mariamne chatted, but she was not listening. Twice she dropped the spindle at a momentary memory of Yosef's hands upon her body.

'Is something troubling you, my daughter? Your hand is usually so sure. Today it is like soap.'

Leah steadied her thoughts. 'I was considering how quickly Yosef is recovering from his injuries. It is good to see him able to move about again.'

'Indeed, and these bright days of *Nisan* will only speed his recovery, praise the gods.' She rubbed the golden idol hanging about her neck.'

After the evening meal, when the animals had been fed and the household had quietened for the night, Leah prepared herself. She brushed her hair until it fell over her shoulders like a silken cloak. She dabbed perfume on her neck, her wrists, her ankles—not too much lest the fragrance linger in Yosef's room. She filled a tiny jug with olive oil and draped her finest robe about her, re-arranging it over and over until it hugged the curves of her body. She waited until the moon was high. Then, tiptoeing down the stairs and across the courtyard, she crept into Yosef's room.

He had pushed his mat aside and in its place was an ornate rug scattered with soft, coloured cushions. She did not care how he had managed to obtain the furnishings or how he would hide them in the morning. He rested on one elbow, his eyes fixed upon her as she loosened her robe and let it fall to the ground. Naked, she walked towards him, holding only the jar of olive oil. She knelt at his feet and poured out the oil, smoothing it over his legs, brushing the jagged scar with her lips. Her hands moved higher, pushing aside the thin blanket that covered his strength.

'Waiting only makes the moment sweeter, my husband,' she whispered, planting kisses like tiny seeds on his thighs, his navel, his throat.

He pulled her to him and her body melted like oil warmed in the sunlight, like nectar dripping from the vine.

Afterwards they lay collapsed in each other's arms. 'I wish we did not have to hide our love,' whispered Leah. 'I want the whole world to see that I am yours and you are mine.'

Yosef nuzzled her neck. 'I have been yours alone from the moment we met by the mandrake. But, my neshama, it is only right that my mother hope for an heir from Simeon.'

'It is a hope in vain. Simeon did not sleep with me in those last weeks. He touched me only to hurt me.' She could not bear to add that he would often steal away, returning before dawn with the stench of sex upon him.

Yosef held her close. 'Let's not speak of my brother now. We will have a son to bear his name but not his nature. We will bring him up in a way that would make my father proud.' He grinned. 'And then we will have many more!'

He kissed her skin moving his mouth slowly over the mounds, into the valleys, slowly lower and lower until Leah's back arched in anticipation and only the livestock in the nearby stable heard their veiled cries of love.

Chapter 14

Night after night, as the full moon waned to a sliver, Leah went to Yosef. Each morning she stole back to her room and lay dreaming of their night together.

One morning, as she lay on her bed listening to the crow of the rooster, she heard another sound—a foreign sound. It drifted through the still morning air across the fields and into the courtyard. It was the sound of hushed voices. Leah sat up, at once on guard. She listened again and heard a man's laugh, low and ugly. Beads of sweat broke out on her forehead. Her heart drummed a deadly beat.

Could they be travellers, passing the night nearby? Yet who would make a journey through here? It was far from the main route for travellers. She leaped from her bed and stepped out onto the roof, straining for a glimpse of whomever it might be. The voices were closer now. Could it be visitors from the nearby village? Not at this early hour. Her heart thumped harder. Thieves stole crops and livestock at night but bandits attacked in the early hours, when households were in the midst of morning duties and the gates were open. Her gaze flew to the courtyard below. She gasped. The gate stood ajar. One of the servants must have gone to collect wood or water. Beyond, she saw three cloaked figures, swords at their sides, run from the trees. She raced down the stairs desperate to beat them to the gate, screaming with all her strength.

'Bandits! Bandits!'

She reached the entrance at the same time as one of the servant girls and slammed the gate shut. They were too late. A muddy boot wedged in the gate. A sword swished close. Leah sprang back and the bandits stormed in. They grabbed Leah and the servant girl, twisting their arms behind their back and menacing them with their swords. The servant girl cried out but Leah kept silent. *Show no fear*—her father's battle instructions echoed in her mind. The third man kicked the gates wide open and whistled. Leah heard the sound of horses' hooves; there were more. She held her breath, trying to still her hammering heart, and silently cried out to *Yahweh* for help. The bandit's hands were greasy around her wrists and his wild beard, so close, scratched her cheek. He reeked of dried sweat, sour milk and animal dung. The bandit holding the servant girl looked much the same but the third man wore an ornate robe and his beard was trimmed. In the marketplace at Sychar he might be mistaken for a prosperous merchant, except for his filthy boots and sword. He turned to Leah and smiled the smile of a snake.

'This is the household of Simeon, master of the olive grove, is it not?'

Leah shuddered. His voice was as well oiled as his beard. 'Why do you wish to know?'

The man holding her twisted her arm harder and raised his sword to her throat. 'Answer with the truth, if you want to live.'

'Yes, yes, this is the home of Simeon,' Leah managed to croak against the press of sharp metal.

The man in the ornate robe extended a hand, the smile fixed like a mask upon his face. 'My master is not a violent man. He only wants his money returned as was agreed.'

Her mind raced. What money? Who was his master? Then she remembered Simeon and Yosef's argument over money, the one that had incited Simeon's violence against her. The Jewish merchant whom Simeon had refused to repay must have commissioned these men of violence to collect the debt.

'Simeon is dead …'

'Silence! I will not listen to a woman's lies.' He nodded to two of his men. 'Find him.'

The men ran into the house and Leah prayed that Yosef had hidden or escaped. One injured man was no match for this band of thieves. She must try to appease them with words.

'I can get you the money.'

The man turned towards her, his eyes glittering. He flicked his wrist and the man holding Leah lowered his sword. Leah seized her chance.

'Sir, I can see that you are a man of reason. Please allow me to find the money we owe you. Simeon kept it up there.' She pointed to the roof.

The man rubbed his oiled chin with a filthy thumb and forefinger. He squinted at her with beady black eyes, and pursed his lips. 'Let us see what you have, and if it is enough. My master requires full repayment, with interest.'

She dared not ask what type of interest he expected. She only prayed that Simeon had not spent all the money. Shouts rang out from the house, a scream and then silence. The bandit's beady eyes darted like a bird of prey from her to the house to his horsemen.

'You two, get inside! Capture that swine!'

They had no time to obey. An arrow flew across the courtyard, striking one of them in the knee. With a cry he dropped to the ground, clutching his leg. A second arrow followed, piercing the other in the thigh. He wailed and writhed like a worm, the arrow lodged deep, still quivering. Leah did not smile but within her sparked an ember of satisfaction and relief. Yosef had overcome his assailants and his aim was as true as his heart. Better to cripple than take a life.

The man in the robes took cover behind the horses. 'Simeon, you will pay for this,' he shouted. 'Come out or we will kill the woman.'

The bandit threw his thick arm over her chest and pressed the sharp edge of his sword to her throat. Sweat broke across her brow. Her neck stiffened and pulled backwards. His hot breath rasped in her ear. 'You're too delectable to waste on death, even for a Samaritan.' His tongue slithered across her skin and her gut curdled.

'Let her go!' Yosef strode from the house, gripping his sword and trying to hide the limp that would mark him as easy prey. His face was as grim as the grave.

The man in the robes smiled his snake smile and waved his hand as though swatting a fly. The bandit withdrew his sword and Leah let out her breath. She blinked away a tear. She would show no fear.

'What do you want?' Yosef stood a sword's length from the robed bandit, his weapon at the ready.

'You know what I want, Simeon.'

'Simeon is dead. I am his brother.'

'You lie!' The bandit spat at the ground. 'My master never mentioned a brother. No, you are Simeon and I have come to collect your debt.'

'I will gladly pay whatever money we owe,' said Yosef. 'Just let the woman go. She will gather what we have and bring it to you.' He caught Leah's eye, a fervid stare. What was he trying to tell her? To escape? She would never leave him to face these bandits alone.

'It is not only money that you owe, Simeon.' The man stretched his arm high. The sleeve of his robe slipped back revealing a reddened stump below the elbow. The man had no arm. 'Did you think I would not recognise the dog that attacked me in the night? You took my arm. Did you hope the lions would take the rest?' The man took a menacing step towards Yosef, wielding his sword.

The bandit holding the whimpering servant girl threw her aside and advanced towards Yosef.

'I am not Simeon.' Yosef stood firm, his sword at the ready.

Leah's mouth went dry. She knew. The blood on Simeon's tunic, the tunic she had thrown in the lion's den, was the blood of this robed bandit. *Show no fear.* Her father's words flew away, like a feather in a storm.

The two bandits lunged at Yosef, their swords clashing in furious combat. Yosef pushed them back, striking the robed robber across the cheek. He bellowed, blood streaming from his face and charged forward. Yosef jumped sideways. His injured leg gave way. He crashed to the ground and Leah's heart stopped. With a savage roar the man in robes swung his sword and brought it down on Yosef's arm. Blood spurted out. Leah screamed. Her hands clutched her chest. She tried to break free but the bandit held her fast. Yosef's arm hung like a rag, almost severed from his body. Blood drenched the ground. Her heart tore in two. She could do nothing to help him.

'An eye for an eye, a tooth for a tooth, and an arm for an arm.' The bandit smeared the blood from his face with his one arm and smiled his serpent's smile. 'One debt has been repaid, and now for the other.' He shouted at the man holding her. 'Hurry. Get the money and all her jewellery.'

Loosening his vile grip the bandit prodded her up the stairs to the roof. She stumbled to the corner where she had seen Simeon lift the tiles, rubbing the tears from her face. These thieving dogs could take the money but they could not take her beloved Yosef. They would pay for the evil they had wrought upon him. She crouched in the corner and saw that the edge of one tile was roughened by use. She prized her fingers into the tiny gap between the tiles and lifted it, praying she would find the money. A small goatskin pouch lay tucked amongst the straw. Her heart sank at the size of it. The bandit shoved her aside and grabbed the bag, tugging it open and tipping the coins on the ground.

'Scarcely enough to feed our horses,' he said, dropping to his knees and scooping the coins back into the bag. His eyes were off Leah and his sword lay unguarded. In one swift movement she lunged for it, swinging the heavy weapon in a wide arc and smashing the flat side of it down on his head. He slumped silently to the ground. Her blood rushed. Her heart raced. She ran to the edge of the roof, ready to throw the sword like a spear at the serpent below.

He stood over Yosef, his sword poised over his heart. A quivering cold coiled through her.

'It is you, is it not, Simeon? Are you not the lion that stalks the road to Jerusalem; the wild beast that attacks innocent men on their way to worship at the holy temple?'

Yosef struggled to speak, his words forced out between laboured breaths. Blood ran from his severed arm in a crimson stream. 'I am not ...'

'Do not deny it!' the bandit roared. 'There are witnesses. And on the testimony of two or three witnesses you shall be put to death!'

'No! He's not Simeon!' Every part of Leah screamed. Every muscle, every sinew, every fibre. But it was no use.

The bandit plunged the sword into Yosef's chest. He let out a strangled sigh and his head slumped to the side. Silence.

'No, no!' Leah screamed a wretched wail. It rose up from the depths of her soul, a wrenching, tortured tearing in her heart. Her hands tore at her robe. Yosef lay as still as stone; his eyes fixed and without light. A dark stain spread out from the hole in his chest. The robed bandit stood over him, his sword still dripping, a foul smile on his face. A cold, black chill fell upon her. An icy shroud that crushed her to the ground.

***

Rough, calloused hands grasping her legs and arms jarred Leah awake. The bandits were hauling her across the courtyard. She slumped between them like a sack of grain. There was no reason to fight. If they wished to kill her also, it would be a blessing. Yosef was dead and she had no desire to live. She kept her eyes firmly shut praying for the blackness to engulf her once more.

'Take her to the house,' growled the bandit in charge. 'Bind her and search the place. We need money and jewels. And do not delay.'

The men dragged Leah inside, dumping her in a corner and binding her hands and feet. She heard them stamping through the rooms above and the crash of Mariamne's loom. Mariamne! Had she escaped? Had she witnessed the murder of her one remaining son? A surge of fury roused her. She struggled to loosen the cords. They chewed into her flesh. The men lumbered back down the stairs, carrying a pile of Mariamne's woven mats.

'She is a choice morsel,' said one of the men. 'And I hunger …' He stepped towards Leah. She shrank back in the shadows, not daring to breathe.

'We have no time for that,' replied the other. 'You can quench your thirst tonight in Jerusalem.' They staggered outside with the mats. Leah heard a cry of rage from their leader.

'You asses! Is that all you could find? Even if we could cart them all the way to Jerusalem they would bring us no money. We need coins, gems, jewellery! Keep searching!'

She heard them thundering up the stairs. They would surely find her gold and ruby earrings, the wedding gift from Simeon. They could have them; they held no value for her. But her father's gift to her, the turquoise studded bracelet, was precious beyond measure. She twisted her fingers, straining to slip the ropes over her wrists. Her arms ached from being stretched behind her back. Her struggles yielded nothing.

Shouts of glee carried from the roof followed soon after by the sounds of the men preparing to leave. What had they done with Yosef? Was he still lying abandoned in the courtyard? Her eyes blurred with tears. She strained against her bonds. She had to get to him.

The bandits were still outside, the leader barking orders. She wormed her way across the floor, the ropes gnawing her skin.

'Well done, my friends. Load those men onto the horses; they will soon revive.' She heard grunting and groans and a flood of curses. 'And mind your pouches. If you lose even one gem, you will pay for it.'

She heard horses' hooves and fading cries of elation, and something else.

What was it? She reached out and grabbed the door post, dragging herself to the entrance. The courtyard was empty apart from Mariamne's discarded mats. No Yosef! The strange noise was louder now, a fierce crackle coming from the storeroom and animal pens. Flames erupted.

'Help! Fire!' she screamed into the deserted courtyard. Where was Yosef? Surely they had not put him in the flames. 'No, Yosef! Yosef!' She screamed his name over and over, a guttural, wailing cry. She dragged herself from the building, choking in the clouds of smoke. Flames licked the roof, feeding on the straw like a ravenous beast. Two figures hurried towards her through the gate.

'Leah! Thank the gods you are safe.' Mariamne whipped out a knife and cut her free. 'Quickly,' she ordered the servant. 'Bring out all the fabrics you can carry. I will follow shortly. Hurry!'

'Yosef.' Leah clutched Mariamne's arm. 'They killed Yosef.'

Mariamne's mouth dropped open, her face crumpled. 'Not my son, my only son.' Her hands shook. 'Where is he?' All around them the buildings burned. She shook Leah. 'Get up, get up! We must find him.' Her voice was frenzied, pitched higher than a screeching owl. 'Get water!'

Leah stumbled to her feet and raced to the water jars, filling two jugs. She ran into the house after Mariamne, to where the servant was gathering piles of fabric and precious dyes. Smoke seeped through the roof making her eyes water and throat burn but there were as yet, thankfully, no flames. She ran through the rooms that opened out onto the courtyard, searching for Yosef. They must have dragged him into the fire. Was it not enough to kill him? The cords of death encircled her, squeezing from her an anguished cry. She ran across the courtyard to the storeroom and the animals. The flames were most fierce here, with thick black smoke and the hissing and cracking of oil jars and collapsing beams. The heat forced her back. It was too late to save anything or anyone. She fell to her knees, her hands clawing at her hair, talons tearing at her heart.

'Yosef, Yosef,' she screamed over and over.

Mariamne staggered through the smoke and gripped Leah's arm. 'We cannot save him,' she cried. 'We must go. If we stay, we also will die.'

'We cannot leave him to burn,' Leah wailed.

'We must.' Mariamne dragged her to her feet, her face ashen and smudged with smoke. They stumbled towards the open gates, stopping only to gather up in their arms as many of the salvaged fabrics and rugs as they could. A mighty crash. A surge of heat. The walls gave way. They fell in a fiery heap sending up showers of sparks. Beside her, Mariamne let out a torn, ragged sob. Their home was destroyed and so, Leah knew, was her life.

Chapter 15

Once again Leah wore the harsh sackcloth of a widow and sat with Mariamne, barefoot on the floor. She was unable to eat or even smile at the generous hospitality of Mariamne's friends. They housed them and tended to them as fragile plants uprooted by a storm. She had no desire for comfort. She wanted only to kneel in the smouldering ruins of her home and scoop ashes on her head. But there was nothing there for her now. All that remained was a fuming heap of rubble. The flames had consumed everything.

The workmen found Yosef in the stable, his body charred beyond recognition. They insisted on wrapping him in linens before she or Mariamne could see him. They sought to spare her added distress but not being able to see his face one last time, as destroyed as it might be, had been just as heart wrenching.

Now it was the third day and once again Leah was walking with the women to the tomb. On this final day of attending the body she carried an alabaster jar filled with precious myrrh and spices. The fragrance seeping through the loose clay seal brought with it memories of their nights of passion, his strong arms beneath her, his warm breath upon her neck, his whispered words of love. Tears flooded her eyes, spilling down her cheeks. She stumbled and Mariamne caught her arm.

'Take care, my daughter.' Mariamne's eyes were dry for the moment. The storm waves of grief broke upon each of them at different times.

The sun was lukewarm and the morning air crisp when they arrived at the family tomb. Two of Yosef's workmen waited for them as they had each day. It was the season for spreading sheep dung around each olive tree, a laborious task, and she was grateful for their sacrifice of time. They dropped their knucklebones, sprang to their feet and hurried to the tombstone, heaving it aside.

Mariamne stooped to enter and Leah followed, leaving the other women outside. Their small oil lamp illuminated the gloomy space. Carved into the walls were niches large enough to hold a body. Some were empty. Some held simply carved stone boxes, the bones of past ancestors. Some were sealed with slabs of stone. Behind these lay the bodies of Simeon and his father, waiting to be placed alongside their ancestors, waiting for the flesh to fall from their bones. One held Yosef, his body wrapped in linen cloths. Mariamne anointed him with oil and unbidden tears. Leah unstopped the jar of perfume. Fragrance filled the room. She dripped the precious perfume over Yosef's body and bitter tears burned her eyes. It could not conceal the acrid smell of charred flesh. With weeping words they recited the prayers for the dead.

When they had finished Leah left Mariamne alone with Yosef. She waited at the entrance watching Mariamne tenderly stroke her fingers over his head as a mother does with her child. From outside she caught fragments of whispers.

'… what man would have her now?'

'… two husbands dead …'

'… and now the brother …'

'… a curse on the family…'

The muted mutterings pierced her heart. She drew in a breath and listened.

'But she is beautiful … two olive groves … a Roman citizen …'

'I am ready.' Mariamne interrupted her eavesdropping. Her face was as grey as a stone in shadow, lines etched upon it like the carvings which marked the entrance to the tomb.

Leah took a final, lingering look at Yosef, and then stepped outside. The waiting women stopped mid-sentence, caught in their idle speculations. They opened their arms and Mariamne fell into their consoling embrace. Leah sank onto a nearby rock allowing the sun to warm her chilled bones. A sudden wave of nausea came upon her and she bent forward, taking quick breaths, hoping the other women would not notice. Their words still pecked at her—small, sharp jabs in her wounded soul. *What man would have her now?*

She could not contemplate marriage. Her heart was forever Yosef's. Yet without a man to represent them, would she and Mariamne be able to manage the olive grove? They were widows with no-one to plead their cause. And where would they live? It would take months, perhaps years, to rebuild but they had no money; just the few smoke-tainted fabrics they had snatched from the flames. Her head pounded. The women's voices grated. She rose unsteadily to her feet. She and Mariamne would stay no longer than the week of mourning. Like carrying a dim lamp along an unlit path, she could see only the next step. They needed to be with family, and the only family that remained was her mother.

***

By the seventh day, Leah could cry no more. She was a wrung-out rag, weary with sorrow, yet dry eyed. The haze of grief was clearing a little and on this final day of mourning, they sat outside, their bare feet tucked beneath their robes, watching the children playing in a gnarled oak tree. In a secluded part of the garden, dappled with sunlight, Mariamne's friend had set up a low bench with several platters of food. Each day she had brought delicacies which, despite her urging, they had barely touched but today, Leah felt a pang of hunger. Rays of light danced over the freshly baked bread, steaming lentil and barley stew, pistachios and a cluster of raisins. She scooped a small portion of stew into a bowl and broke the bread.

'Will you not eat something, Mariamne?' she asked. 'It is truly delicious.' She smiled at their hostess. 'Thank you.'

Mariamne plucked one raisin from the stalk and, staring at it for a moment, placed it in her mouth.

'That is hardly enough,' chided her friend, setting a tiny serving of stew before her. 'Please, my sister, eat a little or you will not manage the journey tomorrow.'

'You are like a pair of old hens,' said Mariamne. She dipped a spoon into the stew. 'I will eat, if only to stop you fussing.'

Leah smiled. Already she could feel the goodness of the food reviving her spirit. She had not cared about the dust clinging to her skin or the tangled mess of hair beneath her head scarf. But now, after a week without bathing or wearing shoes, she looked forward to washing away the smell of smoke and with it, she hoped, enough grief to allow her to make some decisions. They would make the journey to her mother tomorrow. It was surprising that she had not visited during the week of mourning. Perhaps she had not heard the news or perhaps she had no-one to accompany her. A woman did not travel these roads alone.

She watched Mariamne peck at her food—little sparrow's mouthfuls, hardly enough to sustain her. Had her mother also stopped eating? She too had lost both her husband and son. She, her mother and Mariamne were alone. All their men had gone to the grave. Who would protect them now?

Memories of chasing through the olive trees with Atticus flooded back. He had come to her rescue and it had caused his death. A shadow of sorrow passed across her. It had been barely three cycles of the moon since Simeon had killed Atticus and caused her father to drop dead with grief; barely three cycles of the moon since she had last cleansed herself after a week of mourning; barely three cycles of the moon since she had needed to cleanse herself from her monthly bleeding.

She stopped, arrested by the thought.

She raised her eyes to the cloud studded sky and counted. Was she with child? Her heart leapt at the thought, pouring hope through her like a late winter stream. If she was pregnant, it would not be Simeon's; it would be Yosef's.

She could claim the child as Simeon's and pray that no-one, especially Mariamne, calculated the months too closely. Surely the joy of a child to continue the family name would outweigh any suspicion. She turned her face to the sun and closed her eyes, letting it warm her whole body.

The children's cries carried through the garden. They held an air of excitement. Leah opened her eyes to see the boys in the highest branches of the tree pointing beyond the compound's walls.

'Look, a Roman! See his sword!'

'He's coming here, he's coming here!'

A little girl ran over to the women, breathless and blanched. 'Shall we shut the gates?'

The gates were open, ready to welcome visitors. The mourners had dwindled over the week to barely any on this final day. It had been a blessing, a day of rest, and now a Roman was coming—to a Samaritan household.

'A Roman? On his own? Coming here?' Mariamne's friend straightened her robe and tightened her head scarf. The Roman strode through the entrance, the spring of youth in his step despite his sparse grey hair. His legs were solid and sturdy beneath his short tunic and on his feet he wore the distinctive sandals of a soldier. Behind him, standing tall and straight, was a well-groomed servant holding two donkeys. Leah stared across the courtyard at the man. He spoke quietly to Mariamne's friend and looked somehow familiar. He gestured to his servant who responded as a soldier receiving orders and led the donkeys to a nearby trough of water. The children gathered around, keeping a cautious distance, their eyes fixed on his glinting sword. He unsheathed it and they jumped backwards. He balanced it on his outstretched palm and beckoned the children closer. At that moment Leah recognised him. She and Atticus had touched the same sword on the same outstretched hand.

'Marcellus!' The sight of her father's closest friend filled her with joy. She had seen him amongst the many mourners of her father and Atticus but it had been several years since she had spoken to him. She recalled the rare occasions that her father had taken her and Atticus to the magnificent villa on the hill. He had held them captive with his tales of battle and adventure. She set down her dish and hurried to him.

'Marcellus. Greetings.' She wanted to grasp his hand in welcome but she withheld, not wanting to risk offending her hosts.

'And you also, Leah.' He bowed his head slightly, his eyes warm and kind in his solemn face.

'The overseer of our olive grove informed me of the attack. Was it bandits as they said?'

'They were brutal.' Leah's lip quivered. She could say no more.

'I am deeply sorry. Trouble has heaped itself upon you these past months. Your father and brother are greatly missed by the people of Sychar, particularly me.'

Simeon's name hung between them, unspoken. Better to say nothing than to speak ill of the dead.

He continued. 'And your brother-in-law killed also; it is a tragedy.'

'Yes,' Leah said, her throat clamping tight.

'How is your mother-in-law? To lose both sons is a heavy burden to bear for any mother. I have seen it too many times.' His voice held the weariness of too many wars, too many battles, too much bloodshed.

Mariamne's friend returned from scolding one of the children who had been trying to ride the dog like a donkey. 'Sir, come. Refresh yourself. We have water, wine and an abundance of food.'

'Thank you. It has been a long journey for an old man,' said Marcellus.

After Marcellus had eaten, he sat with Mariamne for a time. Leah rested in the shade, observing their lengthy conversation. They would be speaking of the olive grove. With no men remaining, Marcellus would now have to discuss matters with Mariamne directly. Mariamne leaned towards Marcellus, her attention focused. She smiled, the first true smile in a week.

Leah's eyes drooped. She was so tired. Her thoughts ran to Yosef and a desperate longing for his touch overwhelmed her. She was like a well without water, forever to be denied her source of life. She fought back tears. The effort brought on a surge of nausea, and with it a tiny surge of hope. She prayed silently to *Yahweh*: Please, please, please let me be with child.

'Leah,' Marcellus called. 'Come and join us. We have much to discuss.'

She joined them, curious at the glimmer of life in Mariamne's face.

'I confess that I have come here not only to mourn the dead but also to propose an arrangement,' said Marcellus. 'Your father was like a brother to me, and as a brother I am obliged, indeed, I want to ensure the safety of his family and his finances. As you know we were partners in the olive grove. Since your father's death I have taken control.'

'My mother trusts you,' said Leah. 'I am not surprised she asked you to take care of her affairs.'

Marcellus's eyes grew tender in his battle-lined face. 'Leah, your mother has not spoken since the death of your father. If it were not for the efforts of her servant girl, she would remain in her bed all day and night. As it is, she must be helped outside each day where she sits like a statue until someone takes her in again.'

'*Ima*? It cannot be!' Shadows closed in on her. Was she cursed to lose everyone dear to her?

Marcellus leaned forward, his elbows resting on his thighs. 'Sorrow has stolen her spirit. She needs the care of her family but when your sister offered her hospitality, your mother stubbornly refused.'

'I, too, would not wish to leave my home. It is all she has left,' said Mariamne.

Leah laid a hand on her arm. Mariamne too had lost her home, her husband and sons. 'You are right, Mariamne. It is too much to bear. We will go to my mother tomorrow. We will take care of her.'

'You have always had a good heart, Leah,' said Marcellus. 'But women living alone, with no men to protect them—it is not safe … as you both well know.'

'What else can we do? Where else can we go?'

'You can come to live with me.' Marcellus spoke with the boldness of a decision already made.

Leah gasped. 'We cannot! Three women living with an unmarried man … it is not possible. It is not permitted.'

'Not unless one is married.' Marcellus looked at her with a directness that made it clear he was serious.

'Marry? You?' She could not have been more horrified if he had asked her to eat roasted pig. She had no desire, no room in her heart for any man except Yosef.

Mariamne clasped her hand. 'Do not fret, my daughter. Listen to what he has to say. His proposal is honourable.' She rose stiffly and with a fleeting smile, left them alone.

Leah stared after her. Mariamne knew his plan and approved. She could at least listen to him.

'There are many forms of marriage amongst Romans, as amongst you Samaritans,' said Marcellus. 'Those who bear the favour of the gods marry for love. Your parents were blessed to be among these. Other marriages are more pragmatic.'

Leah nodded. She knew well enough of this type of marriage.

'Our marriage would be one of mutual benefit, a business arrangement if you like.' He lowered his voice but not his gaze. 'As your husband I would demand nothing from you.'

'Nothing?'

'Leah, I am old enough to be your grandfather. Your father saved my life on the battlefield. I would not dishonour our friendship or his name by demanding what you would not wish to give.'

'But why would you do this for me, for us? It is charity beyond all expectation.'

'It is not charity, it is sound business. By marrying you I maintain my interest in your husband's olive grove. I do not wish it to fall into the hands of some distant relative who might bring it to ruin. Neither does Mariamne. As for your father's interest, it would have gone to Atticus. Now, with no males remaining, ownership reverts to me. By marrying you, the two olive groves become one. We will manage them together; I will teach you.'

'Does Mariamne not wish to be involved?'

'She does not wish to consider such matters and your mother cannot. Both are too fragile; both need a place of rest. My villa is too large for one old man with his servants. It would bring me great pleasure to share it with you and your mother and Mariamne.' He leaned closer to her. 'It is not you who will benefit most from this arrangement, Leah; it is I.'

'Will my mother agree to leave her home? Have you asked her?'

'We have agreed that she will be close enough to walk there each day if she wishes. And if she chooses to sit under the vine at the edge of the garden she will be able to see the house in the valley below.'

Leah sifted through a tumult of thoughts. He was offering her a secure future, a luxurious place of residence and a way to care for both her mother and Mariamne. And he required nothing in return. Was he being honest or, like Simeon, would he change as soon as she became his wife?

No, Marcellus had only ever been kind and generous. But to marry such an old man when she was barely eighteen years of age? While other young women were eagerly preparing themselves for their first husband, a man they hoped would give them love as well as children, she was contemplating a third contract of convenience. Thoughts of Yosef swirled through her mind, the weight of him upon her, the tang of their bodies, and the tenderness of his words. She would never again experience such love.

She stared at the children playing in the courtyard, the boys sword-fighting with sticks, the girls threading their hair with flower chains. If she carried Yosef's child she would need the security Marcellus offered. Would she prefer to raise a child as an unmarried Samaritan widow or as the wife of a wealthy Roman?

She looked at the man before her. His hair was thinning and streaked with silver but he had the physique of a man many years younger, his muscles carved, his skin taut. His gaze upon her was confident and calm, neither the ravenous gaze of Simeon nor the timid gaze of her first husband. There was strength about him, like a sturdy rock in a sweeping tide. He offered her security. She could trust him, she was sure.

'There is one other matter of which you must know … I may be with child.' She held her breath, studying his face for signs of concern. She saw only joy.

'So Mariamne will have a grandchild and, with the benevolence of the gods, a son to continue the family name and claim his inheritance.' He clapped his hands together in the way of the men at the city gate. The matter was settled. 'This is excellent news and a more compelling reason for us to marry. If he is a boy I will teach him the skills of the trade, the art of negotiation and the ways of a warrior—all necessary to ensure a prosperous olive grove.'

His eyes danced and she yielded.

'Yes, Marcellus, I will marry you.' She strained to return the smile that broke out upon his face. Her head said yes but her heart still struggled.

He took her hand in his. 'I promise to take good care of you, Leah. You are like a daughter to me but to the world, you will be my wife. Let us tell Mariamne the good news.'

Leah had other news to tell her, and as soon as possible. Mariamne must believe that the pregnancy was well along. She must believe that the child she carried was Simeon's.

Part 2

Chapter 16
AD 26 Three years later

It was not yet summer and still the sun beat down on the fields of barley and wheat, hastening the ripening of sheaves from green to gold. Soon it would be *Shavuot*, the harvest festival when everyone made their second pilgrimage of the year to Mount Gerizim. Everyone that was, except Leah, her mother and Mariamne. They had celebrated the holy festivals in the sanctuary of Marcellus's villa, avoiding the shallow sympathy and curious gossip of the other Samaritans.

This year they would gather at the edge of the villa's carefully groomed gardens overlooking the fields below and utter prayers to *Yahweh*, thanking him for his bountiful provision from the land. This year Leah would tell Benjamin how the great prophet Moses brought the Law down from Mount Sinai, inscribed on stone tablets by the very hand of *Yahweh*. This year, his third year, he might help her recount the stories that her mother could not. She remained mute, unable to speak since the death of her husband and Atticus. Her face fell away to one side, like the melting of wax, and saliva seeped from the corner of her slack mouth. Yet her hands were quick to mend a garment or tend the gardens, and quicker still to gather Benjamin in her arms, kissing his bruises and wiping away his tears.

Benjamin had arrived three weeks before his time. A surprisingly robust baby, he had allayed Leah's fears that Mariamne might detect the discrepancy of dates.

'A little late, just like his father,' she cooed. 'Simeon would be proud.'

Her words settled the matter: the child was Simeon's and any suspicion otherwise was extinguished. Leah praised and thanked *Yahweh*. She had clasped the truth to herself sharing it only as she lay alone in her bed, her precious secret whispered into the darkness.

'Benjamin is ours, my beloved Yosef. You would adore him. He is as strong and handsome as you are … were.' The dreadful word bore down upon her sharper than any birthing pang. She would wrap her arms tightly around her curled-up body, stifling the sobs.

She could barely remember, indeed was relieved to forget, that first year of grief. The birth of Benjamin had brought but a brief respite of joy soon overwhelmed again by tormenting thoughts that permitted no sleep. Thoughts of thieving Jewish bandits; bloodthirsty, arrogant men with their crooked religion. The sooner the Messiah came and set them straight the better; something along the lines of Sodom and Gomorrah. Images of flaming sulphur raining down on Jerusalem brought a glimmer of light to her dark nights.

It was not until well into the second year, months after they had taken the bones of their loved ones and placed them in the sacred stone boxes alongside their forefathers, that the heaviness had started to abate.

'*Ima.*' Benjamin's sweet voice drew her from her dark memories. A tiny plump hand touched hers. She reached down and scooped the little boy up into her arms.

'My love, what have you been doing?' His hands were blackened with soil, his face too.

'I am playing with the worms. I built them a house. I will show you.' He squirmed out of her arms and ran off past the carefully tended beds of purple hyacinth and bright yellow narcissi, stopping to lift his hands to catch water sprinkling from a fountain and then ducking behind a hedge dotted with tiny fragrant flowers. Leah chased after him. His youthful exuberance was the sweetest medicine. She found him crouched over a pyramid of soil, poking it with his chubby fingers. Dirt clung to his tiny tunic where the fountain had sprinkled it.

'What a beautiful home you have built,' she said. 'Do you think the worms like it?'

'Oh yes, *Ima*, look!' He dug into the rich soil and carefully extracted a thick, writhing worm. 'See, he is smiling!'

The poor worm didn't look especially pleased but Benjamin beamed with such pride in his construction that it made Leah laugh, sending ripples of warmth through her as soothing as her daily massage.

'He looks hungry. Let's put him over here where he can find food. He must stay strong and healthy to do his work—just like you.'

'What work, *Ima*?'

'He has very important work. He is like a tiny plough that keeps the soil healthy. A garden without worms is a very sad garden.' Benjamin stared solemnly at the worm burrowing into the dirt. Leah tickled him. 'And your *savta* will also be sad if we do not go inside and eat her delicious soup.' She took Benjamin's hand and they skipped along the paving stones that led to the villa of Marcellus. Even now after three years of marriage she still did not think of the magnificent villa as hers despite the ring of topaz and gold that circled the third finger of her left hand, the finger from where, Romans believed, a sinew ran straight to the heart. Marcellus had seen too many sinews of slashed open bodies to believe such a myth but his intentions to honour her as his wife were sincere.

The savoury scent of soup seasoned with herbs wafted from the villa. Benjamin tugged at his mother's hand.

'I am as hungry as a war-horse, as hungry as a war-horse.' Benjamin skipped along beside Leah. His singsong voice was like the sun in spring, filling her with joy.

'Who taught you that?'

'Marcellus. He says it all the time, like this!' He rubbed his tummy round and round.

'He would know; he rode many war-horses when he was in the Imperial Roman Army, just as your grandfather did.'

'Tell me another story, *Ima*, please.' She had told Benjamin every story she knew about her father's exploits. Benjamin never tired of hearing them, over and over.

'I will if you eat all your soup, including the leeks.'

'They taste like worms.' He screwed up his little face.

Leah decided it was better not to know how he knew the taste of worms. They entered the rear courtyard. It was paved with large brick-coloured tiles and dotted with painted earthenware pots from which spilled trails of coloured flowers, trimmed bushes of rosemary and abundant bunches of dill, coriander and mint. In one corner stood a brick woodfired oven, large enough to bake six loaves of bread or to roast a lamb. Through the wide wooden doors was a small coquina, complete with benches for preparation, a raised fire pit and an oven. It was rarely used; Leah's mother preferred the fresher air of the outside fire. She was standing over it now, stirring the soup and flipping the flatbread onto a plate. She held her arms out to Benjamin who ran to her, chatting away about worms. She scooped him up; hugging him close. Wrinkling her nose at his grubby face she threw Leah a questioning look.

'He was playing with worms in the dirt.'

Her mother rolled her eyes and her face eased into a knowing smile. Had Leah and her brother not also played day after day with worms in the dirt? Had they not also been caught up in her strong, loving arms, sniffed by her straight, sturdy nose? Had their bumps and bruises and aches and pains not also been cured with her kiss? A gentle warmth spread through her—the warmth of a spring day by still waters. These three years had restored her soul.

Yet one concern remained. It poured in only when her thoughts were clouded and grey, when she lay alone and awake in her bed, far from the chamber of her husband. Marcellus remained steadfastly true to his promise; his kisses remained affectionately on her cheek, his arms respectfully about her waist, never above or below. But now she felt a change in her body, a welcome thaw, and with it a growing readiness to give herself to her husband. Surely Marcellus would desire children of his own. She could think of no better way to repay him for his generosity and kindness. She was past twenty years of age. She could bear many more children. But he had not once shown desire for her. Did he not want her? Was he not drawn to women?

She walked through the atrium, past carved pillars and fine frescos, the matron of her household preparing to inspect the olive grove with her husband. And as she walked she determined one thing: she would not let this day pass without determining if she was capable of quickening her husband's desire.

Chapter 17

It was dark when she and Marcellus returned from their inspection of the olive grove. The trees were bursting with blossoms, the workers were content and Marcellus had included her in every discussion with the buyer from Italia. A Samaritan would never include his wife in this way. Indeed, from the discomfort displayed by the prospective client, it seemed few Romans did either. Marcellus, however, had continued to ask Leah to explain the figures on the scrolls estimating the number of jars, the cost per shipment and the expected delivery time. He listened like a proud teacher, offering words of support and encouraging the buyer to sample the golden green oil. They had secured an excellent price and now, filled with exhilaration, gratefulness and several cups of wine, she strolled close to Marcellus through the lamp-lit gardens.

'When I married you I did not expect you to teach me, even encourage me in the affairs of men. It brings me great joy to help you oversee the welfare of the workers and to deal with our clients.'

'It brings me joy also, to have you by my side,' replied Marcellus, 'as a companion and as a wife.'

'Then let me be truly your wife.' She reached her arms around his neck and kissed him, a lingering kiss, a kiss awaiting a response. His mouth softened beneath hers, drawing her in, and tiny glowing embers tickled her belly. Suddenly he stopped. He placed his hands gently on her shoulders and held her at arm's length. The fledgling embers flickered and died.

'Leah, I never imagined that I would marry, especially a woman as beautiful as you. The gods have looked on me with favour.' He pressed his lips tight, his gaze sombre and strained. 'Remember how I promised that I would demand nothing from you?'

'You have been true to your word but ...' She wanted to tell him things had changed, she had changed.

Marcellus pressed his fingers to her lips. 'I knew that you would welcome such an arrangement at the time. And I hoped that it might continue; that I would never have to reveal to you the true reason for such a proposal.'

The true reason? Her heart stepped up a beat—a soldier's quick march, alert, on guard. She did not know if she wanted to hear the truth.

'When I was much younger, and your father younger still, I was injured in a battle. An alliance of Germanic tribes ambushed us. It was a disaster— almost three legions wiped out and our auxiliary army decimated. Your father saved my life.'

Leah remembered the remnants of story of which her father had rarely spoken.

'The doctor did the best he could in the circumstances but he could not fully repair the damage. For many days I hovered by the shore of the River Styx. When I recovered, my men were astonished. In their eyes I was whole again, divine mercy from Mars. Only your father knew the truth.' He looked away, his mouth pressed thin and straight, his jaw set hard as a shield. 'Like any young man I was hot-blooded and fond of women. But that part of my life was forever changed by my injury. I would never be able to father a child, never be able to provide a woman with all she should expect from a husband.'

She saw on his face shame—raw, naked shame—and her heart welled within her. 'Oh Marcellus, that is truly a tragedy.' Children were a man's crowning glory, a reward from *Yahweh*, and Marcellus was condemned to have none.

'I do not want sympathy; it is for the weak. It is why I have retained this secret, despite the rumours and taunts that my appetite lay not with women. I diverted all my energy to war and trade knowing I could never have a wife.' He turned now to Leah and squeezed her hand. 'So now you see why my proposal that seemed so generous was in fact selfish. You were the one woman that I could marry and not disappoint because I knew, I assumed, you had no interest in me, in that way.'

Leah drew back. Not disappoint? Had he imagined she would never desire children? Had he hoped his advanced age would repel her? Her grief for Yosef had finally retreated to a precious corner of her heart allowing space for Marcellus' attention and kindness to kindle … What was it that she felt for this man who was older than her father?

Marcellus continued. 'You are the daughter of my trusted friend, a man I considered a brother. Although you are to the world my wife, to me you will always be a daughter.' He took a deep breath as though preparing for some unsavoury task. His gaze was directly upon her, his jaw set stiff. 'If you wish to bear children, the one thing I cannot offer, I will not stand in your way. I would willingly sign the papers for divorce.'

'Divorce?' The word was as bitter as gall upon her lips. 'How can you imagine I would ever wish such a thing? How can you suggest it?'

She flung her arms around him.

'You have pulled us from the depths of despair and brought us to this place of respite. You have taught me the skills of trade and the art of negotiation. You have provided for our every need, and … you are my closest friend. I do not wish to leave you, Marcellus.'

Would she discard this secure life, this kind man, for the sake of bearing more children? To whom would she bear them? Would she risk suffering with another like Simeon?

Marcellus held her close, his arms encircling her like a strong tower. 'I am relieved to hear you say such things. I do not wish to divorce you, Leah, but every young woman expects to bear children. I would not wish to stand in your way, to deny you.'

Leah rested in his embrace, his voice tender against her hair.

'Leah, when your father died I thought I would live out my days here alone and with no one to confide in, no one I could trust. But you have brought the spring back into this wintery old place: you, Mariamne, Benjamin and even your dear mother, as afflicted as she is. The house is alive as it has never before been.'

'But I am not your daughter; I am your wife. Surely you desire affection?' she whispered, brushing her lips against his neck.

'As every human does,' he sighed.

Sympathy and love swelled in her heart. She held him close and realised it was as he had said: their love was not the passionate, possessive love of eros but the brotherly, affectionate love of phileo.

He kissed her tenderly on the forehead. 'It is better if we remain as we are, as the closest of companions. I am sorry I cannot give you more.' He turned quickly and strode towards his quarters. She wrapped her arms around herself, suddenly cold, and retreated in the other direction.

Benjamin's room was close to hers and she looked in on him as he slept. His tousled curls, so like Yosef's, brought a sad smile to her face. He would never know his father. It was Marcellus who showed him the tender love of a father. It was Marcellus who taught him little phrases and songs and allowed him to hold his bow and arrow. Children were like a quiver of arrows, the number of them bringing honour to the parents who bore them. She would be grateful for this singular, sweet arrow for—the thought settled like a sad stone in her heart—while she remained Marcellus's wife, she would bear no more children.

In the quietness of her room she removed her outer garments, extinguished her lamp and climbed into bed. Questions swirled in her mind. Marcellus craved affection but did desire not also stir within him? Had he never sought comfort through his many years? He was old but he was still a man. She wanted to bless him as he had blessed her, to comfort him in whatever way he wished. Her eyes grew heavy. She pulled up the sheet and drifted into sleep.

The creak of the door woke her. Through the haze of sleep and the darkness of night she saw a figure standing there. A cry of fear rose to her lips and then fell away.

'Marcellus,' she whispered.

'Will you hold me tonight?' His voice was broken, stilted, like scratches in the dirt. She reached out her arms and he came to her, wrapping his arms about her and drawing her near. He buried his face in her hair and sighed. Sleep tugged at her mind, clouding her thoughts. She took his hand and guided it to her breast. He moved it away but held her close.

'Just hold me, please. It is enough.'

Leah pressed her body against his; allowing the rise and fall of his breathing to lull her to sleep. If it was all he wanted; it was all she would give.

It was still dark when a sharp blow to her back jolted her awake. Marcellus remained asleep but his arms and legs thrashed the covers as though threshing grain. His head tossed side to side like a ship in a storm, his mouth muttering wild commands. She reached through the dimness to soothe him. He grabbed her arm and wrenched it with fearful force. She cried out and shook him, trying to loosen his grip.

'Marcellus, wake up!'

He opened his eyes and relaxed his grasp.

'It's just a dream, a bad dream,' she soothed.

He did not hear her; his eyes were focused on events long past and he uttered frantic fragments of words. She jumped out of bed and poured a cup of water, raising his head and encouraging him to drink. He took a sip and then with a wild shake of his head, threw himself back, sobbing in his sleep. Water soaked his tunic and seeped into the linens. She lay next to him, holding his hand, watching his face contort in anguish and sweat break out upon his brow. And then she understood. His bed could never be a place for pleasure; it would always be a place of torment, a place where every night he continued to fight the brutal battles of his youth.

***

Leah rose late the following morning. Marcellus had gone and sunlight streamed through the shutters. Visitors were arriving from Sebaste in the late afternoon. Before they arrived she had to help Mariamne with the weaving and take Benjamin to search for woad. She would slice the green leaves from the splaying plant and he would hold his hand over hers. She would squeeze the dye from the torn, boiled leaves and he would do likewise, waving his hands around like two blue birds.

Leah entered the weaving room, chewing her lip. It was a spacious room, flooded with sunlight so that even during the cooler months it remained warm. On this mild, almost summer day, Mariamne had pushed back the doors and opened the windows so a cool, gentle breeze blew through. Mariamne stood at the loom, casting the spindle back and forth. When she saw Leah she stopped, wiping her brow with the back of her hand.

'I am glad of an excuse to rest! It is hot work.'

'Let me help,' said Leah, 'although you may not want my help after my last effort. Where was my mind using the blue thread instead of the red? Have I ruined it?'

'All is well, Leah,' Mariamne said. 'Your error has become a blessing.

Come and see.'

Leah studied the fabric on the loom. The pattern was so unusual, so exquisite, that she could only touch it in surprise.

'You made that from my mistake?'

'I did not want to undo your work so I thought of a way to turn the mistake into something new. Is it not wonderful?' Mariamne beamed.

'It is,' Leah agreed, amazed at how the threads that had seemed so out of place, so wrong, were now an intricate part of the pattern. She grasped Mariamne's hand. The idea she had been considering for the past few weeks spilled from her lips.

'No-one weaves flax with such skill as you, Mariamne. Marcellus says that in all his travels never has he seen such beautifully coloured cloth as we have created this past year. Let us share this talent with others, and make a profit from it.'

'Would Marcellus approve?' Mariamne looked concerned.

'He will be proud of us. He has no reservations about allowing women to make money. It is what he has taught me these past few years.'

'How do you suggest we go about selling our cloth? We live too far from the market in Sychar.'

'We do not need to take our wares to the market; the market will come to us.'

Mariamne looked puzzled. Leah continued, excited that she was finally speaking out her plan.

'Marcellus entertains guests from all over the world. I know they are mostly men who admire a stola purely for the promise of what lies beneath, but sometimes they bring their wives. If we can entice even a few of these women to purchase our wares, we might soon have a steady trail of customers.'

'It is a good idea. When do you hope to start?'

'Tonight! Marcellus has invited two patricians, and one is bringing his wife. I will use the red cloth we dyed last month.' She pulled it carefully from its storage basket and draped the fine linen across her shoulder and around her waist. 'It is a sin to keep such skills purely for our own pleasure.'

Mariamne laughed. 'You are becoming as wise as your husband in matters of trade. He has taught you well.'

'He has,' agreed Leah. 'I can balance the accounts for the two olive groves and it is a joy to talk to the workers during our inspections. We are blessed to have such loyal labourers. They are like family.'

'It is because Marcellus is so generous to them, exceedingly more generous than we ever were.' Mariamne's voice held a hint of regret.

'Marcellus has means beyond all of us,' Leah reassured her.

'Yet it seems that the more he gives away, the more he prospers.'

'I too have noticed it,' said Leah. 'It is a strange principle but one that seems never to fail. I see the same generous spirit in Benjamin.'

'Indeed,' replied Mariamne. 'He may have inherited the appearance of his father but he has the heart of his uncle Yosef.'

Leah turned away so Mariamne would not see the moistness that sprang to her eyes. 'Benjamin is indeed a blessing to us all.'

Chapter 18

Leah strolled beneath the grapevines of the inner courtyard to her chamber. The guests had arrived, dusty and irritable after their journey from Sebaste. The capital of Samaria was ten or twelve miles to the west; through the valley between Mount Ebal and Mount Gerizim. From Sebaste the carriages travelled readily along the paved highway until they passed Jacob's well at the eastern end of the valley and the grain fields outside of Sychar. There, they veered onto a rough, rutted road. It rattled the iron wheels of the carriage so violently that most found it less torturous to walk the final few miles despite the steep incline.

Whenever guests arrived, Leah detected in Marcellus a hint of humour at the dishevelled hairstyles and breathless wheezing of these men and women of wealth. They endured the journey to discuss matters of finance and politics with this highly regarded Equestrian knight. The men hoped to gain his patronage while the women attempted to draw from him stories of slaughter to impress their friends. In return for venturing far from the security of the city, Marcellus rewarded them with generous hospitality and liberal quantities of food and wine. These guests were no different. Upon their arrival Leah had instructed that the sole woman in the party be immediately escorted to the guest quarters to refresh herself. Roman women were accustomed to being seen only at their best, not after panting up a steep, rutted road.

Leah entered her chamber and smiled at the sight of the stola lying on the bed. Mariamne had woven it from the first flax leaves of the season and together they had gathered enough of the madder plant to dye it a rich red. It was soft with a subtle shine, as though it had been polished, and because Leah had cut the cloth on an angle instead of square, it fell from her shoulders in graceful, fine folds.

Adjoining her chamber was a small private courtyard inlaid with mosaics of rich blue and orange. Leah removed her tunic and sandals. From a brass urn she scooped water into a large marble basin and bathed, cleansing her skin with a sponge. She rubbed lavender-scented olive oil into her arms and legs, the same oil the servant used for her daily massage. It had been a new sensation, allowing a stranger's hands to touch her body. Mariamne had embraced the Roman ritual first, constantly praising its virtues to Leah, insisting that it soothed not only the body but the mind. Her hesitation at the impropriety of it gradually waned. Now she wondered why she had wavered for so long.

She stepped into the red stola, fastening the golden clasps at each shoulder, and allowing the fabric to drape in soft folds across her breasts. She twirled slowly admiring how the fabric swirled with the movement. She arranged her hair, fastening it with ivory pins inlaid with pearls—a generous gift from Marcellus. Opening a carved jewellery box, she selected a turquoise bracelet almost as beautiful as the one her father had given her, the one the bandits had stolen. Holding a small bronze mirror she rubbed kohl over her eyes and pressed rouge across her cheekbones. She slipped her feet into a pair of soft leather shoes. She was the wife of an Equestrian knight, ready to greet her guests.

Leah crossed the expansive courtyard and heard lowered voices coming from a corner of the garden, beyond the hanging vines and the bronze statue of Mars.

'Stop complaining, Drusilla. We are here for only one night. It will do you no harm to miss a day or two from your friends at the baths.'

'You did not tell me we would have to walk. My feet are aching and my shoes are ruined.'

'It was you who insisted on accompanying me. You may gather your gossip about this Samaritan wife but while you are a guest in his house, I insist you honour our host.'

'Well,' huffed the woman, 'if this plebeian's clothes do not rival those of Rome, as Livia claims, I will rip every hair from Livia's head and demand she replace my ruined shoes. I wonder what potion she brewed to snare Marcellus. He could have had any Roman women of status and yet he chose this impoverished foreigner.'

'Silence!' the man's voice was as sharp as a blade. 'Our host is an important patron of Sebaste and we are here to maintain his favour. Seal your lips and fix a smile on your face.'

Leah fought back her fiery thoughts. No matter. It was better to know these people's true nature than fall for false flattery. She would attend this evening in a position of strength.

The aroma of freshly baked bread carried from the kitchen. The baker was a loyal servant and excellent cook, skilled in transforming common vegetables, eggs and grain into dishes Leah had never before tasted. At the request of Marcellus their daily meals were simple and light. It was only when they entertained that they indulged in the delicacies so prized by the Roman elite. Tonight she smelled roasted meat, not the succulent roast lamb that permeated every Samaritan festival, but the lighter scent of roast fowl or pheasant. Marcellus, thankfully, refrained from the garish display of unclean animals such as wild boar whose heads, she had heard, frequently graced royal Roman tables.

She entered the atrium where Marcellus conversed with a distinguished, silver-haired man. Both wore white togas but only Marcellus wore the narrow reddish purple stripes on his tunic that marked him as an Equestrian knight. He saw her and placed his hand on his guest's arm, halting him mid-sentence.

'Leah, you are here.' He clasped Leah on the arms and kissed her on the cheek before turning to his guest.

'Please meet my wife, Leah.'

Before Leah could respond there was a rustling of loose clothing and hurried footsteps across the marble floor. It was the couple she had overheard in the courtyard.

'Forgive us, Marcellus, we were admiring your statue of Mars. The god of war. Most appropriate for a man such as yourself.' The flustered man bowed, almost tripping over his unadorned toga. His wife followed, her plain woollen stola clinging to her ample frame.

'I thank you for your generous words,' replied Marcellus. 'Since my retirement I pray more for his blessing on my olives than on my battles.' He swept his arm across the expansive view of rolling hills dotted with olive trees.

'Of course, of course,' the man simpered.

'May I present to you my wife?' Marcellus placed his hand on Leah's arm, a gentle gesture of encouragement. She was still unused to these public displays of affection. She held out her hand allowing the man to bow over it, his hot breath and moist lips sending through her a quiver of distaste. She forced a smile. Marcellus demanded so little from her; this unsavoury task was but a small sacrifice with which to return the generosity of her husband.

'It is a pleasure to meet you.' She looked directly at the panting couple, as Marcellus had instructed: *You are neither servant nor slave. You are a Roman citizen and my wife. Do not lower your eyes.*

She met Drusilla's eyes. They sank in her puffy face like dates in dough, darting away and back again, stealing envious glances at Leah's stola. She caught Leah watching her and a high colour rose in her powdered face. Leah smiled a generous smile, giving the woman grace to retain her dignity. A servant stepped discreetly into the room, hands clasped before him, a serving cloth draped over one forearm. She touched Marcellus lightly and he acknowledged the young man.

'I believe our dinner is prepared. Come, let us dine.'

He led the way along the marble colonnade and into a room overlooking the southern hills of Samaria. They settled themselves on three embroidered couches arranged around a low table laden with delicacies. The aroma of fresh bread welcomed them—knotted rolls piled high in the centre of the table. Bowls of oil from their own olives glistened golden green. Platters of goats curd with fresh thyme and honey on the comb reminded Leah that she had not eaten for many hours. There were plates of sweet roast fennel, leeks in a delicate liquid and eggs coloured with saffron. Taking the place of honour was an enormous pheasant, its skin roasted and crisp with a stuffing of pistachios and pomegranate spilling onto a bed of moist lentils.

Leah reclined next to Marcellus on the centre couch and sipped her goblet of wine. At her direction a servant dished a little of each food except the meat onto her plate. Marcellus selected with similar restraint, made all the more obvious by the repeatedly heaped platters set before the guests. They talked and ate, laughing at Marcellus' jokes and draining their cups of wine.

'Have you heard the news from Caesarea?' slurred one of the men. 'Sejanus, that lap dog of the Emperor, has appointed a new prefect for Judea.'

A grimace passed across Marcellus' face. It was unwise to ridicule those close to the Emperor.

'Who is it?' asked Marcellus, dipping his bread into the olive oil.

'Pontius Pilate, an Equestrian knight like yourself. Have you heard of him?'

'Indeed I have,' said Marcellus. 'Our legions fought together many years ago in Germania. He was young and ambitious, loyal to Rome and zealous for the law, sometimes to his peril. He will make a good prefect for this remote part of the Empire.'

The woman laughed. 'Remote, yes that is the word …' She broke off at the sharp look from her husband.

'Speaking of remote, there are reports that Tiberius has removed himself from Rome to his palace on the island of Capreae,' said the silver-haired Roman.

'The young boys of Rome have a reprieve then,' laughed the other, biting into a fat pheasant leg dripping with glaze.

'I would be slow to believe such accusations,' said Marcellus. 'When he was in Athens I recall he preferred the banter of Greek philosophers to the babble of boys.'

The men's conversation shifted to the dramas of the latest chariot races at Sebaste's stadium and Leah turned to her female guest who was wiping a trickle of honey from the corner of her mouth. Her elaborate hairstyle was impressive although to Leah it looked much like a beehive with so many clasps and flowers scattered through it.

'Drusilla, I trust your journey here was pleasant.'

'Most pleasant, thank you.' The woman dipped her fingers into a silver water bowl, pressed them dry on a napkin and drew herself up on the couch. 'It is a great pleasure to be here, and to meet you at last. It is a shame that Marcellus has not yet brought you to Sebaste.'

'It is I who has preferred not to travel. I am well enough occupied with settling the accounts and caring for my child.'

'You settle the accounts?' The woman's eyes bulged wide.

'My husband insists that I understand the workings of our olive groves. Do not all Roman women take an interest in their husband's affairs?'

'But you are not …' The woman stopped herself mid-sentence. Her face coloured.

'Roman? I am a Samaritan but also a Roman citizen. My father earned his citizenship through his service in the Imperial Roman Army.' Leah smiled, trying to ease the woman's embarrassment. She needed her patronage for the success of her plan.

Drusilla regained her composure. 'I am surprised Marcellus did not mention this.'

'I expect he has matters more important than his wife to discuss.'

'Of course,' she sputtered. 'Certainly the repairing of the stairs at the temple of Augustus has been an enormous project. My husband said that it would not have been completed without the generous contribution of Marcellus.' Drusilla paused, her eyes once again studying Leah's attire. She cleared her throat. 'I hope you will forgive my directness but your stola is exquisite. From where did you obtain such fine cloth? I did not think it was possible to acquire such quality in Samaria. And the colour—it is splendid.'

'I am honoured by your compliments. It is my mother-in-law who weaves the linen. She is teaching me her skills but I still have much to learn.'

Drusilla's eyes glittered. 'So it might be possible to create such a garment for others; if they were prepared to pay?'

'It is a laborious process as I am sure you understand. We may be able to make one or two ...' Leah let her voice trail off, luring Drusilla with her delay. 'They would be quite unique.'

Drusilla rubbed the fabric of her own stola between her fingers. 'I brought this with me from Rome—the best Roman wool—but it is nothing compared to your linen. If you could make me a stola I would be pleased to pay whatever price you ask.'

Leah leaned forward fully aware that her stola now draped enticingly low, drawing lascivious glances from the men. Their lust was purely for what lay beneath. It was Drusilla and her acquaintances who she wished to attract, lured by the promise, the hope that a skilfully crafted piece of fabric would make them the envy of their friends and an object of desire for men. She took Drusilla's plump hand.

'I will make you a stola like no other. It will cling in the right places and fall with the grace of a dove. I have several fine linen skeins dyed a beautiful blue, the plumage of a peacock. It is the perfect shade for your skin. And perhaps you might consider a palla for the cooler months in shades of autumn, edged with blue. You will most certainly be the envy of every woman in Sebaste.' Drusilla's eyes glistened, almost teary with anticipation.

'Yes, a palla too,' she panted. 'How long must I wait?'

'Four months would be sufficient,' said Leah, knowing that the cloth was already woven and could be dyed, cut and sewn within a few weeks. Marcellus had taught her that a high price and a long wait, within reason, created value. She would apply the same principles to her dealings in cloth.

'Could it not be sooner? I would dearly love to wear it to the birthday games in honour of Augustus. The stadium will be filled for the occasion.'

Leah allowed a silence to fall between them, an appearance of hesitation.

'It may be possible, if we take measurements tomorrow before you leave.'

Drusilla beamed, her eyes almost disappearing into her cheeks. 'That is excellent.'

Later that evening, when the guests had stumbled to their quarters, Leah strolled again with Marcellus in the garden. She would not speak of the other night. It was better to look forward, to draw hope from the future, rather than dwell on disappointments of the past. She breathed in the warm night air, sweet with lavender and rose.

'The evening was a success, was it not?' Marcellus held her arm, taking the path towards the edge of the gardens, far from where they had stood the night before. 'It is good to have you by my side at these dinners, especially on these rare occasions when my friends bring their wives. Drusilla appeared quite jubilant.'

'It is because I have agreed to make her a stola and palla for the Emperor's birthday celebrations,' said Leah, linking her arm through his.

'That will certainly impress her friends,' said Marcellus. 'You may soon find other women seeking your skills.'

She looked at his face softened by age, the jaw less defined, his hair sparse, his skin leathered by weather and war. Yet he was still strong and his gaze was gentle. He could not give her everything she desired but he would certainly support her desire to sell stolas.

'That is my plan, if it is acceptable to you,' she replied.

'Of course,' said Marcellus. 'The craft and skill of selling differs not between stolas and olive oil.'

'Indeed,' Leah grinned at Marcellus, 'it was most effective.'

'You may be stepping into a den of lions with those women of Sebaste, but I expect you will soon have them lapping from your hand like kittens. It is a sight I am eager to see. In fact, why do we not attend the celebrations? I am always invited but rarely attend. Let us attend this year and see for ourselves the effect of your creations on the citizens of Sebaste.'

Chapter 19

The months swept by like clouds on a warm wind. Grapes ripened and hung heavy on the vine. The fig tree by the statue of Mars bore a bountiful harvest in deep purple hues, and the pomegranate tree drooped with brilliant scarlet orbs. Benjamin's tunic and fingers were constantly sticky and stained with sweet juice. All through the summer months Leah rose earlier than usual, eager to complete as much work as possible before the sun sapped her strength. There was much to be done to ensure Drusilla's stola and palla were ready for the celebration of Emperor Augustus' birthday.

Whenever she sat with Marcellus in the library going over the accounts, she would study the scroll that told her how many days she had left until the 23 of September—the birthday of the Emperor. Marcellus had explained to her this strange Roman calendar, named in honour of Julius Caesar who had devised it only sixty years earlier. He had consulted with a famous astronomer from the Egyptian city of Alexandria, who suggested that the calendar be based on the Earth's revolutions around the sun. Leah preferred the proper way of counting the months, in tune with the cycles of the moon. The Emperor's birthday celebrations would be in the month of *Tishri* coinciding this year with the Samaritan Feast of Tabernacles.

This year, for the first time in her life, she would miss the week-long festival. It was a necessary sacrifice, she assured herself. They had not made the pilgrimage up Mount Gerizim for the past three years. *Yahweh* had not seemed to mind this limited fulfilment of the requirements; their lives had been filled with peace and prosperity. He would surely not mind if she missed just this once. She promised herself that she would spend the week in Sebaste remembering *Yahweh* with gratitude in her heart. Surely that would be acceptable?

Now she had a more pressing problem: the blue dye which so readily retained its colour on wool had faded on the linen. She would have to dye the stola again, and pray that the shade was right. There was no time to weave another stola. Marcellus had clients to meet in Sebaste and affairs with which to deal before the celebrations. They would be leaving within the week, on the eleventh day of Tishri, the morning after the Day of Atonement. It was the most holy day of the year—a sombre day of fasting from one evening to the next. She could not work during this most sacred assembly when atonement was made for every Samaritan before *Yahweh*. The law said that *Yahweh* would destroy anyone who worked on that day. Isolated in their Roman villa, no-one except Mariamne and her mother would know if she pressed a palla or folded a stola, yet she dared not. She had only a few days remaining to prepare for the journey.

The early morning air was warm and Leah was pleased she had not given into the temptation to lie a little longer in her bed. The rising sun splashed amber streaks across a slate of blue. How she desperately desired the same colour, the stark, clear blue of a dawn sky. Compared to the handiwork of *Yahweh*, her stola looked as though it had been dyed in muddied water. She followed the pathway to the rear of the villa and took several deep breaths of fresh air before wrapping a scarf over her nose and mouth. At the end of the path, far from the house, was a large copper bath sitting on loose stones under a shelter. She pinched her nose and tried to breathe through her mouth. The stench was overwhelming— stale urine fermenting with woad leaves. She picked up a wooden stick and prodded at the stola soaking in the greenish yellow dye, lifting a corner to check the colour. This time she had used more woad and more urine, commanding all the servants to contribute. Perhaps some people's urine was better than others for setting the dye fast in the fabric. It had been soaking for three days now and she could wait no longer. She lifted the stola from the bath and draped it over a taut rope stretched between two trees. Green dye dripped onto the pebbles below, soaking through them into the ground. Carefully she spread out the fabric, ensuring every part was evenly exposed to the air. Now she would have to wait to see what shade of blue she had produced.

She hurried back to the villa, relieved to escape the putrid smell. A wife was permitted to divorce her husband if he became a dyer and she could understand why; the smell lodged in the clothes and clung to the skin. Fortunately her dying efforts were infrequent and her family forgiving. When her mother saw her blackened hands she stopped setting the fire, motioned Leah to sit and poured water into an old bowl. She set the bowl at Leah's feet and gave her a coarse horsehair brush. It took more than water to remove the stains and the stinking stale urine.

With relief she breathed in the smell of spiced incense. It rose over the rosemary bushes from the altar, beyond where Mariamne worshipped faithfully each morning. She soon appeared, stretching her arms, arching her back, presenting her serene face to the sky.

'Shalom, my sister.' Mariamne kissed Leah's mother on each cheek.

Did she perceive the fleeting shadow that passed across her mother's face? Or was it only Leah who noticed her mother's discomfort at Mariamne's worship of the Greek god?

Leah dried her hands, still smudged with black, and stood up to kiss Mariamne.

'Shalom, my daughter,' said Mariamne, pinching her nose. 'I hope this is the last of our dying for a while.'

'We must have dyed enough cloth to last forty summers,' Leah laughed. 'My hands will never be the same.' She held them before her in display.

'A few treatments of olive oil will soon restore them,' replied Mariamne. 'How is the shade of Drusilla's stola?'

'We will know in a few hours. The colour is deeper this time and I am praying the air will turn it a rich hue of blue.'

The dying process was unpredictable, affected by so many things: the youth of the woad leaves, the heat of the water brought barely to boiling, the fermentation of the urine which enabled the colour to adhere to the linen. Had she allowed the fabric to soak long enough? Surely three days basking in the putrid yellow-green liquid was sufficient? It had to be; she had yet to wash the cloth in a bath of water and vinegar, hang it in the shade to dry and then press it under a heavy, heated roller of iron until it was without a crease. Then she would carefully fold it and place it along with Drusilla's palla in a soft bag.

It was not the only bag she would take to Sebaste. She and Mariamne had worked relentlessly through the hot summer months, beating the dried flax into fine fibres and spinning, dying and weaving beautiful combinations of colour: bold shades of scarlet, saffron and amber; greens as deep as the forest and as pale as cucumber; and soft hues of snow, cream and the palest gold, as though they had captured the moonlight. These she would also take, wearing a selection to draw the women of Sebaste as moths to light.

She tipped the bowl of blackened water into the bushes and took from Mariamne a cup of olive leaves steeped in hot water, a bitter brew known to ease stiffened shoulders and restore strength.

'I have been considering our work,' said Mariamne, drawing Leah's attention, 'and wondering if there is a better way.'

'I would be happy if there is a way to avoid smelling like a neglected stable,' said Leah. 'Although the results have been worth every one of my blackened fingers.'

'Certainly we have never produced such an array of colours in our cloth. And I am sure we could continue to create even more beautiful shades. But is it the wisest use of our talents?' Mariamne sipped her drink and continued. 'We can weave the finest linen and create garments of great beauty, garments that I am sure the women of Sebaste will desire. I suspect you will return with more orders, perhaps beyond what we can handle. It is the dying that takes most of our time and, in our unskilled hands, is the most unpredictable. If we are to make many garments, I think we should find someone else to dye our thread.'

'But we will need to pay them and, as yet, we have earned nothing for our work,' said Leah.

'That is true. However, do you not take a portion of the payment for the olive oil in advance? Why not apply the same principle here? Require half the price as a pledge. I am sure the women of Sebaste will oblige. Then we can take our thread and woven cloth to a trusted dyer, and give our attention to weaving and design.'

'How will we find a skilled dyer, one whom we can trust?' Leah could hear the grumbling tone of her own voice. She was not usually given to complaining but she struggled with the thought of abandoning the dying process, of handing it over to another after these months of learning the art. And yet she knew Mariamne was right. By holding onto every time-consuming process themselves, they stifled any opportunity to grow.

'You can find one while you are in Sebaste.' Mariamne plucked a handful of grapes from the vine that sprawled over the stone wall. She offered Leah a small cluster. 'Rouse yourself, Leah. Perhaps all that dye has dulled your senses.'

Leah smiled at her teasing and ate a grape, allowing the sweet juice to fill her mouth. Mariamne placed a hand gently on her shoulder.

'I know we will do well with this new work of ours but there is more than one path up the mountain.'

Leah wandered back to check the stola, still pondering her words. It was dry now. She lifted it carefully from its hanging place and held it before her. The colour was as though of the deepest pool of water. It was perfect.

Chapter 20

It was the morning of the eleventh day of Tishri. Leah and Marcellus set off late, the two-wheeled carpentum jumping and jolting down the rutted road behind the sure-footed donkey. Leah and Marcellus walked until they reached the smoother, flatter road. It cut through the harvested grain fields—now fields of stubble and sticks—all the way to Jacob's well.

The well was at the crossroads of all who journeyed through the Samarian hill country. To the west, through the valley between Mount Gerizim and Mount Ebal, was the main road to Sebaste. To the north-east, travellers traversed treacherous ravines, deep furrows that gouged their way down to the Jordan River, and the road to Jericho. To the south was Jerusalem.

Nearing the well, the carpentum slowed, negotiating its way past a crowd of people. People with water jars, people with skins, people laying up supplies for the Feast of Tabernacles, and a mob of people haranguing a family of Jews. Marcellus ordered his servant to halt the mules. He charged into the midst of them, unsheathing his sword. The sudden sight of a Roman turned them to stone. Their mouths dropped open and the rocks fell from their hands. Marcellus parted the crowd of Samaritans like Moses parting the sea, striding straight to the well and drawing water. Nobody argued. He carried it to the Jewish family huddled together, the younger children crying, an older boy cradling a blood-stained arm.

'Is this how you treat your brothers?' Marcellus turned on the mob, his voice thundering with imperial authority.

'They are no brothers of ours,' replied a youth, sneering in the manner of Simeon.

'They are more your brothers than I,' said Marcellus. 'Are they not on their way to celebrate the same festival as you?'

'They are going to the wrong place. This is the holy mountain.' He pointed to the slopes of Mt Gerizim where Leah could see Samaritans already setting up huts in preparation for the Feast of Tabernacles.

'And does your God require you to murder those with whom you disagree?'

The crowd drew back, a bodily gasp at the accusation. Murder was strictly forbidden and the law decreed severe punishment for those who broke it.

'They are not hurt. It is a scratch only.' The youth puffed out his chest and lifted his chin, refusing to look at the Jewish boy whose mother was binding his arm with a length of cloth. She tied it around his neck, securing his arm like a wounded wing against his tunic. He looked pale and in pain.

'The next stone may have hit his head,' said Marcellus, his tone deliberate and dark. 'Consider that before you act so righteously.' He glared at the crowd. 'And you who stand by and approve are equally at fault. I will be informing the next Roman patrol we meet of this incident. It would be to your advantage to ensure these brothers have a safe journey to Jerusalem.'

Leah pulled her palla closely around her head, anxious that no-one would recognise her. She was not yet ready to face the accusing eyes of the more pious Samaritans who might consider her marriage to a Gentile a sin as grievous as murder. She watched the judgmental scowls marring the faces of her people. The frightened Jewish family stumbled south towards Jerusalem, and Leah wondered with whom *Yahweh* was more pleased.

'I pray for their safety, even though they are misguided,' said Leah.

'Who is to say it is not you who is misguided?' said Marcellus.

'How can you say that?' Leah stiffened in her seat. 'We have the mountain where *Yahweh* pronounced blessing on Israel, we have Joseph's tomb, we have Jacob's well.' She pressed her lips tight, biting the soft flesh. Surely if Jerusalem was the true place of worship, *Yahweh* would have blessed it with a steady supply of water. But it was here at the base of Mount Gerizim, the mountain of blessing, where the water ran abundant and pure. This was surely where *Yahweh* wished them to worship.

'Did *Yahweh* not pronounce blessing on all the tribes of Israel? The Jews are your brothers, yet you argue over the mere matter of a mountain.' Marcellus took her hands in his and smiled. 'I challenge you only to consider.'

'It is true we are brothers,' said Leah. 'We all descend from the sons of Jacob, the twelve tribes. They are from Judah and Benjamin, and I from the tribe of Manasseh, of the house of Joseph. But they deny our bloodline.' She pulled her hands from his and crossed her arms. 'They claim they are purer. They claim they know better. They claim Jerusalem as the true place of worship. Where in the law is that written? Why should I not believe our teachers, our experts, those learned in the law?'

'A religious Samaritan, a religious Jew, a religious Roman—each believes fervently that they hold the truth,' said Marcellus. 'For twenty-five years I commanded a cohort of foreigners—Scythians, Syrians, Samaritans and Gauls— some ready to fall on their swords for their gods, others ready to spit on them for doing so. What a man worshipped, where and why, were not my concern. I measured a man's worth by his actions. Did he spare the children or slaughter them? Did he plunder the spoils? Did he spout lies? Or did he bridle his bloodlust, rein in his tongue, act with dignity and honour?' He took her hand again and his eyes held hers fast. 'Leah, surely you must agree no army, no nation, no group of people is all good or all evil. It is the heart of each person that matters.'

The rays of the setting sun cast an orange glow over the city when they finally arrived at the eastern entrance of Sebaste. The East Gate loomed above them, sombre in shadow. Roman guards stood at attention either side of huge marble columns. High above, in the massive round towers of the city wall, soldiers paced with bows and arrows. Marcellus descended stiffly from the carpentum to greet the approaching centurion guard. They clasped each other's shoulder in respectful familiarity.

Leah brushed the dust from her stola and rubbed her back. Her ears rang; her body ached from the endless jarring of iron wheels on Roman roads. She would rather have walked beside the donkeys than in this covered cart but Marcellus had insisted—the manner in which they arrived at the city would be noted. Travelling alone, he would have ridden his horse. It was an acceptable form of transport for a former commander of an Ala, the auxiliary cavalry of the Roman army, but not for his wife.

Marcellus and the centurion were clapping each other on the back now and laughing like old friends. People bustled in all directions. Some dragged donkeys into the city, others pushed past them in the opposite direction, hurrying away along the paved road which stretched straight as an arrow, cutting east through the terraced hill country all the way to the mountains of Ebal and Gerizim. She hoped their journey was short. Darkness was the domain of bandits and beasts.

Marcellus returned to the carpentum and held out his hand to Leah.

'No carriages are permitted within the city walls; the citizens cannot cope with the clatter. We will walk from here.'

He looked at the donkey, its head buried in a bucket, snorting and slurping the water. It lifted its head, shaking and showering him and the servant.

'It is a generous donkey who refreshes his master,' said Marcellus, laughing and brushing the droplets from his toga. 'Follow us with the bags as soon as you are ready. We will be staying at the usual place. And take care with those.' He pointed to the sturdy, tent-cloth bags resting on the seat beside Leah. Inside lay her carefully folded and wrapped linens.

'I do not wish to leave them,' said Leah. 'Can we not carry them ourselves?'

Marcellus rubbed his chin. 'It is not the usual way I would arrive at the home of the Prefect but I am willing to ruffle the plumes of these peacocks that strut the streets, if you are.'

It was Leah's turn to hesitate. 'I am sorry. I did not think of your reputation.'

Marcellus laughed. 'My reputation is robust enough in this city. It is yours I am thinking of.'

'If I have any reputation at all, it is as your wife.' Leah passed the heavy bags to Marcellus, and descended from the carpentum. She may be the wife of a Roman but was also a merchant of fine cloth. Let the people of Sebaste gossip; it would serve her purposes better than any herald trumpeting from the city towers.

The servant unhitched one of the donkeys and tied the bags onto its back. The soldiers stared. Marcellus led the laden donkey through the gaping gates and onto the most majestic street Leah had ever seen. It was lined on each side with ornate marble columns forming a colonnade which stretched seemingly forever westwards.

'I have never seen anything like it! There must be hundreds of columns.'

'Six hundred,' replied Marcellus, 'all the way to the West Gate and tower at the other end of the city.'

Further on, the colonnade opened out into a large forum. Even at this late hour people filled the spacious square, innumerably more than Sychar on its busiest market day. Men in short tunics with muscular legs, men in rich robes with ebony faces, men in white togas with stately bearing. Some strolled in groups, some strode with purpose, some lowered their tent flaps and loaded their mules with unsold wares. The women were distinctive only by their elaborate hairstyles. Their stolas blended with the buildings—shades of wheat and stone and sand. She glanced at the bags resting securely on the donkey—the women who bought her stolas would surely shine like sapphires among the people of Sebaste.

'What is that building?' asked Leah, watching people stream to one of many marble buildings gleaming in lamplight.

'Those are the baths,' said Marcellus. General Pompey rebuilt this city from ruins around ninety years ago and it was one of the first buildings he commissioned. He built three aqueducts to supply the water—a colossal undertaking.'

'Did we not pass them today?' It would have been impossible to miss the huge stone arches stamping across the fields and up into the hills.

'Indeed, that is the very one that feeds these baths, direct from the springs at Mt Gerizim.'

'I would very much like a bath now,' said Leah, 'but without all the people.'

Marcellus laughed. 'The public baths are as much for banter as for bathing. There is no better place for discovering the secrets of the city.'

Leah surveyed the press of people, imagining the secrets that swirled among them. Her gaze strayed across the crowds. It caught on a camel, or more precisely the man astride it. He stared at her, a piercing stare that snared her breath. His face, except for his eyes, was concealed in a coloured cloth.

A darkness fell upon her, a sudden raven in the night. The Jewish bandit, the one who had murdered Yosef, who had stolen her life—could it be him? Had he come to finish his task? She shook her head, trying to rein in her fear. It was unreasonable, unfounded. Few Jews would be found in Sebaste and bandits favoured unguarded, unwalled places. Places far from their neighbours. Places with women and children. Places like … her heart stopped cold. A cord crushed her chest. Her hand flew to her throat. She tried to breathe. Benjamin, Mariamne, her mother. Why had she left them? Bandits could attack and no-one would know. No-one would hear their cries. No-one would come to their aid.

She squeezed her eyes shut and took a deep breath, taming her thoughts, recalling the words of the holy prophet Moses: *Do not be terrified. Do not be afraid.* She opened her eyes to look for the man on the camel. He had disappeared.

They followed the colonnade, column after column. A hill rose on their right, a crown of massive marble walls towering over clusters of closely set houses. The sky had faded to flint and the city gleamed under the light of thousands of lamps set high on posts.

'Up there is the palace and the temple of Augustus,' said Marcellus. 'Herod built it fifty years ago, when I was a boy like Benjamin. It is famous for its steps. They are a sight like no other.'

'Are they the ones of which you funded the repairs?' asked Leah, trying to put the man on the camel out of her mind.

'Indeed. I am told they had five hundred men working day and night to finish them in time for these celebrations. I am interested to see the results.'

Leah did not answer. A name filled her mind, attaching itself to the man on the camel. Calev. Could he have returned from his uncle in the east?

They left the colonnaded street and followed a narrow cobblestone lane. It opened out into a small square, a fountain sparkling in the centre, its water flowing over the stone feet of a naked Greek god. Marcellus knocked on a carved wooden gate set along one side of the square. It opened, swinging inwards to reveal a sweep of marble leading up to a villa. Lamp light lit up the entrance and the sound of music and laughter drifted from beyond. A tall man in a toga hurried towards them, a golden goblet in his hand.

'Marcellus, my friend.' The men clasped each other on the shoulder. 'I trust your journey was uneventful.'

'Apart from a quarrelling crowd at Jacob's well and an overturned chariot on the road. The driver suffered only a few cuts and bruises despite driving like a madman. Truly he had fortune on his side.'

Their host laughed. 'It is a familiar tale at this time. Everyone is on the roads. Let's pray that next year's New Year celebrations do not clash with the Jewish and Samaritan festivals. Speaking of which …' He looked at Leah.

'Ah yes, please allow me to present my wife, Leah, a Samaritan and a Roman citizen by birth.'

'I am delighted to meet the woman about whom everyone is talking.' He raised her hand to his lips. 'I am Cornelius. My wife, Livia, and I have been waiting to meet you with great expectation.'

'I, too, have looked forward to this day,' said Leah, holding her head high and masking a fluttering of unease with a gracious smile. *The woman about whom everyone is talking.* She patted the donkey beside her. She had not needed its assistance to stir the tongues of Sebaste.

Chapter 21

Marcellus left early the next morning, accompanying Cornelius to the garrison to inspect the troops. It was another warm day, the heat already rising despite the early hour. Leah dressed, selecting a cream stola with an edging of pale sunlight. Thoughts of the man on the camel hung about her like flies on a sticky day. She swept them to a corner of her mind. She had matters of more importance to consider.

Today, Drusilla was coming to the villa to collect her stola and palla. Livia had invited several others also, telling Leah that they would willingly pay for quality clothes that did not require a sea voyage of several months. She pinned her hair back in a loose knot at the nape of her neck. Unlike Samaritans, these Roman women did not cover their hair; rather they displayed it in ever more elaborate styles. Perhaps it was their way of distinguishing themselves despite the bland uniformity of their dress. If today went well, soon they would be able to compete also in their style of stola.

The guest quarters opened onto a broad portico surrounding a paved courtyard. A stream of sparkling water flowed into a large pool and broad leafed green plants interspersed carved marble pillars. Livia sat at an enormous stone table sipping from a delicate cup. She rose to greet Leah.

'My dear, you look greatly refreshed.' She kissed Leah on each cheek, enveloping her in a heavenly scent which Leah did not recognise. 'Come, join me.'

Set at one end of the table was a jug painted in bold crimson stripes, two matching cups and a platter of pistachios, grapes and tiny rounds of a white cheese.

'I would be delighted,' replied Leah, rolling her tongue around the foreign Latin words. She rarely had an opportunity to practise the language—only those from Italia spoke Latin, and prided themselves on doing so. Greek was the language of commerce and Aramaic the language of her people. 'What is the scent you are wearing? It is truly from the heavens.'

'It is rose,' said Livia, touching her throat, the skin as fine and pale as alabaster. Each evening I apply a cream of crushed petals and almond oil. It is said to reduce blemishes, although I doubt that even a whole rose bush would be sufficient to prevent the ravages of this harsh Samarian sun. My face has become as speckled as a sparrow's egg.'

'You are too harsh on yourself. I see no speckles,' said Leah, sipping the cool, mint-flavoured water. She selected a date from the platter, biting into the rich flesh.

'How long have you lived in Sebaste?'

'We arrived from Rome almost two years ago. Cornelius had just returned from a successful campaign in the province of Africa. His troops managed to capture Tacfarinas, the leader of a group of tribes who constantly raided the Roman grain fields. Grain was scarce, bakers went out of business, Rome was in uproar.' She smiled, fine lines fanning out from her eyes like rays of light. 'It is better to hide in a hole than speak to a Roman without bread in his belly. When Cornelius returned to Rome he was hailed a hero. I expected we would retire to the country on a generous stipend but instead he was promoted to administer the regiment here in Sebaste. No one dares refuse a promotion from Caesar.'

She refilled Leah's cup and smiled that same gentle smile. 'The wife of a prefect is a life of change. We must sway like a reed in the tide but never break.'

***

The morning flew by in a whirl of draping and fitting, tucking and pinning. Drusilla's round face beamed at the compliments the other women showered upon her. The blue stola fell in soft pleats, hiding the folds of fat and drawing the eye to her full breasts and hips.

'You are the image of Venus,' said Livia, and Drusilla beamed even brighter.

They pored over the samples, touching the fine fabric, rubbing it between their fingers, holding it to the light as though it were treasure. Only one woman stood apart, her narrow face set hard and haughty, framed by such an elaborate construction of curls that Leah feared it would crush her thin frame. She held up a stola of saffron and scarlet.

'Allow me to help you,' said Leah, taking two gold clasps from a small box. She draped the bright cloth over the woman's bony shoulders and fixed the clasps so her flat chest appeared full. The other women gasped.

'Have we ever seen anything like this in Rome?'

'Octavia, you must have it. You will be the envy of all of Rome.'

Octavia's thin lips parted in a strangled smile. 'And they will know that even in this backwater of the Empire our tastes remained refined.' She ran her jewelled fingers over the bright cloth. 'I may even forgive Valerius for dragging me up here.'

'Surely the journey from Caesarea is nothing compared with the journey to Rome,' said Livia. 'Do you not leave soon?'

'We return to Rome as soon as Valerius hands over the reins of Judea to Pontius Pilate. Let him deal with those temperamental Jews. It is only Caiaphas, their high priest, with whom my husband can speak any sense.'

Livia took Octavia's hand. 'It is wonderful that you were able to come to Sebaste once more before you leave. The New Year celebrations are always a welcome distraction. I can think of no more fitting way to end your time in Judea.'

'I have heard there will be Syrian archers,' said Drusilla, helping herself to a fistful of grapes from the platter offered by a servant.

Octavia ran her hands over her waist and hips, over the saffron and scarlet stola. 'I have seen them in Caesarea. They can hit a target at the opposite end of the stadium while riding their horses at full gallop. There is one with the physique of a god.' Her eyes glittered like a crow. 'I hope he is here. He can wrap his taut thighs around me anytime.'

Drusilla brayed with laughter, grape juice dribbling down her chin. 'Perhaps we may view his virility at the baths this afternoon.'

Leah smothered her shock at the women's lewd comments. Was this the usual way the respected women of the city spoke? She glanced at Livia, relieved to see a serene smile fixed on her face. She did not join in the ribald talk but seamlessly steered the conversation onto payment. Soon the women were thrusting their hands into their pouches and counting out coins of silver and gold. Drusilla picked up two coins, one a valuable aurius of gold, the other a silver denarius.

She turned them over in her hand, examining the images engraved upon each.

'I have always admired the elegance of this aurius.' She held up the gold coin, twisting it to view both sides. 'Most coins are crude in design but this amphora and grape vine leaf are quite delightful.'

Leah imitated Livia, fixing a polite smile on her face to hide her bewilderment. Why was Drusilla praising a coin? Who noticed such a thing?

'I agree,' said Octavia. 'I consider it the most inspired of the many coins my husband had minted, although, of course, he insists that this one is the best.' She held up a silver denarius with a palm branch on one side and the name of Tiberius on the other. 'There is no better way to further one's career than to cast a coin with the sign of Caesar.' She grasped Leah's hand. 'And for a craftswoman of such skill there is no better way to further one's name than for the people to see your stolas on the wife of the Prefect.'

'I thank you for your patronage, Octavia. You have made a splendid selection. I am sure you will be pleased.'

'I am extremely pleased,' said Octavia, stroking the saffron and scarlet stola, 'and I expect you will be too when you, and all Sebaste, see me wearing this at the games.'

Chapter 22

Leah fanned herself with her hand. Even the tent cloth which Livia's servants held above them could not shelter them from the heat which rose from the marble seats of the stadium. They were seated in the women's section, in the uppermost seats, where it might be possible to catch a breeze, but there was none to be had. Drusilla sat in the row below them, flustered and panting.

'Why they chose not to build a decent portico up here, I do not know.' She waved a fleshy arm at the few highest rows of seats shaded by the narrow roof. 'It's impossible to see anything from that distance but I am tempted to move just to escape this dreadful heat.'

'I believe there was not enough money to construct a full portico,' said Livia. 'They were forced to be more frugal than they planned.' She glanced at her servants who subtly shifted the shade cloth to fully cover Drusilla, leaving Leah and Livia partially exposed to the harsh sunlight.

'That is a little better,' said Drusilla letting out a relieved sigh and flapping her arms. The sour smell of sweat carried through the sticky air.

'We should be grateful that we can even attend the games,' said Livia. 'Augustus feared our womanly desires would be inflamed by the sight of naked men. If not for the persuasion of his wife, we may have also been banned from the stadium.'

'It is difficult to be inflamed from this distance,' replied Drusilla. She leaned forward, her excessively adorned head swivelling from one end of the stadium to the other. 'I have not yet seen Octavia.' Then, distracted by her neighbour, she fell into animated conversation about the weather.

Leah peered over the raucous crowd below to the front platform filled with what looked like the senators, distinguished guests and leaders of the city. They were all clothed in white togas, some bordered with the distinctive, and costly, purple of the murex. Rising up immediately behind the dignitaries, in the first row of seats, she saw Marcellus wiping his hand across his forehead. There would be no hope of a reprieve from the heat down there. He spoke to the men around him. All were dressed in the obligatory white toga and on every man's tunic were the narrow purple stripes marking them of equestrian status.

She had seen little of him these past few days. If he was not at the barracks with Cornelius, he was at the basilica meeting with senators or prefects. Each day he had appeared a little more tired, a little less at ease.

That very morning, he had sighed. 'The city never changes. It seethes with gossip, slander and discontent. The basilica, the baths, everywhere I must endure it. It is a necessary duty which I find more tedious each time I visit.' He had held her hands. 'I had hoped to be able to show you the city myself.'

'Do not be concerned; Livia has taken good care of me.'

'She is a woman of virtue, and Cornelius a man of honour. Such qualities are rare these days.' The lines on his face deepened.

'You are troubled about something. Can you not share it with your wife, if not your friend? ' Leah stroked his arm. 'It may lessen the burden.'

Marcellus had remained quiet for a time. Leah waited. Finally he spoke.

'There are rumours of a plot to kill Valerius Gratus.'

'Where? Why?' Leah gasped out the words, her body at once tense.

'This is not the first time an attempt has been made on his life. A millstone was dropped on him in Jerusalem, narrowly missing, and he never takes food or wine without first having it tasted. He has created many enemies during his prefecture, especially among the Jews who despise his interference in appointing a high priest. He deposed several before appointing Caiaphas who, they believe, is as corrupt as the prefect himself. This is his final official appearance, a final opportunity to kill him.'

'And if they succeed?'

'Rome does not tolerate anything that threatens the Pax Romana. The repercussions would be violent, public and swift.'

Could Octavia be involved? From the tales Livia had told her it seemed that Roman women of influence frequently murdered their husbands and even their own children or grandchildren to obtain a new lover or more power. No, Octavia had bragged of her husband and his career. She surely relied on his position and power. If anyone wanted him dead it would be one of those zealously misguided Jews, not Octavia.

She looked about the enormous stadium heaving with people, restlessly waiting for the games to commence. Only once had she seen such a gathering of so many men: on the night of *Pesach* when Simeon had almost caught her spying on the men. Yet here the Romans allowed their women to attend the festivals. They may be restricted to the upper seats but unlike Samaritan women they were not restricted to bending over the fire or chasing after the children.

Her gaze caught on a man below, surrounded by a group who appeared to be listening intently to whatever he was saying. Among the mass of dark-haired men his golden hair stood out like a lamp. He looked her way, as though he had felt her stare. She could not clearly see his face but she felt his eyes upon her. Her heart beat strangely fast and she looked away, reassembling her thoughts, steering them to safer ground.

Over the past days she had roamed the forum's shops and stalls hoping she might see the mysterious man on the camel. She had lingered by the towering temple of Augustus. She had stood in the marble shadow of his statue searching the crowds that ascended and descended the sweeping stone steps. Still, there was no sign of him, no hint that it might have been Calev. Now she cast her gaze across the stadium, across the sand, to the forest of faces on the far side. Finding Calev, if indeed it was him, would be like finding a leaf in a thicket. Her thoughts drifted to Marcellus' fears of a plot and a chill crawled through her heart. Finding a murderer would be just as impossible; this was the perfect place to kill the prefect.

A blast of trumpets resounded through the stadium. Every voice silenced, every eye turned to watch the musicians with their trumpets sounding, their drums beating, their cymbals clanging, their feet marching in precise formation. The flag bearers followed and then the entire garrison, led by Cornelius in full military regalia, sitting rod-straight on his horse. The soldiers marched shoulder to shoulder, six abreast, the sun glinting off their shields. Hundreds of studded sandals beat the ground in unison. The seats shuddered. Behind them six sleek horses, their braided tails swishing high, pulled an open carriage bearing two men dressed in white togas, one trimmed with a broad purple stripe, the other decorated with purple and gold. Behind them sat two women, one overshadowed by the splash of colour adorning the other. Livia grasped Leah's arm.

'Heavens!' she exclaimed. 'It's Octavia. I did not expect such a grand entrance, even for the Emperor's birthday. Does she not look magnificent in her new stola?'

It was difficult to see Octavia's face but her hand was raised in a regal gesture of greeting. The crowds clapped and cheered, although Leah noticed some stood silent. She shuddered. Even she knew the risk they took in refusing to acknowledge Caesar's appointed prefect.

The carriage circled the stadium and came to a stop in front of the platform. Slaves ran out onto the sand dragging an enormous construction of wooden steps which they set in place leading to the platform of dignitaries. Valerius Gratus ascended first followed by the man in purple and gold.

'That is the sponsor of this year's games,' whispered Livia. 'I expect his wife is regretting her decision not to see your designs. She appears like a sparrow next to a peacock.'

Octavia swished up the steps, holding out her hand for the dignitaries to kiss. The plain woman followed but all eyes were on Octavia.

A blast of the trumpet and a flash of fire at the far side of the stadium caught Leah's eye. A huge altar burst into flame, the bright orange blaze leaping skywards and forming fingers of black smoke.

'Are those sacrifices to your gods?' asked Leah.

'Just one god today,' Livia replied. 'Augustus.'

The smell of charred animal flesh drifted through the air, reminding Leah of the holy festivals of her own people. Valerius Gratus was speaking but not loudly enough for Leah to understand his rapid Latin over the hushed mutterings coming from the plebeian section.

'Where is Octavia?' asked Leah. She was no longer among the dignitaries on the platform.

'She will soon join us,' said Livia.

'Is she not entitled to remain with her husband?'

'Do the leading Samaritan women accompany their husbands on matters of state?' asked Livia, her voice genuinely curious.

Leah strained to imagine the chief priest's wife standing with him at the synagogue altar or the wives of Sychar's leading men sitting with them at the city gates. She smiled at Livia. 'That would be impossible. I have been the wife of a Samaritan and am now the wife of a Roman. I much prefer the freedom of being a Roman wife.'

'Yet we are still constrained by the laws imposed by Augustus. My mother spoke of sitting with her husband at the Colosseum in Rome before the Emperor outlawed it. He wanted to deter the licentious behaviour of the spectators.'

'And has it succeeded?'

'There is a way around any rule if one is so inclined.' Livia spoke in low tones behind a raised hand.

'You surely do not mean Octavia?'

'Let me just say that she prefers to sit closer to the plebeian men, unencumbered by her husband.' Livia directed her gaze to the rows of men seated close by. A few wore dull, dark coloured togas but most were dressed in short tunics, exposing their muscled arms and legs.

'Does her husband tolerate such behaviour?'

'The gossip is that they have an arrangement. He chooses to allow her to seek the same variety of pleasures as he does, so long as it is in secret. If he discovers a lover he would be required to divorce Octavia and have the lover crucified.'

'A precarious position,' said Leah.

'But not without its benefits. To gain the patronage of the prefect's wife is to gain power.'

A flurry of activity behind them interrupted their discussion. It was Octavia descending the marble steps, drawing gasps of admiration. She continued down the steps, lifting her stola above her ankles and drawing the stares of several young men from the plebeian section.

'Greetings, my dear friends.' She leaned over to kiss Livia and Leah on each cheek, allowing her stola to slip from her shoulder. She had fastened it loosely and Leah wondered if it was intentional.

'Octavia, you were magnificent!' Drusilla tried to rise from her seat to greet her but sank back like a sack of grain. 'My heart is still racing. Your stola and palla…'

She touched Leah's arm with her sweaty fingers. 'Look at us; we are like beams of the rainbow amongst these women. Leah, you will soon have a stream of customers, I am certain.'

Another blast of trumpets rang out and the stadium filled with lions, leopards and men brandishing a variety of weapons. The crowd screamed and shouted. The animals prowled. A beast pounced, then dropped to the ground, a spear through its throat. Blood spurted and formed a dark pool in the sand. Another reached its target, clawing out the throat of a man. He stumbled and fell on his own weapon, the deadly fork piercing his chest. Octavia and Drusilla cheered.

The gruesome display dragged on. There seemed to be a never-ending supply of men and beasts to replace those slaughtered. The smell of blood and entrails mixed with the sweat of the over-heated, over-aroused masses. Leah looked at her feet, at the beads of moisture staining Drusilla's stola, anywhere but at the scene below. She could see only Yosef laying there, his arm severed, his life blood draining from him. She squeezed her eyes shut.

'You look pale,' said Livia. 'The games are not to everyone's taste.'

Leah forced herself to smile. 'It is the heat. I just need some water.' She searched for one of the vendors who wandered the stadium selling food and water but there were none to be seen.

Livia tapped Octavia and Drusilla. 'We are in need of refreshment. We will soon return.'

'No, no, no,' commanded Octavia, snapping her eyes briefly away from the writhing mess of men and beasts below. 'You must stay for the next event. It will be the highlight of the day.'

'What could it be?' Drusilla's knowing tone made it clear that she knew exactly what spectacle lay ahead. Leah yearned to leave but Livia gave her an apologetic look. It would not do to upset this woman.

The sun beat down. Leah tried to ignore her parched throat and the ache in her head. She peered through the crowd but could not catch even a glimpse of Marcellus. Finally the cries of battle and the moans of death subsided. The crowd sat back in their seats, temporarily satiated. A swarm of slaves carried the dead away and raked sand over the blood stains. The crowd became silent, watching with anticipation what might be next.

Slowly the huge wooden doors at the far end of the stadium swung open.

'Crucifixions,' a plebeian cried.

Excitement rippled through the crowd. A long column of half-naked men, each bowed beneath a huge wooden cross, staggered across the sand. One collapsed, his thin legs folding like a spider's—he was no more than a boy. A soldier cracked a whip across the boy's legs. A stripe of red appeared and the crowd cheered.

Octavia had gone quiet, her neck strained like a scrawny goat, as though she was searching for something or someone. The prisoners were herded across the stadium until they stood evenly spaced apart, the crosses on the ground before them, all the way around the perimeter. Leah noticed a few people leaving; chatting about what food might be available outside to satisfy their hunger. Most stayed and stared.

At the sound of a trumpet, the guards standing by each prisoner shoved them onto the wooden cross, securing their wrists and ankles with rope. Then the hammering began. Leah looked away, blinking back tears and trying desperately to block out the screams of agony. Did Marcellus condone such forms of punishment? Had he been forced to crucify men as a commander in the Roman army? Had her father? She pushed the thoughts away.

'There he is!' Octavia clapped her hands in delight. 'May his end be slow and painful, and a lesson to all those who think they can bribe me.'

'Who is he?' Leah whispered to Livia.

'He is a nobody, who thought he was somebody.' Octavia tossed the caustic comment over her shoulder. 'But he had the attributes of a stallion … such a waste.' She sighed. Drusilla tittered.

Like a deathly dance, the crosses were raised up one by one around the stadium. The crowd jeered.

'You may go now, if you wish,' said Octavia. 'Some people find the next part tedious but I find it fascinating, especially when they use their spears to speed any lingerers' passage to the next life. The masses become unruly if it drags on too long.' With a wave of her bony hand she dismissed them and turned back to feast upon the agony below.

Chapter 23

Relieved to escape, Leah followed Livia to the rear of the stadium and down four flights of stairs to the ground. Stalls were set up under a row of leafy oaks and people jostled to buy wine and beer, dates and grapes, salted fish and roasted nuts and rounded loaves of barley bread. Livia stopped to talk to a woman who stood over a fire roasting almonds. They spoke in hushed, earnest tones while Leah waited, surprised that Livia would speak to someone of a lower rank. Perhaps Marcellus was not the only decent Roman.

'You go on and buy whatever you wish,' said Livia. 'I will be here when you return.'

Leah walked towards the stalls of food, weaving between the people. The smell of roasted pig flesh and the screams from the stadium turned her stomach. She searched for somewhere that might sell water but all she could see were dubious looking vendors of wine and beer and soured milk. Her lips were cracked and her mouth dry as dust. A sudden roar from the crowd inside the stadium made her start. She stumbled over an exposed tree root and let out a cry. A strong arm grabbed her, halting her fall and holding her steady.

'Take care. The ground is uneven around here.' The man's voice was deep and melodious like the strings of a harp. He stood a little shorter than she but he held her without effort. His nose was straight and strong but what overwhelmed her attention was his closely cropped hair, the colour of sun kissed sand, and his scent. It turned her blood to fire and her knees to water. It was the man she had glimpsed in the stadium.

'Thank you, sir,' she stammered, taking a step back. His eyes held hers and a wave of desire surged through her. Her heart raced at the strength of it, this overwhelming yearning that she assumed had died with Yosef. His gaze swept across her and she felt his eyes trace every curve beneath her clothes. She should have been offended or at least modest enough to look away but all she could feel was her flesh singeing. He stood with his hands on his hips, his scrutiny steady and sure.

'What is your name?'

'Leah Marcellus.' The words spilled out before she could object to his direct manner. 'And what is yours?' she asked, combating his directness with her own.

'Gaius Apollos.'

'And are you enjoying the games, Gaius Apollos?' She could barely believe her boldness. She sounded more like Octavia than herself.

'I am enjoying conversing with you more,' he said.

'And yet you do not know me, or I you.' She tilted her chin, struggling to maintain her composure. What had come over her? She should not be speaking so foolishly to a strange man. What would Marcellus think?

'That is a situation possible to change.' His gaze held her captive.

From the corner of her eye Leah noticed a group of men watching her with interest. What if they thought she was a prostitute or worse, recognised her as the wife of Marcellus? Her behaviour could bring gossip and shame upon his head.

'Thank you, sir, for your kindness. I must return to my friends.' She dragged her eyes from his and walked away, casting a withering look at the group of men.

It was not until she and Livia were once again settled in their seats that she realised that she was still thirsty. She searched for Marcellus, as though that might atone for her behaviour. There he was, still seated behind the podium of dignitaries, still conversing with those around him. Her head throbbed a heavy beat. She turned her attention to the games, hoping they would soon be over. Most of the crosses with their crucified corpses had gone. Slaves lowered the final few to the ground, slowly releasing the ropes. One rope slipped through their hands. The cross fell with a thud. The body split apart. Blood and entrails spewed out. The crowd cheered and clapped.

'They do it deliberately, you know,' said Livia. 'It keeps the crowd amused.'

She did not look amused. She looked hot and flustered like everyone else, even Octavia, who was waving furiously at an attendant to bring her wine. The attendant wandered over and at Octavia's command, filled four cups from a wine skin.

'Well thank the gods—finally some sustenance.' She tipped the cup down her throat and held it out for the attendant to refill.

'Keep our cups filled and I will do likewise with your pocket.' She withdrew a handful of small bronze coins and dropped them into the attendant's outstretched hand. He nodded in deference and hurried away. The wine was weak and sweet. Leah finished her cup quickly and hoped the attendant would soon return.

'I expect the baths will be brimming with patrons after this,' said Livia. 'They are a welcome refreshment after the games.'

'Indeed,' said Drusilla who was wilting in her seat.

Trumpets sounded, announcing the next event. With a loud heralding the wooden gates burst open again and a throng of swarthy, bare-chested archers astride sleek horses galloped through, each displaying his bow and arrow high above his head.

Octavia sprang from her seat, joining in the wild stamping of feet and cheers of encouragement. Leah could barely hear her over the noise.

'There he is! The one from Caesarea.' Octavia clapped her hand to her chest, her face raised as though in worship. 'Have you ever seen such magnificent thighs?'

It was difficult to see which archer she was pointing to. They were so fast, flying around the stadium, shooting arrows over each other with great skill. None of them held the reins with their hands. Instead they gripped the horse with their legs and somehow directed them into tight turns and over large obstacles: pools of water, leaping flames and high wooden jumps. The man with the wine appeared again. Leah gulped down her refilled cup. He topped it up a third time.

'Ooh, yes,' squealed Drusilla. 'What skill, what speed, what … what is *that*?'

One horseman had separated himself from the others and was galloping at full speed towards the podium where the dignitaries sat, his bow raised high and arrow drawn back, poised to shoot. Two other horsemen chased after him, riding at a furious speed to cut him off.

'Murderer!' screamed Octavia. 'He is trying to kill my husband! Stop him. Stop him!'

The man released his arrow. One of the pursuers threw himself at his horse. It reared up, knocking the man off balance. The arrow flew straight and fast, not at the podium but just above it, towards Marcellus. A cold dread hit Leah.

Octavia was hysterical; Drusilla was trying to calm her down. Leah could see nothing for the huddle of men, some crouching, some urgently waving and shouting for assistance. She could not see Marcellus. Please, please let him be safe. Panic strangled her throat. She leapt from her seat.

'It's Marcellus, I know, I just know. I must get to him.'

Livia reached out to reassure her. She pulled away and pushed through the women who crowded the aisles trying to see the commotion below. She heard Livia calling her name. She heard Octavia calling down curses and screaming to be taken to her husband. She did not look back.

Soldiers swarmed the stadium and sand, swords drawn, screaming orders. The masses streamed out—satiated with the day's spectacles, thrilled with the rogue Syrian archer, eager to drink.

'I knew it would happen, as soon as I saw him break off.'

'There were rumours of a plot to kill the prefect, you know.'

'And not the first time; he has upset many in Judea.'

Leah sidled and strained and squeezed against the mass of bodies. It was like ploughing uphill. At this rate she would never get to Marcellus.

'Get out of my way!' she yelled at the men in front of her. She did not care what they might think. 'I have to get to my husband. Let me through. Now!'

They stepped aside, their mouths agape, and Leah felt a sliver of satisfaction. Perhaps men responded better to boldness than submission.

At the entrance to the equestrian section soldiers barred the way.

'No one is permitted up these stairs,' said one, his hand moving to his sheathed sword.

'My husband is up there. I need to see that he is safe. Was anyone hurt?' Leah heard the panic in her voice and the burning of imminent tears. She blinked them away. Boldness worked better. She lowered her tone and spoke deliberately. 'My husband is Marcellus of Attica, an Equestrian knight and patron of this city. I must see him.'

The soldier's eyes flickered in recognition. 'He is not here. They have taken him to the garrison.'

'Is he injured? Is he alive?'

The soldier looked at her with compassion. 'I am sorry. I cannot say.'

Leah turned back and hastened through the thinning crowd to the street.

People still spilled from the stadium, some strolling, some stumbling from hours of sunshine and wine. One tripped and fell to his knees, his companions laughing at his blood-stained toga. Another vomited onto the cobblestones directly in front of an approaching litter. The bearers deftly side-stepped the mess and hurried along, ignoring the shout of annoyance from whomever reclined behind the curtains.

Leah's head pounded, her vision blurred. She stumbled to a wall and leaned against it, closing her eyes and praying to *Yahweh* for strength, and for Marcellus.

'Leah!' She opened her eyes to see Livia hurrying towards her. Her servant followed at a trot.

'Leah. Thank the gods you are here. I thought I might never find you in this swarm. Is Marcellus safe? It was not him, was it?' Livia looked around as though expecting to see him close by.

'They have taken him to the garrison. I know nothing else. I must go there at once.' Her parched lips could barely form the words.

'My dear, you look as pale as a ghost.' She took her arm. 'Come, let us return to the villa before you collapse.' Leah opened her mouth to protest but Livia cut her off. 'We will find no answers at the garrison; no woman is permitted to enter. Cornelius will certainly be with him and he will send word as quickly as he can.' She turned to her servant. 'Go to the garrison and find Cornelius with all haste. But first, summon a litter to take us home.'

Soon they were being carried along the street at a rapid, jarring pace. Leah gripped the seat to steady herself. When they arrived, Livia called for refreshments. By the time the servants had washed the dust from their feet and given them fresh household sandals, a feast had been laid out. Leah could not eat. How could she when Marcellus might be fatally wounded ... or worse?

'That is a welcome relief,' said Livia, sipping from a cup of water.

Leah drank also, the cool water washing away the dust and dryness, quenching her thirst but not her anxious thoughts. A shout from the gates drew both women to their feet. They dropped their cups and ran outside. Livia's servant raced towards them.

'He's alive!'

Leah's heart leapt with relief.

The servant stopped in front of them, trying to regain his breath. He sucked in great gulps of air, his chest heaving in and out. 'He's alive,' he repeated. 'The physician says he will recover.'

Later that afternoon Cornelius arrived home and apprised them of the details. The arrow had hit Marcellus in the chest but the surgeon had managed to extract it. The bleeding had been stemmed and Marcellus was conscious although drowsy from the opos. Leah remembered Marcellus describing the wondrous pain numbing effect of the poppy juice during his battles in Germania. She remembered him sitting with Benjamin under the grape vine recounting tales of victory. She remembered Benjamin's enraptured face—it had been almost a week since she had held him in her arms and promised to bring him a gift from the big Roman city. How she yearned to return home but Marcellus was not well enough for the journey. She would have to wait in the city several more days.

'And what of the archer?' asked Livia.

'He has been arrested and will be crucified as a deterrent to others. Somehow he slipped in among the Syrian archers, pretending to be one of them. They suspected nothing until he broke off and headed towards the podium. The rumours were true: he was from Jerusalem and one of those whose purpose was to destroy Roman rule. If it were not for the Syrians' quick intervention Valerius Gratus would be dead.'

Leah slept fitfully that night, tormented by dreams of death—Yosef bleeding in the dust, Syrian archers trampling mangled corpses, Marcellus pierced with polished arrows.

She woke drenched in sweat, her hair knotted and tangled. Tossing aside the crumpled linens she poured water into a basin, dipped in a scented sponge and smoothed it over her face, her throat, her shoulders. She dipped the sponge in the water again, inhaling the strange fragrance. Strange yet familiar. She ran the sponge along each outstretched finger in long sweeps towards her body. What was that scent? It held a masculine, herbal note, hidden beneath the sweetness of flowers. She moved the sponge over her breasts, closing her eyes and breathing deeply. Her body remembered before she did. Her knees weakened and a flush of heat ran through her. It was the scent of the man with the hair of bronze.

Chapter 24

The litter swayed gently from side to side. Livia had insisted she take it; it was not safe for a woman to walk alone in the dyers and launderer's quarter. She had apologised that she could not accompany Leah; she had pressing matters to attend to, preparing for the *convivium* that she and Cornelius were hosting that evening. It was the final event in the week-long celebrations for the Emperor's birthday.

Unlike the day before, there was no urgency in this outing, no dreadful reason to race through the streets. That morning Cornelius had taken fresh clothing and a basketful of food to Marcellus, returning to reassure her that he was doing well. He had passed on her letter, written in haste on a small scroll, telling Marcellus of her anxious thoughts and prayers for his quick recovery. It was all she could do—she could not visit, she could not speak to him, she could not wipe his brow.

Leah reclined on the cushions, surveying the dyers and launderer's workshops from behind the partially draped curtain and trying to ignore the foul smells that assaulted her. The streets were narrow here, on the southern outskirts of Sebaste, where the stench that distinguished the quarter could not taint the main city. Men in grubby tunics and frayed cloaks laboured over enormous tubs set on smoky fires. Some prodded with sticks, others poured in gold coloured liquid from enormous clay pots. She recognised them as the same pots that stood on many corners of the city's streets, attracting a regular flow of men eager to lift their toga and relieve themselves. A row of ragged children, their tunics tucked up and each standing in a large tub, stamped on the cooled, urine-soaked clothes while others rinsed and hung them on large wire frames set over burning sulphur. The fumes stung her eyes and tore at her throat. Two dogs chased each other around wooden barrels spilling over with murky water. It splattered mud-coloured spots over a rack of hanging clothes. An old woman shook her stick and cursed.

Farther along, the clothing changed to dull hues of red, saffron and blue. These dyes were far from the quality she required. They continued through the alleys and lanes, Leah hoping she might see colours as vivid as those she had created herself. Surely there was a skilled dyer somewhere in this city. They turned into a broader, busier street and she saw a sagging line of bright red cloth in front of a large workshop. She called out and the bearers halted, lowering the litter so she could step out.

'Greetings, sir,' she said to a man arranging layers of folded scarlet cloth on a table. He was considerably better dressed than the other workmen she had passed. 'I am Leah Marcellus, wife of Marcellus of Attica. I can see that you are a dyer of superior ability.'

He grinned, exposing a crooked row of broken and missing teeth, 'Woman, you are right. I am the best *flammarii* in Sebaste. No-one surpasses my skill in scarlet.' His shallow chest puffed out.

'Do you specialise only in red?' Leah looked around hoping to see other colours. She needed more than just red.

'No-one dyes a range of colours. If you want blue, see the *violarii* over there.' He waved at a shop displaying fabric of a dull, indistinct blue. 'If you want saffron, see the *crocotarii* down the street, and if you want purple you will have to go to the *purpurarii* in Tyre.'

Leah shook off her disappointment. She had hoped for one dyer to do all colours but if she could obtain a cheap enough price she could consider using several dyers. She picked up a length of red wool. It was of inferior quality, coarse to the touch. 'What is your price for dying this length?' she asked.

The man flicked his eyes over her. She knew this look; she had seen it in the traders who came to the olive grove. He was summing up how much he could ask.

'Two hundred denarii.'

His price was outrageous. A skilled labourer in the city could earn as much as fifty denarii a day, so Livia had informed her, but this was hardly a day's worth of work. Two hundred denarii was almost as much as she had charged Drusilla for her finely woven and uniquely dyed stola! But the quality of the man's work could not be denied. If she could lower his price …

With a thoughtful sigh she leaned over to stroke the rough crimson wool, allowing her stola to slip a little from her shoulder. If it worked for Octavia it might also work for her. She smiled at the man whose eyes were now fixed on her exposed skin.

'I did not ask the price for weaving as well, only the dying.'

The man coughed harshly and cleared his throat. 'Well,' he said, scratching his beard with red stained fingers, 'without the weaving the price for such a length would be one hundred denarii.'

'I expect you would reduce the price for a regular supply of more lengths,' she said, standing up and slowly rearranging her stola.

'Of course.' His eyes followed the path of her hands and he scratched fiercely at his beard, his rapid breathing a harsh rasp.

'Forty denarii,' she said.

'It is not possible. My wife and children would be beggars in the street.' He flung his arms wide, a dramatic gesture, but his eyes remained fixed on her. He was still interested.

'Fifty denarii then, for the sake of your family.' It was a fair price but she could see the curious stares of the nearby shop owners watching their negotiations. This *flammarii*, clearly the best in Sebaste, could not be seen to capitulate to a woman. She lowered her voice. 'There is no need to settle on a price at this moment. I was hoping for a dyer who could do every colour but I see this is not possible. I will consider the matter and, if necessary, return in private to complete our negotiations.'

The man tilted his head in acknowledgement then raised his voice for his neighbours to hear. 'One hundred denarii and not a bronze *as* less!'

It was a relief to leave the putrid air of the launderers and dyers behind but her concerns outweighed her relief. There was only one dyer whose work was of the standard she required and although she had managed to beat down his price—she felt a small glow of victory at her success—she needed more than just red. She sighed. If she wanted the range of colours, and the quality, she would have to continue the dying herself. Mariamne would be left with all the weaving and they would continue to be constrained in how much cloth they could produce.

Octavia had ordered two more stolas as well as a tunic for each of her young daughters. She wanted them before she left Judea 'to astound those stiff-necked women of Rome'. Leah had not seen Octavia's daughters, indeed she had seen neither the children of Drusilla nor Livia, but she had heard them boasting of their children's achievements and complaining of the demands of having so many. They spoke with such assurance, with the assumption that the bearing of many children was usual for every woman. Their words had cast a pall of shame over Leah.

The sound of bellowing, grunting and moaning caught her attention. They were passing a small herd of camels resting by a large water trough, their turbaned riders reclining nearby. The camels carried large baskets filled with exotic wares in vibrant colours. She called for the litter bearers to stop. The turbaned men stared at her with hostile faces. For a moment, she hesitated, aware of the impropriety of her behaviour. Would they even speak to her? It had been many years since she had wished she carried a dagger. Her heart thudded in her chest. She strengthened herself. One of them might know of Calev. She had to find out.

'Sirs, I am Leah Marcellus of Sychar,' she said.

'Why do you speak with us? You are a woman,' growled one of the men in a thick foreign accent. Another spat on the ground.

'I am searching for a friend. His name is Calev, also from Sychar. He travelled to the east to join his uncle, a trader as you are. Do you know of him?'

The men spoke among themselves, gesticulating, frowning and finally laughing. Leah waited, hoping they were discussing Calev and not some more sinister subject. She glanced back to check that the litter bearers were nearby, silently thanking Livia for her insistence on safety.

'Does he have a temper as foul as a camel?' said the man. The other uttered something in their language and they all laughed. 'And a mind as sharp as a sword?'

Was this the same Calev they spoke of? She had never taken much notice of his mind. She did remember him and Atticus always laughing and teasing each other. They had been happy back then, before that terrible time, before Simeon.

'I have not seen him for three years. But I thought I saw him here in Sebaste a few days ago.'

The men chattered again with more gestures and laughter. 'He was here but now he is not. He has returned to Palmyra. That is where his uncle, may Ba'al bless him, has his home. But he will return. Sebaste consumes treasure from the east as a camel consumes water.' The man reached into a sack and pulled out a length of the most beautiful cloth she had ever seen. It was purple and pomegranate and the richest blue, woven with strands of gold. He held it out to Leah. 'This is what we bring from the east—the finest silk.'

She took it, her heart thudding now with excitement. The fabric floated over her fingers like running water. With the right adjustments it would make the most exquisite stola for Octavia. But the price would most certainly be high. Would Octavia pay? She hesitated but a moment. She would wear it tonight, cut and pinned and draped so Octavia could not help but covet such exotic beauty.

'Is it for purchase?' she asked.

The man turned to his companions, exchanging a string of foreign words and much waving of hands. Finally he replied.

'It is not for sale.'

'Oh.' It was all she could say. The man grinned at the disappointment that surely showed on her face. She handed the beautiful cloth back. He took it, folded it with great care and then presented it to her.

'Take it; it is our gift to you. Any friend of Calev is a friend of ours.'

'How can I accept such a treasure?' she stammered.

'How can you refuse without insulting us?'

'Sir, you are exceedingly generous.' Leah bowed her head, amazed at their spontaneous kindness.

'It is nothing. Many times in the treacherous desert regions, we have been blessed by the quick sword of Calev. This is but a small gesture of our gratitude.'

After obtaining an assurance from the traders that they would ask Calev to visit her, she left with the silk carefully secreted in a purse and with a lightness of heart. If she could purchase silk and other exotic cloth directly from Calev, she and Mariamne would have less need to dye their own.

They neared the forum and the litter bearers negotiated their way through the increasingly crowded streets. This was the heart of the city, throbbing with vendors, merchants, nobility and slaves. Voices cried out in foreign accents, calling attention to their brimming baskets and tables heaving with strange foods, fine spices, precious stones, ivory tusks, embroidered work and multicoloured rugs with cords twisted and tightly knotted. Incense mingled with the sharp scent of sweat and animals. Sheep milled in wooden pens, waiting to be sold for sacrifice; camels drank deeply from broad barrels of water, war horses snorted and shook their manes in protest at having their hooves shod.

She alighted in front of the baths where she had arranged to meet Livia and pressed a bronze coin into the sweaty palm of each of the six litter bearers in thanks. Around her, helmets and tunics mingled with turbans and togas. Leah clutched her purse tighter. People trickled up and down the grand marble steps of the baths which led to a sweeping, shaded colonnade. She watched a man of enormous girth, wrapped in a robe of scarlet and surrounded by fussing slaves, emerge from the grand entrance. He waddled across the colonnade and down the grand stairs where he was hoisted into a litter and carried away.

A flash of flame caught her eye. In an area marked off by statues of naked Roman gods, their muscles chiselled and their heads wreathed in tight curls, a group of people were applauding a man in flowing dark robes. He stood on a rostrum and in one hand held high a flaming stick. Curious, she drew closer to the crowd.

'Who is he?' she asked two women.

'It is Simon of Samaria. He is a pupil of the holy man, Dositheus of Arabia, but claims to be even greater. His Samaritan followers say he is the divine power, the promised prophet.'

'Those Samaritans follow a strange religion, if you can call it a religion at all,' said the other woman. 'They worship an invisible god and have been waiting thousands of years for this promised prophet.'

'Strange indeed. What is the benefit of following a god you cannot see, and why worship only one? It may incite the jealousy of the others.'

Leah remained silent, not wishing to reveal her accent that might mark her as one of those strange Samaritans.

'I have heard he healed a man of blindness,' continued one of the women, straining to get a better view of the man on the rostrum.

'And he claims he can fly,' said the other.

'Then he would truly be a god.'

Like inquisitive birds the women bobbed up and down, peering around the heads of those in front.

'What sort of magic is that?' a man called out. 'It is just a burning stick.'

The crowd laughed. The magician swivelled to face the accuser, his eyes like burning coals in his shaded face. Leah shuddered. There was a dark power in those eyes. The magician raised his free hand to the burning stick. His fingers were so close to the flames yet he did not flinch. Another flash of fire and the crowd gasped. Flames flickered from the magician's fingertips. He held his hand high for all to see and then slowly brought his outstretched arm down until his flaming fingers pointed at his accuser. He spat out a single, incomprehensible word and the accusing man crumpled to the ground.

'Is he dead?' whispered the women among themselves. A man swung around to answer them.

'Certainly not; who would pay to hear a murderer? Simon has come to teach and heal us, not harm us.'

Leah was not so sure. She did not like the tinge of pride in the magician's face; it reminded her of Simeon. The fallen man's friends dragged him to his feet and hauled him away. She caught a glimpse of gold. The tightly curled hair stood out like a lamp on a stand. Her heart beat faster, her breath caught in her throat. Gaius Apollos stared at her from across the crowd, his gaze as powerful as the midday sun. She had no time to bask. A touch on her arm and a voice at her side made her jump.

'I see you have found our famous philosopher's corner.'

'Livia!' Leah clasped Livia's arm in greeting. 'I am glad you found me in this crowd.' She glanced at the man on the rostrum whose smooth speech now held his audience captive. 'This one is certainly … interesting.'

'The rostrum is never without a philosopher or holy man,' said Livia. 'They quench the people's continual thirst for new knowledge.' She laughed and linked her arm through Leah's. 'Come, let us bathe before the masses arrive.'

They ascended the grand stairs of the baths and started along the broad colonnade. It was lined with statues of marble and bronze, standing guard over shaded seats where men with oiled skin and damp hair sat talking.

'Do men and women bathe together?' asked Leah.

Livia's answer was cut short by footsteps behind them and a deep voice calling her name. Leah turned and her heart bolted like a horse in an open field. Striding along the colonnade, a broad grin on his face was Gaius Apollos.

Chapter 25

'Livia, what fortune! It has been too long.'

'Heavens, Gaius Apollos! You are a long way from Athens. What are you doing here in Sebaste?' Livia greeted him with a kiss.

'I have come to learn from the philosophers of the east and take their teachings back to the Areopagus. As you well know, we Greeks have ears that itch for the latest ideas.' He looked over Livia's shoulder at Leah and winked.

Leah did not know where to look. His gaze was so bold and below it he wore the attire of a Greek philosopher, a toga draped over one shoulder, exposing a broad athletic chest and golden arms as finely chiselled as any of the statues that surrounded them. Livia stepped aside and held out her arm in introduction.

'Leah, this is Gaius Apollos, the son of our very good friends in Athens.'

'I am pleased to meet you, Gaius Apollos,' said Leah, struggling to maintain her composure. 'I am Leah Marcellus.'

Gaius gave a small bow while Livia continued.

'Leah and her husband have been staying with us for the Emperor's birthday celebrations, but yesterday they suffered a dreadful misfortune.'

'Do you speak of the attempted assassination of Valerius Gratus? The drinking houses were full of the gossip last night.'

'Then you will have heard that the arrow hit another. It was Leah's dear husband.'

'A misfortune indeed,' said Gaius. His brow furrowed and his tone softened. 'Is it serious?'

'Thankfully the surgeon says that he will recover,' said Leah. 'Livia and Cornelius have kindly extended their hospitality until he is fit to return home.'

'It is our pleasure,' said Livia, giving Leah a motherly smile. 'Now tell me, Gaius, are your parents well?' She turned to Leah. 'Our families were very close when Cornelius was stationed in Athens. Gaius even tutored our son in philosophy for a time.'

'My parents are well although I see little of them now that I live in Corinth.'

A shadow crossed Livia's face. 'Corinth?'

Gaius laughed. 'Ah, the den of wicked pleasures. I can assure you, not all Corinthians are so lacking in restraint.' His eyes flicked to Leah again and she wondered with which Corinthians he associated.

'I am pleased to hear it,' said Livia. She glanced at the growing stream of people entering the baths. 'We are hosting a *convivium* tonight. If you do not have more pressing matters, you are most welcome. I am sure Cornelius would like to hear the latest news from Greece.'

'I would be honoured.' Gaius kissed Livia on both cheeks and then took Leah's hand and lifted it to his lips. 'Until tonight.' His breath brushed across her skin like flames. Her lips parted. She pressed them together, terrified that her voice might betray the fire within.

Inside the baths, determined to put Gaius far from her mind, Leah marvelled at the gleaming mosaic floors of the atrium, the palm trees cradled in turquoise pots and the magnificent fountain. Sunlight streamed in from the open air above, dancing off the water like silver bells. Just off the atrium was a generous airy room where women were in various states of undress. Assistants were busy hanging stolas on pegs and placing the women's shoes in alcoves set along the walls. Leah followed Livia's lead, removing her clothes and putting on a light woollen garment that allowed, thankfully, some modesty. An assistant with skin of gleaming ebony handed her a pair of sandals with thick soles. 'For the heat,' she explained in a strong foreign accent.

Leaving the apodyterium they entered a room that was as warm as a summer's evening.

'We start with the tepidarium,' said Livia.

The walls were painted scarlet and lined with bronze seats where women sat chattering and leaning into each other. Above them the ceiling displayed all kinds of birds and flowers in spring shades of yellow, rose and sky blue. Livia's friends congregated around them, questioning Leah about her fabrics.

'Was it truly you who designed the stola that the prefect's wife wore at the games?' asked one.

'It was an honour that Octavia chose to wear it for the occasion,' replied Leah. The women pressed closer.

'How did you achieve such brightness of colour?'

'And such diversity,' added another.

'With much pegging of the nose,' said Leah. She joined in their laughter.

'Will you be making more? Such a garment is sure to draw my husband to the cubiculum with more fervour.'

'If that is the case, you will soon have a scroll full of orders!'

'I am pleased to assist in such matters of importance,' said Leah and they all crowed with delight.

From the tepidarium the women moved into the caldarium. Everything was hot: the walls, the floor, the air. Sweat beaded on her brow and she was glad of the thick soled sandals. She eased herself into the almost scalding water of the pool and watched drips of water sizzle on the mosaic floor. Like the breath of Gaius on her skin. The thought slipped through her defences, her resolve to not think about him. How could she be thinking of another man when Marcellus, her husband, lay wounded and alone? She sank lower in the steaming water feeling the light garment cling to the curves of her body, the same curves over which Gaius had swept his gaze.

They emerged from the heat and entered the frigidarium. The change from hot to cold was a welcome slap on the face, exactly what she needed to arrest her disloyal thoughts. In the centre was an enormous round bath with water spilling from the mouth of a bronze lion. Some women swam in casual frog-like movements. Others ducked their heads under and splashed each other like small children. Leah plunged into the chill water, and jumped out just as quickly, gasping for breath and grinning with the exhilaration.

With her skin still tingling she allowed a slave to rub her skin with a coarse linen cloth and massage in scented olive oil. The slave's fingers were skilful on her shoulders and arms and legs, and the fragrance of lavender filled the room. She slid into her stola, combing her damp hair and tying it in a loose knot. She joined Livia in the atrium and they strolled past sculptures and frescoes and flowering plants, their conversation relaxed and light-hearted.

'It is wonderful to be cleansed of the dirt of the city,' said Livia. 'These baths are as splendid as any in Athens, or Rome for that matter. We are blessed to have such skilled craftsmen here in Sebaste.'

'Never have I seen such splendour in one building, apart from the Temple of Augustus,' said Leah. 'And never have I seen such high ceilings.'

They continued to chat about the magnificent artworks adorning the atrium, but Leah's attention wandered to the far end, to a cordoned off space filled with mats and iron bars with lead weights at each end. Multiple sets of wide, wooden doors swung open to the outside. Beyond the doors she glimpsed men running and wrestling, their bodies glistening with sweat. Three men strode in through the open doors, jesting with each other and clothed only in loincloths. Leah stared. Livia's stories of artists and sculptors and painters faded to a dull hum. One of the men hoisted an iron bar effortlessly above his head. She could not tear her eyes away.

She was transfixed, feasting on every taut, golden muscle and curve of Gaius Apollos' near naked body.

Chapter 26

The lamps were lit, the tables laid, the wine jars filled. All was ready for the final evening of Emperor Augustus' birthday celebrations. Leah hovered in the hallway, securing her swept up hair with an ivory and pearl pin and smoothing the silk stola over her hips, ensuring it fell evenly to her ankles. She had spent the afternoon draping, cutting and pinning the precious fabric until it was transformed into the most beautiful stola she had yet created. She walked across the mosaic floor to where Livia and Cornelius were greeting guests, the silken stola embracing her body like a lover.

'Leah, how delightful to see you!' Drusilla sailed towards her, her arms outstretched like oars. 'What a magnificent stola; another of your wonderful creations I am sure. You must meet my friends. I have told them all about you and how it was I who first discovered your most excellent talent.'

She kissed Leah on both cheeks, embracing her as though they were the closest of friends. The odour of rose water and rotten teeth assaulted her. Drusilla, her chest puffed with pride, introduced her to the other women. Leah replied in her best Latin, enjoying the startled look of Drusilla's friends. It was clear they did not expect a woman from this region to speak the language of Rome. The conversation eased into Greek, mingling with the other talk in the room. It seemed that Latin was spoken only as a statement of status and once established, was discarded in favour of Greek.

'And how is Marcellus?' asked Drusilla. 'Such a terrible thing to have happened. I was so occupied with calming Octavia … the wife of the prefect, Valerius Gratus,' she explained to her friends, '… that I did not see who had been hit. I only heard later that he had been taken to the garrison. Is it serious?'

She placed her hand on Leah's arm in a gesture of concern. It was more likely she wanted to acquire information to impress her friends.

'He is much improved, thank you. He will be able to leave the garrison tomorrow.'

'Praise the gods for that,' said Drusilla, clapping her clammy hands. 'You must be altogether relieved. I expect you are anxious to return to the quiet of Sychar where he can recover in peace.'

'Indeed,' replied Leah.

A servant offered her a goblet of wine. It was sweetened with honey and slid down her throat with ease. While Drusilla flitted to other subjects Leah's thoughts remained with Marcellus. According to Cornelius, as soon as the physician had declared him well enough to travel, he had arranged for a carpentum to carry them back to Sychar. They would leave tomorrow. She lifted her cup. The wine flowed like a warm river, easing her irritation.

She and Livia had made plans to attend the baths again with the promise of introducing Leah, and her garments, to more of the women of the city. Could she not have just one more day at the baths; one more day to meet with the women; one more day to bathe in the water ... one more day to see Gaius? She lowered her eyes, afraid that the guests who swirled about her might somehow know what filled her mind. She could think only one thought: Gaius would soon be here.

She excused herself from Drusilla and moved outside to the portico where Livia was instructing a servant. The evening was clear, the warm air fragrant with incense from candles set all over the garden. Servants glided among the guests offering platters of food and goblets of wine. A group of musicians played a lively tune which only elevated the animated talk.

'Leah, you look wonderful,' said Livia. 'I hope you are enjoying our *convivium*, despite the absence of our dear Marcellus. Do not fret; I will ensure you are looked after. Now you must try these.'

From a platter she took a stick-like purple-green vegetable, slightly charred, glistening with oil and sprinkled with tiny rocks of salt. 'It is called asparagi. It is prized by both Romans and Greeks.'

Leah bit into the stick expecting it to be bitter and hard. Instead it was tender with a burst of sweetness, salt and olive oil. She took another bite.

'*Velocius quam asparagi conquantur.* Faster than asparagi can be cooked.' The voice behind her was deep and melodious. The asparagi caught in her throat.

'Gaius, it is a pleasure to see you here,' said Livia.

'The pleasure is truly mine,' he said, raising Livia's hand to his lips. 'And, Leah, how much more pleasure can I endure?'

'I am sure you will manage,' said Leah, unable to restrain her delight.

'I am impressed by your knowledge of our Roman sayings,' said Livia. 'I expected Athenian philosophers to read only the ancient works.'

'Are not the sayings of the Emperor Augustus of equal worth?' He laughed. 'In truth, it was my mother who used to say it all the time.' He picked up an asparagi spear and ate it. 'A most appropriate choice for his birthday celebrations, a fact I am sure is not wasted on your guests, Livia.'

'I do not think all are as astute.' Leah followed Livia's glance to a group of guests stuffing the slender stalks into their mouths and smearing the oil from their faces with the back of their hands. They called out to a servant to refill their cups and Leah wondered how long their togas would remain unblemished.

'The art of living is in the pleasure of each moment,' said Gaius. 'To not appreciate that is to lose life.'

'And what of the moments that are devoid of pleasure?' asked Leah.

'They serve only to enhance pleasure when it comes. We cannot fully appreciate pleasure unless we have experienced the lack of it.'

'It is too late in the day for me to struggle with such ideas,' said Livia. 'Leah, I will leave you and Gaius to debate the finer points of pleasure while I attend to the less cerebral duty of ensuring we do not run out of wine.'

She smiled and moved towards the chief steward who stood by a marble column, discretely observing the servants. One threaded towards them and Gaius inclined his goblet. The servant refilled both their cups. The wine slipped down like warmed oil, soothing her mind, loosening her limbs.

'Your opinions on pleasure are intriguing,' she said. 'I would like to hear more.'

'Then let us go to a quieter place,' said Gaius. With his hand at her back he guided her away from the guests to a secluded corner of the garden. It was the lightest of touches but it was all she could feel. The music and laughter dimmed behind them. She breathed in the scent of him beside her, more powerful than any wine.

'What would you like to know?' asked Gaius

'I would like to know… what it is like in Athens,' said Leah, grasping for an able response.

'It is a city clinging to the glories of its past. Only the meeting of the Areopagus can entice me away from Corinth. It is highly respected, a place where people congregate to discuss and debate the latest ideas.'

'And what have you learned?'

'I have learned that philosophy stimulates the mind but not the body.'

He moved closer to her. Her heart raced but she stepped away, restoring a respectable distance between them.

'I have heard there are many schools of thought stemming from the great Greek philosophers. Which do you follow?' she asked. The lamplight caught on the shadow of gold across his jaw and above his lip; amusement tugged at his mouth.

'I do not consider it necessary to restrict myself to a single school. There is knowledge to be gained from many. I have sat with the Epicureans and also with the Pythagoreans and the Stoics. During my recent travels I have discovered new ways of thinking. There are certain philosophers from the east here in Sebaste from whom I wish to learn more. It has persuaded me to stay on here in Sebaste for the winter.'

'Do you not have responsibilities in Greece?'

'I have few responsibilities. Livia's friends, who I now call my parents, produce wine and olive oil. Their vineyard and olive groves are extensive and their eldest son manages it all. They are pleased to assist me and proud to have a philosopher in the family.'

'And your true parents?'

'They died when I was young.' There was vulnerability in his eyes.

'I am sorry,' said Leah, resisting the urge to comfort him. 'We also have olive groves on the slopes south and east of Sychar. You may be interested in seeing them,' said Leah.

'Is that an invitation?' He stepped closer again, this time tracing her face with his fingers. She dared not speak, dared not break the moment.

'Leah.' Her name upon his lips, the strain in his voice, the heat of his fingers: it was overpowering, untamed. He pulled her to him and kissed her.

His tongue grazed hers. She felt the strength of his muscles beneath his toga. She opened her mouth, inviting him in. His hand slid lower. The pleasure, so close to pain, was exquisite. A bell clanged and they broke apart. Leah glanced around to ensure no-one had seen them.

'It is nothing,' said Gaius running his hand down the exposed skin of her chest and slipping it beneath her stola. She pressed against him.

'Gaius.' Her voice was a hoarse whisper. His eyes smouldered and he took hold of her, bruising her mouth with his kiss. The bell rang out again. She pulled away from him and peered across the courtyard. The guests were wandering inside.

'We must go,' she said.

'Stay with me. Stay here. We will not be missed,' said Gaius, catching her hand in his.

Her resolve faltered. She cast herself against him, clutching the breadth of his arms and kissing him one last time. 'I must go.' She could not risk being caught. She hurried towards the light determined not to look back.

Inside the guests had gathered near the grand entrance. Leah straightened her stola and smoothed her hair, re-adjusting the pearl pins to catch up the strands that had escaped. She took a deep breath to settle herself, hoping that no-one would notice the flush of her face or the creases in the crushed silk. Applause broke out and Octavia swept through the doors on her husband's arm. She was wearing the crimson stola and Leah could see women among the guests staring at the daring colour and design. They stopped in the middle of the crowd. Valerius Gratus raised his hand for silence.

'May the gods be with you for your warm welcome. It is our pleasure to enjoy this final evening of celebrations with such excellent hospitality. Our gratitude to you, Cornelius.' He extended his hand towards Cornelius and Livia in a regal gesture.

'We are saddened to leave Sebaste but our great Emperor Tiberius, may the gods bless him, has recalled us to Rome as soon as we have installed your new prefect, Pontius Pilate, in Caesarea.'

The guests clapped politely, with a little less vigour. Valerius Gratus smiled at the assurance that he was the preferred prefect.

'As most of you are aware, an attempt was made on my life at the games. Thanks to the quick reaction of a Syrian archer, the plot failed, and tomorrow you will be able to see the traitor nailed to a cross outside the East Gate. As for the archer whose courageous deed saved my life, I have granted him Roman citizenship.' The guests cheered and raised their goblets. The prefect held up his hand and the noise subsided again.

'There was, however, one man who fell to the blow of the arrow and is at this very moment in the garrison recovering from what might have been a mortal wound. He is a good man, a man of great esteem in this city and an Equestrian knight of the highest order. Let us honour Marcellus of Attica.' He raised a clenched fist and brought it across his chest, striking it in the Roman manner of respect. 'And to his wife, Leah, our deepest respects at this time of distress.' He followed Octavia's subtle nod in her direction, staring for a moment before he continued. 'And who, my wife tells me, makes the best garments outside of Rome.'

Leah inclined her head, graciously accepting the tribute, aware of the many eyes upon her. She masked her elation with a demure smile. She could have spread no better report of her fabrics. The prefect clapped his hands signalling the end of the speeches and a return to the festivities. Soon she was surrounded by women clamouring to capture her attention. She glanced past them searching among the guests for Gaius, but he was gone.

Chapter 27

Leah gently closed the door to Marcellus' room. She walked through the inner garden and out to the dark courtyard where Mariamne crouched over the fire. A rooster crowed, splintering the pre-dawn silence.

'How is he?' asked Mariamne.

Leah rubbed her eyes. They burnt with fatigue from her all-night vigil. 'His breath is shallow and more rapid than yesterday. Oh, Mariamne, I do not know what else we can do.'

'We are doing all the physician instructed. We can do no more, except pray.'

'I have been pleading with *Yahweh* all night,' sighed Leah. 'I do not think he will listen without a sacrifice at the synagogue and the prayers of the priest.'

'Go if you think it will help,' said Mariamne. 'But *Yahweh* is the god of the Samaritans, not the god of Marcellus. Would not Aphrodite or Mars be more inclined to heed our prayers for a Roman?' She reached out her hand. 'Come, help your stiff old mother-in-law to her feet. We will offer a grain sacrifice to Aphrodite and call on her to appeal to the other gods. Then I will take my turn with Marcellus and you can sleep.'

Leah walked with Mariamne to the inner garden where the fountain tinkled and the bronze statue of Mars loomed. Set in one corner was a small altar where, if Leah rose early enough, she would find Mariamne worshipping. No-one else used it except the occasional religious guest. Mariamne placed the grain offering next to the incense and lit both with a flame. They knelt together, Mariamne raising her hands in worship.

'Blessed Aphrodite, Queen of Heaven. We humbly kneel before you praising your great power and love for those who worship you. You know my devotion to you, my daily sacrifices and prayers. We ask you to have mercy on Marcellus. Heal his wounds, restore his strength, save him from the grave.' Mariamne lifted the gold pendant from around her neck, kissing the image of the goddess. 'Without him, we are three women and a child alone.' She bowed her head and continued her petition, a low stream of melodic mutterings.

Leah bowed her head also. Was it her fault that Marcellus had slipped into decline? Had she betrayed him unto death with her thoughts of Gaius? The journey home had been hot and dusty. Despite the rough journey, Marcellus had slept much of the way, waking only to sip from a skin of water. He spoke little and did not eat at all. When they arrived late in the day Benjamin had run out to greet them, his little arms waving with delight. She had picked him up and hugged him to her, planting kisses all over his sweet face. He soon squirmed out of her arms and ran to Marcellus expecting another great hug. Marcellus had only smiled, reached out his hand to squeeze Benjamin's shoulder and then closed his eyes with a ragged sigh. The servants had carried him to his bed while Leah explained to Benjamin why he could not yet show Marcellus his newly built fortress.

'I made it all by myself. It is in a secret place, just for me and Marcellus, just for the men,' he had said.

'He will feel better tomorrow,' she had assured him.

But he hadn't. Now a week later, he slipped in and out of sleep, his body shivering and soaked with sweat, his breath short and shallow. They had dressed and redressed the wound in his chest, bathing it with salted water and applying the ointment provided by the garrison's physician. They had held a cup to his cracked lips, encouraging him to drink, but he could manage only a few feeble sips. Only a miracle could save him now.

Mariamne groaned, drawing Leah from her thoughts. 'My old knees are complaining,' she said, grasping the altar to help herself rise. 'Now off you go to your room, Leah. A few hours sleep will soon restore you. Your mother will see to Benjamin and I will see to Marcellus.'

Despite her reluctance to leave Marcellus for too long, she obeyed. She collapsed onto her untouched bed and closed her eyes.

***

'*Ima, Ima!*' Benjamin's voice stirred her from sleep, his hand tugging at hers. '*Ima, Ima*, everyone is crying, everyone is crying.'

Leah's heart plunged. It could mean only one thing. She leaped to her feet, gathered Benjamin in her arms and raced towards Marcellus's room.

'Don't fret, my lamb, everything will be alright.' But she knew it would not. She saw the servants sobbing outside his room. A sure spear pierced her heart and she knew. Marcellus was dead.

The women wasted no time in wrapping his body, with spices and myrrh, in strips of linen. The days were still warm. Warm enough to curdle a corpse left unattended for too long. They laid him to rest in the family tomb alongside Leah's father and Atticus. There was no need for hired mourners. Every worker from the olive groves, their families and many of the inhabitants of Sychar joined the lamenting procession.

The following day a party of the leading men of Sebaste arrived, along with Cornelius and a contingent of Roman soldiers.

'We did not expect his body would be burned so soon,' they said, dismayed not to find the body of Marcellus on display in the house. 'Where is his urn? We must at least honour his ashes.'

'I am sorry,' Leah replied. 'We did not follow Roman practice. He has been laid in his own tomb, next to my father. He was his closest friend and fighting companion. They hewed it from the rock together.'

She led the way to the tomb, the ground shuddering with the beat of the soldiers' feet. In reverential file they followed Leah into the stone cave. Her mother was anointing the body with oil and spices.

'*Ima*, these men have come from Sebaste to honour Marcellus,' said Leah.

Her mother dipped her head in acknowledgement and gathered up the anointing oils, a look of peace on her face. She laid a tender hand on the stone boxes containing the bones of her husband and son—a greeting, an embrace, a farewell. Later, after the soldiers and dignitaries had left with Cornelius proclaiming that a statue of Marcellus would soon stand in Sebaste's basilica, her mother's expression remained with her. How could she appear so peaceful? Without Marcellus they were a family adrift, exposed, unprotected. Yet her shoulders were not stooped, her face was not furrowed, her mouth was not pursed. If only she could speak.

The days stumbled with sadness. Benjamin hid in his fortress, a bundle of sticks erected between two bushes. He spoke to a friend who was not there, emerging only when he was hungry. He did not understand when Leah explained that Marcellus could not play with him.

'Please wake him, *Ima*. He needs to wake up and come home. He cannot sleep in the tomb forever.'

'He can't wake, little one. No-one wakes from the tomb.' He would shake his dark curls in protest and run back to his fortress.

Mariamne also withdrew, speaking little and eating less. There was no peace in her eyes, only fear. Aphrodite had not answered her prayers.

At the end of the week of mourning, Leah bathed and put on clean garments. The olives were ripe and the harvesters needed to see her, to be assured that all would continue as usual. She arrived home late in the afternoon and heard Mariamne in the atrium. After days of sorrowful silence it was a relief to hear her voice. She was speaking with a visitor, a man. Who might it be? She refreshed herself, dipping a cloth into cool water and wiping away the dust of the day before joining Mariamne.

'Leah, I am glad you are here,' said Mariamne, her voice bright, her words hurried as though running along a taut rope. 'I would like you to meet my relative, the son of my father's cousin.'

The man creaked to his feet. 'I am honoured to meet you, Leah.' He bowed his bald head but made no attempt to kiss her hand. Leah smiled at her unmet expectation. Why would he? He was a Samaritan, not a Roman.

'And I you, sir,' she replied. His beard was long and grey, and his skin was tough and leathered from years of sun.

'My heart grieves for your loss,' he continued. 'Mariamne sent word of the death of your husband and I came as quickly as I could.' His words were smooth and hollow; they did not reach his heart.

'That is kind of you,' she replied, giving Mariamne a questioning look.

'Yoachim has come from beyond the Jordan,' said Mariamne. 'He has land there and a family but sadly no longer a wife.' Her words spilled out like a stall keeper in the marketplace. 'I have explained our predicament; that we are three women and a child alone, with no man to speak for us, no man to negotiate with the workers of our olive groves or the buyers of our oil.'

Leah's neck stiffened. She tried to temper her tone. 'I have just this hour returned from inspecting the olive grove, as I have done these past years with Marcellus. Our supervisor is trustworthy and well able to manage the workers. As for the buyers, I will continue to deal with them.'

'I know you understand the management of the groves as well as Marcellus,' said Mariamne. 'But you are a woman.'

Yoachim nodded in agreement, his fingertips pressed together in front of him.

'Sir, are you offering to be our patron?' asked Leah. She strained to maintain a friendly tone.

Yoachim glanced at Mariamne, perched rigidly at the edge of her seat. He cleared his throat. 'I am not offering to be your patron, Leah. I am offering to be your husband.'

Leah stepped back, her legs suddenly weak, a vile taste in her mouth. She stared at his ancient, wrinkled hands pressed imperiously, insincerely together. They would never touch her.

'Please consider it, Leah,' implored Mariamne. 'You are young. You need a husband, and more children. By marrying Yoachim we ensure that our groves remain in the family. We must safeguard this inheritance for Benjamin and for the family name.'

Leah stared at them. By what authority did they dare to arrange her life? The authority of a father? No. The authority of a husband? No. The authority of a mother-in-law? That was no authority. Her fists clenched. A cold fury took hold, talons of ice gripped her.

'No.'

She stormed from the room, leaving Mariamne stunned and Yoachim spluttering.

Only when she reached the end of the garden where she could see the fields and her childhood home far below did she stop. She crossed her arms, fists still clenched, and chewed her lip. She had insulted a guest—a shameful act—yet it was Mariamne who had caused her to do so. Her nails dug into her palms.

'Leah.' Mariamne marched towards her, her voice raised in reprimand. 'This is no way to treat our guest.'

'Marcellus is barely cold in the tomb! You are not my father. If I need a husband, I will choose him myself.'

'Where will you find a husband in Samaria? You have already had three husbands. You are almost beyond marriageable age.'

'I will not marry another old man and especially one I do not know or trust. You have never spoken of him. Do you even know him yourself?' She spat the words like hailstones.

Mariamne dropped her gaze. 'I have met him only once, many years ago, at a relative's wedding. It is true—I barely know him—but, Leah, we cannot remain as three women and a child. We need a man. He is the only one I could think of.'

Leah heard the fear. Her heart thawed, not completely, but sufficient to soften her reply.

'Do not fear, Mariamne. I will not let us become desolate. I will not let anyone take our land. I will not let Benjamin lose his inheritance. But please understand, I do not need your help.'

***

Leah sat at the table in Marcellus' study, a fresh parchment spread out before her. She dipped a bronze pen into the inkwell and carefully formed each letter, silently thanking her father and Marcellus for teaching her the skill. The light from her freshly trimmed lamp glowed on the parchment. She adjusted its position so her hand did not cast a shadow over the writing. She could wait not a night to set her plan in motion. It was so clear, so simple. She should thank Mariamne for forcing her so quickly to a decision.

It was true: the olive oil traders expected to negotiate with a man, any disputes had to be represented by a man, and Benjamin needed the influence of a man. But what Samaritan would allow her to retain her interest in the olives, the negotiations and the keeping of accounts? What Samaritan would encourage her trading in cloth with the Romans? No honourable Samaritan man would allow his wife such freedoms.

Yet she needed to marry. She needed more children to ensure that the land and the family name were continued through the generations. If anything happened to Benjamin, all would be lost. She needed a husband who understood the workings of an olive grove, who was proficient in negotiations, who would be a good father to Benjamin. A man who she desired.

She rolled up the letter and sealed it with the seal of Marcellus.

Chapter 28

The month of *Kislev* arrived bringing a chill to the air that equalled the chill in the villa. Barely a day passed without Mariamne praising Yoachim's attributes: 'He sits with the elders at the city gate', 'He is skilled in the dealings of trade', 'He would be a good father for Benjamin', 'You do not have the same choices as of a younger woman'.

Her mother kept to herself, that strange look of peace on her face. She rose before daybreak, taking long walks over the hills, and returning with gifts of coloured stones and vibrant autumn leaves for Benjamin. Leah poured out to her all the reasons why she should not marry Yoachim. Her mother would stroke her hand and smile. Leah could almost hear her words: 'You are strong, Leah. I trust you.'

Leah watched over the olive grove and spent days dying cloth. She avoided Mariamne as much as she could except to agree they should try selling their fabrics in the marketplace at Sychar. It was a bold step; they had neither a stall nor a patron. Mariamne offered to go, eager to visit the town and an old friend. Leah seized the fortuity of her imminent absence and sent word to Sebaste.

***

Gaius Apollos arrived in the crisp of morning, galloping up the steep road to the villa, his horse puffing and blowing and steaming with sweat. Leah was helping Mariamne secure the last of the baskets onto the donkey. They were filled with carefully folded fabrics and brightly coloured cushions, ready for the market.

'Who is this man arriving at such an early hour?' asked Mariamne.

Leah, too, was surprised. He must have left Sebaste well before dawn. 'It is Gaius Apollos. He has come to honour Marcellus at the tomb and to see the olive grove. His family grows olives in Greece and he is interested to compare methods.'

'And you intend to accompany him on this inspection?' said Mariamne.

'Gaius follows the Roman way, not the strictness of the Samaritans. He is happy for me to show him the groves on my own.'

'The workers will talk.'

The approach of Gaius ended their debate. Leah introduced the two and after exchanging greetings, with Gaius expressing his sorrow over the death of Marcellus, Mariamne set off for Sychar with a servant and a scowl.

'I am glad you received my letter,' said Leah, holding out her hand for Gaius to kiss, striving to maintain formality in front of the servants. 'It is good to see you.'

'And you also,' said Gaius, his eyes dancing.

'Let me arrange refreshments. You must be thirsty after the journey.'

'Assuredly, I am,' said Gaius brushing his hand against hers.

His touch set off a flurry of sparks. They walked through the atrium to an intimate side room filled with low couches. Gaius reclined against the embroidered cushions. Leah sat opposite, listening attentively to Gaius recount the gossip of Sebaste. She did not miss his gaze slipping every so often to her breasts. She described the details of Marcellus's death and her tears welled. He reached for her hand and she clasped it tightly.

'And now Mariamne wants me to marry her ancient relative to ensure the security of our property. I do not know if I can bear it.' She dabbed the tears from her face.

'That is no reason to marry. Epicurus has a saying: *It is not what we have but what we enjoy that constitutes our abundance.* What enjoyment could this man give you?'

'I am certain, none, but I can see no other way.' She withdrew her hand and sat upright. 'But you did not come to listen to my troubles. Let me show you our olive grove. The trees are stripped bare but you will be able to see the last of the fruit being pressed.'

'I have no interest in the olives,' said Gaius, moving to sit next to her. He cupped her face between his hands and kissed her. 'Is this not what you invited me for?' His words were warm and sweet against her ear. She felt his teeth and then his tongue.

'I invited you to …' His lips silenced hers and they sank together onto the cushions. His kiss, his scent, his body hard against hers was intoxicating but it was not yet time. She steeled herself and pulled away.

'Gaius, I cannot give myself to a man who is not my husband.' Her hand rested on his thigh.

He coiled his fingers around a stray strand of her hair and looked into her eyes. Was desire enough to draw a man into marriage? Her three previous marriages had been for practical purposes: a favour for a friend, an acquiring of land, the security of her family. Even her marriage to Yosef, if not for those thieving Jewish bandits, would have been seen simply as following Samaritan custom. No-one had known of their secret love. She shut away thoughts of Yosef and fastened her mind on the man before her. Surely Gaius needed to see what a life as her husband would entail. And yet her heart beat in dread of his answer.

'Come, I will show you the olive grove.' She took his hand. 'Let us go before the heat of the day rises.'

Later, when they returned, Leah led Gaius down a narrow corridor to the library. The room was semi-circular with doors opening onto an east-facing terrace. An expansive painting overlooked Marcellus' desk and carved into the curved wall were niches, each housing a papyrus scroll.

'What a collection. There must be hundreds of papyri here.' Gaius crossed the mosaic floor, touching the ebony knob on one papyri with reverence. It was wrapped in a purple cover, tied with scarlet string. He lifted the thin metal label. 'Aristotle?' He swung around to Leah. 'Marcellus studied the philosophers?' His voice held the excitement of a child.

'Marcellus was interested not only in the philosophers but also astronomy, history and literature. See there in the Latin section is one of Livy's books on the history of Rome, and a translation of the *Phenomena* by the poet Aratus of Cilicia.'

'By Hercules!' exclaimed Gaius, studying the precisely inscribed labels.

She pointed to the niches closest to the desk, filled with simple scrolls tied with plain cord. 'These are our contracts and accounts for the olive oil.'

'And you administer this alone?' asked Gaius.

'Without Marcellus, I must. It is not difficult but it leaves me little time to help Mariamne with the weaving and dying.'

Gaius caught her in his arms. 'Then let me help you.' He brushed his lips against hers. 'Leah, I have thought of you every day since we met. I cannot sleep for thinking of you.' His breath was warm and spiced with the scent of cloves and craving. 'Be my wife. Together we can manage the olives and I will bring my friends here to buy your fabrics. We will fill this house with laughter and …' he brushed his lips over hers again, '... with love.'

'Love,' she whispered, the possibility sprinkling her soul like the first autumn rains.

***

'You are foolish beyond imagining,' said Mariamne, stabbing her needle into a torn tunic. 'You barely know this Gaius Apollos.'

'I know him better than Yoachim,' said Leah, her body warming at the memory of their kisses the day before.

'But we know Yoachim's family. A husband brings to the marriage not only himself but his family and friends. Who is this man's family? Who are his friends?'

'Gaius's family are friends of Cornelius and Livia. They consider him a son. I am sure Marcellus would have respected Cornelius's judgement on matters of character.'

'Marcellus is not here. It is me, your mother and Benjamin who will have to live with this man. You are bringing him into our home, to be the head of our household. How could you make such a decision without first consulting us?'

'I am consulting you now, am I not?'

'It is not consulting when the deed is already signed, and with only a servant as witness!' Mariamne tugged at a thread. It snapped and she cursed.

'The servant is a Roman citizen; the law permits him to bear witness,' said Leah. Marcellus had often used him to witness documents.

'The law of Rome perhaps, but what of the Law of Moses? You are marrying a foreigner who does not understand our Samaritan ways. Will he allow us the freedom that Marcellus did?' She rubbed away a tear. 'Will he raise Benjamin in the ways of his fathers? Marcellus respected our ways but what of this Roman?'

'He is not Roman; he is Greek.'

'He is not Samaritan.' Mariamne tied a knot in the torn thread. 'And what of Benjamin's inheritance? Will this new husband of yours demand our land?

Can you be sure he is not marrying you for your wealth?'

'He has enough wealth of his own. He will one day inherit his family's olive groves; he does not need more.'

'Some men are never satisfied,' muttered Mariamne.

'He loves me,' said Leah. 'And I love him.' The words were out before she could check herself; a foolish statement, an argument that held little weight, she knew, for her mother-in-law.

'It is love from the loins,' Mariamne scorned. 'Better the love that ripens like a fig on the vine than that which springs up like the flowers of the field and falls quickly away.'

For a moment doubt assailed her.

'Do not worry, Mariamne. You will soon see what a good man he is.'

'I pray so, for all our sakes,' said Mariamne, raising a hand to her chest and rubbing the golden image of Aphrodite.

Chapter 29

Leah opened her eyes and sighed with content. Her bed, her body, her heart—all was filled with the joy of Gaius. Her husband's arm was under her head, his other arm embracing her even in sleep. Morning light streamed through the shutters. It was well past sunrise but she felt no compulsion to rise. Benjamin did not need her; he would be well cared for by his two savtas.

Last night they had danced and drunk until the moon shone high in the night sky. Guests spilled into the gardens, some swaying to the musicians' rhythms, others swaying from too much wine. The villa had never been so full. Every bed was occupied, so, too, were the rooms leading off the atrium where the servants had laid soft rugs and cushions as extra sleeping space. The party had been at its height when Gaius had caught her from behind.

'Ah, my wife,' he said. 'We have stayed with our guests long enough.' He handed his goblet to a man standing close by. 'Drink it, my friend, I have no more need of wine.'

The man grinned. 'Who needs wine with a wife as beautiful as yours.' The woman standing beside him scowled but he seemed not to notice. He raised the goblet in salute then tipped the wine down his throat. 'To Gaius and Leah, may the gods favour you with health, wealth and an endless feast of love.'

Gaius put his arm around Leah's waist and walked her away. The guests laughed and cheered. A twinge of sadness plucked at her heart, like a solitary note of a flute. She had no family here to celebrate this final and most important part of the wedding ceremony. Her sisters had made excuses of distance and the demands of family, but she knew the true reason. They refused to attend a gentile wedding. Her mother and Mariamne had already retired and so there were only Gaius' friends to cheer them to their chamber.

Husband and wife walked through the inner courtyard and Gaius took her in his arms, kissing her with hunger and running his hands over her hips. It extinguished her momentary melancholy. The music, the laughter, the voices, all faded. She had been dreaming, thirsting for this moment for weeks. They entered their chamber and fell upon the bed. The lamplight flickered. The room darkened. She wanted nothing, cared for nothing, felt nothing, except Gaius. It was as though he had known her forever, his fingers skilfully tracing the curves of her body.

None of her husbands, no not even Yosef, had carried her to such heights of pleasure. This is how it would be for the years to come. She gazed at the shafts of sunlight dancing across their tousled sheets. Nothing could be more perfect.

***

The guests had all gone by the eleventh hour, hastening to leave before the rain clouds looming in the west gathered strength. Gaius strode between each carpentum clasping shoulders with the men and kissing the women.

'What a night! As good as any in Sebaste,' said one couple, swaying slightly and squinting in the sunlight.

'Or Athens,' added another, jovially slapping Gaius on the back. 'Take care of this beautiful wife of yours or next time I may steal her from you.' His crumpled toga bore evidence of too much wine and his reddened eyes of too little sleep.

'Next time I expect you to be married yourself ...' said Gaius.

'Married or not, I would not miss your next *convivium* for all the virgins in Rome.'

'My friend, do not expect an invitation until at least the spring. My wife and I will be occupied.'

Leah cringed at the barely veiled innuendo. She lifted her head high and set a smile on her face. 'I trust you have a safe journey. I must see to our other guests.' She left them to their laughter.

A movement at the side of the villa caught her attention. It was Mariamne, tight-lipped and stiff-necked, holding Benjamin's hand. She let the little boy go and turned away before Leah could greet her. Her early retirement the night before and her absence this morning spoke louder than any words.

'*Ima, Ima.*' Benjamin ran to her, his grubby hands outstretched. She scooped him up and sat him on her hip, sending off the final few guests with promises to send word as soon as she had more stolas ready to sell. The carriages clattered down the hill and Benjamin flung his little arms around her neck,

'*Ima, Ima*, come and play with me.'

'What are we playing,' asked Gaius, walking over to them and kissing Leah lightly on the lips. Benjamin's arms tightened around her neck.

'Just *Ima*,' he said, his voice as imperial as any Emperor.

'It seems I have a worthy rival for your affection,' said Gaius. His smile and the depth of his gaze flooded her with heat. She prayed for night to come quickly, for when they would again lie together.

'Let us make a bargain between men,' said Gaius, looking seriously at Benjamin. 'You have the day with your beautiful *Ima* and I will have the night.'

Benjamin clung tighter to Leah's neck and said nothing. Leah kissed his soft curls. He still spent hours in the garden, hidden in his hut, still grieving for Marcellus, the only father he had known. As with Mariamne, it would take time for him to accept this new man into his life.

'Come, my little lamb, show me what fortress you have made today.' Benjamin beamed. He squirmed from Leah's arms and, gripping her hand, pulled her towards the garden. 'I will see you soon,' she called over her shoulder to Gaius.

He stood with his hands on his hips, his tunic taut across his broad body, a grin on his face. 'You will find me with Aristotle.'

Leah and Benjamin had barely an hour gathering sticks and dry autumn leaves to embellish the tiny shelter before the first drops of rain splattered on the dry soil. Benjamin squealed with delight, raising his arms to the skies, letting the heavy drops fall on his face.

'Rain, *Ima*, rain. *Yahweh* sent the rain!'

'He did,' said Leah, surprised at his words. She realised that she had not spoken to him of *Yahweh* for many months. The autumn rains had so far been sparse and scattered, barely sufficient to replenish the soil after the months of summer. The olives had been pressed and the jars of oil safely stacked in the storehouse. Now the barren trees thirsted for rain. Leah copied Benjamin, lifting her hands to the sky and thanking *Yahweh* for the life-giving water.

The rains lasted for weeks as though making up for their late start. Leah spent her days with Gaius, showing him the workings of the household. In the mornings they would rise and eat together, sometimes with Mariamne, her mother and Benjamin; at other times on their own. Mariamne showed him the workings of the loom and seemed pleased with his questions and compliments on her handiwork. Gaius sat with her mother, speaking of Athens, Corinth and the cities of the east. He took Benjamin into the library and read him stories of Hercules, Apollo and Mars. Leah would find them bent over a parchment, drawing pictures of great gods with swords and fire, stretching out their hands to the earth below.

The almond tree blossomed, the flax flowers bloomed, the olive branches budded. The warmer months brought traders eager to inspect the olives before harvest. Gaius charmed them with his philosopher's tongue. Never had they procured such prices for their oil. In their bedroom each night their passion flared, only cooling when Gaius sighed over the delay in conceiving a child. Leah brushed aside his complaints and the condemnation they brought.

The olives were harvested. The first rains fell. The earth grew moist, the air crisp. Gaius withdrew to the study, to the scrolls of Socrates, Hippocrates and Plato. No longer did he invite Benjamin to draw. No longer did he retire with Leah. He remained with the scrolls until the moon was high and the lamp oil low. Leah curled under the covers, sleeping fitfully until he came, sliding his hands over her skin, embracing her with kisses, driving away her doubts.

The high snows melted, the streams ran full and fast. The second spring of her marriage had come and Leah at last felt the blooming of new life within.

Chapter 30

AD 28 The month of Nisan - Spring

'I must go to Sebaste.' Gaius rolled over and kissed Leah's closed eyes.

'Again?' she mumbled, trying to rouse herself. Sleep was the only time she did not suffer sickness. Each night she sank gratefully into slumber. Each morning the gall stirred, gnawing at her empty stomach. 'What calls you back so soon? It has been but a few weeks since your last visit.'

'Obligations, my love, and sadly they cannot wait. I must go today.' His kisses moved to her lips, prising open her mouth while his hands found her tender, swollen breasts. 'I will be a few days only. I could not leave you for any longer.' His hands slid over the curve of her belly, gently swelling with child in this fourth month, and moved lower. Her excitement built but so too did her sickness of stomach.

'I'm going to be ill.' She pushed Gaius away and rushed out to the garden, expelling her stomach's meagre contents in great heaving spasms. By the time she returned, Gaius was dressed in a chiton and cloak. He was ready to leave.

***

He returned, as promised, a few days later, his handsome face ruddy and radiant. He strode into the villa and Leah ran to greet him.

'My wife, how I have longed for you.' He took her in his arms and kissed her ravenously, ignoring the servant waiting to take his cloak. The young man studied his toes, shifting uncomfortably at such a public show of affection. Gaius noticed too.

'*Carpe diem*, boy,' he laughed. 'Now go before you fall over those feet.'

The servant scurried away.

'Don't mock him, my husband,' said Leah. 'He is only doing his duty. Now, tell me about your journey. Was it successful?'

'Indeed,' replied Gaius. 'My friends insist we have sequestered ourselves out here long enough. They are anxious to see us again and as you are unable to travel I have invited them here. They will arrive tomorrow,'

'Tomorrow?' Leah's mouth dropped open. She scrambled to assemble her thoughts. 'There is so little time to prepare. I will need to inform the servants at once. I expect we can quickly make up the guest room.'

Gaius smiled and pulled her close. 'We will need more than one guest room. It is all my friends, and a duo of philosophers from Alexandria on their way to Rome. We have wintered long enough, Leah. It's time to open our arms and extend our hospitality.'

All his friends! Her body stiffened. His arms felt like chains around her thickened waist. Had he considered her at all?

'The servants will need to go into Sychar today,' said Leah, her thoughts tumbling through the necessary tasks. 'We will need more supplies.'

'Do not worry about the wine. I have a cartload following. It should arrive before sunset.'

'A cartload! Are they staying a month?' Leah pushed Gaius away. Her stomach stirred.

'By Hercules, we would never survive a month!' Gaius laughed. A carefree laugh—a carefree laugh seasoned with scorn. 'They will all be gone within the week.'

'A week!' What would she tell Mariamne and her mother? Their home was to be overtaken by a crowd of strangers who only Gaius could vouch for. Bile rose in her throat, cutting off any attempt at argument. She clamped her hand to her mouth and raced for the stone basin.

***

They arrived the next afternoon, one carpentum after another. Several of the men had ridden up earlier on horseback and Gaius had immediately called for refreshments. At the clattering of carriages, the men strolled out to the entrance, cups of wine in hand. Leah was already there, waiting to greet the visitors, ensuring that they knew this was her home and that they consider it as such. Mariamne's words, when she had told her of the visitors, echoed in her head: 'It is as I feared. This husband, in whom we should find rest, is instead bringing into our home his heathen ways and his foreign friends. This house will soon be a home no longer.'

Watching the carriages snaking up the hill, a trickle of doubt diluted her defence of her husband. There were as many people as at their wedding party. Gaius introduced them and she welcomed each one, their names flowing past her like stalks in a stream. The women hugged her, expressing their great joy at seeing her and their sincere appreciation for such hospitality, but it was Gaius on whom their hugs lingered. No-one seemed bothered by this and Leah admonished herself for such childish irritation.

The afternoon flowed into the evening on a river of wine and food and gossip. The philosophers debated with vigour, paying special attention to the two from Alexandria. One was a woman with kohl-rimmed eyes that slanted in her fine, pale face. The men leaned forward when she spoke, eager to hear from her the latest ideas from Egypt. She curled on her seat like a cat, stretching out her cup for more wine, and staring down her slender, straight nose at the men around her. Gaius reclined next to her on the couch and every so often the woman's hand would brush his.

Leah was caught at the other side of the room with a group of women discussing the misfortunes of one of their friends. The tale was tedious in its detail but the women were so engrossed they barely noticed Leah rise. A crushing tiredness swept over her and she swayed a little, holding out her hand to steady herself against the wall. She looked to Gaius but he was turned away, his attention wholly given to the pale philosopher, speaking words that made her viper-like tongue lick her lips. Leah motioned to a servant.

'Please tell your master that he is needed in the atrium. At once.'

The servant nodded and Leah made her way to a small marble seat in the atrium, reviving a little in the cooler air.

'My delectable wife.' Gaius strolled across the marble floor. He took her in his arms and pulled her close. 'What is it that cannot wait?'

Leah's concerns melted in his arms. 'I have barely spoken to you all evening. I wanted a moment alone.'

Gaius kissed her. 'We will have all night alone with each other, and I cannot wait, but for now we must be with our friends.'

'And that philosopher ...'

'Surely you are not jealous,' he laughed. 'Leah, you are my wife. She is simply a guest among many.'

He ran his hand over her hair. 'It is late and I can see you are tired. Do not feel obliged to remain with my over-imbibed friends. Go and rest. I will see them safely settled in their rooms and then I will be with you. It should not be too many more hours.'

'I hope it is sooner than that,' said Leah.

'As do I,' said Gaius, kissing her on the cheek.

She watched him stroll back to the *convivium* and sighed. Many husbands would have insisted that their wife stay, ensuring an air of gracious hospitality. She ran her hand over her stomach. They were married and she carried his child. Surely she could trust him.

***

She woke in the depth of night, reaching out to Gaius. The bed was cold and empty. Sleep tugged at her eye-lids begging her to return but she could not. She rose from her bed, wrapped her cloak about her and opened the door of her chamber. A woman's muffled laugh carried along the corridor and she realised that this was the sound that had awakened her. With her heart thumping in her chest, she slipped through the shifting shadows, following the hushed whispers to the courtyard.

They were pressed against the statue of Mars, their faces so close to each other. Her heart froze. Her breath froze. She heard Gaius whisper, his voice deep and low as it was when they were alone together.

Her heart started beating, fast and furious and wild. She saw a jug by the fountain. She marched over, dipped it in deep and threw the contents at the two. The woman screamed. Gaius swore and spun around, water dripping from his head.

'Leah! I thought you were asleep!'

'Asleep! I have most certainly been asleep.' Her voice was raw, hard, tearing at her throat like shards of glass. 'Asleep to your true nature.' The threat of tears stung her eyes. She forced them away. She would not show weakness in this foreign woman's presence.

'You are mistaken, my love,' said Gaius, moving towards her and taking her hand in his. 'We were only discussing the teachings of Epicurus.' He turned to the woman who was wiping water from her face, smearing across it dark streaks of kohl. 'Let us resume our conversation in the morning.'

'It will be my pleasure,' she replied, her head held high, a silken smile on her kohl smeared face. 'Leah, you are welcome to join us.' She walked away, the bracelets on her ankles jingling with each mincing step.

Leah glared at Gaius. 'Do not think you can fool me with your lies,' said Leah. 'I am not blind.'

She pulled away from his grip but he held her tight, drawing his arms around her and kissing her. She struggled to escape but his grasp was firm and his kisses insistent. 'Do not be upset, my wife. You are the only one I desire. Sit with us tomorrow. Leave Mariamne to attend to Benjamin and the servants to our guests. Allow a little wine to pass your lips. It is good for a wife to be by her husband's side, and in his bed.'

'I was in your bed. It is you who was elsewhere!' She wrenched herself free and marched away.

'Leah.' He chased after her and seized her arm. 'Our guests are here for but a few days. It is an opportunity to impress them with our generosity, to establish ourselves as hosts of distinction, worthy of honour in Sebaste and beyond. Can you imagine the benefits that might come from such a reputation? It was a duty, not a pleasure.' He kissed her again. 'You are my only pleasure.'

Her resolve faltered. Had she been too quick to judge? She surrendered to her husband's kisses. Soon his friends would be gone and everything would be as it was.

Chapter 31

Leah rose early, leaving Gaius sprawled across the bed, a sheet moulding to his fine form. She sighed, trying to ignore a creeping shadow of sadness. Simeon had been unfaithful but she had never loved him, neither had she chosen him. Her pain had been purely that of failing in her duty as a wife. With Gaius it was different. She wanted him, she desired him and she had chosen him against Mariamne's counsel.

She dressed and hurried through the silent halls to find her family. She would do her work, instruct the servants, see her son, embrace her mother and Mariamne and be ready to spend the remaining day with her husband and his friends. She would join them in their debates, their dining and their drinking. She would make sure that every guest returned to Sebaste with an excellent report of their hospitality and their marriage.

'*Ima, Ima*!' Benjamin dropped his child-sized broom, fashioned from a short leafy branch, and ran across the courtyard, leaping into her outstretched arms.

'What a welcome,' said Leah, kissing his warm little face. 'It is as though you have not seen me for a week.'

'He was calling for you last night,' said Mariamne, sweeping the paving stones clear of the barley chaff. 'The noise of our guests woke him. I took him to my room; I did not wish to disturb your entertaining.' Disapproval edged her words. She stopped her sweeping and limped over to Leah.

'What has happened, Mariamne? Have you hurt yourself?'

'It is nothing; a little stiffness. It will ease.' She leant on the broom and rubbed her hip. Her face was drawn with deep lines, like that of a much older woman. 'When are they leaving?' She nodded towards the sleeping villa. 'I could not sleep last night, neither your mother. This cannot go on, Leah. These friends of your husband are overtaking our home.' She whisked her broom at the scattered husks.

'I am sure they will leave soon and all will return to normal.'

'Normal? What is normal for us is not normal for Gaius. Do you not see that? Does a man change his ways when he is married? No, it is the wife who must change hers. Do not think he will forever be content to remain here with us alone. He will continue to bring his friends and we will continue to have no rest.' She looked at Leah with reddened eyes. 'I fear you have made a grave mistake, Leah. We are to be strangers in our own home.'

'That is not true,' said Leah with more conviction than she felt. 'Truly this is our home and Gaius respects it as such.'

'Am I free to work in the garden when drunkards stagger about? Is Benjamin free to run through the halls?'

'He can run wherever he likes. These people are of no danger to his safety.' She hugged Benjamin and he rested in her arms. 'We are going to the olive grove later. Would you like to come?'

'Yes, *Ima*. I want to stay with you.'

She kissed his forehead and looked at Mariamne. 'I will be busy with the guests this evening. Let us hope that the wine jars run dry. Then they are sure to leave.'

Mariamne did not smile. She resumed sweeping the chaff with a force that sent it swirling like a storm.

***

They set out for the olive grove at midday, Gaius leading his friends through the flower-laden trees, answering their questions about the pressing process and accepting their compliments on the rich soil. Only a handful of the men had come, the others pleading tiredness or simply not appearing at all. Irritation knotted inside Leah. The land was his but only because of his marriage to her. He had not spent years working the land; he barely knew the labourers. No-one noticed when she and Benjamin slipped away. She spent the next hour chasing Benjamin through the olive trees, searching for him as he hid, and standing with arms ready to catch him should he slip from his precarious clambering in the branches.

They returned in the afternoon, joining the other guests in the garden where they reclined on upholstered couches, brought out to take advantage of the warm spring sun. The pale philosopher was not there and Leah breathed a sigh of relief. Benjamin tugged at her hand.

'I'm hungry, *Ima*.'

'I am not surprised,' laughed Leah. 'You have not stopped running since we left.' She knelt down and gave Benjamin a hug.

'Your *savta* will give you something to eat.' She kissed his warm cheek and sent him running off.

'Leah, come and join us,' called Gaius, 'And bring more wine,' he said to the servant, taking the last cup from the tray. He tipped his head back to down his drink.

'You should have come, you sluggard.' He slapped his neighbour on his thigh. 'The fruit of the vine tastes never so sweet as when one has thirsted for it.'

'Indeed you appear to have thirsted plenty since you left us,' said the man. He gripped Gaius' arm. 'Your physique has not suffered the absence of the gymnasium. I think the life of a farmer suits you.'

Gaius stretched his broad arms and clasped them behind his head. The sun caught the stubble of gold across his face. 'It is the life of a married man. You should try it, my friend.'

'You are living proof of the wisdom of Socrates. Did he not say by all means marry. *If you get a good wife, you'll be happy; if you get a bad one, you'll become a philosopher.*'

The guests clapped and laughed while the man cast Gaius a knowing look. Leah accepted the wine offered to her by a servant and took a sip. It was sweet and cool. Gaius extended his arm to Leah.

'Come here, my lovely wife, sit with us.' He pushed his friend aside with a force that made him tumble off the seat, sending everyone into fits of laughter.

The man rose with his cup raised high and bowed with an extravagant sweep of his free arm. 'Not a drop spilled.'

Everyone cheered and the conversations continued, loosened by ceaseless jugs of wine. Leah emptied her cup and took another, and another. It slid down smoothly and eased her mind. Perhaps Gaius and his friends were right in their following of Epicurus. They were free from the compunction to worship or appease any god; the gods were not at all interested in the affairs of men. Instead, as Gaius repeatedly expounded, a person's abundance resided not in what he had but what he enjoyed. Why should she not follow their example and enjoy the pleasures of this gathering—the intellect and wit of the men, the envy of the women, the passion of her husband.

The sun dipped low in the sky and they moved inside where the servants had laid out a banquet of delicacies. They feasted on freshly roasted barley and bread dipped in olive oil, platters of beans, lentils with fresh herbs and roasted meats. Leah felt no hunger but instead filled her cup again and again. The house was filled with mirth, the guests doubling over in laughter at each other's wit, the women flattering each other's dangling earrings and gem studded bracelets.

'Leah, when are you next bringing your garments to Sebaste? Everyone is anxious to see your new designs,' said a young woman.

'Everyone?' asked Leah.

'Has Gaius not told you? Your name echoes through the baths, both your fine work and your marriage to the most eligible philosopher in the city. Do not think your hiding away here diminishes your reputation.'

'I did not expect to have a reputation,' said Leah, the wine dulling a jot of concern and making her giggle.

'A Samaritan woman with a Samaritan child married to a Roman nobleman and now a Greek philosopher, and a merchant of fine fabric.' The young woman rested her hand on Leah's. 'There is much to talk about and I am honoured to be invited to meet you.'

There was admiration in her eyes and a note of respect in her voice that surprised Leah. Did this explain Gaius' frequent visits to Sebaste? Yet he had not once suggested she accompany him to Sebaste to show her designs. But she had not asked. She had few fabrics to show for the past year. Instead her attentions had been taken captive by her new husband.

A crash across the room interrupted her muddled thoughts. A couple lay sprawled on the floor surrounded by puddles of wine and shards of smashed pottery. They rolled over, the man helping the woman to sit up and fumbling to help her adjust her stola.

'Leave that for the bedchamber,' laughed one man, throwing almonds at them.

Others joined in and soon almonds covered the floor. A servant moved to clean up the mess and they pelted him also. Leah looked around to find Gaius. He should be stopping this. The man on the floor dragged himself upright, staggered over to the mocking guest and punched him in the face. Blood spattered from his mouth and he reeled backwards into another group. They tripped against each other, cursing and spilling wine over their togas. Soon there was a confusion of flailing fists and shouts of encouragement from the onlookers. The *convivium* had descended into an unruly *comissatio*.

Leah searched for Gaius. Where was he? She ran into the courtyard, her vision blurred, her head heavy. Out of the shadows stepped a figure. She stopped short.

'Benjamin!' What are you doing here? You should be in your bed.'

'I was looking for you, *Ima*.' He clung to her leg. 'Why are they shouting? Gaius wouldn't tell me.'

'You have seen Gaius? Where is he?'

'He went this way.' He ran off. Leah followed, stumbling over the paving stones and steadying herself against a wall as they entered the villa. Benjamin was ahead, running through the lamp-lit vestibule towards the farthest end. It led to the chamber of Marcellus. The door stood ajar and he ran through it pushing it wide open. Beyond was Marcellus' bed and on it was Gaius with the pale philosopher. The woman let out a startled cry and grabbed her stola to cover her white skin. Gaius leapt from the bed, his nakedness exposed.

'Get out!' he yelled. He swung his arm at Benjamin, sending him headlong into the wall. His head hit with a heavy thud and his little body slumped to the floor like a rag.

'No, no!' Leah screamed, rushing into the room and kneeling over her son. He was as still as death. She picked him up and cradled him in her arms. His head lolled back and his mouth sagged open. Leah hugged Benjamin to her, kissing his lifeless face. 'Wake up, my little lamb, wake up.'

'He should not have come in here,' said Gaius, his voice as hard as iron. The woman had scurried from the room. 'And neither should have you. Now leave and take your son with you.'

'You are the one who will leave!' She threw herself at Gaius, raining blows upon him and screaming curses.

'Stop these hysterics,' he said, grabbing her arm and wrenching it hard behind her. She twisted and brought her knee up into his groin. He gasped, his face contorting in pain and fury. He curled his fist and struck her with force. She doubled over, clutching her stomach. 'You are my wife and you will do as I say. Now take the boy and get out!'

The short distance to Mariamne's chamber stretched forever. Behind her she heard Gaius cursing and crashing about the room, then his heavy footsteps stumbling back to the *comissatio*. Benjamin's eyes flickered open and shut, mournful whimpers coming from his mouth. Leah staggered along the corridor carrying him in her arms. Her legs were unsteady. Pain seized her stomach.

'Mariamne!' She stumbled into the darkened room. 'Mariamne. Please. Help.' She had barely stammered the words before Mariamne was at her side.

'What has happened?' She peered at Benjamin, limp in Leah's arms. 'Oh, my heavens! My precious child.'

Another cramp seized Leah. She hunched over with a groan. Mariamne took Benjamin and laid him on the bed, stroking his head and tucking the covers around him. He opened his eyes and moaned.

'My head, *Savta*. It hurts.' He started to cry.

Mariamne soothed him with kisses. 'Close your eyes, little one, and sleep. I will bring a poultice for your head and you will feel better in the morning.'

'*Ima*, I want my *ima*,' he cried.

Leah slumped on the edge of the bed and held his hand. 'I am right here, Benjamin. I will always be here.' She gripped his hand more firmly. She would never abandon him the way she had these past few months. This was all her fault.

'You are hurt also,' said Mariamne, helping her to rest against the pillows. 'Tell me what has happened.'

'Gaius was in the chamber of Marcellus with one of the guests ... a woman.' Leah looked away, ashamed. 'Benjamin ran in and Gaius threw him against the wall. Then he hit me.' She drew in her legs at another cramping pain. 'I am sorry, Mariamne. I have been a fool. He is not the man I thought he was.' Tears trickled down her face. She wiped them away.

'I have prayed for you to see the truth but I did not wish it to be in this way,' said Mariamne. 'He is clever and charming but without wisdom. His heart is shallow and dry; it has room only for himself.'

'What am I to do?'

'You will do nothing tonight but rest.' Mariamne lit her lamp. 'I will return soon with herbs and honey for Benjamin and for you. We can only pray that the poultice will lessen that lump and the herbs settle your baby.'

Leah curled up next to Benjamin. He was sleeping now and Leah put her face close to his so she could feel his gentle breath against her cheek. Nothing, no-one was more precious to her in this world—this child of her beloved Yosef, this son who would ensure the family name did not disappear from the town records. Her hands moved over her belly. Would she be able to rejoice as much with this child of an unfaithful, lying husband? Would she not always favour Benjamin? Yet the infant was innocent; he should not suffer for the sins of his father. A violent pain gripped her, worse than any other, sucking her breath from her in a guttural gasp. A sickening flush of warmth flowed from her body. She clamped her legs together.

'No, no!' she cried. 'Don't leave me, don't leave me. I do love you. I will love you. I promise. I promise.'

She lurched from the bed, searching for something to stem the flood of blood. Tears streamed down her cheeks. Another spasm came upon her and she fell to the floor. It was too late. The pain of childbirth took hold and cast her baby from her.

Chapter 32

The light of the new day roused Leah from a fitful sleep. Benjamin was asleep beside her, his little chest rising and falling with each breath. She stroked his cheek and he opened his eyes as though from the deepest dream.

'Benjamin.'

He stared at her, for a moment without comprehension, before his face formed a smile, as weak as the winter sun. 'My head hurts.'

'Yes, my lamb, but it will soon feel better. Are you hungry?'

'I have a headache in my belly too,' he said, and pulled his knees to his chest.

'I also,' said Leah, stroking his arm.

The events of the night before were a nightmare she wished were not true. She looked at the floor where she had lost her baby. It showed no trace of the blood; no trace of Mariamne wrapping the tiny blood-soaked form in cloth. No ghost of the perfectly formed body under the light of the lamp. Leah touched her stomach. There was no sickness, no pain, only emptiness. Would Gaius even care? He cared for no-one but himself and he was a danger to Benjamin. She could not stay married to such a man. Her heart was as hollow as her womb.

She washed and dressed, braiding her hair and pulling her sash firmly about her waist. She had no desire and no need of Gaius. She would divorce him this very day. He would forfeit his claim to the estate as the Roman law of *sine manu* demanded. The olive grove would remain in her name and he could leave along with his unwholesome guests.

The morning sun streamed into the library. Leah pulled out a clean papyrus and wrote the terms of divorce upon it. With each stroke, every letter, her resolve strengthened, her sight cleared. She had been blind, unable and unwilling to see

Gaius for who he truly was. He would not bring safety and security; he would bring only trouble. She signed the scroll and rolling it up in her hand, went in search of Gaius. He was not in their chamber—the bed was untouched. Neither was he in Marcellus' room—the bed was dishevelled.

She marched towards the atrium, following the sickly odour of stale wine and incense. Her stomach did not turn; her sickness had been scourged from her. She saw him lying alone on a couch, snores rolling from his slackened mouth, a tilted goblet in his hand, its contents a pool on the floor below. She shook him awake.

'Leah,' he smiled. 'Is it morning already?' He reached out to touch her but she stepped away. He frowned. 'What is wrong?'

'What is wrong? You lie with another woman. You almost kill my son. You cause the death of your own. Everything is wrong.'

'The death of our child?' Gaius leapt up, grabbing both her arms. 'What do you mean?'

'You hit Benjamin and you hit me. The baby passed in the night.' She reported the words without emotion, despite the wrenching in her heart.

'My son is no more?' he said.

'Your daughter is no more.' The relief in his face fuelled her anger.

'There will be others, my wife.' He moved to kiss her. She pulled away.

'There will be no others. I am no longer your wife. This very day I have drawn up a proclamation of divorce. You can leave with your friends.'

Gaius stepped back and rubbed his unshaven jaw. 'Divorce? Why would I wish to divorce? This place has brought me great pleasure. You have brought me great pleasure. Why would I leave?'

'You are an unfaithful, violent drunkard. You have no place in this home.'

'Do not be foolish, Leah. You need me. You cannot manage the groves without a husband.'

'Husband?' said Leah. 'You are the least of all husbands. These past evenings of wine have revealed your true nature.' She thrust the scroll at him. 'You will sign this and leave.'

Gaius unrolled the scroll and read it. A scornful smile spread across his face. He tore it slowly from top to bottom, dropping the pieces to the ground. 'You are upset. Now is not the time to make rash decisions. I will accompany my friends to Sebaste and allow you space to recover your senses. I am your husband and I intend to remain as such.'

Leah stared at the torn papyrus at their feet. Could he refuse to divorce? No, she would never submit to that. She needed advice. She needed a patron to stand up for her and plead her cause. But she did not, ever again, need a husband.

Chapter 33

They made their escape the following week. Leah and Mariamne had agreed: the decision could not be delayed. If Gaius insisted on returning, they were powerless to stop him but they could not risk being trapped with such a man in this place. They had no-one near to help, no-one to save them. They would go to the home of Dinah and her husband. Despite the years since she had last seen her friend, Dinah had replied to her message within the day: certainly she and her husband would welcome them into their home.

Leah gathered up the accounts and records of transaction, and informed the chief steward to direct any matters of business to her in Sychar. She summoned the overseer of the olive groves and affirmed her steadfast trust and approval of his position. In return he assured her that his loyalty to her father and Marcellus extended also to her. Benjamin's inheritance would be safe in his hands.

Her concern was not only for Benjamin's inheritance but for his health. He had risen from his bed but the following evening, while eating his meal, he had stiffened like a corpse, the spoon clattering to the ground. It was only a moment and then he had recovered, picking up the spoon with a puzzled look on his face. Just this morning another shaking had come upon him. Again it was for only a moment but his vacant stare afterwards worried Leah. Was it an evil spirit that seized him? She prayed not. Was it a sickness that Dinah could cure? She walked in the way of her grandmother, in the ancient secrets of healing herbs. She prayed Dinah could help.

They entered the gates of Sychar late in the afternoon and followed Dinah's directions through the cobbled streets. The houses were close together, joined by mud brick walls which thrust the narrow streets into shadow. Benjamin rode on the donkey, his little head lolling in sleep. Leah walked beside him, holding his arm so he did not fall. Mariamne hobbled along behind, assisted by Leah's mother who was silent but sure of foot. They knocked on the wooden door and heard the excited shouting of children.

'*Ima, Ima*, they are here!'

The door swung open and Dinah threw her arms around Leah.

'Peace be upon you, Leah!' She kissed her on both cheeks, her heavily pregnant belly pressing against Leah. 'Come in, come in. Welcome to our home.' She greeted the older women and led them to a stone bench. 'Please, rest here and I will bring you water. You will be tired after your journey.' She hurried away, calling to the children who were chasing each other up and down the ladder which led to the roof. 'Come down here, you two, and welcome our guests.'

They clambered down and ran over to where Leah was lifting Benjamin from the donkey. At the sight of the children his pale face broke into a smile.

'This is Benjamin,' Leah said to the children, setting him down. Immediately one of the girls took his hand.

'Do you like lambs, Benjamin? We have three. Would you like to play with them?' They ran off without a glance back.

'He looks just like his father, may he rest well with his ancestors,' said Dinah. She took Leah's hand in hers. 'Too many winters have passed since we last met. I heard rumours that you had married your father's Roman friend. And now here you are, with your belongings and without a man. What has happened?'

'Tragically, Marcellus died more than a year ago,' said Leah.

'Oh, my dear friend,' said Dinah. 'It seems that death stalks you like a lion—three husbands taken. What will you do?'

'I have already done something and it was a foolish mistake. I feared that it was not good to be three women and a child alone in the country, so I married again in haste … against the wisdom of my elders.' She glanced at Mariamne.

'It is done now,' said Mariamne.

Leah continued. 'He is not the man I thought he was. He is unfaithful and violent. He threw Benjamin against a wall and his blows caused me to lose my baby.'

Dinah let out a small cry, her hands flying to her own distended belly. 'May his seed be sowed with salt!' She clapped her hands to her cheeks. 'Forgive me,

Leah. It is not for me to reproach your husband.'

Leah smiled. The years had not mellowed Dinah's tongue nor her fervent loyalty for her friends. It was as though they had never been apart. 'He is my husband no more.'

'Surely he has not also died?'

'He is very much alive but he refuses to divorce. He destroyed the deed before my eyes.'

'You demanded divorce?' said Dinah, astonished. 'What Samaritan woman dares demand divorce?'

'Remember I am also a Roman citizen, as is he. I am entitled to divorce him but I cannot enforce it. He insists he will remain in our home and continue as my husband. We can never return while he is there; it is not safe. We must stay here in Sychar until I can find a way to persuade him.'

'There are men here who specialise in persuasion,' said Dinah, 'but they are difficult to find and demand a hefty fee, so I am told.'

'It will be worth it, whatever the price,' said Mariamne, a scowl on her face.

The sound of children's squeals carried on the breeze, so joyful, so innocent. Leah took Dinah's hand in hers. 'Gaius is not the only reason we came here. Benjamin needs to be with other children. It is not good for him to be alone. And we are worried; since he hit his head, he has been moonstruck. We know of no treatment. Can you prescribe a remedy?'

'I have a balm that might soothe him but the cure is more from the gods than the ground,' said Dinah. 'We could take him to the synagogue and have the priests pray over him, although they often shun such people for fear a seizure will disrupt their reading of the scriptures.'

'Let us try the herbs first,' said Leah, cringing at the memory of her last time before a priest. She would not subject her son to that.

'And for you, I will prepare a special medicine,' said Dinah. 'It is no small thing to lose a child but once it is gone you must ensure no part remains. Some Egyptian myrrh and Ethiopian cumin will soon restore your strength and heal your wounds.'

'My dearest friend,' said Leah, hugging Dinah, 'it is a joy to be here with you. It is as though I have at last come home.'

The door to the street swung open and a tall, bearded man entered, reaching out to catch up the children, one in each arm.

'Abba, we have a new friend!' they cried.

The man kissed them and set them down before striding over to the women. Dinah rose to greet her husband.

'Ashur, this is my friend Leah, and her mother and mother-in-law.'

'Shalom.' Ashur bowed to them all. 'Dinah has spoken of you many times. Our home is your home.'

'Peace be to you and your family,' said Leah. 'We are deeply grateful for your hospitality.'

Leah rested in the warmth of the family as they ate the evening meal and afterwards settled the excited children to sleep. Her mother and Mariamne also retired, and Leah sat with Dinah and Ashur sipping a fragrant tonic that Dinah had prepared for her.

'We plan to settle in Sychar for at least the summer months,' said Leah. 'We will rent a house and hope to establish a stall in the marketplace to sell our fabrics.'

'To find a house is simple,' said Ashur. 'To set up a stall is not so simple. You must first seek the permission of Judah ben Levi. He sits at the city gate and is highly respected among the elders, even more so since he built our town wall. We have not been attacked by bandits since; the whole town is grateful for his generosity. His name is engraved on the city gate and it is his word that determines who can trade in the marketplace.'

'How can I speak to him?' asked Leah.

'You can seek an audience with him at the town gate, if you can find a male to represent you.' Ashur cleared his throat. 'I would help you if I could but my presence would only hinder your cause. Judah ben Levi cannot abide any whom dare question his conduct.'

Leah did not ask how he had upset this Judah ben Levi and Ashur did not offer any further explanation. That night she lay under the stars, warmed by a heavy blanket, breathing in crisp air tinged with the sour scents of the city. Benjamin lay beside her, his body warm against hers. She kissed his soft curls, so like Yosef. If only Yosef still lived they would by now have many precious children like Benjamin. She would be a contented mother and wife like Dinah. Their children would be roaming the hills of Samaria, as she had. They would be clothed in fine wool and linen. She would have made beautiful coverings for their beds. Yosef would have taken his place among the men in the synagogue and their lives would have been full.

Instead, it was she who must provide for the prosperity and protection of her family. If it required the favour of this Judah ben Levi, then so be it. She had no man to introduce her but, as she had learned from the women of Sebaste, there were other means by which a woman could obtain what she desired. She closed her eyes and drew her son close. She would do whatever was necessary for the safety of her son.

***

Leah woke to the smell of fresh bread. It wafted up from the street, climbing over the cluster of roofs, nudging her awake. Voices below exchanged husky shaloms amidst the clearing of sleep thickened throats. She heard scraping, a clang of heavy metal and the rumble of cart wheels over cobblestones. She rose, leaving Benjamin asleep, and descended the stairs. The fire was set and a pot of swollen chickpeas rested on the stones. The door to the street was ajar and as she wondered if she should close it, Dinah entered, holding a basketful of bread. 'Shalom, my friend,' she said, lowering the basket and kissing Leah on the cheek. 'Did you sleep well?'

'Wonderfully,' said Leah. 'I had forgotten how refreshing it is to breathe the night air.' She pointed to the basket. 'I hope you have not bought all this bread for us— our appetite is not so great.'

'It is enough to last for tomorrow's Sabbath,' said Dinah. 'I praise *Yahweh* that we have a baker as our neighbour, especially every Friday.' She picked a bunch of mint and dill from the garden.

'Friday already,' said Leah. 'I had lost track of the days.' She hoped her light-hearted excuse would cover her oversight. How long had it been since she had observed the Sabbath? The practice had slipped away gradually like the seeping of water through clay. Since her visit to Sebaste the previous summer, with the demands of caring for Marcellus and later the distraction of Gaius, it had been so often a burden and inconvenience to join her mother and Mariamne in setting the day apart.

'Well, I am glad you are here to celebrate it with us,' said Dinah. 'These herbs can go in with the chickpeas. They can cook while we go to the well. I am grateful you are here to help me carry the water jars. I usually have to make two trips on Fridays.' She laughed. 'Twice the time for gossip!'

The women of the town flocked through the city gates and along the road to the well. Dinah knew everyone and they all wanted to meet Leah. Their welcoming smiles and talk of family, food and the preparations for *Pesach* warmed Leah's heart. These were her people, her customs, her place. Despite the early hour, women were already returning, their water jars balanced on their heads or resting over their shoulder. One appeared harried, hurrying past, her face set with worry.

'That is the servant of Judah ben Levi's wife,' said Dinah. 'She is as sullen as her mistress is sour. Of all the women in Sychar, the wife of Judah ben Levi has the most reason to be content and yet I do not think even the return of the Messiah could sweeten her disposition. Her husband sits at the city gate and provides her every desire. Her home is filled with every ornament and treasure. Her family is clothed in fine linen and purple, and her sons excel in their learning of the scriptures. She parades them proudly at the synagogue before us all.'

'I am pleased that my son is not so quick to learn,' said one of the women walking with them. 'I do not want the priests to choose him for their training. Better he should learn his father's trade than become a hypocrite.'

'Hypocrite?' said Leah.

'How do you think our synagogue is gilded with gold? How is it that certain priests reside in fine houses and fatten themselves?'

'They claim to know the law but deny it by their actions,' said Leah, recalling the perverted priest who had submitted her to the test for an unfaithful wife. It should have been done in the light of day, with a number of reliable witnesses. Instead Simeon had dragged her to the synagogue at night where there would be no witness to the bruises which proclaimed his violent hand. He had surely paid the priest abundantly for his trouble.

'It takes only a pinch of yeast to leaven a whole batch of dough,' said Dinah. 'Yet there are those who remain faithful to the law. Surely the Messiah will reward them when he returns.'

The women muttered in agreement. They wandered on to the well and

Leah considered their conversation. The wife of Judah ben Levi wanted only the best. If she were to see the finery of Leah's linens, would she not desire them for herself? Yes, Leah thought, the way to Judah ben Levi was through his wife.

Chapter 34

Two Sabbaths had passed and Leah, once again, rose early to draw water from the well. Praise be to Jacob, her ancestor, for digging the well that was the envy of all Samaria. Even now, two thousand years later, cool, clear water flowed into it.

It had been years since she had needed to walk daily to a well. Marcellus had constructed the villa with an abundant cistern, supplied with fresh rainwater not only from the roof but also from a nearby spring. She rubbed her hand over the thickening callous on her heel and watched Benjamin play a hopping game with Dinah's youngest. They chanted a verse of scripture, over and over, in time with their feet. Leah smiled. Benjamin had learned more of the holy word in this past week than she could imagine. It was truly good for him to be here with other children. Next year he would be able to attend the school and if he continued learning in this way, he would not flounder. It was yet another reason why they must stay in Sychar. She replaced her sandal and wiped the dust from her hands. Aching feet were a small price to pay for Benjamin to be educated and for their safety.

She gazed beyond the children to the spreading oak, a wooden hut hidden among its leaves, steps fixed against its trunk, a swing hanging from a sturdy branch. Ashur was forever at his workbench constructing, creating, caring for his family. This was a true family—stable, safe; a mother, a father. Her blood smouldered. Her mind seethed. She needed to rid Gaius from her home. From her life.

She checked that the children were safely occupied and went inside to where their belongings were stored. Thankfully it would not be long now before they had their own home. Just this morning Ashur had taken Mariamne and her mother to inspect a house at the other side of the market. It had a spacious roof for drying flax and fruit, a generous courtyard and vegetable garden, and a light-filled inner room that would be ideal for spinning and weaving in the winter months. If they approved, Ashur would negotiate with the owner a fair price.

She searched through the bags, withdrawing a linen stola the colour of pale sunlight and shaking out the creases. Removing her tunic, she ran her hands over her flat belly. Flat where there should have been a swell. Flat because of the hand of Gaius. She would not grieve. It would be worse if she still carried his child. It would have permitted him the right to claim part of her property. Now she had every legal right to retain the entire estate for Benjamin. She squared her shoulders. Let his fountain overflow in the streets of Sebaste or Corinth or Rome. She wanted no part of him.

She slid the stola over her head, fastening it with a plaited belt. Every day of the previous week she had accompanied Dinah in collecting her son from the synagogue. Every day she had worn a different stola. She had chosen carefully, avoiding the bright colours that would draw needless attention in a Samaritan town, selecting just enough colour and difference of design to catch the eye of Judah ben Levi's wife. Indeed it had worked. On the second day she had approached Dinah and Leah, briefly enquiring after Dinah's family and barely waiting for an answer before turning to compliment Leah on her attire. Leah had responded with restraint, baiting the woman's curiosity so that the next day and the next she converged upon them, extracting from Leah the source of her exquisite garments, her hopes to establish a stall in the marketplace and her concern that she had no patron to plead her case. Leah had relinquished the information a little at a time, gradually reeling in the pinched-faced woman like a fish on the line. Today she would accompany Dinah again.

Like all Samaritan synagogues, Sychar's was on the outskirts of the town, positioned on a small rise with a clear aspect of Mount Gerizim. Its bronze doors opened towards the holy mountain as if embracing it. A broad stone pathway led to the entrance, but Leah and Dinah, holding the hands of the younger boys, followed the other women off to one side, to the more humble entrance of an attached building. It was here that the sons of Sychar learned to read and recite, to calculate and write. They were not inside today but sitting under a spreading tree listening to a tall, thin man, stooped with age and turbaned in the style of the East.

'They have a different teacher today,' said Leah. 'From where does he come?'

'He comes each year from Mesopotamia to share the ancient stories, the mysteries of the stars and the Eastern understanding of the body,' said Dinah. 'The boys' teacher believes it is important for them to learn not only the writings of Moses but also those of our more recent ancestors—those who settled here from the five cities.'

Leah well remembered the ancient stories. She and Atticus would sit at the feet of their father as he recounted tales of wild animals attacking their ancestors because they did not know how to worship *Yahweh*. The people of the five Assyrian towns had each brought their own god to this new land. It was only when they also worshipped *Yahweh*, the god of the Israelites, that the attacks ceased. Then her father would pretend to be a wild lion, roaring and chasing them around the courtyard. Her mother always smiled at her husband's tales of heroes and gods but at night, as she tucked them into their blankets, she would speak softly to them: *Do not think those stories are true. Your ancestors did not follow the Assyrian gods. They only ever worshipped Yahweh. We Samaritans retain the truth of Moses in its purest form, purer than the Jews. When the Messiah comes, he will prove our cause.*

Leah watched the turbaned teacher hold up a small bronze figure, perhaps an Assyrian god. He recited a verse and the students repeated it in chanting tones. The teacher brought his hands together, fingertip to fingertip, palm to palm, and bowed low. It seemed not everyone held the same view of worship as her mother.

'Greetings, Leah. I am glad you are here.' Judah ben Levi's wife sidled up to Leah, her eyes sweeping over the sun-coloured stola. 'That colour—it is magnificent. How the women of this town, indeed the whole province, would flock to buy such a garment.' She reached out to touch it, like a child reaching for honey. 'I have spoken to my husband about your fabrics and your wish to set up a stall in the marketplace. Come to our home tomorrow morning at the tenth hour. That is when he sees his clients and that is when he has agreed to see you.'

Chapter 35

Leah returned to town with a light step, allowing the chattering of the children to flow about her. She had an audience with Judah ben Levi tomorrow. A weight lifted from her and she laughed along with Dinah at the older boy's stories of school. They walked through the artisans' quarter, past potters at the wheel, carpenters at the saw and forgers of iron dripping with sweat. Smoke drifted into the street along with the hammering of ploughshares and the sharpening of swords. Ahead, the street opened into the marketplace.

'Let us see if old Ruben has any early figs,' said Dinah, weaving through the hawkers and traders. 'He insisted they would be ready this week, as though he is the one who determines when they ripen!' She sidestepped a pile of dung. 'His produce is the best in Sychar, and he makes sure everyone knows it.'

They passed a stall displaying a jumble of jewellery alongside lengths of linen. Leah slowed her step and called to Dinah. 'You go ahead. I will catch up with you.'

'I will meet you at Ruben's stall.' Dinah waved at the far side of the marketplace and carried on with the three children.

Leah lifted a length of linen. It was of inferior quality, coarse to the touch and dull in colour.

'Are you the only supplier of linen in Sychar?' she asked.

'I am,' said the stall holder, rubbing his nose with the back of his hand and scratching his beard. 'Not a lot of demand for it in this town. The women here prefer to spin their own wool.' He eyed her up and down. 'They would rather spend their money on this fine jewellery.' He picked up a gold pendant inlaid with blue and red gemstones. 'Lapis lazuli and carnelian—try it, try it.'

He held it out to her.

'Sir, it is beautiful but I am only interested in linen.'

She smiled and walked away. With such poor samples of linen it was no surprise the local women preferred to make their own woollen garments. There was certainly an opportunity here for her fabrics.

She wandered on, imagining how she might set up her stall. She did not hear the shouting. She did not see the skirmish or the flurry of fists. A tattered trader reeled into her. She stumbled and a strong arm grabbed her.

'Steady, woman.' The man continued to hold her, past the point of propriety, seemingly unconcerned to be seen doing so. His sash, secured around a generous girth, was the colour of emerald. His onyx eyes glittered beneath thick eyebrows, sweeping over her before resting on the trader who was cradling his blood covered nose. 'Be careful, my friend. You almost felled this graceful willow.'

'Forgive me, Judah ben Levi,' said the man, nodding apologetically to Leah. With a scowling glance at the foreigner who had punched him, he scurried away.

'Peace be upon you, sir,' said Leah, withdrawing her arm from his grasp and pulling her scarf more firmly over her head. 'You have saved both my dignity and my dress. I am truly grateful.' She did not lower her eyes but instead looked straight at him. By the hand of *Yahweh*, here was the man she would petition tomorrow. She must present herself as respectful yet sufficiently bold to secure his favour.

A broad grin broke across his face and he stretched wide his arms. 'Woman, it is my honour to help you.' His voice rose above the din of the marketplace, turning the heads of those nearby. 'If, while in our fine city, you find yourself in trouble again call the name of Judah ben Levi and I will be your willing servant.'

He raised his hand to his heart, his mouth and then towards her—a gesture of humble service. He turned to the traders who were loosening the girth straps on their camels and unloading their wares.

'Men of the East, I beg your forgiveness for the insults of that scoundrel. Do not judge Sychar by his actions. We are a welcoming city, eager to encourage trade from every part of the world. Please accept my humble invitation to dine with me this evening ... as a gesture of our goodwill.' He bowed.

'Sir, we are pleased to accept your hospitality,' said the tallest trader, stretching and clenching his bloodied fist. 'May prosperity blow across your path like sand in the desert.'

Judah ben Levi sauntered off through the crowd, raising his hand in greeting to one person and then another.

Leah stared at the tall trader, his head and face wrapped in a deep blue turban. His voice sounded familiar, not foreign. Her heart skipped a beat. Could it be Calev?

She lowered her basket to the ground and pretended to rearrange its contents. A shadow fell upon her and she looked up to see him standing close.

'Leah, is it you?' He spoke quietly and, unlike his parting words so many years ago, with no note of bitterness.

'Yes, Calev, it is I.'

Tears of joy sprang to her eyes, memories long past sprang to her mind: Calev racing with Atticus across the fields, Calev devouring her mother's date cakes, Calev coming to her defence against Simeon.

'My friends gave me your message on my return from the east. I was on my way to see you. I did not expect to find you here.'

'There is much to tell,' said Leah. 'I am staying with Dinah whom you must surely remember from our youth. Follow us when we leave the marketplace. We can speak at her house.'

She picked up her basket and walked through the bustling buyers to Ruben's stall. Pyramids of fiery saffron, ground cumin and lentils towered over piles of pistachios and pomegranates. Dinah jostled with the other women to fill their baskets with the choicest leeks, garlic and baby figs.

'There you are,' she said. 'Did you find anything that caught your eye?'

'Yes,' said Leah. 'I found Calev.'

'Calev! Goodness—it's been years!' said Dinah. 'Where is he?' She looked around.

'He is there with those traders and ready to follow us to your home so we are able to speak in private.'

'Let us go then,' said Dinah. 'I have enough vegetables here to feed the whole Roman army.'

All the way home the boys kept turning around, staring at the richly robed man in the blue turban who followed them. They pushed through the door ahead of Dinah and Leah and ran to their father.

'Abba, Abba, an Arabian is coming! He's got a sword!' They skipped around him like lambs let loose.

After the introductions, a courteous greeting from Mariamne and a tear filled hug from her mother, Leah sat with Calev.

'It is truly a joy to see you, Calev,' said Leah, offering him a cup of cooled water. 'It has been many years.'

'Years indeed,' said Calev. 'When I left here, I vowed never to return. It took the trials of the trade routes, the danger of the desert and the passing of the moons to teach me. And, I admit, the lure of profit in the cities of Samaria.' He drained his cup and smiled, the same mischievous smile, now worn at the edges. 'When I saw you in Sebaste, I thought I was dreaming. I could not understand why you were dressed as a Roman, and why you were with Marcellus. Were you not given to Yosef?' He drained his cup, his dark eyes demanding an explanation.

'I was given to Yosef,' explained Leah, 'but men came demanding debts we knew nothing about. They burned our estate to the ground. They murdered Yosef.' The memory seared like the parting of a wound, a wound she had thought well put to rest. Not all Jews were evil. Not all Samaritans were good. Her reasoning told her so. Yet a putrid, fetid hatred flowed from the torn open tomb of her heart.

'Curse the dogs! May they die a thousand deaths. Tell me who they were and I will hunt them down and slit their throats.' Calev's hand moved to his sword.

'Revenge will not return Yosef,' said Leah, warmed by his heated response. 'Mariamne and I escaped to the nearby town. Marcellus heard of the tragedy and offered us shelter and a home. I married him for propriety, to secure the olive groves and to provide a home for Mariamne and my mother. They had both lost everything.'

'There is no worse curse than to lose all your sons,' muttered Calev.

'She does have a grandson,' said Leah, pointing to Benjamin who was wrestling with one of the boys. 'His name is Benjamin.'

'I see Marcellus has already taught him the art of war.'

'Marcellus taught him many things but he, too, has died. He was wounded while we were in Sebaste and did not survive. We buried him with my father and Atticus.'

Calev reached out his hand as though to touch her. Instead he gripped the wooden bench. 'So now you are again three women alone. It would be wise to stay here in Sychar where there is the protection of people and the city wall.'

'That is what we intend,' said Leah. Before she could speak further, Ashur sauntered up, rubbing sawdust from his hands.

'So Calev, tell me about your travels. I am curious to hear a Samaritan's perspective of the cities across the great desert.'

Leah left the men to talk and went to help prepare the meal: leek and lentil soup, steaming flatbread, chopped cucumber with mint, watered wine and dates. Later, while the children dipped bread into their soup and picked the mint leaves off the cucumber, Calev told them tales of stinging sand storms, golden-skinned fruit shaped like a waxing moon and emperors' palaces filled with treasure.

Leah watched his face, weathered by the desert, lines fanning from his eyes. She looked at his sinewed arms and battered knuckles. He was as tough as any Roman soldier. Could she ask him to help her deal with Gaius? No, he had already rescued her from one husband and it had cost him the life of his closest friend, and almost his own. The pain of her brother's death stabbed her, as sharp as the day it had happened. No, she could not ask him to save her from another husband. It was shameful to even admit to this foolish marriage.

The children left the table to play and the conversation continued with Calev answering their questions: 'I journeyed last year to the Stone Tower at the western edge of Serica, the land of the Han,' he said. 'It took many months over mountains, rivers and desert. I secured trustworthy partners at each trading stop along the route. It has allowed us a steady supply of silk without our profit being corroded by greedy middlemen.'

'Your friends generously gave me a sample of your silk in Sebaste,' said Leah. 'It is truly exquisite. I have wanted to ask you if we could purchase more. We plan to set up a fabric stall here in the market. Tomorrow I am meeting with Judah ben Levi to request his permission,' said Leah.

'I am eating with him tonight,' said Calev. 'He is, without doubt, eager to secure our trade for the city. I will mention our requirement for a single, reliable stall owner, someone trustworthy.'

'He envisions Sychar as a mighty trading town,' said Ashur. 'He will do anything to bring in more money.' His voice held a hard edge.

'Is that not to the benefit of all?' asked Leah.

'Our town has prospered but Judah ben Levi has prospered more. The townspeople revere him but he is not all he seems.' Ashur emptied his cup and rose from the table. 'It has been an honour to meet you, Calev. Please stay as long as you like. As for me, I have a roof to repair.'

'And I have camels that need feeding and watering,' said Calev. 'My men have taken them to the well. Leah, if you wish, you can come with me now and select your silks. We leave at daybreak tomorrow.'

Leah accompanied Calev through the streets to the city gates. They stood open, dominating the spacious square and the ancient oak tree. The leading men of the city sat in its shade, in sedate conversation or in earnest debate. Some spoke with foreign travellers, discernible by their manner of dress. There were Romans among them, older men in white togas that reminded her of Marcellus. Judah ben Levi was there also, and as she and Calev walked past his eyes followed. He was a man who missed nothing.

'Leah!'

Hurried footsteps came from behind.

The accent was Greek. It set her heart to ice and her teeth on edge. Surely he could not be here. She lowered her head and kept walking.

'Leah!' He strode up to her, halting her progress.

'Who are you?' demanded Calev. 'Why do you cry out this woman's name in the street?'

'I am her husband,' said Gaius, his face contorted with fury. 'And who are you?'

'I am a friend,' said Calev, his hand clenching into a fist.

'A friend? I leave my wife for but a few days and when I return she has abandoned our home and made a desert dweller her "friend". Do your camels not provide enough comfort that you would steal my wife?'

'I am your wife no longer,' said Leah. She turned to Calev. 'This man is an adulterer. He beat Benjamin and caused me to miscarry.' She glared at Gaius. 'You are no longer my husband.'

'You cannot discard me so easily, woman.' Gaius gripped her arm. 'Return with me now to our home.'

'It is not *our* home, it is mine,' said Leah as though explaining to a child. 'We are divorced, Gaius. You have no authority over me or the estate.'

'You will come with me now,' said Gaius, pulling her away.

'She is not going anywhere,' said Calev, grabbing her other arm and sliding his free hand to his belt. Leah saw the glint of a blade and held her breath.

'Shalom, my esteemed friends.' Judah ben Levi appeared beside them placing his hands together and bowing deeply. It was a clever ploy, requiring Gaius and Calev to release her in order to reciprocate his greeting. He looked from one to the other and smiled. 'I have had the honour of meeting you, my brother,' he said to Calev, 'but not yet you, sir.' He turned to Gaius, appraising his toga draped in the manner of the Greek philosophers. 'I can see you are a man of learning and from your accent, a visitor to our parts. Have you come to share your wisdom with the humble people of Sychar? We do not often receive such distinction.'

Leah watched Gaius waver under the accolade. His eyes moved from Calev to the town elders, to her and back to Judah ben Levi. His shoulders straightened and his face relaxed into a broad grin.

'I am Gaius Apollos from the city of Athens, and a follower of the great philosophers Epicurus, Pythagoras and Plato. I would be delighted to share my knowledge with the citizens of this fine city, sir. However, I came here on other business: to accompany my wife back to our home.'

'She is not your wife and she is not going with you,' said Calev.

Judah ben Levi held up both hands. 'Men, this is not the place to debate such delicate matters. Woman, you are an inhabitant of this town, are you not?'

'I am, sir,' replied Leah, refusing to look at Gaius.

'Any townsperson who has a dispute can bring it before me. I will hear both sides and make a just decision.' He smiled at Gaius. 'Sir, allow this woman to go on her way for now.' Judah ben Levi waved over a young man, not yet old enough to grow a full beard. 'Accompany this woman safely to her home.' He turned back to Leah. 'Do you have someone to represent you; this merchant here, perhaps?'

'I appeal to present my own case,' said Leah. 'I am a Roman citizen and prefer to speak for myself.'

Judah ben Levi took a step back, his thick eyebrows disappearing for a moment up under his head covering.

'She will have to,' said Calev. 'I am leaving at dawn.'

Judah ben Levi studied Leah, his hands stroking his oiled beard. 'Very well, then.' He turned to Gaius.

211

'Now, my friend, come sit with me. It is not often that we men of Sychar are able to speak with a Greek philosopher. And if you do not have more pressing matters, I would be honoured if you would come to eat at my house tonight. My guests, and this noble merchant here, will be eager to hear your ideas.' He clasped Gaius on the shoulder. 'We will settle this matter quickly, I assure you, my friends.' He bowed to Calev.

Gaius glowered at Leah before strolling away with Judah ben Levi, their heads bent together in earnest discourse—his vanity more pressing than his disobedient wife.

'It would be wise to do as he says,' said Calev, looking at the young man who stood by waiting to carry out Judah ben Levi's orders. 'I will bring the silks to you later. You will have to trust that I will choose well for you. And I will have to trust that my newest client will manage to remain in Sychar.'

'Most certainly,' said Leah, annoyed that he doubted her ability. His face broke into a teasing grin. She pressed her lips together. This was no time to jest. 'Do not expect a denarius more than those silks are worth.'

Chapter 36

Leah arrived at Judah ben Levi's house well before the appointed hour. Ashur had directed her through the streets until they arrived at double brass doors set in a whitewashed wall. The doors stood open, broad and welcoming. Townspeople came and went from their morning salutatio with their benefactor. Some hurried off on errands. Others wandered away in small groups, praising aloud the name of Judah ben Levi. Leah walked across the paved courtyard, past a gardener who was tending brightly flowered plants that spilled from boldly glazed pots.

The young man who had accompanied her home the previous day stood before a closed door painted a vibrant blue. He held a wax tablet in one hand and rolled a stylus between the fingers of the other. Two men were seated on a wooden bench waiting their turn to enter. They stared at Leah. She could see their disapproval—they would never allow a wife of theirs to seek an audience alone with a city elder.

'Shalom, sir,' she said to the young man, causing him to almost drop the stylus. 'I am here to speak to Judah ben Levi.'

'He is expecting you,' said the young man, inclining his head. 'Wait here. He will see you after these men.'

Leah sat opposite the men. They shifted uncomfortably, averting their eyes. Time passed and a man of short stature emerged from the house, a scroll clutched in his hand, a look of satisfaction on his face.

'Praise Judah ben Levi for his open hand,' he said, waving the scroll at the waiting men.

Their faces lit up and they entered the house with a light step. Leah looked down at her tightly clasped hands. The skin on her fingers had softened since her time with Gaius. She had abandoned the loom this past year, leaving Mariamne to the weaving. But now, with Calev's delivery of the most beautiful silks, their workload would lessen. They could sell both the imported silk and their own weaving with which from now on, Leah vowed, she would always assist Mariamne. She recounted Dinah's questions the day before as they inspected the luxurious cloth, holding it up to the sun and watching the light dance off the delicate threads of gold.

'Why go to all this trouble to set up a stall?' Dinah had asked. 'Surely you have enough income from the olive groves?'

'Without Marcellus our income has been unreliable,' said Leah. 'Our regular buyers discerned quicker than I the dubious charm of Gaius. Our orders have diminished. We have enough to pay our labourers and maintain the groves but little else. Mariamne and I had already discussed selling our fabrics. This trouble with Gaius has forced us to a decision that we might have made anyway.'

The door burst open and the two men stomped past without a word, without a smile. Leah closed her eyes and breathed in deeply, allowing the air to fill her chest, calm her mind. She had chosen red today, the colour of a setting summer sun, woven with ochre, gold and green. It was no surprise that the local men had stared. Their own wives had no access to such colours. Surely Judah ben Levi would agree to this stall and the trade it would encourage. Surely he would benefit more from her remaining in Sychar than judging in favour of Gaius.

'Greetings, woman,' said Judah ben Levi as she entered the room. Like Pilate without the palace, he stood behind a large table strewn with scrolls and papyri. A bone stylus stood in a jar next to a wax tablet and a solid brass seal ring. 'Twice we have met and yet I do not know your name.'

'I am Leah Marcellus, a Samaritan of this region,' said Leah.

'And yet with a Roman name.'

'My father took the name as a gesture of honour for his commander in the Imperial Roman Auxiliary,' said Leah. 'Upon their discharge, Marcellus and my father purchased an olive grove on the slopes towards the south.'

'Ah-ha, the olive groves of Marcellus,' said Judah ben Levi. 'So you are the daughter who married her father's friend after a bandit attack. I heard talk of it in the marketplace.' He scratched his neatly trimmed beard. 'But this man who claims to be your husband is a philosopher from Greece, not a centurion of

Rome.' He pulled out the padded chair at his desk and sat, hands spread wide, palms down, a picture of power. 'Be seated, and tell me your story.'

'Marcellus died over a year ago leaving me to provide for my mother, my mother-in-law and my son. In my distress I acted with foolish haste and married this man. He is a man of charming ways and clever words, but he has proven himself unfaithful and violent.'

'You should have waited for a good Samaritan man.'

'What you say is true, Judah ben Levi. I cannot defend my actions in marrying Gaius, only my actions in demanding a divorce. It is not safe for us to remain with this man. He threw my son against a wall and almost killed him.' She kept her tone sober, calm, business-like—displays of emotion would not further her cause.

'You did not provoke him?' asked Judah ben Levi.

What lies had Gaius poisoned this man with? Had Judah ben Levi already determined his verdict? She ignored the beating of her heart, the clamminess of hands. 'I provoked him only by finding him lying with another woman.'

'That is an unfortunate circumstance,' said Judah ben Levi, the corner of his mouth twitching.

'Except for my son's injuries, I consider it fortunate to have discovered his true nature. As a citizen of Rome I have a legal right to divorce him, even without his consent. I have borne him no children. He can claim not one pebble of my estate. However, as a woman, I have no means to enforce the law and so he remains in my house, the house of Marcellus.'

'And what is it you want of me?' He folded his arms across his broad chest.

'I have brought my family here to this city to take refuge, and to contribute to its prosperity,' said Leah. 'I am asking for your patronage to protect me from Gaius Apollos and to set up a stall in the marketplace. I will bring to this city the finest silks from the east as well as the finest garments from our own loom. I have sold stolas to the wife of Valerius Gratus and to the women of Sebaste. I am certain that when they hear of my stall they will come … with their purses full.'

'My wife extols your handiwork and I must agree with her,' said Judah ben Levi, looking Leah over with an approving eye. 'Such craftsmanship would benefit this city. However I do have an obligation to Gaius Apollos.'

Leah maintained a mask of indifference despite the roiling within. What agreement had Gaius charmed this man into last night?

'I have promised him a podium in the marketplace. It is a delicate situation.' He laced his fingers together. They were clean and smooth, not those of a man of the soil or the sword. Yet for a man of the city he was well built with a strong jaw, a straight nose and a fine robe falling over muscular legs. What would convince him that he would gain more from supporting her than Gaius?

'Gaius Apollos will be here but a season. I intend to stay in Sychar, to bring a steady stream of customers to the streets.'

'He is a man of influence, from the very birthplace of philosophy. The people of this city, and many from far off, will flock to hear him speak. It will bring prominence to our city and the people will applaud me.' He reached for the seal ring, absently rubbing the engraving and slipping it on and off a thick finger. 'Certainly violence is a worthy case for divorce; more worthy than the woman who divorces her husband for taking up the trade of tanner or coppersmith. But it is not my place to enforce the man's removal from your home.'

'Sir, I can see you are a man of great acumen and influence. Surely your wife and the many women of Sychar will applaud you for making their city the centre of the finest fabrics in the land. Surely it is within your power to appease Gaius Apollos.'

Judah ben Levi leaned back in his chair, stroking his beard. 'I will grant you a stall for a fee of five shekels a month and a tenth of the profits.' His black eyes gleamed. His demands were excessive and he knew it.

'Five shekels! I am not redeeming my firstborn!' said Leah.

'I am impressed that you know the Law of Moses,' said Judah ben Levi, his eyebrows arching. 'For that alone I will drop the amount to three shekels a month.'

'One shekel is all I can afford until I am able to trade.'

Judah ben Levi rose from his chair and paced the room. 'Leah Marcellus, you are unlike any other Samaritan woman. You are ambitious, as am I, and your Roman citizenry gives you a boldness most intriguing. I am willing to offer you my protection and my patronage. I wonder, what can you offer me in return?'

He came close and took her hand, raising it to his lips. His kiss was hard and dry. It did not cause her to shiver with delight; neither did it repulse her. What was she prepared to do to assure the safety and security of her son? The women of Sebaste seemed at ease with the secret sharing of their bed. She must be as wise as a serpent. She smiled at Judah ben Levi, clasping his hand and pressing it to her chest.

'You are a married man, Judah ben Levi, and I am a merchant of silk who must be seen to be upright. I can offer you only my steadfast loyalty.'

His breath was hot against her skin. 'For the moment, Leah Marcellus, your loyalty will suffice.'

Chapter 37

Over the following months Leah resisted Judah's advances, intending to assure his favour through the promise of profit from her thriving silk stall. It might have remained that way except for the schemes of Gaius. He, too, had the ear of Judah ben Levi, impressing him with his oratory and the crowds he attracted. Leah saw through it: the repeated phrases, the same arguments served up as new. Judah ben Levi, however, was pleased to offer his patronage. The shekels he paid into Gaius' greedy hands bestowed on him praise from the townspeople for bringing such new ideas to Sychar. He had given Leah her stall and at a fair price but he delayed in dealing with Gaius.

'It is a thorny issue,' he said, when Leah petitioned him at the weekly meeting every client was obliged to have with their benefactor. 'Have mercy on the man and permit him to stay in the villa. He has agreed to leave you in peace.'

'He is no longer my husband; he has no right to live there. I want him out of my home.'

Mariamne, too, wanted him out. 'Who knows what state the villa is in with that pagan carousing there. And now he comes here, as brazen as a brass snake.' She would hit her stick on the ground. 'The longer he remains there, the harder it will be to evict him.'

At each visit, Leah encouraged Judah in his grand boasts, listened to his complaints of his wife and, as the summer months cooled to winter, comforted him with an occasional touch. But still he would not yield on the matter of Gaius. Her demands were met with a helpless raising of hands.

'What can I do?'

She knew Judah ben Levi could do much ... if it suited him.

On her walk to the well, when she stood at her stall, day after day, month after month, the problem of Gaius pressed heavy upon her. Calev kept bringing silk from the east – a round journey of three to four weeks; longer if caught in a sand storm or attacked by desert raiders. Whenever the time drew near, she would rise early, hastening to the well to see if he had arrived overnight. If he was there, they would draw water together and speak of his journey, his trading – never of Gaius. He would bring silk to her stall and stay to see Benjamin. Then he would go, taking swords, glass and gold back to his uncle who waited in Palmyra. He could never stay and of this she was pleased. She did not need Calev's judgement; she did not need his help.

The arrival of the chief steward of Marcellus finally drove Leah to action. It was a crisp winter morning and the almond trees bloomed. He sidled up to her stall and pulled back the cloak that shrouded his furtive face. Leah started in recognition. She had not seen him since they had left the villa almost a year ago.

'Shalom, Leah,' he said, his words rushing out like a rain-flooded stream. 'I cannot stay long. I cannot be caught here.' He withdrew a scroll and untied the cord, spreading it out over the fabrics on the stall table. 'I have seen Gaius speaking with some of your buyers. They have been to the villa. I suspected he was making his own contracts with them so I took it upon myself to search through the scrolls. 'You must see these figures for yourself. They do not agree.' He stabbed at the columns of numbers.

Leah studied the scroll, noting the waxed seal of several of their principal buyers. She saw the discrepancies and chewed her lip, a cold rage curdling her insides. He had no right to interfere; the olive grove was not his to control, not his to gain from. He was skimming the earnings like cream from cow's milk. For a year he had remained entrenched in the villa, assuming the role of master, and why not—there was no-one to stop him.

She could tolerate it no longer. She had to persuade Judah ben Levi. Gaius had to go.

***

Few carriages ever entered Sychar – even Judah ben Levi did not use such transport. So when Drusilla's carriage clattered through the gates, the whole town stopped and stared. Leah lingered with the crowd, watching and waiting for her plan to unfold. Drusilla and her friends stepped from the carriage, shaking out their pallas and smoothing their curled and pinned hair with jewel-laden hands. The town elders were instantly on their feet, hurrying towards them, Judah ben Levi leading the way, bowing so low his nose almost scraped the dirt.

'Shalom, fine women. Welcome to our humble city and may the peace of the gods be upon you.'

'We have come from Sebaste to see Leah Marcellus,' said Drusilla, raising her fleshy nose in the air and regarding her surroundings with squinted eyes.

'Leah Marcellus?' said Judah ben Levi, drawing his head sharply back and raising his eyebrows. 'You have come all this way to see her?'

'Have you not seen her fabrics? There is no-one in all Samaria who can rival her linens. As soon as we received word she was here, we came. Although …' added Drusilla, 'it is a mystery why she has settled on this small town rather than Sebaste for her trade.'

Leah watched Judah ben Levi's face flush and his jaw clench at her words; to him, Sychar was a city. His city.

'Drusilla, shalom and welcome,' she said, strolling over from where she had been waiting. She hugged each of the women. 'It is a joy to see you. How is Sebaste? You must tell me all the news.'

She tucked her arm into Drusilla's and turned to Judah ben Levi whose mouth was opening and closing like a fish in a net.

'Sir, you must surely have more important matters to deal with.'

He stammered out an answer and, as she hoped, a hasty invitation for the women and Leah to take refreshments at his house.

Later that afternoon Drusilla and her friends stumbled into their carriage, replete with the best of Judah ben Levi's food and wine. Leah brushed her hand against Judah ben Levi's and sighed.

'My friends have left with their arms full and their purses empty. Word will soon spread through Sebaste and many more from that city will come. I am grieved to think their journey might be wasted.'

'Why?' Judah ben Levi looked at her sharply. 'Did they buy everything? Can you not procure more?'

'They did indeed fill my money bag and diminish my stocks, but Calev is coming soon with fresh fabrics. That is not the problem.'

'Then what, woman?' He stood before her, regal in bearing but with a worried look on his face. She moved to a nearby bench and sat, positioning herself as Octavia might have done, displaying the attributes of her figure to full effect.

'Is not the goodwill and wealth of these Roman women of greater worth than one Greek philosopher of little standing?'

'Their custom is invaluable but what has that to do with Gaius Apollos?'

'His presence in this city is like a thorn in our side. My son is afraid of him and my mother-in-law will give me no rest until he is removed from our estate.'

She drew three silver coins from her purse and pressed them into Judah's palm. 'This is your portion of today's earnings. Is it not more than all the earnings of Gaius? The people flock every day to my stall and the numbers will only increase when it is known that even Roman women buy their fabrics here. For this past year, and for the benefit of the city, I have endured Gaius's unlawful habitation of my villa. I can do so no longer. If he stays, then I must go.'

'He pleases the people and brings status to Sychar.'

'There are other philosophers.'

'There are other sources of silk.'

Leah contained her concern and set a serene smile on her face.

'Would the women of Sebaste come this way for another?' She sighed and pushed a strand of hair behind her ear, slowly tracing her finger past her earring, running it down the length of her neck. Judah ben Levi's eyes followed. His lips parted, his breathing quickened.

'I could withdraw my patronage … but to evict him from your villa.' He spread his arms wide. 'I am a man of clean hands.' His gaze was greedy, his brow beaded with sweat.

'Judah ben Levi,' said Leah, bringing her face close to his and slowly stroking the back of his neck, 'if the reward is great enough there is always a way.'

It did not take long for Judah ben Levi to act. The following week he informed her that she would have no more trouble from Gaius Apollos. She did not allow herself to wonder at the method of persuasion; she did not care.

Judah ben Levi's dark eyes gleamed as she broke the seal of Marcellus and read the letter from the chief steward confirming that Gaius had indeed gone. In the seclusion of his rooms Judah ben Levi took Leah in his arms and claimed his reward.

Chapter 38

10 months later, 29 AD The month of Kislev – Winter

Leah gathered up her belongings into her basket and turned to kiss Judah ben Levi on the cheek. Her touch awakened him and he opened his eyes.

'Stay with me.' He reached for her hand. 'It is not yet dawn; I hear no birdsong.'

'Your ears are too old,' said Leah. 'The rooster finished his crowing while you were still snoring.'

'I am not snoring now,' said Judah ben Levi. He grabbed her and pulled her onto him. Her loose hair cascaded over the bronze amulet nestling in a forest of chest hair. 'Stay.' His voice held the huskiness of morning, his breath as pungent as sun-warmed curd.

'Should we birth rumours to fester in the streets?' She pushed him away, rising to her feet and straightening her stola. 'I have a stall to attend and you have a wife to meet.'

'She will not return from her sister's house so early. They will first take the children to the synagogue. And then they will gossip in the marketplace and spend all my money.' He yawned and sat up. 'Why will you not marry me, Leah? At least then I would be able to sleep longer.'

'You have no need for a second wife. Is one not trouble enough?' she said, tying her hair back in a loose knot and covering it with a shawl.

They spoke without conviction; both well aware that the husband of but one wife was a more praiseworthy state for a city leader and that in occasionally warming Judah's bed, Leah maintained his favour without marital constraint.

'Trouble indeed. She is like a constant drip on a rainy day.'

'As a wife, I may be just as wearisome.'

Indeed his wife, with her superior ways and idle talk, was like a thorn in Leah's sandal. She heard the whispers of the women as they walked through the market, as they gathered at the synagogue: *she did not have a husband; she had had many husbands; she had only one child; she was barren; she was cursed; she consorted with Romans.* The rumours swirled like dust borne on the wind but as long as she brought them beautiful silks, it would never settle.

'It is the wanting and waiting that stirs your loins, Judah ben Levi,' she said.

She picked up her basket and stepped out into the dark, rain washed street, stealing along a narrow alleyway towards the marketplace. It was a familiar route now, one she followed whenever she and Judah ben Levi spent a few hours together. The wheat, the grape and the olive harvest had passed since she had first lain with him. He was an eager bed mate; not as adept as Gaius, neither as callous as Simeon. She smiled at the thought of his panting body and his husky pledges. Men thought they were in control but the glimpse of a shoulder or the graze of a finger could bend them like barley in a breeze. But he would never make her heart sing as it had with Yosef; no man ever could. She cursed under her breath; it did no good to resurrect such memories.

From a side alley a shadowy figure stepped forward and grabbed her arm. Before she could cry out a hard hand clamped over her mouth.

'Be silent, Leah.' The man's voice was familiar but it did nothing to quiet her pounding heart. 'What are you doing stealing away from Judah ben Levi's house at this hour?' he whispered, his voice cutting her like a blade.

'Calev! Why are you lurking in the shadows? Why would you presume such a thing?' said Leah.

'Do not consider me as foolish as you,' he said, glaring at her. 'Judah ben Levi's attendant was overheard in the marketplace boasting of the secrets he holds. Your name was mentioned and rumours are already taking flight. This morning I see that they are true.'

'Can a woman not walk through the town alone without being accused of waywardness?'

'Do not lie to me, Leah,' he growled. 'Why would you do such a thing? How could you stoop to this?'

His look of disgust seared like a flaming arrow, reigniting a shame she had succeeded in suppressing each time she explained away her absences to her mother and Mariamne. What right did he have to accuse her? He was a supplier of silk, a partner in trade, nothing more.

'I stoop to nothing. Judah ben Levi and I help each other, that is all.'

'How has he helped—by dragging your reputation into the mud?'

'He rid me of Gaius.' Her angry retort was out before she could withhold it.

'Gaius?' Calev laughed—a scoffing, bitter laugh. 'You slept with the snake for that?'

Leah slapped him. 'I do what is necessary for my family. You have no right to judge. You turn up a few times a year bringing trinkets for Benjamin and then you return to the desert. I could think of no other way.'

'Did you consider how he persuaded Gaius to leave?' said Calev, glaring at her. 'Did you think he would dirty his hands himself?' He grasped her arm, shaking it as he spoke. 'It was I who persuaded Gaius. It was I who drew my dagger for your great patron. He convinced me not to tell you. If I had known why ...'

'You?' A gust of wind swept down the street. Leah clutched at her cloak but it was not the wind that chilled her. Judah had deceived her. She warmed his bed for no just cause. Her legs weakened beneath her and she was glad of Calev's fierce grip on her arm.

'Why did you not tell me of your troubles with Gaius?' said Calev. 'Did you not think I would help?'

'You saved me from one husband, and it ended in death. If not for me, Atticus would still be living and you would not have fled to the desert in anger. How could I ask you to save me from another? I had to take care of the matter myself.'

'By acting as a harlot and a fool?' said Calev.

Leah snatched her arm from his grasp. Tears stung her eyes. 'I need you neither to condemn nor rescue me.'

'You need someone to turn you from this foolish path before you lose everything you have built.'

His words stung more than her tears. 'You bring me silk and I pay you. That is all your responsibility to me.'

'Do not tell me my duty, Leah.' He pressed her against the wall, his face so close she could feel his beard against her skin. His eyes burned into hers and for a moment she thought he would kiss her. Her heart pounded like a hammer on the anvil. Her thoughts tripped and staggered, astonished at their course: *she wanted him to kiss her*. Instead he stepped back, his hands clenched. 'My camels are at the well. I will bring them to your stall this morning and you will have your silk.' He turned and strode away.

Leah stumbled off in the other direction, taking deep breaths of the chill air, her anger moving from Calev to herself to Judah ben Levi. She had been a fool to trust him. She had been a fool to believe she held sway over him. She had been a fool not to ask Calev's help.

The early morning marketplace was astir. Traders led laden donkeys through the open town gates, men tightened tent pegs, merchants laid out their wares. The fires were lit and the smell of roasted meat drifted through the market along with the crackling of locusts in hot oiled pans. Old Ruben was unloading sackfuls of dates, olives and garlic from a cart. His heavy cloak hung off his thin frame, hampering his steps, and he threw it off in exasperation. Leah made her way to a stall surrounded by a huddle of traders. They cupped their hands around rough-hewn cups, their breaths steaming out in the crisp morning air. As soon as he saw her the toothless stall keeper ladled out a cupful of the brew.

'This will warm your bones this fine morning, Leah.'

She handed him a bronze coin and raised the steaming drink to her lips. The sweet mixture of date honey and herbs turned bitter in her mouth. Curse Calev for his silence. Why had he not told her that it was he who had expelled Gaius? She could have maintained the favour of Judah without lying with him, without risking her reputation, without suffering shame. Calev's fury and his face so close to hers, filled her mind. She had wanted to hit him. She had wanted to kiss him.

The drink caught in her throat and she spluttered. She preferred anger. Anger at his judgement, anger at his condemnation, anger at his making her feel shame. She wiped the liquid from her face, calming her rushing thoughts, her racing heart. No-one need know. Judah would soon suppress the flapping tongues. Raising her head high, she sipped the drink and caught the conversation of the traders.

'If they choose to travel this way, those Jews are asking for a fight,' growled an unkempt trader, crunching on a locust.

'Is it not fitting to strike on the jaw those who brand us half-breeds?' asked another. He had a cut on his cheek and a bruised, bloodshot eye. 'They drink from Jacob's well as though it is theirs. They should keep to their own country and leave us to ours.'

'Surely they have as much right as you to walk through this land? Was not Jacob the father of the Jews as well as you Samaritans?' asked an ebony-skinned man.

'You are well informed, my friend,' said the grubby trader. 'We do have the same ancestor but those Jews claim to be more pure. Was it not they who were taken away to Babylon? Was it not us who remained in the land? We are the true upholders of the law and Mt Gerizim is the true mountain of worship.' He wiped his mouth with the back of his hand.

'Does your law tell you to insult those who claim a different truth?' asked the dark stranger.

'They are all the same. Their mouths boast in arrogance and their callous hearts are closed. If the Messiah himself came and sat in the shadow of the holy mountain they would still refuse to accept the truth.'

'If your Messiah comes he would do better to rid us of those iron-fisted Romans. They are the ones who extort our money and trample us in the dust.'

Leah walked over to her stall and hauled back the sturdy tent cloth, fastening the ropes firmly and allowing the morning sun to spread its gentle rays over the table. She had more important matters to worry about than when the Messiah might return. They had been waiting thousands of years; it might be a thousand more.

She reached into her basket, drawing out the lengths of silk and carefully arranging them over the table. One was the colour of the forest with swirls of sapphire as though the rains had washed through it. She held it up, feeling it glide through her fingers. These past few years had seen her trading prosper, and with it, her standing in the city. What standing would she have if she was exposed?

The law would not condemn Judah for sleeping with her because she did not belong to another. But the law could not protect her reputation; that was in the hearts of men.

She sighed and looked at the silk, crushed in her clenched hand. She tried to smooth out the creases. She was no better than *him*. She had deceived Dinah, her mother and Mariamne. She had hidden her absences by visiting Judah only when it was Mariamne's turn to fetch water from the well. Even now Mariamne would be returning with the heavy water jar and hurrying Benjamin along to the synagogue before joining Leah at the stall.

Still in his first year of school Benjamin was in awe of his teacher, arriving home each day reciting the adventures of the holy prophet Moses or the ancient songs. Dinah's sons watched out for him and Leah had never seen him more content, except when he was taken by a fit. He had a demon, some said. *What sin did his father commit for this to afflict him? Who was his father?* Leah heard the whispers in the street. All the medicine of Dinah did not help, neither Mariamne's entreaties to Aphrodite. Her mother sat by Benjamin as he slept, her hand upon his head and her mouth forming soundless words. If she were praying, her prayers, too, were fruitless.

Leah watched a priest walk through the marketplace, his hands clasped piously at his belt. Since her family's return to Sychar she had observed every Shabbat, offered every grain and dove sacrifice, dutifully taken her son up the holy mountain for every required feast, hoping that *Yahweh* would be pleased. But how could he be pleased with her observance of the law when her own heart condemned her? If the Messiah, on whom all their hopes rested, returned would he not also condemn her?

The leaden beat of Mariamne's stick on the ground and the call of old Ruben drew Leah from her sombre thoughts.

'Shalom, esteemed woman of the cloth,' he called. 'Will you not make me a new tunic? See how mine is torn.' He raised his robe revealing knobbly knees and withered legs. 'Would you not like to take my measure?' He gave a wicked grin.

'Away with your brazen talk,' said Mariamne, shaking her stick at him. 'I have better things to do than to listen to an old goat like you.'

Ruben laughed as she deposited her basket on the stall table and greeted Leah with a kiss.

'Shalom, my daughter. You rose early this morning.'

'I could not sleep,' said Leah, cringing at the lie that had previously fallen so easily from her lips.

'Neither I,' said Mariamne. 'Our linen supply is low. These are all that remain.' She pulled out the coloured cloths and laid them on the table. 'We have no flax to make more. We must wait four months until the harvest and pray these will last.'

'Do not fret, Mariamne. We have enough silk and…' Leah stopped herself saying Calev had brought more. Mariamne could not know she had seen him that morning. Mariamne would have to keep fretting until he arrived.

The grunting and groaning of camels carried across the marketplace. Calev was leading the animals through the swarming crowds. Mariamne clapped her hands in delight and hurried out to greet him.

'Where have you been for so long—to the land of the Han and back again?'

'I was delayed in Perea. Bandits on the King's Highway.' He hoisted the bulging baskets from the camels and deposited them on the ground, dusting off his hands. They were blackened and his knuckles bore harsh red marks. Leah imagined the bandits had not fared so well.

'We are glad to see you,' said Mariamne. 'And Benjamin will be overjoyed. He does not stop asking about you.'

It was true, thought Leah, recalling Benjamin's constant queries. *Where is Calev? He promised to take me over the hills on his camel. He said he would bring me a bow and arrow. He is going to teach me how to shoot a bird.* She was pleased to delay her son learning to shoot—he was not yet six years of age.

'You will stay with us tonight?' continued Mariamne.

'I have goods to deliver to Tyre,' said Calev. 'I cannot stay.'

He caught Leah's eye. What was it she saw there? Anger? Disapproval? Why did it grate at her heart? It was easy for him to admonish her; he would soon depart again. It was she who must live in this town. It was she who must ensure the success of her stall. It was she alone who would have to deal with Judah ben Levi.

'We have several undyed skeins of yarn which are no value without colour,' said Leah. 'Perhaps you could take them with you to Tyre and have them dyed.' She turned to Mariamne 'If we weave the Tyrian blue with our last few skeins, it will fetch a high price and carry us through the winter.'

'That is an excellent idea, daughter,' said Mariamne. 'Will you be returning this way, Calev?'

'In the next few weeks,' said Calev, clenching his jaw. 'If you need my help you need only ask.' His hard stare told Leah that he did not speak of the linen.

Chapter 39

The following week Leah was, as usual, perched in the marketplace watching the haggling of merchants with traders, traders with stall keepers and stall keepers with townspeople. She patted the piles of coloured cloth before her, rearranging a length of purple so the tassels hung in a lavish fringe over the edge of the table. Fine gold thread wound through the cloth in intricate patterns, catching the sun. Calev's latest delivery of silk was the finest yet. Yet it brought her no joy. Shame bore down on her like the weight of a thousand waters. Shame that she had only one child, shame that she had no husband, shame that the husband she had was not hers. She lowered her head, careful that no-one would see the tears that welled, careful that no-one would hear her cry for help, her now constant prayers to Yahweh, forever falling from her lips.

'Leah.' The voice was right beside her. She spun around.

'Calev?' He could not be back from Tyre so soon, and yet her heart beat a little faster at the thought.

'Leah.' It was a gentle whisper, soothing and rich. She lifted the tent flap. Nothing but an old dog curled up next to the shady stone wall. It opened a sleepy eye, ever hopeful for food, then drooped back to sleep. Her name came again and she stopped. The voice wasn't beside her or behind her; it was within. Was it the voice of her father—a memory of words spoken long in the past?

Soon you will know the truth and the truth will set you free.

'What truth?' She thought she had spoken softly enough but as she dropped the tent flap she caught the complicit smile of old Ruben adjusting the thick garlic plaits that hung above brimming baskets of olives, coriander and mint. He grinned a toothless smile.

'Talking to yourself at this hour of the day? You should join the priests up on the mountain.'

'And you should mind what you say or the gods might wither your melons.' She peered across the marketplace, watching for Judah ben Levi. Over the spread of silks she had whispered to him her concerns. His smile had faded and he had hastily assured her he would swiftly deal with the bearers of any idle gossip. Now several days later he was yet to bring her a good report. Finally she saw him, striding through a knot of merchants, clapping one on the back in a jovial greeting. A man roasting skewers of lamb called out to him. He threw up his arms in mock regret and patted his paunch.

'Shalom, Judah ben Levi. You are late today. Did your discussions go well?' She inclined her head towards him in greeting, picking up a length of crimson silk and running it through her hands.

'Ah, my feisty one, straight to the point, I see.'

'Not at all, sir. I merely noticed that your sash is crushed as though you have been sitting for too long. I was concerned.'

Her concern was not at all for him. Her concern was only for how she would disentangle herself from him without consequence.

He leaned forward and his hand brushed hers, leaving a trace of sweat. 'The city elders and synagogue leaders are dining with me tonight. It is a tiresome obligation that will leave me in need of refreshment. Perhaps, after my guests have departed, you will come to me and I will tell you the good news.'

'Perhaps,' she said, wiping the sweat from her hand as soon as he sauntered away.

The women soon crowded around her stall eager to be the first to inspect the newly arrived silks. She cut lengths, draping them over slender shoulders, arranging the fabric to show off their waists, their hips, their ankles. The coins grew heavy in her purse, as heavy as the thoughts that pressed upon her. What was this good news? If she did not go to Judah tonight, if she broke their agreement, he could withdraw his patronage, he could demand a greater part of her takings, he could bring false testimony against her. He could bring her family to ruin and shame. Yet knowing the truth of his deceit she could not, she would not ever return to his bed.

And what of this voice? This truth that would set her free? It could not be the truth of Judah's deceit. She was still as trapped as a caged dove.

The afternoon passed by and the sky clouded over, threatening rain. These were the early rains, falling gently on the dried out ground, softening it in readiness for the planting of seed. As Leah extended the tent to shelter the fabrics she heard a curt voice cutting through the market like a scythe through maize. Mariamne.

'Move out of the way, you great sluggard. Can't you see there's an old woman in a hurry?' She swung her stick at the legs of a sprawled-out youth. He sprang up as though stung by a bee.

'Mariamne, what are you doing here? Is something wrong?' She saw the older woman's pinched lips, the barely concealed distress.

'It's Benjamin. He's had another seizure. It threw him into the fire.'

Leah's hand flew to her heart. Mariamne clasped her hand, glancing sideways to check that no-one had heard her.

'Remain calm, my daughter. Your mother is with him and he is recovering. I was planting seeds in the garden when I heard your mother cry out. She had already pulled him from the fire and laid him on his side. The shaking did not linger, thank the gods. Brave little lamb, both legs are burnt but I do not think too badly. We doused the burns with the last of the water and your mother made a poultice of bees honey, wine and aloe.

'I must go to him at once.'

She hugged Mariamne, leaving her to take care of the stall, and hurried away, ducking behind the stalls to avoid the curious stares—hungry for gossip.

Why must her son suffer so? Did he truly have a demon, as some said? Were the gods punishing her? Was Yahweh? She was the one who had withheld the truth of Yosef from Mariamne. She was the one who had brought Gaius, that smooth-tongued viper into their home. She was the one who now lay with a married man. All her efforts to secure her family's future had been fruitless.

Lifting her tunic above her knees, she ran through the town, past the mud houses and brick walls, and along narrow alleys, her leather sandals slapping the hard ground in staccato. She pushed through the gate and ran into the house. Benjamin lay in his grandmother's arms, whimpering like a puppy, his eyes vacant as they always were for a time after a fit. His legs, usually so busy running, climbing and exploring, drooped without life. Her mother held him as she had when he was a baby, rocking him gently and humming a soothing tune. She raised anguished eyes to Leah and released Benjamin to her.

'My little dove, my precious boy.' She kissed his face, breathing in his innocent scent, blocking out the acrid smell emanating from his legs. 'I am here now. Your Ima is here.'

His vacant eyes focused and he started to cry. 'It hurts, Ima. The fire is eating my legs.'

Leah's heart wrenched, her eyes welled. 'I know, my lamb. It will hurt for a little while but I will make you a special drink to take the pain away.'

'I am thirsty.' Benjamin's whimpers turned to sobs. Her mother looked at her with pleading eyes. Pleading for Leah to hurry to the well and draw more water. 'I will return soon with mandrake for the pain and with water,' she said, kissing her mother and Benjamin.

Grabbing a basket and the empty water jar, she hurried towards the town gate. Curse Judah's magnanimous insistence on building a town wall. It provided protection, and for that the townspeople were indebted to him; they had not been attacked since. But she could no longer escape to the countryside unnoticed. Everyone had to pass through the gate that bore the bold inscription of their benefactor.

She hurried past the town elders, still debating under the ancient oak tree. She hurried past the guards yawning at the gate. She hurried down the potholed road, past the ploughed wheat and barley fields with their straight furrows stretching into the distance, waiting to be sown with seed. She hurried up a barren slope scattered with rocks. Rolling to the south, olive trees dotted the slopes in rows as straight as lines of Roman soldiers. It was here that she had grown up running through the grass, climbing the trees and throwing unripe olives at her brother. It was here that she had first kissed Yosef and it was here, at the edge of the stone wall, that she would find what she was looking for.

There it was: the rosette-shaped plant with the deep green curled leaves, bright purple flowers and tiny fruit like fragrant balls of sunshine. She would not dare to pull up the human-like root of this mandrake plant. It would be too potent for her little boy. All she needed was a few leaves, boiled with thyme, to ease his pain. She gathered what she needed and hastened to the well.

Chapter 40

The shadows were lengthening. The sun dipped low. It was the sixth hour and the well was deserted. Deserted except for one man. She approached with caution, the reassurance of her dagger at her belt. This was the time to be preparing the evening meal, not wandering in the countryside where hungry lions and strange men lurked. She did not look at him. She did not speak. She attached the leather bucket to the rope, ready to lower it into the well.

'Will you give me a drink?'

The accent was Galilean. His face was drawn and tired and his clothes bore the dust of a day's journey. But the dust did not hide the blue tassels at the hem of his cloak—the man was a Jew. Surely he would sooner die of thirst than ask a Samaritan woman to draw water for him?

'You are a Jew and I am a Samaritan woman. How can you ask me for a drink?' She reached for her dagger. The last Jewish man who had spoken to her had murdered Yosef.

'If you knew the gift of God and who it is that asks you for a drink, you would have asked him and he would have given you living water.'

The gift of God? Living water? The man had asked her for a drink and now he held out this strange offer. Was he a holy man? Was he a lunatic?

'Sir, you have nothing to draw with and the well is deep,' she said. 'Where can you get this living water? Are you greater than our father Jacob, who gave us this well and drank from it himself, as did also his sons and his flocks and herds?'

The man smiled and in his eyes she could see amusement. He had no need for her reminder of their common ancestry or the fact that the well of Jacob provided the purest water in the land.

'Everyone who drinks this water will be thirsty again,' he said, 'but whoever drinks the water I give him will never thirst. Indeed, the water I give him will become in him a spring of water welling up to eternal life.'

Eternal life? No man lived forever—that she well knew. What he offered was impossible.

'Sir, give me this water so that I won't thirst and have to keep coming here to draw water.'

She held her breath waiting for his response. Would he raise his hand and shower her with water as had Simon the sorcerer with fire? Would he pray over her the blessing, or curses, of Yahweh as had the Samaritan priest? She looked at his face, shining in the setting sun. There was a strength and assurance about him, as though he feared nothing. He looked at her with eyes so warm, so powerful that it set her heart ablaze. It was as though he could see her very thoughts.

'Go, call your husband and come back.'

'I have no husband,' she replied. The flame in her heart faded; he did not know her at all.

'You are right when you say you have no husband,' he said. 'The fact is, you have had five husbands, and the man you now have is not your husband. What you have just said is quite true.'

His words pierced her like a two-edged sword. How could he know? Her insides curled. She saw Judah ben Levi's wife, the suspicion that tormented her thoughts, the tears that soured her face. How had she not imagined his wife would suspect her husband's unfaithfulness? She herself knew such pain and yet she had brought the very same on another. Was she any better than Gaius? The truth laid bare her heart, slicing it open with the skill of a slaughterer. Yet the conviction held no condemnation.

She looked at the man and, like a scroll unfurling, she saw, one after the other, each of her husbands.

He knew of the first sickly youth her father had given her to. He knew her desperate effort to conceive, the mandrake she had secretly eaten, the anguish when her body expelled the child.

He knew Simeon: his heavy hand, his violent death. He knew Marcellus: his noble character, their separate beds. He knew Gaius: his lust and his deceit.

Four husbands and yet this man had said five. The words of the law filled her mind: 'If brothers are living together and one of them dies without a son his widow must not marry outside the family. Her husband's brother shall take her and marry her and fulfil the duty of a husband's brother to her.'

Yosef! This man knew Yosef and was acknowledging him as her husband. Despite deceiving Mariamne, despite disobeying her request, the law still stood. Tears pricked her eyes, caught in her throat. No ordinary man could know this.

Could he be the Messiah?

No. He was a Jew. Surely the promised one would come down from Mt Gerizim.

'Sir,' she said, 'I can see that you are a prophet. Our fathers worshipped on this mountain, but you Jews claim that the place where we must worship is in Jerusalem.'

The man smiled at her and she felt a flow of love—warm, golden, light-filled love. 'Believe me woman, a time is coming when you will worship the Father neither on this mountain nor in Jerusalem. You Samaritans worship what you do not know; we worship what we do know, for salvation is from the Jews.'

Salvation from the Jews? She could more easily drink vinegar. The prophet continued and she marvelled that he spoke to her. No holy man spoke to a woman. 'Yet a time is coming and has now come when the true worshippers will worship the Father in spirit and truth, for they are the kind of worshippers the Father seeks.'

How did one worship in spirit and truth? What of the law, the holy festivals, the sacrifices? She wanted to ask him but first she needed to know the one hope that burned in her heart.

'I know that the Messiah is coming. When he comes, he will explain everything to us.' She held her breath. Could he truly be the Anointed One, the Messiah? He looked so ordinary with his weary face and worn sandals. Yet in his eyes, in his words, there was something extra—extraordinary.

'I who speak to you am he.'

I am. These were the very words the holy prophet Moses had heard from the burning bush. They set her heart on fire. Greater than the embrace of Yosef, greater than the joy of Benjamin, her heart filled to overflowing. It bubbled up and spilled over, flooding her with peace, with joy, with life. After thousands of years of waiting could he be right here by this well speaking to her? She was unable, unwilling to move, basking in the strange warmth, drinking in the living water.

'Rabbi.' A man's voice from behind made her jump.

A group of rough-looking men strode towards them from the direction of the town. They crowded around the teacher, staring at her with dark, questioning eyes. She could stay here no longer. She pulled her shawl over her head and hurried away, her heart racing, her thoughts spinning. She could not let this holy man pass by the town. This was not a secret to keep to herself. She had to tell her mother. She had to tell Mariamne. She had to tell the whole city.

Chapter 41

'Ima, Mariamne! Come quickly! Come quickly!'

'What is it?' said Mariamne, hurrying from the house. Her mother followed, holding high a lit lamp.

'At the well. I met a man. You must come.' Her breathless words tumbled out. 'Where is the water jar? Have you suffered an accident? Have you been attacked?' Both women's faces were filled with concern.

'I have not been attacked. I have been …' How could she explain the joy that sprang within, the hope that lifted her up and carried her like a bird on the wind? The words she had heard earlier repeated over and over in her mind: *Soon you will know the truth and the truth will set you free.* She gripped Mariamne's arm. 'He told me everything I ever did. He knew of all my husbands. He even knew about Yosef.' She stopped, her heart sinking at her untimely confession.

'Yosef?' Mariamne tilted her head, her countenance creased.

'I am sorry, Mariamne. We disobeyed your wishes. We did not wait as you asked. Yosef fulfilled his obligation as a brother-in-law, and as my husband. I carried no child from Simeon. Benjamin is the seed of Yosef.'

Mariamne recoiled. Her face clouded. 'Why did you not tell me?' It was too late to turn back; she ploughed on.

'When Yosef was killed I saw no reason to burden you with the truth. I carried a child to continue the family name and that was enough, so I thought. I am sorry Mariamne, to have held this secret to myself for so long.'

'It is your lying that hurts more than your actions,' said Mariamne, clamping her hands on her hips.

Leah winced at her words.

'And now you say that this stranger speaks of all this? How could he know what I did not know myself?' said Mariamne.

'You must come and see. Everyone must see,' said Leah. 'Go tell your friends and I will tell the city leaders.'

'Did you bring the mandrake and the water?'

Leah threw her hands to her face in dismay. 'See how my mind is in turmoil! I have forgotten my own son. How is he?'

'He is asleep, thank the gods,' said Mariamne, her tone still severe. Would she forgive her for withholding the truth?

Leah clasped her mother's hands. 'I will return very soon.' Her mother squeezed her hand, her expression that of an excited, expectant child. She cast her dancing eyes to the gate and back again. She was telling her to go.

Leah ran through the streets, arriving breathless at Judah ben Levi's house. The attendant at the gate inclined his head in recognition and relaxed his grip on his sword. She hurried through, following the sound of revelry across the courtyard and into the house. She ignored the servants' shocked stares and burst into the room filled with guests. This was no time to concern herself with Samaritan convention; they would certainly want to hear this news. Judah ben Levi reclined with his guests at the head of a table laden with food and wine. She rushed up to him and the voices of the men faded to silence.

'Leah Marcellus, our notable merchant of silk,' said Judah ben Levi, his cup of wine suspended in mid-air, his eyebrows rising. 'What brings you here?'

'Come, see a man who told me everything I ever did. Could this be the Messiah?' She looked around at the religious leaders and elders, their expressions changing from disapproval to interest.

'The Messiah, here in our very own city?' said Judah ben Levi. 'And you say he told you everything you ever did?' He stared hard at her; she knew what he was asking.

'Everything,' she said. 'He knows everything about me.'

Judah's face paled. His eyes darted anxiously around the elders but their attention was on Leah. One of the elders propped himself up and stroked his beard. 'The lives of the other woman of Sychar are open books: their ancestors, their husbands, their children, all their comings and goings,' he said. 'But with you, Leah Marcellus, there is only conjecture. Who in this city knows everything about you; how much less a stranger? We must hear what this man has to say.'

'If you were any other woman I might dismiss your claims as wild imagination kindled by too much wine,' said another, glancing towards the women in the adjoining room.

'Indeed, Leah is not one to question,' said Judah ben Levi, his look of unease displaced by a greedy glint.

'Imagine if the long-awaited Messiah has chosen Sychar as the place to reveal himself; we will be acclaimed throughout the world.'

One of the priests stood up and addressed Leah. 'Where is this man who told you everything you ever did?'

'He is at the well, with his followers. They call him rabbi,' she said. She did not add that he was Jewish. Let them judge for themselves.

'Through the ages there have been many false prophets claiming to be the Messiah,' said the priest. 'He may be yet another. However, if he is truly the promised one we would not want to miss him. Come, my brothers, let us go at once and see for ourselves.'

With a clamour of voices, the men rose from the table, pulling on cloaks and tying their sandals. Curious, the women in the other room ceased their chatter and watched. Only the wife of Judah ben Levi arose and came near, enquiring of her husband in pressing tones. He dismissed her with a curt word. She pressed her lips together and, with a bitter glance at Leah, returned to her guests. As though scales had fallen from her eyes Leah saw the woman's submission to a husband who provided security and status but little love. Her heart caught like a fish in the net. She could not escape the truth. It had suited her to believe Judah's criticism of his wife. Now her behaviour filled her with shame. There was only one man she wanted to please—the man who knew her every thought, the man at the well.

They made their way to the well, men and women, a swelling throng as word spread through the town. The priests and elders led the way holding high their lamps. They neared the well and the excited chatter subsided. The Jewish rabbi stood, his motley group of followers flanking him. The chief priest greeted him and a hush fell over the crowd. Caught at the back of the group with the other women, Leah strained to hear their exchange. She thought she heard her name and then, through the crowd, she saw the rabbi look at her, a gentle smile playing on his lips.

She breathed a prayer: 'Yahweh, if he is truly from you, show me.' Immediately her mind filled with thoughts of Benjamin: the fits that felled his frail body, the burns that ate into his legs, his plaintive cries. If this man was truly the Messiah he could heal Benjamin. But now he was surrounded by the elders and priests, the men of the town also pressing forward to hear him. She could not reach him and even if she could, no woman was permitted to speak to a rabbi in public. She watched Judah ben Levi move to where everyone could see him.

'Men and women of Sychar,' he called out in an imperious voice, 'do not think you will miss out on hearing this fine rabbi from Galilee. At our urging he has agreed to stay in Sychar. Go to your homes. Tell your friends and relatives. He will be speaking in our city tomorrow.'

The crowd dispersed and Leah hurried to the well, helping Mariamne to draw the water and fill the jar. Soon they were walking back along the road. Ahead she could see the rabbi. He was talking to one of the elders.

'I must speak to him,' she said. Before Mariamne could protest she hurried ahead, her thoughts only for Benjamin. If she was dragged before the leaders for breaking one of their sacred rules, so be it.

'Teacher,' she said.

He stopped and turned around, calming with a touch the elder who blustered in outrage.

'Let her speak,' he said.

'Sir, have mercy on my son.' She fell to her knees before him. 'He has seizures and is suffering greatly. Just today he fell into the fire and his legs are badly burned.'

'Woman, you have great faith. Your request is granted.' The rabbi looked at her with such love, such approval. She, who did not deserve it. The elder watched with his mouth agape.

Leah rose on shaky legs. Did she have great faith? She was no priest. She did not know the whole law. She had not fulfilled every sacrifice. She had sinned.

'Do you really think he can just say the word and Benjamin is healed?' whispered Mariamne. 'Without prayers, without burnt offerings, without sacrifices?'

Leah did not know. All she knew was that her dry heart now brimmed with hope.

As soon as she arrived home she crept into Benjamin's room. Carefully she unwrapped the bandages around his legs and, holding the lamp close, inspected the burns. They did look less angry, or was it just her hopeful imagination? That night a tumult of thoughts kept her tossing for hours before she finally fell into a restless sleep.

Leah woke the following morning to the sun warming the room and the smell of her mother's flatbread wafting up from the courtyard. So, too, did the sound of Benjamin's laughter. Laughter, not tears. Leah leaped from her bed, hope rising in her heart. She wrapped a woollen shawl over her shoulders and hurried down the stairs. She saw Benjamin jumping over a pile of sticks. She saw his legs—no bandage, no burns.

She called his name and he ran to her. It was impossible. She ran her hand over the newly healed skin.

'Ima, my head is like the sky.' He waved his little arm at the cool, clear sky above. 'No clouds.'

Before she could reply he ran off again. Could it be that the seizures had left him?

'It is a miracle!' she said to her mother who was tending the fire. 'I asked the rabbi ...' Rabbi? He was more than a teacher, of that she was certain. 'I asked the Messiah and now Benjamin is healed.'

Her mother beamed, her eyes brimmed, her hands clasped to her chest as though clasping a precious pearl to her heart. She raised her eyes to the heavens. She was praising Yahweh without words.

'Children heal quickly,' said Mariamne, coming out of the house carrying a basket filled with fabrics, ready to open the stall. 'The burns were most likely not as severe as they seemed.'

'How can you doubt? You saw the man. You heard what he said,' said Leah.

'We must be cautious to believe.' Her pinched lips, her flint-edged tone, her sharp stare told Leah that she still smouldered at her deception.

'And yet you believe Aphrodite. Did she heal Benjamin? Does she know the things this man knows?'

'Aphrodite is a distant god. She looks upon us from afar and chooses to help us when it pleases her. It is not wise to speak ill of her.' Mariamne touched her precious pendant. 'Neither will I speak ill of this man until I have heard more of what he has to say. Perhaps he is the Messiah, perhaps he is not.' With a swing of her stick and a swish of her cloak she marched off to the market.

Leah helped her mother douse the fire, wrap in cloth the remaining flatbread and ready Benjamin for synagogue. Surely that was where the prophet would be speaking. She hurried Benjamin from the house and saw her mother waiting at the gate, her best scarf tied over her head. She too was coming to see the man Leah had met.

The man who was surely the Messiah.

Chapter 42

The crowd of people spilling from the synagogue announced the presence of the prophet. Had a Jewish rabbi ever been invited to speak in a Samaritan synagogue? Leah walked Benjamin beyond the crowd to the school, leaving her mother to join the throng. The other mothers were doing the same, depositing their children with haste and hurrying back.

'Leah, is it true?' One of the mothers touched Leah's arm. 'Did he tell you everything you ever did?'

Leah stopped and more mothers gathered around her, eager, hopeful, transfixed on her reply. Only Judah ben Levi's wife held back, a stiff scowl on her face.

'He did, and not only that …' She wanted to tell them how Benjamin was healed, how no-one but the promised one could perform such a miracle. But if Mariamne, who had seen it for herself doubted, neither would it convince these women.

'How do we know that this man does not know her from elsewhere?' muttered Judah ben Levi's wife.

'From where?' asked one of the women. 'What would a Jewish rabbi ever have to do with a Samaritan woman? It is not possible.'

'I tell you, this man knows things about me that no-one could know,' said Leah. 'But do not believe my word alone. Hear him for yourselves.'

The people jostled and strained and squeezed into the synagogue, eager to hear what the rabbi was saying. Leah raised herself high on her toes and caught a glimpse of her mother's bright headscarf; she had managed to work her way to the front.

'Who is he?' asked someone in the crowd. 'What is his name? Where does he come from?'

'He says he is Yeshua, from the town of Nazareth.'

'Nazareth? From Galilee? You would sooner get milk from a ram than a prophet from that place.' The people around laughed.

'The leader of the synagogue must approve; he has allowed him to speak,' said a grey-haired man leaning on a stick. 'Now be silent. I cannot hear what he is saying.'

The crowd quietened and listened. The rabbi was speaking of the law, of Yahweh's promises to Abraham and the teachings of the holy prophet Moses. People asked questions, even the synagogue leaders, and although Leah could not hear she saw their astonishment at his answers. Whispers travelled back through the crowd.

'He says he has come to fulfil all that is written in the Law and the Prophets.' 'He teaches as one who has authority, not as our teachers of the law.' 'What is this wisdom that has been given to him?'

Leah had no need to hear more. She had heard his words, she had seen his power, she needed no further convincing. She retreated through the enraptured crowd, her heart at once light with the thought of the Messiah and heavy with thoughts of Mariamne. How could she atone for the hurt she had caused? The city gates were some distance ahead when Leah saw a huddle of men and women blocking the path and muttering among themselves.

'Who is this fellow who claims to be greater than Moses?'

'What right does he have to claim that it was he who our holy prophet Moses spoke of?'

'He is a Jew. It is blasphemy.'

From the midst of the huddle Judah ben Levi's wife stepped out, hands on her hips, her face as hard as a stale crust. 'Ah-ha, look who comes. If that man were truly the Messiah, he would know what manner of woman this is. She has fooled the good people of our city with her false claims. Who can believe anything that falls from the lips of a harlot?'

A chill coursed through Leah. Had Judah not appeased her, persuaded her, lied to her? Her blood froze. She fixed her eyes on the stony path and tried to pass. A rough hand grabbed her.

'A harlot, you say?' The man grinned, a lascivious glint in his gaze.

'I am no such thing,' said Leah. She pulled away from the man's grip. He held her fast and her heart struck a fearful beat.

'She has the brazen look of a prostitute in all her finery,' said another woman, her worn clothes and rotten teeth marking her as ripe for bribery. She flicked a filthy finger at the Leah's robe. 'You men need not tire yourselves in pursuing this one.'

'Woman, do not accuse us of such evil,' said the man, in an indignant tone. 'We are faithful to our wives. We are faithful to the law and what it commands us to do to such a woman.'

'Take her away!' cried Judah ben Levi's wife.

'Have mercy,' cried Leah. 'I am innocent,' she screamed, knowing she was not. Her heart thundered like a thousand charging chariots. 'You cannot do this. You cannot condemn me on the testimony of one. There must be witnesses.'

Judah ben Levi's wife thrust her furious face close. 'You, who are so well versed in the law. You, who the people acclaim for your fabrics.' Spittle flew from her lips. 'Without me you would have never had a stall in this city. And how do you repay my generosity?' She lowered her voice to a vicious whisper. 'By sleeping with my husband. And now the people praise you for bringing this prophet to our city as though you were a woman of virtue. You are a woman of vice, a viper to be trampled, a serpent to be stoned.' She stepped back. 'Do to her as she deserves.'

The filthy group hovered, ravens ready to attack. A second man fixed his grip on her. She struggled like a sail in a storm, held fast between the two brutes. They dragged her off the path, across a stretch of ground and threw her down a stony slope. She stumbled on the loose stones, twisting her foot and tumbling into the hollow. She had to escape. She jumped to her feet. Pain speared her foot. It gave way beneath her and she fell on her hands and knees.

'I am not guilty! You cannot do this!'

Surely someone would hear her cries. Surely someone would see what was happening. She could not die this way. She could not leave Benjamin. She wanted life, not this life of deception but one of truth and … marriage.

In the midst of her terror, the thought astounded her, and the name that accompanied it: Calev.

She gritted her teeth and pushed herself upright, ignoring the pain. A stone flew hard and fast hitting her on the arm.

'Stop, stop!' she screamed.

She hid her head under her hands. 'Help me, Yahweh,' she cried. 'Save me.' Rocks pelted her back like heavy hailstones. She crawled away, her hands still over her head, stones scouring her skin. The rocks kept falling. 'Yahweh! Calev! Someone! Save me!'

She heard a fierce shout. The pelting stopped.

'Get away from my daughter or the next stone will be at your head!'

The voice was rasping, like gravel in a grinder. Leah looked up. There stood her mother, her arm raised, a rock in hand.

The attackers hesitated, glancing first at each other and then at Judah ben Levi's wife. She turned and scurried away, shrouding her face with her scarf. A wave of pain overtook Leah and she slumped to the ground. She heard a muttering and a shuffling of retreating feet, and then an approaching scrambling of stones.

'Leah.' Her mother placed a gentle hand on her back. 'What have they done to you?'

'You are speaking, Ima. How can it be?' Leah grasped her mother's hand and drew it to her lips, tears filling her eyes.

'I touched the hem of his garment.' Her mother's face glowed with gladness. 'And then I spoke his name. It was like a knot unravelling in my throat. I am free!'

Leah tried to smile. Instead tears burst from her in great sobs. What blessing was this? First Benjamin and now her mother. She had done nothing to deserve it. She had not kept the law and the commandments. She had lied and deceived those who loved her; she had justified her impulsive marriage to Gaius and her sleeping with Judah ben Levi as necessary for the security of her family.

Yet what choice had she had? Her father had arranged her first two husbands for his own purposes. She had fulfilled her duty as a daughter and a wife. Had she ordained their deaths? Had she summoned the bandits to kill Yosef or the archer to shoot Marcellus? She could put her hope in no-one except herself.

The truth will set you free. The words returned to her mind as clear as though someone spoke them aloud.

She had put her hope in herself to find a husband, to bear or not bear children, to provide for her family, and where had it led? To this stony hollow and almost death. Was the truth that she could put her hope in Yahweh, in the Messiah? But how? His purpose was to restore the glory of Israel, not care for a Samaritan woman.

'Come, my daughter.' Her mother stroked her face, gently wiping away the tears. 'I do not think those cowards will return but it does no good to stay out here.' Her mother helped her to her feet and they made their way into the city.

They did not go home but instead, at Leah's insistence that she was well enough, went to the marketplace. It was alive with talk of the Messiah.

'Woman, you were indeed right,' said a man, stepping into their path and grasping her hand in his excitement. 'Never has any man spoken like this man.'

'Now we believe, not only because of what you said,' said his companion. 'We have heard him ourselves and know that this is indeed the Messiah, the Saviour of the world.' He turned to the men gathered around. 'Surely he is the one who will cleanse the land of our Roman oppressors.'

Leah and her mother left them to their eager debate and hobbled on to the stall. When Mariamne saw them she dropped the fabric she was folding.

'Leah! You can barely walk. What has happened?' Her concern held not a trace of her earlier resentment.

'A band of cowards were stoning her,' said her mother. 'Praise Yahweh that I returned when I did.' A smile as wide as the city gates lit her face.

Mariamne grasped both her arms, her mouth gaping. 'My sister, am I dreaming? After all these years—you speak!' The two women laughed and hugged and kissed each other before Mariamne again turned to Leah.

'Stoning? On what accusation? On whose authority?' She took Leah's arm. 'Sit here before you collapse.'

With relief Leah slumped onto the stool and took the cup that Mariamne pressed into her grazed, bloodied hands.

'My daughter, you need not explain what happened just yet. Thank the gods you are safe. Now I ask you to listen to what I have to say.' Her eyes were moist. 'All this long morning I have considered your actions and searched my heart.'

Leah grasped the cup, the pain running through her body dulled by anxiety. Had Mariamne forgiven her or would there forever be a rift between them?

'I have cried with sorrow for the tragic deaths of my beloved sons. And I have cried with joy for you and my grandson. If you had heeded my words and delayed fulfilling the law, our family name would have died with Yosef. As it was with our ancestor Tamar, you and Yosef did a more noble thing.'

'Our withholding of the truth was not noble,' said Leah. 'But our intentions were true. If Yosef had lived we would have blessed you with many more grandchildren. We spoke of such a future.' Her heart gave a familiar tug, fainter now, a sweet shadow of past pain.

'It does no good to look back,' said Mariamne, patting her hand. 'Our future lies with Benjamin.'

'Benjamin! He will be waiting for me.' Leah jumped up. Her legs weakened beneath her and she clutched at the table of silks. Mariamne took her arm.

'Do not fret. Calev has gone to get him.'

'Calev? He has returned from Tyre?' Leah tried to quieten the hope that sprang within. She had seen his anger, his disappointment. He would not want her; no upright man would.

'He said he would walk Benjamin home,' said Mariamne. 'I expect they are waiting at the house and, like all men, wondering where the food is.' She exchanged a look with Leah's mother. 'No-one is interested in buying today. I can attend to the stall on my own.'

'And you, Leah, must rest,' said her mother.

With a firm hand she helped Leah to her feet. In the short time at the stall Leah's body had stiffened. Each step sent through her a shuddering of pain. Her head grew light. She gripped her mother's arm and fixed her mind on the joy of hearing her voice.

From outside the gate, Leah heard laughter. They entered to see Calev standing by the tree holding out his arms to Benjamin who clung to a high branch. 'Ima, Ima!' he cried, leaping from the branch into Calev's arms. Calev staggered and the two fell on the ground laughing. Benjamin recovered first, running to Leah ready to throw his arms around her legs.

'Take care, my child, your Ima is hurt,' said her mother.

Benjamin stopped and stared at his grandmother, briefly bewildered that she spoke. Then he turned a serious face to Leah. 'Ima?'

'Do not be concerned, my son. I need only a little rest.' She forced a smile through the throbbing that beat across her back. His face relaxed into a grin.

'Ima needs only a little rest,' he repeated to Calev who was staring from one woman to the other.

'What has happened?' he asked.

'Leah was almost stoned but, praise Yahweh, I heard her screams,' said her mother.

'You are speaking!' said Calev, staring at her in wonder.

'It is the hand of the Messiah. He has come at last and he has healed me and Benjamin also. Leah met him at the well, and now the whole town has gone to listen to him.'

Calev's eyes widened.

'It is true,' said Leah. 'He told me everything I ever did.'

'Everything?' Calev's face darkened with concern.

'Everything,' said Leah, knowing of what he spoke.

'Did he cause this?' He pointed to her torn, muddied clothes and bruised, bloodied hands.

'He had nothing to do with it,' said Leah.

'Then who?' he demanded. 'Tell me and I will repay them with the side of my sword.'

'How will that help?' she said.

What good would come from accusing Judah ben Levi's wife? It would only heap more trouble on the situation. A wave of nausea came upon her and she swayed, her vision dimming. Strong arms grasped her and she heard Calev's voice so close. She felt him carry her inside and lay her down. She felt her mother's gentle hand dress her wounds and smooth her brow as she had so many times as a child. Her voice, like the sweetest honey, soothed her to sleep.

Chapter 43

The marketplace echoed with emptiness. The stalls abandoned, the tent flaps down, merely a scattering of sellers, a trickle of traders. Everyone was at the synagogue— those who had gathered there the previous day and those they had urged to come on this second day that the rabbi of Nazareth spoke. Everyone, that was, except Judah ben Levi and those of his clients who sought his sanction and his shekels. Leah grasped Benjamin's hand firmly and hurried in the opposite direction, away from Judah ben Levi, away from the marketplace, and towards the synagogue. She had slept beyond dawn and now Benjamin was late for school. Yet her heart was not anxious, neither her countenance creased. It was the Messiah who drew her with such haste. She had woken completely refreshed, with barely a bruise to remind her of her battered and aching body of the previous day. Would the miracles of the Messiah never cease? Her meeting with Judah ben Levi could wait; she had to hear what the rabbi would say today.

'Ima, watch me!' Benjamin pulled his hand free and ran ahead, jumping over muddy pools of water and wetting his coat. He turned, every so often, for her approval and she clapped her hands. His face beamed with life and his eyes held a spark she had not seen since Gaius had thrown him against the wall.

'Ima, can I run to school?'

'Certainly you can!' said Leah. The synagogue was within sight, and the school beyond.

'Calev promised to bring his camels to school. I'm telling all my friends.' He gave her a wave and ran off down the road.

Calev? Surely now that he had sold all his silk he would not wish to delay another day. The camel bags would be laden with silver and gold; payment that his uncle in Palmyra would be thirsty to see. The joy in her heart dimmed like a doused lamp. She side-stepped a muddy pool, splashing mud on her sandals. Perhaps it was better this way. She could not bear to see his disapproval, his disdain. Shame weighed heavy upon her. He would never consider her more than a sister, a woman of many husbands, widowed, divorced and wayward. She was as soiled as her mud-spattered sandals.

The synagogue was packed with people and the rabbi was teaching, his Galilean accent, so similar to their own, soothing those concerned that they listened to a Jew. Leah slipped in unseen. Unseen, that is, until a woman near the front turned and fixed her fretful eyes upon her. It was Judah ben Levi's wife. From across the room Leah felt the force of her wrath, and something else— fear—and it wrenched her heart. The woman was a wife forsaken. If she told Judah of her suspicions he would deny them or declare the law alleged no sin in taking an unmarried woman to his bed. If she insisted on retribution she risked Leah reporting the unlawful stoning of a Roman citizen—a punishable crime.

The rabbi continued his teaching. The leaders and priests sat stiffly, soberly rubbing their beards; a few leaned forward, hanging on every word. The hours flew past. The low afternoon sun flooded the synagogue bathing the rabbi's face in warm, golden light. He raised his hands, ready to pronounce the final blessing.

'If you continue in my word, you are truly my disciples. Then you will know the truth, and the truth will set you free.'

Leah sat transfixed. Here were the same words yet with an explanation of how to know the truth. And what had been his words all day? None other than the Law of Moses. Yet with a difference. This Yeshua of Nazareth spoke of the spirit of the law, of worshipping in spirit and in truth. The law of the synagogue leaders said that she and Judah ben Levi had not committed adultery. But the spirit of the law, the truth, was different. She had grieved Judah ben Levi's wife and in doing so, grieved Yahweh. The truth will set you free. At this moment the truth weighed upon her like a winter coat. She had disobeyed the will of Yahweh. She had gone her own way.

How could she make amends? No dove or grain offering would suffice. There was only one way. She fell to her knees and prayed. 'Yahweh, forgive me.'

A shadow fell upon her and she looked up. Yeshua, the rabbi of Nazareth, stood before her, his eyes dancing with light. He reached out his hand and pulled her to her feet.

'Daughter, your sins are forgiven.'

Her shoulders straightened. She lifted her head. This Yeshua of Nazareth not only taught with the wisdom of a prophet, not only healed the sick, not only knew everything about her, but now also forgave sins? Surely this was the gift of God, the living water of which he had spoken at the well. She wanted to run to him, to thank him, to touch his cloak but he had gone, carried away by the crowd who continued to swarm around him.

Joy streamed through her like the first autumn showers, filling the furrows, settling the ridges, softening the soil. She knew what she had to do.

She ran outside, searching … searching for one woman. There she was, heading towards the school where the children were just now spilling out.

'Naomi!' She called her name and realised that it was the first time she had done so, the first time she had considered her as more than Judah ben Levi's wife.

'Naomi!'

Naomi turned and took a strangled step backwards, clasping her basket before her. Dark moons hung from her eyes, deep lines furrowed her mouth.

'What do you want?'

'Forgive me, Naomi. I betrayed your kindness. You have every right to despise me.' She had admitted her adultery. She had confirmed Naomi's suspicions. 'If I can make amends in any way ...'

Naomi's knuckles whitened on the basket, her eyes widened and welled. 'Make amends? What do you have that I would desire? A stall of silk?'

Naomi's mouth curled cruelly at the edges. 'I have a husband who sits at the city gates, a household of servants and the blessing of many children. Our friends applaud us for our gracious hospitality and the city scrolls record our generous gifts.' She stretched her neck forward, pressing her face close to Leah's. 'You have one fatherless child and no husband. You have nothing.'

Spittle struck Leah's face. She wiped it off and watched Naomi stalk stiffly away. Her heart swelled with sadness for Naomi and with bitter loathing for what she had done to her. Yet strangely, surprisingly, the joy in her heart continued to flow, bringing with it the stillness of sunrise. Naomi spoke the truth: she had only Benjamin, she had no husband, she might soon lose Judah's support of her stall.

But the Messiah had come. Her son was healed. Her mother now spoke.

Her heart no longer condemned her.

Her honour did not depend on a husband, a quiver of children or a purse-full of shekels. It depended on the man she had met at the well. In this, Naomi was wrong. She did not have nothing; she had everything.

Shouts and laughter and a chorus of chatter filled the air. Leah followed the sound past the synagogue school, past the spreading sycamore tree and over a grassy incline. There, seated on a camel adorned with bright coloured tassels, and surrounded by children, was Calev.

He was still here. He had stayed for Benjamin. He had kept his promise. The children soon scattered. Calev tethered the camel and came towards her.

'I expected you to be gone,' said Leah. 'Does not the desert call your name?' Her mouth stretched in a smile.

'The desert can wait one more day.' Calev's eyes sparkled. 'There is another who also calls my name.' He tilted his head towards Benjamin who was feeding the camel thick tufts of grass.

'I am glad you are here, Calev, for Benjamin, and for myself.' He had been right to call her a harlot and a fool, and yet he was here, as he had so often been—from solemnly promising Atticus that he would always look after her, to rescuing her from Simeon, to dealing with Gaius, to bringing her silk and now caring for Benjamin.

'I have made a decision.' Calev stared at her straight. 'I have spent enough time trading in the deserts of the east. I am leaving Palmyra.'

Leah's heart stopped. This was the end of her silk supply but worse, the end of Calev's visits to Sychar. 'Where will you go? What will you do?'

'It is time I married.'

The smile froze on her face. The blood surged in her head. Her heart wrenched within her. Why was it so? He had every right to choose a wife—a woman pure and untarnished.

'And who will you choose? A Palmyran princess? A desert dweller's daughter?' It was better to tease, to keep her tone light.

'I was thinking of a Samaritan.' His eyes grew warm. He held her gaze fast. 'I was thinking of you.'

Leah stepped back. Her breath caught in her throat. A tear flew to her eye. 'You know who I am. You know what I've done. Why would you marry me?'

Calev laughed. 'I know you are wilful and sometimes exceedingly foolish. Yet I know who you are—a woman of virtue and value. I would marry you because I ...' he caught her hand in his, '... because I love you.'

Leah's heart blossomed like a sun brushed bud, each part unfurling and spreading out to the light. Just like the Messiah, he knew her secrets yet did not condemn. Yet with his scarred hands and sharpened sword, he was no Messiah. He could not raise a man from his mat; he could not read the depths of his heart. But he was a man who she cared for, a man who she trusted, a man of his word, a man she could laugh with, a man she could love.

A man she could marry.

Author's Note

The Silk Merchant of Sychar is based on the John 4 account of Jesus speaking to a Samaritan woman at Jacob's well, on the outskirts of the current day city of Nablus. It is significant that this is Jesus' longest recorded conversation.

And perhaps his most outrageous.

Outrageous because Jews did not speak to Samaritans. Outrageous because rabbis did not speak to women in public. Outrageous because a person of the 'wrong' race, the 'wrong' gender, and with no formal religious training became arguably the world's first evangelist for Jesus.

There has been much speculation over who this woman was, and how she came to have five husbands. A close study of the John 4 text, along with research into the Samaritan, Jewish and Roman culture, religion and laws renders many possibilities.

Indeed '…and the man you now have is not your husband' could have been a culturally acceptable situation according to the laws of the AD20's.

Religious scholars debate over the time of day this meeting took place. Was the 'sixth hour' noon or six pm? By comparing every time reference in the gospels, especially around Jesus' trial and crucifixion, I sided with the scholars who conclude that John's gospel is written in Roman time and that the sixth hour is six in the evening.

Then there's the question of the time of year. Are Jesus' words, '…four more months and then the harvest…' literal or a saying of the day? Again scholars have found no evidence of such a saying so I have taken it as literally four months before the barley harvest.

Apart from preventing misleading extrapolations of the character of this woman, none of these matters are crucial to the essence of the conversation.

Jesus is concerned with the woman's personal salvation as well as a matter that is just as relevant today as it was then: arguments, hatred and even murder over religious differences.

Read Jesus' words carefully and discern for yourself the message of this Jewish rabbi who proclaimed himself the long awaited Messiah, and who millions of people from every tribe and nation have since believed.

Note: For further study, refer to the Book Club Notes at http://www.rhizapress.com.au/the-silk-merchant-of-sychar

Acknowledgments

Writing a novel is like having an assignment with no deadline – and that nobody wants!

My first thanks must go to Sarah and the Write-On writers group at Writing NSW. Without your weekly critique and encouragement I would still be procrastinating over a half written manuscript.

Thank you to Kaye Chalwell, Nina Bianco and especially Valerie Forestier for reading the manuscript and catching all the cringe worthy phrases. Thank you to Iola Goulton for your incredibly helpful structural edit, and to the team at Rhiza Press for the essential finishing touches that transform a manuscript into a real book.

Thank you to Hemi and James who endured carrot salad every night for two long years. I hope one day you'll recover from the trauma because it really is very healthy!

And finally thank you to the Lord who truly is where my help comes from.